WOLF

A NOVEL

HERBERT J. STERN AND ALAN A. WINTER

Skyhorse Publishing

In honor of Bernhard Weiss

Foreword

In October 1918, an amnesiac soldier encounters a corporal suffering from hysterical blindness in the mental ward of Pasewalk Hospital. Their friendship based on mutual dependency is the spine of this story that ranges from the founding of the Nazi Party to Hitler's ascendency as Germany's absolute dictator in 1934.

Wolf is the account of German democracy strangling itself in excessive division and discord until, finally, its exhausted citizens turn to a dictator . . . who then eliminates all dissent.

Wolf is historical fiction because there are fictional characters. Nevertheless, the events and vast majority of people depicted are historically accurate . . . more so than many accounts termed "history."

Fiction reveals truths that reality obscures
—Jessamyn West

Prologue

Berlin, February 28, 1933

"I am to meet Bernhard Weiss at this address."

"He doesn't live here," said Lucie. Lucie Fuld-Traumann was a stout, married woman in her fifties. The whites of her eyes became more visible as her gaze traveled from my black high boots to the red swastika armband to the shoulder epaulets and finally to the *SS* lightning bolts on my collar. Her lips trembled in fear. Her gnarled hands twisted a blue-and-white dishtowel into knots.

"Damn it, woman, we don't have a moment to waste. Where is your brother?" I brushed past her and slammed the door before removing my peaked cap. "You don't want your neighbors gossiping that an *Obergruppenführer* was seen standing in your entranceway. Now get Bernhard."

Lucie stood her ground. "I told you, Bernhard is not here."

The house was compact: crystal chandelier above our heads, living area with an upright piano to the left, kitchen straight ahead, and the dining room to my right. The dinner table had been set for three. I knew that Lucie and her husband, Alfred, who must have been cowering in an upstairs room, did not have children. After Bernhard Weiss, deputy police commissioner of Berlin, had been removed from office some months earlier, he sent his wife and daughter to Prague while he sought refuge in his sister's house . . . hiding from the very police he once commanded.

I turned back to Lucie. "Didn't he tell you to expect Friedrich Richard?" I showed her my identification card. "I'm Friedrich." Lucie remained frozen in place, unsure of what to do.

Time was of the essence. "You must trust me. We have a window of opportunity to get Bernhard to safety and join his family in Prague. It's a seven-hour drive through the back roads to the Czech border. If we leave now, we can stay ahead of the men who have been dispatched to arrest him. Now take me to him. *Immediately.*" I glared down at her. "You brother's life is in your hands."

Without further denial, Lucie guided me to the basement door. It was dark. At the bottom, she pushed a button and a small light buzzed to life, casting macabre shadows on the damp walls. She called her brother's name.

Then I bellowed, "It's me. Friedrich. We need to go . . . now."

Clothes rustled from an unlit corner. A soot-smeared Bernhard Weiss emerged from behind the coal stack. He coughed into a handkerchief before he could speak.

"I knew you would come," he said without preamble. We clasped hands.

"Goebbels has ordered your immediate arrest. We don't have much time."

Weiss nodded and pushed passed me. Upstairs, he grabbed a packed bag stashed for the day he needed a quick getaway, snatched a pistol from a side table that he shoved into the back of his pants, hugged his sister, promised he would see her again, and left his beloved Berlin.

*

We headed south in silence, each absorbed in the import of what we were doing. It was a cloudless, cold night. A full moon illuminated the country roads. After an hour, oncoming traffic ceased. We sped along with growing confidence that we would be safe . . . at least until we reached the border.

I broke the silence. "Did you hear about the fire in the Reichstag?"

"Lucie told me Hitler announced that the Communists attempted a putsch. That seems far-fetched. Do they have any proof of such a plot?"

Until six months ago, Bernhard Weiss, slight of frame yet huge of intellect, was the leading policeman in all of Prussia, which included Berlin. He single-handedly brought German police work into the twentieth century by introducing forensic techniques that became standard for criminal investigations throughout Europe. A thorn in the side of Joseph Goebbels, he refused to let Hitler's twisted mouthpiece issue vituperative rants against both him and the Jewish community with impunity. Weiss clamped down each time Goebbels defamed him, successfully suing him, even putting him in jail. The irony! Weiss had fallen from highest-ranking Jew in the police department to a hunted man.

I turned to Bernhard. "Proof of a plot? They are looking for proof. If they don't find it, they'll try to manufacture it. In the end, it won't matter. They'll do what they want."

"Reich President Hindenburg is our last hope. He hates Hitler. He would never let him get away with that."

"Then you haven't heard this morning's news. Hitler got the Old General to invoke Article 48 of the Constitution. All civil liberties in Germany have been suspended."

"Isn't that what you wanted," Weiss reminded me of a past argument, "a dictatorship to restore Germany's greatness?"

"I wanted a temporary dictator the way ancient Romans occasionally summoned one to solidify political power in an emergency. Nothing more. I did not want the suspension of all civil rights of our citizens."

Even in the silver cast of the moon's light, I could see Bernhard grow pale. We rode for a few minutes while he considered the ramifications of a suspended constitution. More than once, he started to say something only to stop and rethink it.

"Let me get this straight," Bernhard said. "By Hindenburg handing him the country, there is no more freedom of the press. The right to object to one's own arrest has just been eliminated. All dissent will be silenced." Then he added, "Legally, if Hitler does half of what he claims he will do, life for us will become intolerable."

I knew "us" did not mean all Germans. Weiss was speaking for his fellow Jews. There was no need to discuss this further. I did not have the heart to tell him that Hitler had already ordered Wilhelm

Frick, his minister of Interior, to draft racial laws forcing Jews out of German life. The first law, ejecting all Jews from the civil service, would be implemented in five weeks, along with laws to prevent Jews from taking bar exams and Jewish doctors from receiving compensation under national health insurance. This would herald the end of Jewish doctors, lawyers, and public servants in German society. I argued with Hitler not to do this, but to no avail.

We lapsed into silence. I had a basket of food in case we got hungry and cans of petrol anticipating that stations would be closed in the dead of night. When nature called, we relieved ourselves alongside the car.

We neared the border crossing as rays of the early morning sun peaked above the horizon. I hopped out of the car and opened the trunk. "Get in. It's better if they don't see you."

While the diminutive Weiss curled into the trunk, he still balked. "Get me out as soon as it's safe. I hate being confined like this."

"Who doesn't?"

I closed the trunk and restarted the car, rounded the bend, and rolled up to a large gate that blocked the road. White, narrow guardhouses flanked either side of the barrier. A sleepy-eyed guard ambled toward the car, wagging his gun for me to roll down the window.

"You must turn around."

"I have urgent matters to attend to. Let me through."

"The border is closed until the Communist conspirators who burned down the Reichstag building have been rounded up."

"I just came from Berlin. You may not have heard: they captured all of them. Now let me pass."

By now, the guard in the other station poked his head out to see what the commotion was about. I opened the door and stood to my full measure, towering over the guard. "Do you know who I am?"

A glance at the uniform of an *SS* General brought the man to heel-clicking attention. But still, he remained suspicious. "I must see some identification."

"This is insane," I muttered under my breath. I handed him my identification card plus my *SS* membership card.

The guard's assuredness evaporated. "You're an *Obergruppenführer*? Other than Himmler, that's the highest *Schutzstaffel* rank."

"There is no time for military lessons. Let me pass."

He compared my face to the picture on the *SS* card. By this time, the second guard wandered closer. "How is it I have never heard of you?" asked the first.

"Because I perform secret missions for the Führer."

"Even so, I should be familiar with your name." He asked the other guard if he had ever heard of me. The man shrugged.

"This will clarify matters for you. Then I must be on my way." I handed him a letter with the *Führer's* unmistakable signature, that validated I spoke as his personal representative. "I assume you have a phone in your guardhouse. Call the *Führer*. Ask who I am. Explain to him why you deem it necessary to detain me."

The guard handed back my identification cards and letter. "That won't be necessary, *Herr Obergruppenführer*."

I saluted. "Heil Hitler."

I wheeled around. With my back to the guards, I made a show of adjusting my cap to wipe my brow. I reached for the car door handle when a muffled cough broke out from the rear.

"What was that?" called the guard.

I cleared my throat. "That was me."

He raised his rifle. "Hold it right there."

The guard motioned for his comrade to keep an eye on me. With my back still to the guard, I unbuttoned my coat. The first guard edged to the rear of the car.

"What's in the trunk?"

"Nothing." I said in a loud voice. "It's not locked. Open it and see for yourself."

The guard lifted the hatch with his left hand and stepped back as the trunk sprung open. Two shots rang out from inside the trunk and the soldier crumpled to the ground. I whipped out my Luger and shot the second guard before he had time to react.

I ran to the back; Weiss climbed out of the car. "Are you hurt?"

Weiss shook his head as he knelt over the guard and pressed the carotid artery. "This one's dead; the other one?"

"Still alive." I had aimed wide on purpose. The second guard lay on the ground attempting to staunch the flow of blood from his right shoulder with his left hand.

Weiss and I approached him, pistols in hand.

He pleaded. "Please, *Herr Obergruppenführer*, I will not report you . . . I . . . "

"Will say nothing," said Weiss . . . who then placed his gun muzzle to the man's temple and squeezed the trigger.

I raised my arms. "For God's sake, why did you do that?"

Weiss scowled. "How could you return to Berlin if that man lived?"

"That's just it. I have no intention of going back."

"We will talk about this later." He looked down. "For now, they can't be found this way. We need to make it look like they were defending the border." Together, we fired a number of rounds from our pistols into the guardhouses, breaking the windows and sending shards of wood flying. Then we grabbed their rifles and dragged each to a guardhouse, propping them against the splintered siding. Satisfied the staging was believable, we resumed our journey without discussing what happened.

*

When we found the address on Kaprova Street, in Prague's Jewish Quarter of Josefov, Bernhard said, "Don't stop. We'll get out a few blocks from here. No need to connect this car to my family's address."

We parked on a street with many stores. As I came around the car to join him, Bernhard motioned me to the other side of the street. "We make an odd couple. People will remember us if asked. Walk over there." He made a valid point. I was more than a head taller than him. I walked at a different pace than him, turning corners a few seconds after he did. After a number of blocks, he looked both ways before entering an aged apartment house. I counted to twenty and then followed through the front door.

"Here." I looked up. Weiss leaned over the railing and pointed to the stairs. There was an open door to the left of the landing. I found Bernhard hugging and kissing his wife and daughter in the salon. After he introduced me, I followed him into a smaller room.

"Close the door." There was a small table with two wooden chairs arranged below medallion macramé lace curtains.

Before he said anything, I blurted, "I can't go back. Not after what we just did."

"Friedrich, no one but us knows what happened today." His steel-gray eyes were piercing as he added, "There were no witnesses."

"I'm not talking about just today, Bernhard. I'm talking about what is in store for your people in the days and years ahead. The Nazis are fanatical in their racial theories."

"That is all the more reason why you have to go back."

"I don't know if I can return to Berlin and look at Hitler or those around him in the eye anymore."

"No one is closer to the *Führer* than you. You're the only one in a position to do something. You must return."

I pushed up from the small table and paced like a caged animal. "If I try to stop them I'll be killed."

"No one expects you to march into a room and wipe out every one. But there will be opportune times when you may be able to affect change. You're Hitler's favorite. There is no one in a better position to speak sense to him. That's your destiny. To make that possible." He raised his right hand. "God help me, I didn't want to, but I had to execute that poor guard."

I went to the window, lifted the edge of the curtain, and gazed out at the city I thought might be my new home. When I dressed in my uniform before fetching Bernhard, I believed it would have been the last time I would wear it. That's why I stuffed my pockets with Reichsmarks, took my precious photo-graph that I had carried since the war, and left everything else, intending never to return.

Bernhard cleared his throat.

I turned from the curtain and faced him.

"There's one more thing you must do, Friedrich. You need to keep an account."

"An account of what?"

"You were there at the beginning. When the Nazis weren't even the Nazis. When they were an aimless group of puny men who met in a tavern to swill beer and discuss politics. No one knows the history of how this happened better than you. Write it down. Don't leave out anything. Then, when this madness is over, share it with the world."

"To what end?"

"To make certain no one forgets."

I thought about the magnitude of what he asked. "There has been so much. I would not know where to begin."

Weiss gave his small smile. "Ah, yes. Begin at the beginning."

PART I

Chapter 1

July 1918

"Where am I?" The words sounded like they were forced through a grinder.

"Berlin," answered the angel dressed in white. "In the facial plastic surgery ward in the Royal Ear and Nose Clinic of Charité Hospital."

I tried to move my right hand but couldn't. I cranked my left hand in fits and starts until I touched my face. It was swathed in bandages. My chin, cheek, forehead . . . there was no skin left uncovered. Shifting to see her better sent a hot poker of pain through my body.

"Am . . . I . . . par . . . alyzed?"

"No."

"Can't . . . move . . . head."

"It's fixed in a splint. For precaution."

I tried to make sense of that but could not. "How . . . get here?"

"You don't remember?"

She leaned over and I smelled a hint of sweet jasmine. She had blue eyes and her blond hair was tucked under a starched white cap. Crow's feet signaled she was something over forty. Her crisp uniform accentuated her ample figure.

I attempted to shake my head to answer her question, but it was fixed in place. "No," I hissed through clamped teeth. My teeth. My tongue tripped over wires and rough edges. I could not move my jaw. My eyes darted to what I could see. Out of the corner of my eye, a bag of clear liquid hung from a pole.

She explained. "You need fluids. There is no way you can drink enough with your jaws wired shut." I could not process her words. Nothing made sense. "Your jaw, zygomatic arch, and right orbital bones were all broken in the explosion. If you move your tongue around, you'll discover you've lost some teeth. We filed the sharp points down. After your jaw mends, the technicians will fabricate replacements for you."

"How . . . long . . . here?"

"A week."

"Don't . . . remember." She smiled for the first time. It was a warm and reassuring smile. I detected the slightest bit of playfulness hiding behind her prim demeanor. "What . . . your . . . name?"

"Anna."

"What . . . happened . . . to me . . . Anna?" I strained to push each word through wires and over clamped lips.

"There was a big offensive in Marne meant to drive the enemy back."

"Did it . . . work?"

She grimaced. "All I know is that scores of soldiers have been pouring in here. From the looks of it, we took a beating."

"Can't move . . . hand . . . right . . . leg throbbing." My breathing grew shallow, more rapid. It was painful to speak. "Will . . . I . . . walk?"

She cupped my right hand in hers; it was warm. "Rest for now. You are one of the lucky ones. You still have your arms and legs, though your right leg and arm were both badly broken. They need time to mend. You also have many fractured ribs. One punctured your lung. When they brought you in, you were unconscious. You lost too much blood; you needed a transfusion. Your reflexes worked, so we knew you weren't paralyzed. Still, we stabilized your neck as a precaution."

Her words reassured me.

She released my hand and eased off the bed. "So far, you are healing without complication, but you're still not out of the woods. There's always the chance of infection." She drew a metal table closer. "It's time for your sponge bath."

Anna opened my hospital gown. She turned to the white porcelain bowl, wetted a sponge, and squeezed out the excess water. She sat at the edge of the bed; I felt her thigh against mine. She put her left hand on my shoulder and with a gentle touch, dabbed my exposed skin. She washed all that she could, closed the gown, and then washed my left arm with care so as not to disturb the IV needle in my arm. Next she pulled the bed sheet aside and washed my left leg and the parts of my right leg not in a cast.

"You can't roll over." With a deft touch she slid her hand under my back to reach most of my backside. She padded to the other side of the bed to reach what she had missed.

She rinsed the sponge one last time, hovered over my midsection, and whispered, "I'm not quite finished."

The corners of my mouth creased upwards. As best I could determine, a most important reflex was still intact.

Chapter 2

There were advantages to being in a coma: I felt no pain. Now that I was awake, the pain ebbed and flowed in torrents. Anna gave me an injection before she left. I spent the rest of the morning in a morphine haze. By late afternoon, prickles of pain twisted back into my consciousness. I begged for more medicine. While I waited for a nurse to administer my newfound friend, I struggled to remember what happened to me. I tried to picture being dressed in a uniform. Carrying a rifle. Marching in formation. Fighting in a battle. Nothing came to mind. Try as I might, I could not remember.

The next morning Anna asked, "How did you sleep?"

"Very . . . little."

"How would you rate the pain?"

"I . . . need . . . medicine." I was desperate to return to that dreamy state where I floated and felt naught.

"Not so fast. The doses need to be spaced out. We don't want you to become addicted."

That scared me. Not the addiction part, going without that magic juice. I needed it. "I . . . don't . . . care!"

"You say that now," said Anna, "but you'll regret it later."

*

Sometime thereafter—it may have been days, for I lost sense of time—a man in his fifties, somewhat balding but still with enough hair to comb, appeared at the foot of the bed. He sported a salt and pepper moustache. Bushy brows heightened his stern gaze. He was dressed in a herringbone suit with a stethoscope draped around his neck. Anna stood behind him.

"I wondered how many more days you would be sleeping," he said.

"Are you my doctor?" My speech had become easier to understand.

He bowed. "Jacques Joseph, chairman of facial and plastic surgery."

"Have you examined me before?"

"Many times."

"I don't remember."

"Between the coma and the morphine, you've been asleep most of the time."

"Can you tell me when these bandages are coming off?"

"You're not fully healed. They have to stay on a bit longer." He glanced at Anna with a look of conspiracy. "Before we change them, would you like a mirror for a preview? This way you won't be shocked."

Why would he say that? I plumbed Anna's face for guidance; she smiled, but said nothing. "Won't I look the way I did before?"

Again, Dr. Joseph glanced at Anna. He cleared his throat. "The truth is, we had no idea what you looked like."

"How different can I be if you put all the parts back where they came from?"

"There was shrapnel embedded in your forehead and scalp. Your right orbit was fractured, as was your cheekbone. Your nose was smashed in. There were deep gashes everywhere. Flesh was hanging loose. Your jaw was broken. You have to understand, there were no landmarks or references I could use except this."

He reached into his pocket and handed me a photo.

I took it with my left hand. "What is this?"

"I hoped you could tell us."

It was a picture of a family: a father, mother, and two children: one boy and one girl. All well-dressed. The father in a suit, the mother in a dress. The boy and girl outfitted in party clothes. The boy, perhaps ten or twelve, was too young to predict his adult features. There was a date on the back: 1908.

I handed the picture back. "Who are they?"

"Don't you know?"

"Should I?"

"There was no identification when they brought you here. Everything was either left behind at the aid station or, most likely, lost in the blast. We found this photo in your boot."

"I can't remember anything that happened."

"That's not that uncommon as a result of severe head trauma."

"How long before I get my memory back?"

Anna stepped forward. "Most of the time, it returns after the heavy pain medication ends."

"And the other times?"

"There's no telling how long it will take," answered Dr. Joseph. "We've come to call you Patient X. Try to remember the town you came from. An address. Somewhere you might have lived."

"Nothing comes to mind."

"Perhaps a nickname?"

I made light of this. "X has a catchy ring to it, don't you think? I could get used to it." Anna's smile lifted my mood.

"Let's change his bandages," said Dr. Joseph.

With care, they removed my mummy-like wrappings. Where the bandage tugged the skin, they cut around it so as not to rip the scab or pull an embedded suture that could open a wound. Anna removed the stitches with light touches.

Dr. Joseph inspected each area with great care. I smelled mint on his breath. He straightened up and stepped back. "There is no sign of infection anywhere."

"What about the bandages on my arms and legs?

"Anna can replace them later."

I wanted to touch my face. My nose. My skin. "How do I look?"

Dr. Joseph nodded to Anna. "You tell him."

"X, you are going to be a dreamboat."

She fetched a silver-trimmed, round mirror and held it so I could see myself. What I saw was a young man who might be between twenty to twenty-five years old. While there needed to be more healing, I now had an idea of what I looked like.

"Are you pleased?" Dr. Joseph asked.

"I don't know if this is me or someone else."

"You will have the *fräuleins* swooning. What do you think, Anna?"

Anna gloated. "Most men would kill for a face like yours. You look like Conrad Veidt."

"Who is that?"

"An actor. He appeared in *The Mystery of Bangalor.*"

"I just want to look like me."

The doctor explained, "I need to examine the rest of you before Anna puts salve and covers the wounds with fresh bandages. You will have plenty of time to admire yourself after I leave."

Dr. Joseph inspected the burn areas and graft sites. He checked my breathing and then issued an order to Anna. "His lungs are not as clear as they should be. Arrange for a chest X-ray."

"I need more morphine."

He grabbed my chart and flipped to the list of dispensed medicines. "You have to wait a couple of hours."

That was not the answer I wanted. The moment Dr. Joseph left, I asked Anna for an injection. "I'll see what I can do," she answered.

"Do you think you have a family? A wife? The picture you carried was not of a woman," Anna asked as she rolled me back from the X-ray department.

"I haven't thought much about any of that. Right now I'm more concerned with how my wounds heal. What about my identification? Didn't I have a wallet or identity tags?"

"No. You were stripped down to your underwear and boots when we got you. Your face was torn apart. Broken bones. All we cared about was saving you. I don't mind telling you those first days were touch and go. We weren't sure you would survive. The last thing any of us expected was that you would have no memory when you came out of your coma."

Over the next few weeks I learned about Anna's personal life. Widowed at the outbreak of the war, married eight years before that, childless, she seemed drawn to me, although there were many years between us . . . or perhaps because of it.

Charité Hospital, October 1, 1918

I remained in the hospital three months. During that time I endured additional skin grafts over burned areas, had facial scars smoothed out, and started a therapy to strengthen my arms, legs, and core muscles.

Eight weeks into my stay, the hospital dentist and technicians fabricated removable bridges to replace missing teeth. My physical progress was great, yet Dr. Joseph continued to express concern.

"I am worried about you," the doctor said. It happened to be Anna's day off.

"There's no need. I've all but stopped using painkillers. Just Bayer once in a while."

He dismissed my statement with the flick of a wrist. "Drugs are not my concern. You need to know who you are."

"Patient X suits me just fine."

"That is part of the trouble. The way you embrace it worries me. We are not equipped to deal with this sort of problem. I've signed orders for you to be transferred to another hospital. You leave today."

My throat constricted. I was terrified to leave the only place I knew . . . and Anna.

Dr. Joseph continued, but I barely heard him. "It's far from here. Pasewalk Hospital. They have doctors who treat soldiers with different kinds of wounds."

I struggled into a hospital-issued uniform, slipped the lone photograph from my boot into a small kit and left without a goodbye to Anna. I had no choice. I did leave a note. It was all I could do.

*

Pasewalk Hospital was more than one hundred kilometers northeast from Berlin, near the Polish border.

Given that it was wartime, it took half a day to travel to Pasewalk. I kept to myself during the train ride, gazing out the window but seeing little of the countryside. Dr. Joseph was right. While I was now free of all bandages . . . freedom would be illusory without an identity. Pasewalk represented that hope.

Chapter 3

October 1918

Pasewalk Hospital, once known as the Firing House for its use as a firing range, was a large, austere red brick building replete with turrets on either side of the entranceway. A row of trees lined the street in front of the haunting building.

I arrived by train in the late afternoon and was transferred to a horse-drawn lorry. Finally, tired and stiff, I found myself on a slow-moving queue that began outside the hospital and snaked its way inside. I staggered to the front desk.

"Name," barked the nurse.

I displayed a sheepish grin. "My name is X."

My response did not jar her. She looked at the nametag pinned to my makeshift uniform, saw that X was my name, checked off a box, had me sign something I did not bother to read and ordered me to Ward B on the second floor. Nothing private this time. The ward had eight beds.

I was assigned to the only empty bed, in the far right corner. I had nothing other than a photograph and my kit of toiletries to put in the chest of drawers next to the bed. The bedsprings squealed from my weight. The thin mattress sagged in the middle. None of the patients acknowledged me. When the chap next to me finally did speak, he had a terrible stutter. The fellow next to him had a nervous twitch that caused him to claw at his shirt top and stretch his neck to the right in a bird-like manner. As a group, my new neighbors exhibited bizarre behaviors. Memory or no memory, my anticipation of help turned to schemes of escape.

*

Sleep eluded me that first night. My neighbors jabbered, cried out, screamed, or sobbed in a cacophony of noises. I had finally drifted to sleep when a nurse roused us up.

She strutted to the foot of my bed. "Welcome to Pasewalk. My name is Gerda. Breakfast is in ten minutes." Before I could answer, she continued. "After you eat, you have an appointment in the clinic with Dr. Forster."

"Who is he?" I asked, still in somewhat of a sleep-deprived fog.

"Your doctor."

In time, a nurse escorted me to a small, windowless office. She pointed to a stiff, wooden chair planted in front of a steel desk devoid of any extraneous artifacts save a solitary folder: my medical records. Given the number of surgeries, the folder was thick.

I continued to fidget when the door opened and a large man almost as tall as me, entered. He struggled into the chair behind the desk, offered me a cigarette and when I declined, fired up his own. "My name is Dr. Edmund Robert Forster. I am a psychiatrist. My job is to help you find out who you are."

"That would be appreciated," I said, my remark laced with both hope and skepticism.

It was as if he had not heard me, for he did not react. Instead, Dr. Forster spewed out a plume of blue-gray smoke. He studied me from behind round black-framed glasses that gave him an owl-like stare. "Do you know who you are?" he asked without preamble.

I gave up on the friendly approach. "If I did, I wouldn't be here talking to you, now would I?"

"On the contrary, it is quite possible you want to be here."

"Surely you don't believe that, Herr Doktor. No one wants to be here unless it is to get better."

Forster lit another cigarette with the embers of the last. He drew in a long drag before speaking again. "You have much to learn, Herr X. The patients here—personally, I would prefer to call them inmates—have one thing in common: none want to get better. They know that if they did, they would be sent back to the trenches. None want that."

There was nothing to like about this man. "That may be true for others, but not me. I *don't* want to be here."

"So you say." He glanced at my file.

My fists opened and closed. I bounded out of the chair, although it caused pain to move so fast.

He held up his hand. "We're not finished."

"We are for today, Herr Doktor Forster."

*

Departing from breakfast the next day, I heard a piercing scream from the bowels of the building. I froze. I turned to the soldier next to me, the one who blinked non-stop. "What was that?"

"Probably the sleeper. He sleeps day and night. The nurses poke him every few hours to use the W.C. so he won't crap in his bed. They hate cleaning it up. The doctor is convinced he is faking it."

"Is he?"

The man shrugged as if to say, *who knows?*

"What are they doing to him?"

"Electrodes."

I knew better than to ask where the wires were attached. One thing was clear to me: I had to get out of this place. I began to push myself. I tried to pry open the window on my memory. I started with what I knew. From the onset, I had the ability to speak. No one questioned that German was my native language. I could do numbers in my head, so that part of my brain worked. But when it came to conjuring up my past, everything was missing.

Back in my ward, I plucked out the photo that Anna and Dr. Joseph had found in my boot from the night table next to my bed. I studied each face as I had done a hundred times before, hoping to ignite a memory. The girl in the picture might have been eight or ten. She wore a light-colored dress that had a high neckline and ended at her knees. The boy stood next to his father; he was already half a head taller than the girl. He looked large for his age, as I might have been, given my oversized frame. From the date on the back of the photo, I knew I could not be the father.

*

The next day a fight broke out during lunch hour. One patient taunted another. The instigator was a thin, small, balding patient who enjoyed annoying those around him. This time he picked on a patient who was a head taller and twice as wide. The big man reached across the table, grabbed his tormentor by the throat with his left hand, and smashed him with his right fist. He didn't stop with one punch even though the agitator was already unconscious. He drove punch after punch into the man's face. Blood poured from the fellow's nose as his limp body absorbed the punishment like a ragdoll.

No one tried to stop it. I could have minded my own business, too. I didn't. I grabbed the big guy by the shoulder and spun him around.

"It's enough! Do you want to kill him?"

He snarled. "Who the fuck do you think you are?" Without waiting for a response, he swung his paw toward my chin. As if I knew how to fight my entire life, my left arm blocked his punch and I connected with a solid right with enough power to drive him to the floor. I readied myself for when he got up, but he lay there without moving. Seeing he was no longer a concern and ignoring the pain shooting through my arm, I scooped up the agitator and carried him to the intake room. When the nurse saw me cradling him, she pointed to the cot.

"What happened?" she asked as I laid him down.

I explained about the oversized brute and the thrashing he gave the man on the cot.

"Must have been Schweinitz. He has manure for a brain. The last one he sent here didn't have a patron saint like you."

"I did what anyone should have done."

"Not many around here would have been brave enough to stand up to that bully."

I rubbed my fist. "He wasn't that tough."

"Let me take a look at that."

"It's just a little stiff."

The nurse ignored me. She had me wiggle my fingers.

"Nothing appears broken. You may not be so lucky next time." She nodded to the man on the cot. "Thanks for saving him."

No one at the hospital fought near me again, and when I walked the halls patients took a wide birth around me. As the days passed, I struggled to recall, without success, how and why fighting came so natural to me. As it turned out, these skills would prove useful in the years ahead.

*

"Has any of your memory returned?" Dr. Forster inquired the next day. I shook my head. I noted a change in his demeanor. It was somehow different, even respectful. "From what I heard, you know how to handle yourself. Look at you. You stand six-foot-seven. Even after being in Charité for some months, you must weigh at least two hundred and twenty pounds. Most men would know not to tangle with you. Perhaps you trained soldiers how to fight?"

"I wish I knew."

Forster continued. "Do you even know why Germany is fighting? Why you and your fellow soldiers are risking their lives?"

"I've heard bits and pieces. Nothing that makes a coherent story."

He lit a new cigarette with the stub of the one already burned down to his finger. The nails on his right hand were nicotine-stained.

"We fight for our Fatherland. For a way of life that is superior to other countries. Our motto is '*Der deutsche Geist soll die Welt heilen*.'"

The German spirit shall heal the world.

"The German spirit may be good for the world, but it is not healing me. Why are you telling me this?"

"Because you have no views, opinions, or information. Here is the truth, Herr X. We are losing this war. But the war is bringing us together. Uniting Germans as we have never been united before."

This talk caused me to wonder which of us was ill. He sounded more like an inmate than a physician, but he gained my attention by changing the subject.

"Let me ask you, do you like being called X?"

"While I don't mind it, I would prefer to have my own name."

"From the army's point of view, you exist because they sent you here. We are even required to pay you, but you don't exist with respect to an identity. As long as you are in this place it doesn't matter. You're safe. But it cannot last forever. In time, anonymity will work against you. To help, I am going to give you a name: Friedrich Richard." He picked up a pen, wrote the name out on a pad, and handed it to me.

"Why this one?"

"Friedrich Richard was a patient here. He died not long ago. Actually, he committed suicide. As far as we know, he had no family. More importantly, we haven't reported his death yet. The army believes he is still here. You can become him and no one will dispute it."

I squirmed in my seat. "I don't see why I have to assume the name of a dead man."

"Look, X, you need to be *someone*. The war will end soon and you must have official papers. Use Friedrich Richard's military identification card. When your memory returns, toss his name and become your old self. No one will be the wiser."

I didn't like it, but it gave me a way out. "You must think that I'm much better or you wouldn't be doing this. I'm grateful for what you've done. So, yes, the identify papers with my new name are a great idea. I'll be able to function like any normal person. If that's the case, isn't it time to release me from this hospital? I could be on tomorrow's train and away from here."

Forster shook his head. "You're not ready to leave." His voice was cold and final.

Chapter 4

My wounds healed. I outgrew physical therapy and turned to weight training as an outlet for my energies. While my body mended, my mind remained clouded. *Squeeze the trigger with gentle pressure.* That phrase wormed its way into my dreams each night. It must have come from my past, but only served to further confuse me. I needed to learn more about myself.

One day, I asked Gerda if she could arrange for me to shoot a pistol. I thought it might jog a memory.

"There is an open area in the back that used to be a shooting range. You were a soldier. It makes perfect sense. Let me speak to the administrator."

*

An aide named Markus marched me to the open field behind the hospital. Beyond it lay a square cemetery with simple gray-granite tombstones. The aide placed an empty bottle on each of ten posts supporting the fence surrounding the cemetery. He handed me a pistol.

"That's a Mauser C96," I said without a second's thought.

Markus was stunned. "How did you know that?"

"I don't know, I just did."

There was a red number *nine* branded into the wooden handle that looked cut from a broomstick. The number was a distinct reminder not to use 7.63 mm ammunition. I seemed to know that, too. With its long barrel and a strip of nine-millimeter brass-shelled bullets serving as a miniature bandolier dangling from the right side of the gun, the Mauser C96 resembled a tiny version of a machine gun.

The gun's weight felt comfortable in my right hand. I was relieved there was no lingering pain as I lifted my arm to aim. I cupped my left hand under my right wrist, aimed, and fired. I missed the first bottle. I dropped the pistol to my side, drew in a calming, deep breath, repeated the steps, and squeezed the trigger with gentle pressure. This time the bottle shattered, as did the next and all the rest. It was rapid and effortless.

"Perfect," said Markus.

"I missed the first one."

"That one didn't count. That was remarkable shooting."

*

Gerda stopped me in the doorway to my ward as I returned from another unproductive session with Dr. Forster. "Friedrich, you are going to have a new bunkmate." She pointed to the empty bed next to mine.

"What happened to the stutterer?"

"He progressed enough to return to the front."

"Shock therapy?"

"Who wants to stay here after that?"

*

A few hours later, I turned the corner on my daily walk around the grounds to witness a caravan of horse-drawn carts filled with new patients pull up to the front. The last man in the rear wagon could not steer his way down without help; his eyes were bandaged. He was thin and pasty-faced. His straight black hair draped across his forehead and he had a thick walrus moustache that drooped beyond the corners of his lips. "Get me down," he ordered to no one, his arms flailing to touch something. The cart driver grabbed the man's extended hand, guided him to the ground, and then forced him to grasp the belt of the patient in front of him.

I followed as they marched to reception. Once registered, each was shown to their ward and bed. Gerda sidled up to the soldier who would soon occupy the bed next to mine.

"I'm Gerda. I will be your nurse." She caught my eye and winked. Without a word, the man took her arm as they shuffled toward our ward. I followed a few steps behind. She patted the mattress hard. "This is your bed," she pronounced in a loud voice.

"I'm blind, Fräulein, not deaf."

Gerda grimaced. She made no effort to hide her distaste for this chap. "Someone will take you to lunch in a short while."

"*Danke schön*," he mumbled to Gerda's retreating backside. I watched him lean and feel around the bed. When he got to the pillow, he oriented himself, swung his feet onto the mattress, and settled down. I could have stayed and welcomed him but instead walked away.

Gerda caught up with me in the hallway. "Friedrich, I need your help with the new patient."

"Why is he so nasty?"

"He was blinded in a gas attack. We are so understaffed. It would be great if you could help feed him and help him navigate the halls."

"I'm not qualified to be a nursemaid. Besides, why was he sent here if he has problems with his eyes?"

She put her hand on my arm. "It's not my job to question why. Now, please, do this for me?"

As it turned out . . . I should have said, "No."

I remember that date as if it were yesterday: October 21, 1918.

*

Reluctant to attend to an unpleasant blind man, I stayed away from my ward the rest of the afternoon playing cards. Gerda found me two hours later. "You can't hide here all day, Friedrich."

I grinned, tossed my cards down, bid my adieu, and followed Gerda. The new man lay motionless with white gauze taped across both eyes. There was no way to know if he was sleeping or awake. I eased onto my bed, trying to be quiet; the bedsprings pinged.

"*Wer geht Dahin?*"

"It's me, your neighbor." While his German was flawless, I detected the slightest of accents.

He spoke without affect or turning his head. "My world is black."

At that moment, Dr. Karl Kroner entered the ward. I often saw this doctor examining new patients when they arrived at Pasewalk. Kroner was a thin man with a handlebar moustache, with gold, wire-rim glasses that made him appear serious. He was a Jewish neurologist, awarded the Iron Cross, First Class. Like the patient in the bed next to me, I later learned that Dr. Kroner was recently the victim of a gas attack and temporarily blinded, too.

Dr. Kroner introduced himself, helped the patient to a sitting position, and removed his bandages. After examining the patient's eyes through an ophthalmoscope, Dr. Kroner scrunched his face into a quizzical, I-am-not-sure-about-this, look. Then he placed new bandages over the patient's eyes and stood tall.

"You have remarkable blue eyes," Dr. Kroner said.

"Will I see again, Herr Doktor?"

Dr. Kroner shifted his weight. "We have the best doctor in all of Germany here to treat your problem. I will arrange for Dr. Forster to examine you."

The blind soldier groped for Kroner's hand. "But will he help me see again?"

"If anyone can, it is Dr. Forster."

The man let go of Kroner. "Then I will place my fate in this man's hands."

I was startled that Forster, a psychiatrist, would treat this fellow's blindness. "What happened to you?" I asked once Kroner left.

In hushed tones, he explained, "I am a regiment message runner."

"What's that?" I asked.

"We run from the commanders to the troops in the field, dodging shells and bullets to deliver their orders. I am one of the longest-lasting runners in the war," he said with pride. "Most get killed."

"How did your injury occur?"

"I was attached to the 16th Bavarian Reserve Infantry Regiment. The List Regiment. We were in the trenches at Wervicq-Sud, in northern France. The other runners and I were about to eat breakfast when we heard the telltale plopping of nearby shells. In moments, I started to cough and then choke. All of us did."

"Didn't you have masks?"

"It happened too fast. In moments my eyes turned into glowing coals; it grew dark around me. We all knew it was *gasvergiftung*." (Gas poisoning)

I swung my feet over the edge of the bed and sat up. "And then what happened?"

"They cut the uniform right off my body, washed out my eyes, and sent me to Oudenaarde. It's a town in Belgium. I stayed there five days before they sent me to see a specialist in blindness here."

I did not have the heart to reveal that his soon-to-be-treating physician was a psychiatrist.

We stopped chatting when a nurse brought my new companion his meal. I cut the food and helped him stab the pieces, which he ate sitting at the edge of his bed. When he finished, he mumbled his thanks. I took the tray, said good-bye, and left for the dining room. By the time I returned, he was fast asleep.

"Help me! Help me! Will someone help me?"

I awoke with a start.

"Won't someone show me mercy and take me to the W.C.?"

No help was in sight. "I'll be right there." I assisted him to his feet. He was all bones. I led him to the toilet and opened the door. "It is right in front of you."

"Is the door still open?"

"It is. I want to make sure you don't trip and hit your head."

"Am I standing in the right place?"

"You are."

"Then please close the door. I am capable of doing this myself."

I shrugged. The worst he could do was soil himself. "The cord is to your left. About shoulder high. And the paper—actually old newspapers—are piled on the right."

I heard the tank flush, but the door remained closed. I knocked, heard nothing, and yanked it back. I was surprised to find him standing toe-to-door, his face in mine. He held out his hand for me to guide him back to his bed.

"You are very kind. What is your name?"

"Friedrich Richard."

A bright smile creased his face. "You have parts of each of my two most favorite people in your name: Friedrich Nietzsche and Richard Wagner. It is an honor to make your acquaintance, Herr Friedrich Richard."

"The honor is mine. And what should I call you?"

"The men in the regiment call me Wolf."

The next day Wolf returned from his first session with Dr. Forster. Patients did not question each other about private sessions, but Wolf volunteered.

"I cannot believe that speaking to a doctor will make my eyes better. He didn't even examine me the way Dr. Kroner did."

"Perhaps he needs to know you better before he can help you."

"I don't see how. I told him that I was an artist and that I needed my eyesight to paint."

"What do you paint?"

The muscles on his taut face relaxed. He ticked off a series of themes. "I paint scenes. Beautiful scenes. Churches. Plazas. Landscapes. And faces." Then his face hardened. "Not a word about my painting. Instead Doktor Forster asked about my parents and if I had been a happy child. What does that have to do with my eyes getting better?"

I tried to reassure him. "After a time, I've learned that there is a method to the Herr Doktor's questions."

Wolf's second night at Pasewalk introduced a trait that remained as long as I knew him: Wolf suffered from insomnia. He would pace back and forth for hours on a route he memorized, while the others slept. And then, when the hospital was abuzz on its early morning schedules, Wolf would sleep 'til noon.

Between conveying him to the toilet, his nocturnal pacing, and feeding him, I had a substantial job.

As the days passed, Wolf continued to report his talks with Dr. Forster, including intimate details about his childhood. "I told Docktor Forster that that I hated my father and was glad when he died. The lout beat me. The times he didn't beat me were when he was too drunk to raise his arm." Wolf said this sitting with his head straight, unmoving.

"Didn't your mother try to protect you?"

"When she did, he beat her, too. When he finally died, his pension sustained us for a time. Then my mother got sick and the money ran out. Breast cancer. I can't tell you how she suffered." As he spoke, the gauze covering his eyes grew moist, and he wiped his runny nose on his sleeve.

*

I had my own sessions with Dr. Forster. "Tell me, Friedrich, what have you learned about your friend, the one they call Wolf?"

"Is it correct for me to discuss another patient with you?"

"I don't see why not," Forster answered. "You would be helping me understand him better."

Dr. Forster saw I was skeptical.

"Let me share what I can," Forster said. "Wolf came from a dysfunctional family. His father was a cruel, brutal man incapable of loving his son or anyone else. A drunkard and a wife beater who openly philandered. When he died, Wolf experienced a great sense of relief. But this respite was short-lived. Soon after, his mother became sick. She had a most painful death."

I tried to remember something Wolf had said. "He did mention a Dr. Bloch to me. He said that the doctor did everything he could to make her comfortable, but that nothing worked."

Dr. Forster leaned closer, a conspirator sharing a secret. "That is part of his problem, Friedrich. On the one hand, this Jewish Doktor Bloch was the kind father Wolf never had. Indeed Wolf continued to have an emotional tie to Bloch long after his mother passed. He sent Dr. Bloch paintings—street scenes—that he painted when he moved to Vienna."

I was impressed. "He didn't have to do that."

"Ah . . . but there's another side to this. Subconsciously, Wolf also resents the doctor because he could not relieve his mother's pain."

"I don't see how any of this bears on his blindness after a gas attack."

"Before I explain, there is something else you should know. Wolf recited a poem from memory that he claims to have written in homage to his mother. It's a touching poem. It talks about a mother growing older and what used to be easy for her now takes a greater effort. The poem goes on to describe that as the mother travels on her last journey, growing weaker and sicker, she may no longer be able to understand what her son says anymore, but the son should remain joyful until the last, bitter hour."

"That is how he described his mother's death to me. But, Dr. Forster, what does this have to do with the fact that Wolf cannot see?"

Forster grew animated as he explained. "Don't you see? Wolf has linked Germany losing this war to his mother's slow death. As a result he transferred his mother's pain to his eyes."

"How can you possibly connect his blindness to his mother dying and Germany's defeat?"

"Because it's not real."

"What's not real?"

"The poem." Forster tapped the side of his head. "That's not how I meant to say it. The poem is very real. The sentiments are beautiful."

"Then what's the problem?"

"Wolf didn't write the poem. Georg Runsky wrote it more than a dozen years ago."

"I don't understand. What are you saying?"

"It means that Wolf's problem is more difficult to treat than I first imagined. He suffers from hysterical blindness. A French physician—Paul Briquet—first described a syndrome seventy years ago in which the mind can do strange things in order to cope with emotional and psychological stresses. Wolf has never gotten over his mother's death and now he is challenged with Germany's metaphorical death. This dynamic translates into Wolf shutting down a sensory organ. In his case, it's his eyes. And to make matters worse, he has taken a poem written by someone else and convinced himself that he is its author."

I followed Dr. Forster's explanation as best I could. "Is there nothing you can do for him?"

Before answering, Forster struck a match and said through a stream of smoke, "Wolf will remain blind for the rest of his life . . . unless something gives him permission to see again."

"Could my memory loss be a variation of what Wolf is experiencing?"

Forster shook his head. "No, it's different. His issues are deeply personal and psychological. Given the head trauma you received, yours appears to be organic. I haven't given up on you. There are still treatments available to try."

*

Dr. Forster began a different approach to help me regain my memory. He read popular children's books out loud to see if any sounded familiar. When that did not work, *I* read the books out loud. Still nothing. Next he showed me pictures of city after city, to see if I recognized a street, a building, or a monument. No image meant anything to me.

Then he tried music. We listened to Mendelssohn, Brahms, Pachelbel, Strauss, Offenbach, Schumann, Wagner, and more.

"Do any sound familiar?"

I nodded. "Many do."

There was excitement in his voice. "Which ones?"

"Actually, they all do."

"Can you picture where you listened to them? Was it in a theater? In your house? Maybe you played an instrument in an orchestra? Who were you with at the time you heard them?"

Try as I might, I could not picture listening to this or that music in any given place, only that I knew each piece well enough to anticipate chords. Dr. Forster assured me that one day something would catapult my lost memories from its recesses to the forefront of my brain.

Chapter 5

Wolf was a complex individual. To me, he was by turns tolerant, then needy, and yet warm when I least expected it. For instance, he could not have been more sympathetic when he learned from me about my amnesia. I continued to help feed him and take him to the bathroom when the urge called. I guided him down the halls, introduced him to the other patients, and listened to his many discourses on art, architecture, and history. The man was well read. It was nearly three weeks after his sessions started with Dr. Forster that he began to make progress. He could see the outlines of shapes.

It was then that he first began to talk about the Jews. He despised them. "Jews identify themselves by blood," Wolf said. "The blood of the mother. They are a race. If they were a religion, blood would not matter. The other great religions—Catholic, Protestant, Muslim, and Hindu . . . all of them—do not use blood to define themselves. Jews are a racial virus. They infest every society they enter. No matter which country they abide in, their loyalty is to their tribe—their race—and they suck the blood out of every country that hosts them."

This was news to me, and I had no way of knowing if he was correct.

When it came to memory, Wolf's was phenomenal. He read hundreds of books, or so he said. He remembered every significant date in German history, every battle Germany fought, and which generals were in command. Wolf quoted Nietzsche and Schopenhauer. He could sing the librettos from Wagner's *Ring of the Nibelung*. And he had the ability to contort his voice and mimic all sorts of realistic sounds.

November 11, 1918

News raced throughout the hospital: The Chaplain announced that the Great War was over. Germany signed an armistice agreement with the Allies to go into effect at the eleventh hour of the eleventh day of the eleventh month. Acknowledging defeat, our army agreed to withdraw behind our own borders.

Although the outcome was bitter, most of us were elated that the fighting ended, including me.

Not Wolf. Wolf's gains of three weeks reversed. The news of the armistice plunged him back into total darkness.

"We have surrendered? That's impossible!" Wolf cried out, raising his index finger to the ceiling. "We're *not* defeated. Foreign troops *never* entered German soil. The war was still ours to win," he insisted. "We have been stabbed in the back!"

I tried to mollify him. "Wolf, it's good the war is over. Too many have died. Now is the time to save lives."

Wolf was inconsolable. He would not stop his tirade. "It was the Jewish press and Jewish moneylenders that sunk us."

*

The next day I reported to Dr. Forster that Wolf's blindness returned moments after learning about the armistice.

"What else did he say?"

"He said that Germany would emerge from this temporary defeat as the greatest nation on earth."

"Friedrich, does he really believe what he says?"

"With all his heart."

The doctor's eyes crinkled with delight. He clapped his hands. "You have given me the tool I need to help him see again."

That night, Dr. Forster summoned Wolf for a special session.

*

The following morning, I rushed to Dr. Forster's office filled with excitement. "It's amazing! When Wolf returned from your last treatment he could see! Not only could he see, but he had a different air about him."

Forster leaned forward eagerly. "Tell me how he has changed."

"Besides seeing everything clearly, he was more formal. More reverent. More focused. What did you do to him to change him so?"

Dr. Forster beamed. "None of my usual techniques worked on him. Unlike others I treat here, he was no shirker. He was anxious to get back to the front."

"Wolf told you that the first day he was here. So did I . . . we both wanted to go back to the front!"

"I didn't believe Wolf at first." Dr. Forster plucked a cigarette from his silver case and tapped it before striking a match. He drew in deeply before he spoke again. "The doctors in the field knew that his comrades were also gassed. Those men not only recovered but returned to their positions in the trenches. When Wolf continued to act out and claim to still be blind, he was diagnosed as a hysteric. That's why he was sent here. His condition is mental, not organic."

"But he started to see shapes. He was getting better."

"Yes. And when you told me he turned blind again upon hearing of Germany's defeat, I knew I had the answer to unlock what was still holding him back. So last night, I summoned him on the pretense of needing to perform another eye examination. The moment he sat down, I drew the blinds and lit two candles."

"To what end?"

"To hypnotize him."

"Did he know what you were doing?"

Dr. Forster shook his head. "Not in the least. When he was under hypnosis, I blew out the candles and sat back. Then I told him it would take a miracle for his blindness to be reversed and that miracles are far and few between. When they do occur, it is because God wants them to happen."

"What did he say to that?"

"Not a word," answered Dr. Forster. "Then I grew firmer. I told him that only a person with Herculean willpower could see again. I challenged him. I suggested he was the anointed one, and that if he had the inner strength to open his eyes and see again, he would be the one to save Germany."

I could picture Wolf sitting there, while Forster spun his web of suggestions.

Dr. Forster grew animated. "All this was said in pitch blackness. Then I relit both candles. I took Wolf's hands in mine and squeezed them. 'If you trust yourself to the divine plan God has in store for you,' I said, 'open your eyes.' I waited a few strokes. 'Do you see the flickering flame?'"

At that moment Dr. Forster stood and took my hands in his, just as he had taken Wolf's the previous evening.

"At first Wolf said, 'I cannot see the flame.' Then he began to change. His breathing grew shallow. He said, 'I see a kind of white, round glow.' I raised my voice louder; I squeezed his hands harder. Like this." Forster put tremendous pressure on my hands. "Then I said, 'That is not good enough. Only when you have absolute faith in yourself will you stop being blind.'" Spent from re-experiencing the ordeal, Forster dropped my hands and fell back.

"Then what happened?"

Sweat rimmed the edge of his scalp and his upper lip. He took out an embroidered handkerchief and swiped away the perspiration before continuing. "He cried out that he could see my face, and even the signet ring on my finger. I told him that he had been cured." Forster collapsed into his chair. "I tell you, Friedrich, this is my crowning achievement as a doctor."

*

Upon my return to the ward, I found an exultant Wolf. "*Friedrichshen*, it is so good to see you, *really* see you, and to know that you will never be faceless to me again. I can never forget your kindnesses. When no one else heeded my cries for help, you were at my side, day after day. Ours is a bond that will last forever."

"I am happy for you, Wolf."

*

I stopped in Forster's office the following day. "What's next, Dr. Forster?"

"What do you mean?"

"For me? Wolf? The rest of the men? The war is over. What's to become of us?"

"Everyone here is still in the army. Treatments will continue. The ones that don't improve will be sent to a sanitarium."

"Wolf is cured. What about him?"

"I need to observe him for a few days to make certain he doesn't relapse. Then he will be released back to his regiment."

"And me?"

"You, Friedrich, are not cured."

"I feel fine. My wounds have healed. You've given me a name. Find a regiment for me to join."

"It's not that simple." Dr. Forster lit another cigarette. His head twitched as he sat straighter. Something bothered him. "You have the name of a dead man. You cannot take his place in the army. You need your own identity."

My right leg started to bob up and down. "You gave me his name. You said I could go about my life with it. Are you taking that back?" I squeezed my leg to stop the bouncing.

"I have an academic appointment at Charité Hospital. I will write orders for you to return there so we can continue your treatment."

"There's nothing wrong with me." I rose to leave. "I will not return to Charité, but I am prepared to make a deal with you."

"Sit down! Friedrich, you are in no position to make a deal."

"Hear me out." I leaned over his desk. "You gave me the identity of a man because you said I needed one to function once the war ended. You said you never reported his suicide, that his papers were still valid. Because of you, I can go out into the world as Friedrich Richard. But now, you don't want to let me go until you succeed in restoring my memory. Isn't that the truth? So here is the deal: you will let me go to Berlin as Friedrich Richard. In return, I will schedule regular appointments with you for treatment."

Forster frowned. I could see that he didn't like it . . . but I gave him no choice.

*

Wolf's sight remained with him. He had a few more sessions with Dr. Forster, as did I, and on November 19, 1918, we were both discharged.

"Where are they sending you?" I asked.

"Back to my regiment in Munich."

I turned playful. "Have you come up with a plan to make Germany great again?"

Wolf answered in earnest. "I don't see how to accomplish that now, but one day I will have a plan." He took my hand. "I will always have a place for you, *Friedrichshen*. Until then, what will you do?"

"I'll look up my former nurse in Berlin. She's the only other person I know. I think she had an interest in me. I hope she still does." He knew all about Anna from our late night talks. "I'll try to get a job in Berlin."

"The leftists are in revolt there. They call themselves *Spartacists*. Whatever you do, be careful, Friedrich. There will come a day when *I* will need you."

We embraced as two brothers who were about to go in opposite directions. While there was something odd about the man, I knew that we had forged a unique bond from adversity.

"One last thing." A wave of embarrassment washed over me. "In all the time we've been together, I never heard your proper name. I only know you as Wolf."

He wrapped his hands around both my shoulders. "It's Adolf . . . which is a variation of Adalwolf. It means 'splendid wolf.'"

"Adolf what?"

"Adolf Hitler."

PART II

Chapter 6

Berlin, November 1918

I left the sleepy town of Pasewalk in the early morning and, hours later, emerged into the central Berlin train station. The only money I had was the five months' pay issued on my release and a photograph of people I didn't remember. On the train I could think of little else other than finding Anna. What would I do if Anna no longer worked at Charité Hospital? Or if she no longer had an interest in me?

I located the hospital on a wall map and set off to find her. I found a city in crisis. There were brigades of men dressed in mismatched jackets and pants topped with every manner of fedora. They marched out of step, shouldering rifles while hooting and hollering like hooligans. Back at Pasewalk, newspaper headlines were alarming:

BERLIN SEIZED BY REVOLUTIONISTS

AND

NEW CHANCELLOR BEGS FOR ORDER

News accounts and Wolf's warnings were one thing. Witnessing the disorder was another.

There was fighting in the streets. Armed Communists knelt behind barricades. Red banners hung from buildings and windows. Every few blocks I was forced to change direction in order to navigate around rowdy gangs of every flavor: Socialists, Monarchists, and Bolsheviks.

When I finally reached the hospital, I inquired as to Anna's whereabouts at the reception desk.

"I'm sorry, *mein Herr*, but hospital staff are not permitted personal visitors." Rather than argue, I turned to leave, dawdling until she was distracted, and then I ducked into a stairwell and trekked up one floor to look around. No luck. Then the second and third floors. Still no Anna. On the fourth try I spotted her leaving a ward.

"What are you doing here?"

"These are for you," I pressed a small bouquet of flowers into her hand. "I had all to do not to crush them getting here from the railway station."

She smelled them and then threw her arms around me, kissing me full on the mouth. My concerns about Anna were answered.

She stepped back and surveyed me from head to toe. "Pasewalk agreed with you." She poked me in the ribs. "You put on some weight. You look wonderful." Then with a look of concern, she asked, "How about your memory?"

"Nothing came back to me."

Her smile turned into a frown. "Not even your name?"

I shook my head. "But I have one now. They gave it to me at the hospital: Friedrich Richard."

"I like it. It's a strong German name. It suits you."

Then she turned me into the light to get a closer look. With a delicate touch she turned my face from one side to the other. "Your wounds have healed without scars." Her fingers lingered an extra second.

"I'm sure Dr. Joseph would like to see how you have healed. I will arrange an appointment."

After muttering that I would like to see him, too, I said, "I'm lucky I made it to the hospital from the train station. Troops are everywhere. People chanting and singing songs. What's happening in Berlin?"

"Too much to tell you about now. It's wonderful that you're here, but I need to get back to work."

I had hoped for more than a hug, a kiss, and a goodbye. Crestfallen, I fussed as if trying to find something in my pocket.

She saw my concern. "Friedrich, my shift ends in two hours." She smiled warmly. "If you occupy yourself for a while, you can come back to my house. I'll feed you and catch you up on the news. How does that sound?"

"Like a wish fulfilled."

"I'll meet you at the hospital entrance."

I set off in a random walk, keeping my head down to avoid contact with the gaggles of men clogging the streets. I found a quiet street and peered through a storefront window. For a time, I watched a shoemaker trim a strip of leather to form the sole of a shoe. He looked up and motioned me to come in.

"May I help you?"

He was old and hunched over, but his thick fingers were nimble. "I was fascinated by the way you used your tools. The precision of your work."

"I've been doing this since before you were born. Hands have their own memories. I don't have to think about what I am doing." He wiggled his fingers. "They do all the work."

"I would like to learn a trade. Is it possible you might have a job opening for an apprentice?"

"As much as I would like to teach someone what I know," he sighed, "there is not enough business to pay wages. I barely pay my bills now."

"It was just a thought. Thank you for your time." I pulled open the door.

"Why don't you try the lighting store across the street? Everybody is converting gas lamps into fixtures. Buildings are being wired for electricity every day. It is a good business."

No matter which shop I entered—the lighting store, a butcher, a men's clothing store, even a barbershop—it was the same. The few businesses that made enough to remain open could ill afford to take someone in. I lost track of time.

I found Anna waiting on the hospital steps. I was about to apologize when she grabbed my hand. "I was worried about you. Let's go. I live a short walk from here, but we still need to watch for roving bands of ruffians."

Getting to her home proved a challenge. We would start down one street only to reverse ourselves, duck into an alleyway or hide behind a garden wall to avoid groups of rifle-toting men. A ten-minute walk from where *Philippstraße* ended at *Hannoversche Strasse* took half an hour.

She pointed. "This is it. Number twenty-three." We stood outside a red brick building surrounded by a six-foot block wall. Her voice turned husky. "I should warn you, I live with someone."

"Oh!"

Anna turned impish. "*She* is out most nights. Marta has a job in an underground nightclub."

Relieved, I asked, "What is an underground nightclub?"

"The Kaiser was very prim and proper. He discouraged nightlife, but that didn't stop Berliners from having a good time. We just did it quietly. Most often in dark cellars. Now he's gone and clubs and cabarets are springing up all over town. But," she laughed, "we still call them 'underground.' My roommate, Marta, works in one."

Anna's apartment was on the second of a three-floor, U-shaped building that overlooked a garden courtyard. White lace curtains covered the windows of the living room. There were two small bedrooms.

Marta was in her mid-twenties. Slender, with a narrow face, her thick lips made prominent by bold red lipstick. Her short blond hair emphasized large gold-colored looped earrings. She greeted me with a broad, bright smile.

"Anna tells me you work in a nightclub."

She shrugged. "I was trained as a dietician, but the pay was awful. I make enough at the club to put up with the lecherous old men that try to paw me every night."

"Are they that bad?"

"Nothing I can't handle."

We squeezed around the kitchen table for dinner. When we finished, Marta rose. "Do you mind if I leave the dishes to you two? I need to get ready for work."

"I am so glad you decided to see me on your return," said Anna, once Marta was gone.

"You have been in my thoughts since the day I left Charité."

She rolled her eyes. "There's not a soldier who doesn't fall for his nurse." Then she reached for my hand. I felt a spark race up my arm. Her dimples deepened. "I had hoped you would return. Stay here with Marta and me, at least until you find work. Where else would you go?"

"What about Marta?"

"She won't care. The apartment is small, but we work opposite schedules. She at night, me during the day. Believe me, it will be nice to have a man here with all that is going on in the streets."

I looked down at the couch.

Without blushing, Anna shook her head. "You can't stay out here. You have to share my bed!" She drew me near. "Will that be a problem?"

*

I awoke to an empty bed in the morning. Anna had gone to the hospital while Marta's door was closed. In the kitchen, a note rested on a linen napkin that covered a plate of food: "Coffee is on the stove. Bon appétit. See you after work." I reheated the coffee, ate with gusto, and rinsed the dishes and silverware.

Having finished cleaning up, I left the apartment in search of a job. The answer was the same everywhere: businesses were hanging on by a thread. There was no work.

*

Anna found me on the couch, sitting in the dark, with a glass of whiskey in my hand.

"There are no jobs out there. I can't eat your food, drink your liquor, and not contribute."

She slipped next to me, her face painted with concern. "Is that what this is about? You paying to stay here? Listen to me, Friedrich. Even though I like you very much—and it has been a long time since I said that to anyone—this is also about me helping someone in need. Until you find yourself, I will provide you a place to stay and food to eat."

I turned away, unable to meet her gaze. "I refuse to be a charity case."

Anna touched my chin and drew my face toward hers. "You've got it all wrong. This is not charity. I am a caregiver, Friedrich. You need help and I am fortunate that I can give it to you. Take it in the spirit it is given." Then her eyes narrowed, her thin brows arched, and she permitted the smallest smile. "Actually, consider last night a deposit on your repayment to me."

*

Anna arranged for me to see Dr. Joseph the next day. When I arrived, she greeted me at the clinic entrance. "He's anxious to see you." She ushered me to an examination room, handed me a hospital gown, and left to see another patient.

"I hear that you now have a name, *Herr* Former X." Dr. Joseph chuckled as he entered the room.

He was as I remembered: professional yet exuding warmth. "It's Friedrich Richard," I said. "Dr. Forster gave it to me at Pasewalk. It's not my real name."

"To quote the Bard, 'What's in a name?'"

I had no idea what that meant.

Dr. Joseph touched the bridge of his glasses, as he often did. "Let me take a look at you." He adjusted the overhead dome-shaped light designed for close inspection. He had me turn this way and that. Maneuvering the gown, he studied the areas that had been burned: my right leg, arm, and back.

While I dressed in front of him, he said, "I am pleased with your progress. From what I hear, so is Anna." He patted me on the back, and then turned serious. "You promised a certain someone to schedule appointments with him. He's been asking for you."

"Could you please tell Dr. Forster that I am doing fine?"

"If your memory was restored, I would. But it's not."

"Nothing he tried worked. Why should I waste time seeing him when I could be out finding a job?"

"If for no other reason than he's the doctor who cared for you."

"No, Dr. Joseph. *You* are that person. As far as Dr. Forster is concerned, I was a clinical experiment that failed."

Chapter 7

January 1919

I still had no work at the end of my second month in Berlin but grew familiar with fellow job seekers also going door-to-door each day. Conversations were struck that turned into shared stories over steins of lager.

Clothes were a premium; I continued to wear an army uniform shirt along with pants Anna bought me.

"You were a soldier," a fellow said one day. "Join us. The leftist *Spartacists* revolt is attempting to take over Germany. The *Freikorps* needs men like you to restore stability. I guarantee it will be better than pounding the streets for a job that isn't there. It's up to us to save the new government from the Communists."

The revolution in Berlin was in full flower. Chancellor Friedrich Ebert's new government survived only because the army backed him. But the army, a shadow of itself, was inadequate to deal with the Communists. In a desperate move against the left, Ebert summoned the *Freikorps* to arms. The *Freikorps* were roving bands of former soldiers led by former officers.

I no longer remember that comrade's name, but he convinced me to join the fight. "The Minister of Defense, Gustav Noske, has asked us to break the Marxist Communists workers' strike. Two Jews head it: Rosa Luxemburg and Karl Liebknecht. If we don't stop this uprising now, the Reds will take over. Berlin will become a Bolshevik puppet like Hungary. Join with us! What do you say?"

For the next several weeks, I became a head-bashing member of the *Freikorps*. I put men into the hospital where Anna, who thought I was job-hunting, ministered to their injuries. We stormed buildings, destroyed barricades, and liberated Berlin . . . block-by-block.

By mid-January, Anna had figured out that I was no longer looking for work, but kept her peace avoiding a confrontation. Then one day she came home early and found me nursing a whiskey.

"You gave me a start. I didn't expect you to be home now. Is everything all right?"

I continued to stare into my glass. "These last few weeks have been rough. I haven't been as attentive to you as I have in the past and . . ."

"That's because you are under so much stress to get a job. It's understandable."

"I appreciate that, but let me finish. You're right. I have been under stress. You and Marta have been generous letting me stay here without expecting me to contribute." She tried to say something, but I stopped her. "No matter what you say, I do not feel good about myself. More to that point, I don't deserve you."

Her eyes puddled. "Friedrich, where is this coming from? I thought if I gave you your space, you would feel better about yourself." She blotted away the tears and straightened her uniform. "I promised myself after I lost my husband at the beginning of the war, that I would not get involved with another man. It was not that I didn't want to love someone else; I couldn't bear losing someone a second time." She looked me straight in the eyes. "Is that where this is going?"

My resolved weakened. "I guess what I have been trying to say is that I hate the way my life has turned out."

"It is not your fault." She leaned into me; I put my arm around her. "The country is a mess. Anarchists almost toppled the government," she said, and then sat up. "Did you hear what happened yesterday?" She didn't wait for an answer. "The papers say that the Spartacist Revolt is over. Their leaders, those Communist troublemakers Karl Liebknecht and Rosa Luxemburg, have been arrested. They say that in three days we will elect a National Assembly and become a parliamentary democracy. Isn't that good news? Then I am certain you will be able to find a job."

I stood, took two paces, and wheeled around. "They didn't just arrest Liebknecht and Luxemburg, Anna, they killed them."

"There was no mention of that in the paper. Are you certain?"

I eased back next to her and took her hands. "I was there, Anna. Luxemburg was clubbed to the ground with a rifle stock and then shot in the head. The *Freikorps* threw her body into the Landwehr Canal."

Anna let out a sigh of relief. "God forgive me. I should feel awful about her murder. But I had convinced myself you were seeing someone else these last few weeks."

She went to the sideboard and poured herself a whiskey. We faced each other. "So what you're telling me is that you are not disenchanted with me, it's just your need to find a purpose in your life." She took a sip before continuing. "Since there are no jobs available, you helped prevent leftists from overthrowing Chancellor Ebert. Do I have it right?"

In large part, she did. "What you left out is that I don't deserve you, and you should be with a man who not only loves you, but can make your life easier."

"You dumb fool. I don't want another man. I want you . . . with all your stupid imperfections."

Chapter 8

January – November 1919

Beyond aiding the understaffed army, the *Freikorps* served another purpose: it provided me with both companionship and another patriotic mission. This time we set out to overthrow the recent Communist takeover of Bavaria. Ernst Röhm led our division of thirty thousand men. Captain Röhm, holder of the Iron Cross, First Class—for distinguished service—stopped at nothing when it came to accomplishing a mission. That he liked boys rather than girls did not trouble me.

Led by Röhm, we overthrew the Bavarian Communist government, while at the same time, Germany's politics shifted yet again. A new constitution was adopted. The seat of government was moved to the town of Weimar, where the government's shaky legs began to stabilize. With their monarchies overthrown, the fifteen separate German states initiated democratic freedoms that raised hopes. There was also a tectonic shift in German mores. It was this swing in values that gave Anna and Marta an opportunity to change my life.

*

One Sunday afternoon, in early September, Marta, Anna, and I set out to picnic in a nearby park. The women prepared a lunch of assorted sandwiches. My job was to carry the blanket, wine, and glasses without breaking anything.

"Friedrich, be a dear and open the Riesling," Anna said.

As I turned the corkscrew, Marta blurted out, "My boss is looking for someone your size to be a bouncer at the nightclub."

I wasn't certain what a bouncer was. After Marta explained, I asked, "All your boss wants me to do is stand there and look tough? And he will pay me to do that?"

"It's more than that. Your job is to keep drunks from entering. We can't have customers harassed or disturbances distracting our shows. Sometimes that means a physical confrontation."

"Mixing it up is not an issue for me."

"I didn't think so," said Marta. Then her pale skin turned crimson. "There is something else you should know. Things can get pretty weird inside the clubs."

"What are you talking about?"

Marta explained. "The new Weimar government is not self-righteous about sex. It has overturned Emperor Wilhelm's moral pigeonholes. With the new republic, the genie has been let out of the bottle, so to speak. My boss wants to capitalize on it."

"In what way?"

"You're aware that my boss closed his underground night-club to open a cabaret." I nodded. "Well, he opened two more clubs: one for gays and one for others. Straights are welcomed at both."

"Whoa! You are going too fast for me. What are *others*? For that matter, what are straights?"

Anna pointed to herself and then me. "You and I are straights. Male/female."

"Others," said Marta, "are everyone else. Lesbians. Homosexual men. Transvestites. Men who like midgets, and those interested in people with disabilities."

I could not credit what I was hearing. "You're talking about a nation of perverts."

"On the contrary," said Marta, "we are talking about freedom of expression. So," she glanced at Anna, "are you going to take the job?"

"You skipped over how things might get out of hand inside the club."

"It's not complicated, Friedrich," Anna interrupted. "You keep the peace in the club. That's the job. Period. From my perspective, that is better than gallivanting around the country in a private army committing indiscriminate violence. For which, I might add, you receive no pay and run the risk of getting killed."

"Let's get something straight," I replied. "The *Freikorps* protects our women and children. Our purpose is to bring stability to our country."

Anna crossed her arms. "Is that so? Rosa Luxemburg was a woman. I was the duty nurse when they brought her decomposed body to Charité. She remained in the Landwehr Canal for five months after your comrades killed her. You can imagine how hard it was to identify her. Your *Freikorps* didn't protect her, now, did they?"

"Are you questioning that the leaders of the Communist Revolution had to be removed?"

Anna turned stone cold. "You accomplished that. The streets are quiet. Now I want your answer, Friedrich. Take the position or leave our flat."

The picnic was a setup. They both knew I had no choice.

*

Marta's boss, Max Klinghofer, owned a grand space that he took from foreclosure during the war. The space needed little in the way of renovation. The Nightingale Party Hall was filled each night not only with Berliners, but also with patrons from all over Europe and even the United States.

When we first met, Max sized me up. "Marta said you were big, but I didn't expect you to be this tall . . . or this broad. I like it. Can you handle yourself?"

"Let's just say I don't shy away from a fight."

"Are you always the winner?"

"So far."

Max was anything but intimidating. He was as wide as he was tall. He waddled when he walked. He reminded me of a King Penguin with a perpetual cigar stuffed in one side of his mouth.

In the brief time I worked there, he presented as a confirmed bachelor, with no entanglements. Later, I came to know better.

"The job is simple," he said. "Don't let anybody into the club you don't think belongs here. From time to time, check to make sure there's no trouble inside, and all will be good."

*

Besides the Nightingale, Max launched two more clubs: one for homosexual men and lesbian women, and one for transvestites named *Club Sei Dir Selbst* (Club Be Yourself). Max's timing was perfect. Berliners had long been repressed. In the aftermath of the war, their latent inhibitions erupted. Business was terrific.

Berlin's sexual revolution attracted partygoers from all over the world. I saw gowned men whom I swore were women, and what I thought were tuxedoed men were lesbians. I often moved around the club to keep the peace. My sheer size was usually enough to maintain or restore equanimity. But there were times when I needed to use my bare fists or the brass knuckles Max had provided me. I kept a Billy in my back pocket as a final recourse.

"I could not expect a better job," Max said one evening after a few weeks. "There has been no real trouble since you've been at the door. Even inside, people either see you or know you're around, and they mind their manners. Take this."

He handed me a wad of cash. I laid the stack on the table. "What's this for? There's no need to pay me extra for doing my job."

Max chortled. "Son, if I give you money, it's for a reason. Since you've been here, the Nightingale has been more profitable. That's not a coincidence."

The club was also profitable for me in ways I did not expect. People slipped marks into my palm to jump the line or for the preferred seating I could arrange. Female patrons, even when accompanied by male escorts, slipped me money to join them at their table once the club had filled and the doors closed. I stopped counting the number of times a woman's hand would caress my knee when I took a seat next to her.

*

On June 28, 1919, six months after I left Pasewalk, we signed the Treaty of Versailles. The treaty was meant to cripple us. It did.

"This is going to hobble us for generations," I told Anna on our Sunday off.

"No one wants another war. The treaty prevents us from rearming. What's wrong with that?" she answered.

"Did you bother to read the terms? We have to accept total blame for the war. We have to pay the Allies for its entire cost, regardless of which side caused the damage. We have to limit the size of our military. Our navy is decimated. They took thirteen percent of Germany's land that includes one tenth of our population. That's close to seven million Germans. Anna, imagine. Seven million Germans have lost their homeland! On top of that, they've stripped away our colonies around the world. They left nothing untouched!"

Anna remained unfazed. "Everyone knows that politicians are politicians."

"What is that supposed to mean?"

"They're words. Do you really believe they will ram all those terms down our throat? You'll see. As time goes on, everything will return to normal."

I had thought the two of us had found a way to coexist, but it was clear we had values that could not be reconciled. There was more. Anna, in her early forties, wanted security and comfort. I figured I was in my early to mid-twenties. I worked nights; she worked days. And then there were the girls at the club. As Anna and I drifted apart, my fidelity weakened. I was not made of stone. I protected the beautiful women who worked in the clubs. Many of them wanted to show their appreciation. In time

I learned that if I had a turn with a girl, it gave her status. Other than Marta, who was too close to home, I took my pick.

Why not? Anna and I stopped being intimate. Did Anna "know" about the others? Of course she did. Deep down, women often "know," even when they don't want to admit knowing, allowing them to continue relationships they should end.

As long as I wasn't blatant about my escapades, I believed things could continue. From my vantage point, there was no need to change. I continued to save money and have fun on the side. I knew Marta had a soft spot for me, and, if I didn't get involved with her, I trusted she would remain silent.

But in my heart, I knew this could not go on indefinitely.

Chapter 9

November 20, 1919

I made a habit of taking daily afternoon walks around the city now that the streets were quiet. I was surprised to find Anna home when I returned to the apartment. Her shift didn't end for another couple of hours.

"What are you doing here?"

"I thought I would surprise you before you left for work."

I tried to make sense of this. "Okay. I give up. What's the occasion?"

"It's our anniversary, silly. We've been together one year today."

I turned sheepish. "I don't have a present."

"The one present I want from you is to quit your job. It's come between us. I want you out of that life and back with me. I'm sorry I ever pushed you to take it." She waited for a reply. But I had nothing to say.

Anna edged onto the kitchen chair; her shoulders slumped. "I had to try. From the time you came to Berlin, I thought maybe you were the one. Maybe we would get married. But this is not working for me. I want more. I deserve more." She fished a white handkerchief from her pocket and dabbed her eyes.

I moved to her and eased my hand onto her shoulder.

Rather than flinch she leaned into it.

"The war messed up so much for so many," I said. "More than anyone else, Anna, you understand what happened to me. For all I know I might be married. Even have children. I need more time."

She shook her head and pushed off the chair. "I have to get back to work. We'll talk about this again."

*

The conversation with Anna lingered in my mind as I marshaled patrons through the entrance door at the Nightingale. I was conflicted about my next steps until fate decided for me.

Three boisterous men turned the corner and headed straight toward the Nightingale. Between their stench and their blood-stained, ripped clothes, I reckoned they had just come off the late shift from the local pig slaughterhouse. I reached for the set of brass knuckles tucked in my pocket.

"Sorry *mein Herren*, this is a busy night. We're full. I can't let anyone else in."

Their leader tottered into his compatriot. His speech was slurred. "All we want is a drink. Now out of the way." He was a brute of a man . . . bigger than me. He tried to brush me aside. I held firm.

"I told you: there is no room for you."

Without warning, he cocked his arm and took a roundhouse swing at me. I ducked and delivered a right uppercut with all my weight behind it. At that moment, he lurched forward. Instead of hitting his chin, the brass knuckles smashed into his throat. There was the unmistakable crunch of his trachea. He dropped to the pavement, clawing at his neck. He struggled for air. His eyes bulged. He soon turned blue. There was no helping him.

The other two stood immobile, their mouths open, transfixed by the sight of him writhing on the ground, frantic to breathe. I whipped out my Billy and raised my arm. "Who's next?" They took one look at me—wide-eyed and snarling—and scattered.

When I turned back, the man on the ground lay still. I checked: no pulse. I grabbed two busboys and, together, we moved the body into the alley. He was not the first they carried away. They thought he was just another drunk that needed to sleep it off.

I had no remorse. If the police were called, I could justify defending myself. But I was a man without a real identity. I could not survive a police investigation.

I found Max, counting cash, in his small office tucked behind the bar. A glass of brandy was wedged between the stacks. He glanced up, nonplused by my appearance. "Looks like you just saw a ghost or worse. Everything all right at the door?"

"I just killed a guy. Dragged the body out back."

"What happened?"

"He attacked me. I hit him."

"With the club?"

"The knuckles."

"Did he have a weapon?" I shook my head. "Wait here." Max returned with a kitchen knife. "Press the guy's fingers around the grip and then leave it close to the body. Get lost for a few weeks. I'll get word to you when it's okay to come back through Marta."

I was too numb to thank Max. I spun around toward the door.

"Not so fast, Friedrich." Max pressed a fistful of cash in my hand.

"How can I ever thank you?"

"Stop wasting time. Get out of here."

*

I managed to put together a travel bag without waking Anna. But as I reached the front door, she called out. "Where are you going?"

Anna stood in a white nightgown. She rubbed her eyes then saw the bag in my hand. "Friedrich, I didn't mean to scare you away with our talk. Please don't leave."

I could not report that I had just killed a man. "Anna, I've tried, but I can't give you what you want until I find myself. I know now I can't do that in Berlin."

"Even if that's true, were you going to leave without saying goodbye? I thought you were better than that, Friedrich. If there is someone else, be a man and tell me."

I took her hand. "I've told you before, Anna, there really is no one else I care about. You have been the best thing that ever happened to me. I would have been *nothing* without you."

Her eyes watered. "Friedrich, will you come back?" I didn't answer. "Did you take your photograph? The one from your boot."

I pecked her on the cheek. "Goodbye, Anna." I turned to the door.

"You didn't answer me. Will you come back?"

I knew she would search. When she found the photograph gone . . . she would have her answer.

*

Brisk steps took me to the street. I froze. Max was clear: I had to leave Berlin . . . but where to go? Then it occurred to me: Wolf rejoined his Bavarian Regiment after he left Pasewalk. Perhaps he was still in Munich.

Although trains weren't running at that late hour, I made my way to the station, found a bench, and snoozed until early morning announcements woke me. I bought a third class ticket on the afternoon train to Munich.

With Munich's Central Train Station behind me I found myself ambling down the wide, tree-lined Maximilian Street. Beyond the statue of Maximilian was the *Hotel Vierjahreszeiten*, The Four Seasons Hotel. Large arched doorways welcomed guests. Everything about this hotel shouted, "Expensive." I had plenty of money from the tips I had saved, plus the wad of bills Max gave me. In fact, I was pretty well off. *Why not?*

They had a room available that faced the back. I could afford to stay a week . . . if it took that long to find Wolf.

I pointed to a poster just inside the hotel lobby. "Excuse me," I said to the clerk at the registration desk, "What is that meeting about?"

"That's the Thule Society. They used to be called the Order of the Teutons. They meet here every week."

"Sounds mysterious."

The man looked about to make certain no one paid attention to us. "I slid into the back of the room once and listened to them. They believe that they are the direct descendants of a super race that had its origins in a lost land mass. Like the missing city of Atlantis . . . but not under water. They call it *Hyperborea* and claim it was located in the furthest regions beyond Iceland. Its capital was known as Thule. Their people are known as Aryans."

This was gobbledygook. "What's an Aryan?"

He pointed to me and then to himself. "You and I are Aryans. True Germans. We are part of the so-called master race." He puffed out his chest as he spoke.

"Being born German makes us Aryans? Is it that simple?"

Again he glanced around furtively before continuing. "Only if you are pure-blooded. They check for that, you know."

"I don't understand."

He reached under his desk and produced a membership application for the Thule Society. Above the signature line, he pointed to the following declaration. "Read this."

> The signer hereby swears to the best of his knowledge and belief that no Jewish or colored blood flows in either his or his wife's veins, and there are not members of the colored races among their ancestors.

The Jewish reference I understood. I heard a lot about that from Wolf in Pasewalk, and, afterwards, from many of the men in the *Freikorps*. Even Anna and Marta made off-handed comments about the Jews . . . mostly about Jews and money.

But colored people? My only experience was with the entertainers at Max's clubs. They were talented and fun to be around. I never heard that Negroes were responsible for any of Germany's problems.

"Can I go to their meeting?"

"As long as you're not Jewish or colored. Walk in and introduce yourself. I'll arrange for your bag to be brought to your room."

I grabbed my room key, headed for the door, and entered a banquet hall filled with rows of chairs. About thirty people milled around. All men. A fog of pipe and cigar smoke hovered over them. There was a table in the front for the speaker.

A stocky man about my age strode toward me. He had a dark receding hairline. "Welcome." He offered his hand, "I'm Hans Frank."

"I'm Friedrich Richard."

"Have you come to hear our speakers, Feder and Rosenberg?"

"I saw the sign when I registered. The clerk explained a little about your Society. I thought I would find out more."

"Wonderful. Gottfried Feder is a noted economist. Alfred Rosenberg talks about the German soul, on what it will take to keep our race pure in order to fulfill our destiny." Just then, there was movement in the front. "We're about to start. Let's sit over there." We took seats next to each other in the back row.

Applause greeted Gottfried Feder as he approached the front of the room. He was a trim man, of medium height; his thinning white hair was in full retreat. His chin had a deep cleft and a small salt-and-pepper moustache punctuated the space between his nose and lip.

Feder had a loud, clear voice. "It has been one year since the politicians signed the armistice with our enemies that ensured the destruction of our economy. Germany has no credit. Our factories are idle. Our skilled workers cannot find jobs. Why is that?" He raised his voice and pointed to the ceiling. "Our country has been crippled by the usurious interest rates banks charge. Who runs the banks? Let me give you their names: Samuel Sachs and Marcus Goldman, Solomon Loeb, Jacob Schiff, Henry Lehman, Jules Bache, the Warburg brothers, the Rothschilds, and the Oppenheim family. Most are German or their families came from Germany." He paused for effect and was rewarded by murmurs of assent from the crowd. "All are Jews! What drives them to do these things to us? We all know the answer: make as much money as they can, regardless of the pain and suffering they cause us. Who bears this pain? I assure you not the Jews. You and I! It is the *Deutsche Volk*!"

While the audience thundered its approval, I was confused. I had no memory of Jews. I did know Max Klinghofer. He was fat and ill mannered. Yet, he had given me work when I needed it, treated me fairly on the job, and helped me escape at the end. I knew Dr. Joseph, admired his skills, and was grateful that he took an interest in my wellbeing. Then I recalled Dr. Kroner at Pasewalk, who tended to his patients with compassion. Was I supposed to hate these men because they were Jews?

Then I thought of Jews like Rosa Luxemburg, Karl Lieb-knecht, and many other Bolsheviks, who denounced these same banks and bankers that Feder railed against. I was puzzled that Jewish Communists and this Thule group made identical accusations against the same people. For the life of me, I could not see the difference between leftist Jews and this group cheering Feder's remarks.

Feder took an extra few seconds to scan the audience, giving a slight nod to signal he was almost done. "Germany will not be great again until we rid ourselves of this plague that infests us. Only then can we fulfill our mandate as the greatest race this world has ever seen."

At this, everyone jumped to their feet and gave Feder a booming ovation. Hans Frank poked me in the arm, and then whispered, "Wait until you hear Rosenberg."

The audience settled down. Alfred Rosenberg shuffled to the front. In contrast to Feder, Rosenberg had the bearing of a taxidermist. Sallow-faced, dark circles rimmed his deep-socketed eyes, and his thin lips were pressed into a grimace.

"Germanic culture," Rosenberg began, "has been crucial to the spread of civilization throughout the ages. Whenever a great empire has arisen, there can be no doubt that Aryanism influenced it. From Caesar to Napoleon and all the great leaders in between, whether they were aware of it or not, their successes originated as direct legacies carried from the peoples of *Ultima Thule*. These first Aryans descended from an alien master race in search of another planet to inhabit as their sun grew black."

Rosenberg's voice dropped, his eyes still glued to an imaginary mark. Everyone tilted his head to better hear. "In the end, they all failed. There is no Egyptian or Roman Empire. There is no French Empire or Ottoman Empire. Why? Because they let the races intermix; their blood became tainted. Impure. We Germans lost the war because Jews brought us to the fateful decision to sign the armistice. We must never let this happen again. Our Aryan greatness is directly descended from the peoples from the lost continent of *Hyperborea*. We must return to racial purity in order for Germany to reach its destiny . . . to rule the world."

The audience stood as one and cheered. Although I barely understood what he said, making Germany stronger sounded like a good thing. I rose to my feet along with the others.

Rosenberg then spun around and faced the flag on the wall behind him. Feder joined him. In unison, they extended their right arms outward, straight as arrows, toward the flag. It bore the Thule Society insignia of a Hindu letter representing good fortune. Both men shouted, "Heil." To which everyone in the audience, including me, shouted back in unison, "Heil."

Frank turned to me. "We are on the lookout for new members, Friedrich. Perhaps you would consider joining us . . . that is, if you pass the test."

"Test?" Then I remembered the pledge.

"You cannot have any Jewish blood in your veins."

"I don't." Dr. Forster had inspected me and told me I was not a Jew.

"Or colored blood."

"It's not possible." I did not know that for sure, but seemed a safe answer based on how I looked.

"If you enjoyed hearing Feder and Rosenberg, join us to hear another dynamic speaker. He's electrifying."

"Is it another Thule Society meeting?"

"No. It's a new political party."

I was grateful to meet people who took an interest in me.

"Tell me where and what time. I will be there."

As we said good-bye, Alfred Rosenberg sailed past. Frank grabbed his arm. "Alfred, don't be in such a hurry. Let me introduce you to Friedrich Richard."

"Are you from Munich?" he asked.

"No, Berlin. I'm here to find a friend. I last saw him a year ago when he was about to reunite with the List Regiment."

"Then he's Bavarian," Frank said.

"I don't think so." I remembered that Dr. Forster told me that Wolf's mother was from Linz, Austria. "I'm not even sure he's still in the army."

"What's your friend's name?"

"Adolf Hitler. Do either of you know him?"

Looking from one to the other, even the grim-faced Rosenberg broke into a toothy grin. Then Frank said, "He's the one I planned to take you to hear. Adolf is our best speaker. Although still in the army, his captain gave him permission to join our party: the DAP. *Deutsche Arbeiterpartei.* The German Workers' Party."

"Is Adolf a member of the Thule Society, too?"

Rosenberg's smile evaporated. "Adolf refuses to join." He checked his watch. "It's late enough, why don't you join us for a drink?"

As we moved toward the lounge, an athletic looking man exited the meeting room with long strides. Frank called out. "Rudolph, Just a minute. Your *Fräulein* can wait a little longer." Rudolph, a young man with dark, beady eyes topped with heavy bushy black brows broke into a soft smile. Frank put his arm around Rudolph and pulled him toward the lounge. "You're coming with us. Tell her I held a gun to your head."

"That's the only excuse she would accept." He acknowledged me for the first time. "Whom do have we here?"

Frank brought me nearer. "Meet Friedrich Richard. He is thinking of joining our group."

"Rudy Hess." He held out his hand.

We moved to a wood-paneled lounge where the hotel served high tea in the late afternoon and beer and cocktails at night.

Frank nodded to the far corner. There was a polished round table with four high-backed, brown leather, nail-head chairs. Just as we took our seats Frank called out to a tall, lean man headed for the bar. "Wilhelm, come join us." After we made room for a fifth chair, Frank made the introduction. "Wilhelm, may I introduce Friedrich Richard."

I rose to greet him. He had a firm handshake.

"Wilhelm Frick, Herr Richard. A pleasure to meet you. Are you new in Munich?"

"Be careful, Freidrich," Frank winked, "Wilhelm questions everyone." I later learned that Frick, older than the others, was a prominent lawyer and a leader in the Munich Criminal Police Force.

"Were you in the war?" Frick asked.

"I was." I wanted the questioning to stop there, without needing to explain my memory loss or making up a history, so I said, "I spent a good part of the time since then in the *Freikorps*. First in Berlin and then in Munich."

Hess's eyes widened. "I was in the *Freikorps* in Munich."

"I witnessed the *Freikorps* overthrow the Bavarian government, though I couldn't participate," chimed Wilhelm Frick. He shrugged one shoulder. "I was with the police."

"I fought under Ernst Röhm," I explained. "Before that, I was in Berlin when Liebknecht and Luxemburg were killed."

This got everyone's attention.

"We're in the presence of a celebrity," said Frank. "You should know that Röhm is one of us. He joined the DAP. Member #625. Hitler is #555."

"I thought you said the DAP was a small group. You have hundreds of recruits."

Hess snickered. "We're not many. Hitler said to start the membership numbers at 500." The others chuckled with him.

"Tell me, Friedrich, what sort of leader was Adolf when you were with him in the army?" asked Frick.

There was no escaping their hunger to learn more about Wolf's past, but I had to stay away from the psychiatrist in Pasewalk.

"It was at the end of the war. We were both wounded. Our beds were next to each other in the same ward. He had trouble with his eyes. I read the newspaper to him every day. He absorbed every article like a sponge. After I finished the paper, he would tell me what was wrong with each politician. Adolf spoke of how our leaders betrayed German workers by supporting the industrialists."

Hess hung on every word. "I'm sure Adolf could not contain himself."

"Oh, he was animated all right. He held back nothing when it came to how we were forced to surrender when we should have kept on fighting."

"You said it was something about his eyes," said Rosenberg. "He doesn't speak about being in the hospital much."

I kept to the facts. "It was a gas attack. He was blinded for many days."

"Then we are all lucky he recovered," said Rosenberg.

I noted Frank's gaze bounce from Hess to Rosenberg to Frick. Each nodded. Then Frank patted me on the back. "It's unanimous. We welcome you as the newest member of the Thule Society."

They took me at face value and did not ask me to fill out a membership application. Though I didn't think much of it at the time, it was a fortunate happenstance: I avoided making a record with my borrowed name. As time went on, I made it a practice to protect my false identity and my murky past by avoiding making records . . . anywhere.

Chapter 10

February 1920

The next day Hans Frank brought me to hear Wolf speak. I hid behind a column in the rear of the meeting hall so as not to distract him.

I was stunned. The men the night before neglected to describe Wolf's full power as a speaker: the feverish pitch of his voice and its powerful effect on his audience. He was nothing like the man I knew in the hospital. His voice was loud. Piercing. It had a guttural quality that evinced power, controlling the audience like a master puppeteer. They hooted when he wanted them to, cheered when he called for that, and rose in unison with thunderclaps of approval at the end.

After the cheering subsided, I wriggled through a circle of admirers—mostly women. Wolf was bathed in sweat, his voice raspy. At first he didn't see me. I waited. When he looked my way, his piercing blue eyes did a double take. In a flash, he brushed aside his admirers and grabbed me by the shoulders.

"*Mein Gott*! *Friedrichshen*. I wanted to get word to you but I didn't know where to find you in Berlin."

Wolf turned to Hess, who stiffened with envy. "This is the good soul who took care of me when I was blind in the hospital. If not for him, I would never have survived."

"He was in the *Freikorps*." Hess tried to elevate himself in Wolf's eyes by being in the know about me. It struck me even then that he was a bit of a toady. Then Hess added, "Friedrich was there when Luxemburg and Liebknecht were killed."

Wolf turned to me. "Is this true?" I bowed. He pinched my cheek as if I were a little boy. "Tell me, Friedrich, what are you doing in Munich?"

"I'm sort of in between things."

Wolf raised his brow. It was his way of asking about my amnesia. When I squeezed my lips tight, he had his answer. Comfortable that our secrets were intact, he slapped me on the back. "Then it's settled. Friedrich will join the DAP and head the detail that guards me."

Wolf introduced me to other party leaders. Hermann Esser stood out. He was about twenty, tall, with black hair and a moustache reminiscent of Wolf's. As he had for me, Wolf had a pet name for Esser.

"*Hermchen* is a tremendous speaker," Wolf said. "Our *second* best, next to me, of course." He let those words hang before continuing. "Esser co-founded the DAP along with Feder and some of the others. We put him in charge of party propaganda."

Later, Wolf took me aside. "Friedrich, you must stay close to me. Always. You are the only one I really trust."

*

Reconnecting with Wolf changed my life. I headed the contingent that protected him. In those days it was common practice to disrupt political rallies. The Communists did it to us and we did it to them. At first we shouted down the protestors. When that didn't work, we used clubs. Troublemakers were dragged out the door and tossed down the stairs.

Wolf decided we needed to be better organized. He addressed us in a side room of the Sterneckerbrau Tavern. "We need filing cabinets. Desks. A phone for members to call us. In short, we need an office. Without this, we will never become a real political party."

"Adolf's right," said Rosenberg. "If we want to amount to anything, we need to function like we are here to stay."

"Evolution of our group fits into Darwinian dynamics," added Hess.

I rolled my eyes. *What did Wolf see in Hess?*

"Even if we agree," said Frick, "how do we pay for it? Our treasury is empty. We can't afford rent."

The so-called "treasury" amounted to a few marks in a cigar box.

"Captain Mayr, my commanding officer, will pay the rent until we get on our feet," Wolf explained.

It was Captain Mayr who assigned Wolf to survey fringe groups as part of an army program to ferret out dissidents, particularly Bolsheviks. When Wolf attended his first DAP meeting, his job was to remain unobtrusive, to sit and listen and report back. According to what I was told, when Wolf heard the nonsense that spewed from the main speaker, he devastated the man, rebutting him point by point. The DAP leaders begged Wolf to join on the spot. Against all army rules, Captain Mayr permitted Wolf to join the DAP while remaining in the army.

Frick smiled. "We all know you don't talk without having a plan. Where will we establish our headquarters?"

"I have already talked to the owner of this tavern." Wolf tapped the table. "He will rent us the cellar room."

Thus, the Sterneckerbrau Tavern's basement became the first home for the German Workers' Party.

*

To preserve cash, I moved into a nearby men's boardinghouse with dormitory-style cots reminiscent of the ward at Pasewalk. Wolf continued to live in the army barracks located on *Luisenstrasse*, unless he was with a woman. On those occasions, he used the apartments of friends. But I will come to that in due course.

Wolf organized DAP's new office with efficiency. In no time, desks, a phone, filing cabinets, typewriters, and whatever else we needed filled the room. But for all that, Wolf kept clear of the Thule Society and its meetings.

One day, in a private moment, I asked, "Wolf, there are so many Thule Society members in the DAP, why haven't you joined?"

His eyes twinkled. "For me, it is not a matter of taking the good with the bad. I take the good and leave the bad. I will make use of their swastika and their greeting of 'Heil.' I agree that mixing races with Aryans adulterated the German people, which must be cleansed. I can accept all that, but I must leave them with their gibberish occult beliefs.

"Even so, what harm is there in joining?"

"Great harm. Their fables and quest for a lost continent are sheer nonsense. One day, when I am called to lead Germany— and that day will come—I cannot be associated with fairy tales or any past blemishes.   The same holds true for you, Friedrich. We can never do anything that will call attention to the secrets we share. Do I have your word?"

"No one will ever know about Pasewalk."

Wolf embraced me to seal our secret bond. Then he pulled on his serious party face. "There is one last thing you can do for me."

"Name it."

"I need another responsible driver. He has to be good with his hands when the situation calls for it. I have a candidate in mind. A young man who approached me at a meeting and asked to join. He's a watchmaker by trade. Look him over. Tell me what you think."

*

In this way I came to know Emil Maurice.

It was easy to like Emil. To begin with, our first and last names were both forenames. We both liked to drink and fight. We both enjoyed women. We spent many off hours in the tavern above the DAP Headquarters, often with Hermann Esser who ran with us from time-to-time. Emil had musical talent. He played the mandolin and sang folk songs. After a few rounds, I'd be tapping on the table top as his percussionist.

One evening, Emil spotted a table occupied by three well-dressed young women. He spoke out of the side of his mouth,

"Watch this." He plucked the strings of his instrument as he sauntered to their table and serenaded them. They loved it. From time to time, one or another glanced at either Esser or me. Emil finished his last song, spoke a few words, bowed, and then returned flashing a thumb's up.

"Nod like you agree to what I just told you. Wave to them."

Hermann and I obediently gestured.

"What was that all about?" I said through gritted teeth.

"They are local shop girls out for the evening. When I explained we were new to the city and have yet to meet ladies as lovely as them, they were quick to volunteer to show us around."

"What are you talking about? We know our way around the city," I said.

Hermann smacked my shoulder. "They don't know that. Besides, I want the blond to help me find my way."

"I'll take the brunette on the left," Emil said.

"That leaves the one on the right." I stole a glance her way. Our eyes met for a moment and then we both turned away . . . she was interested.

"Well done, Emil. Well done," I said.

Even better, the six of us took full advantage of Emil's three-bedroom flat.

*

As good as Emil and Hermann were with women, Wolf was better. Night after night, women fought to sit in the front row when Wolf spoke. Spittle flew from the man's mouth and, still, they beamed at him. And they did this with their husbands beside them. Many times, Emil and I had to peer over our shoulders to make certain he was safe when women pressed against him, slipping notes in his hand. What most didn't know was that his interests were limited to two types: middle-aged dowagers who could contribute to party coffers . . . and teenage girls for his personal fun.

How many times did Emil and I discuss what we came to call the "Wolf Phenomenon?"

"Look at us," Emil said to me over beers in the tavern one night. "We are young. Virile. By all measures women consider us handsome, while he is nothing to look at. And yet, we are nothing when it comes to Wolf and the fräuleins."

"What are you talking about? Women fall all over you," I said.

"Granted this is a great time to be single in Munich, what with all the widows the war created, but it still doesn't account for him."

"There is an answer."

Emil took another swig of his beer. "I'd like to hear it."

"It's not that complicated. Once so-called normal men gain power, prestige, or have money, they are viewed as having this 'star' quality. To women this is an aphrodisiac. And, by the way, it goes the other way, too. Men are attracted to women for the same reasons. I saw this repeatedly when I worked the clubs in Berlin."

Emil scowled. "I don't buy it, Friedrich. Look at us and look at him."

"You're proving my point. When was the last time a woman knocked on your door late at night? It doesn't happen to me, but as sure as the sun rises in the east, it happens to Wolf. Adolf Hitler has that star quality in full measure."

"Truth be told, I have been with some women that I could only bear when the lights were out."

"Why were you with them?"

"They were rich."

"Are you listening to yourself? Rich or powerful pave a two-way street between the sexes."

"And if you have both?"

"It's a speed track."

*

Wolf's celebrity translated into gains for the DAP. He refined his speeches but the themes were always the same. We would have won the war but for the politicians in Berlin who stabbed the army in the back. The Bolsheviks are ready to march from Moscow to conquer us. And then there were the Jews. Always the Jews. Wolf castigated them ferociously, labeling them the "vermin" that infected our will to win. The Jews profited from our miseries; they had to be removed from Germany.

Under Wolf's insistence the DAP became businesslike. New members paid dues and non-members paid admission to hear him speak at rallies. The party now had an income. When he could, Wolf siphoned money from party funds to me saying, "You need this."

I attended every important meeting at Wolf's side to ensure his safety and offer advice when asked, which was rare. He was a great talker but not much of a listener. Emil drove us from speech to speech. While Wolf loved cars, in all our years together I never saw him behind the wheel . . . that included the expensive ones older women gave him. When we were not acting on party business, the three of us often, along with Hermann Esser, went on the prowl for women using Emil's apartment as our secret playground.

Wolf's favorite conquests were girls under twenty. Party members were kept in the dark regarding Wolf's affairs. This was no easy matter. He manufactured the public image of a celibate, devoted entirely to the Fatherland. To protect that image, Wolf often cast a girlfriend aside for the slightest breach of confidence. One might have leaned too close or dared touch his hand in public. A demand for marriage or, worse yet, a baby were *verboten*. The greatest offense was to brag about being Wolf's girlfriend.

None of this would have been a problem—for him or us—if every discarded young woman had been content to pack up and leave without a fuss. But more than one tried to kill herself. The first was Suzi Liptauer. Suzi attempted suicide in 1920 when Wolf dumped her for the beautiful Emmi Mare. Later there were others Fortunately, most came and went without doing harm to themselves: Jenny Haug, Lotte Bechstein, Adelaide Klein, Marlene Weinrich . . . and more. Even as Hitler aged, his taste in women remained constant: athletic and between the ages of seventeen and nineteen. Rarely older. One was sixteen. None of this mattered in the early years, but, as I shall account, this addiction gained heightened importance as he rose in prominence . . . and more than once almost brought us all down.

February 1920

At an Executive Council meeting, Hess made an announcement. "The DAP now has one hundred and ninety paid members." As customary with the good news, we all slapped the table with open palms.

Wilhelm Frick rapped the table for attention. "We are grateful for the good news, but there are new points of business we need to discuss. The first is a proposed name change. Since this is Adolf's idea, I turn the floor over to him."

Wolf explained. "In a few short months, we have evolved from a small group without a purpose into a movement with a mission. We are better organized. We have a following. And as Rudy pointed out, we have grown."

Again the men slapped the table in appreciation; Hess beamed at Wolf's mention of his name.

Wolf continued. "But this is not enough. We must not be viewed as a local *völkisch* party. We must appeal to all of Germany. I suggest that we change our name from the *Deutsche Arbeiterpartei* (German Workers' Party) to become a party that represents all of Germany: the *Nationalsozialistische Deutsche Arbeiterpartei.*"

Hermann Esser rose. "As co-founder of the DAP, I claim the privilege of making the formal motion."

Hess raised his hand to second the motion. Rosenberg and Frank nodded their support. Frick scanned those seated around the table then asked for a show of hands. "It's unanimous," he declared.

And so, our party became the National Socialist German Workers' Party. NSDAP.

Nazis for short.

Frick continued. "That brings us to the last item on our agenda: Adolf has crafted a twenty-five-point platform. We have printed this manifesto on red leaflets. Friedrich," all eyes turned to me, "has a team in place to hand them out. The town will be plastered with red posters to promote the date and time of our next meeting. Hermann Esser has created inserts for the newspapers." Then he added, "We rented the Hofbräuhaus four days from now."

Rosenberg stood up. "While nothing would please me more than to grow our party as fast as possible, how can we spend money we don't have?"

Frank and Feder smacked the table in agreement. No one else followed suit.

Wolf cleared his throat and spoke *soto voce*, forcing everyone to lean toward him. "We are bound for greatness. This cannot be done in a small way." He rose to his feet. His voice grew. "Our twenty-five points are going to rival Luther's placard on the doors of Wittenberg!"

Everyone pummeled the table. We would find the money.

Chapter 11

February 24, 1920

Emil and I were in charge of the security for the big rally at the *Hofbräuhaus.*

"Adolf expects a great turnout tonight," I said as we inspected the rooms behind the stage. "We need to be alert for trouble. Have you worked the details out with Röhm?"

Ernst Röhm carried a well-known reputation for violence. A war wound left a slanted scar on his left cheek that ran from the corner of his eye to the edge of his lip. He had a chubby appearance that might lull the uninformed to think him harmless. Nothing was further from reality. The man was ferocious.

Röhm was a senior leader in Colonel von Epp's Bavarian Free Corps for Border Patrol East—better known as *Freikorps Epp*— the group I joined to overthrow the "Munich Soviet Republic." Wolf recognized Röhm's organizational skills and asked him to create a private paramilitary army. Known as the *Sturmabteilung (SA)*, the *SA* was charged with protecting NSDAP rallies. In time, the *SA* would grow to a force of millions and become a threat to the party itself.

"Nothing must go wrong tonight," I told Emil. "Adolf is counting on us."

"Röhm's men know what to do." They stood around the room in their brown shirts with swastika armbands.

Wolf had redrawn the angles of the Thule Society's swastika. He made it square, bolder, and solid black. Then he placed the symbol onto a white disk superimposed on a red background.

"Does Röhm have enough men for tonight?" My stomach twisted into knots that something would go wrong.

"At least fifty." Then Emil added, "And before you ask, each will be equipped with a rubber truncheon and a whip. Now stop fretting!"

Wolf arrived dressed in his only blue suit. His riding crop—an ugly crocodile whip—dangled from his right hand. In those early days, he carried it most everywhere to augment his image of strength. I thought it made him look foolish but held my peace.

Fifteen minutes before the scheduled start, the room was empty—except for the *SA*. We were in a state of anxiety. Where were the people? Hermann Esser shook his head in disbelief at the empty room. I squeezed Emil's arm when the first person took a tentative step through the door despite seeing no one else. Then another came. Then more. Soon the steady stream turned into a flood of people. Moments later every chair was filled. Latecomers lined the walls. We had drawn two thousand to the rally!

Wolf approached the podium and the room quieted. He stood before his largest audience, yet his face betrayed no nervousness. The moment he uttered his first words, moles from opposing parties erupted into yells and catcalls to drown him out. We were prepared. Without hesitating, brown-shirted *SA* men swooped down wielding truncheons. Emil and I flanked Wolf. Beer mugs flew toward the stage. Wolf ducked and dodged them; Emil and I deflected others. Through all the tumult, Wolf kept speaking, his mighty voice rising above the fracas.

The highlight of the speech was the party's twenty-five-point program.

Wolf ticked off point-by-point, stopping after each one to solicit a reaction from his audience. He hammered the point until he was satisfied it was made. Only when the yeas were greater than the nays, would he continue to the next one. Some elicited cries of protest. The more reckless jumped on chairs to drum up negative support. When this occurred, Röhm's Brownshirts went into action, clobbering heads.

Wolf's twenty-five points laid out the party's blueprint for Germany's return to greatness included the following: all Germans must be united into a Greater Reich; Germany's colonies must be restored; the Versailles Treaty must be revoked; Germany must be treated as an equal among nations; war profits must be confiscated; unearned income abolished; the means of production must be taken from the industrialists and placed into the hands of the workers; old-age health standards must be implemented; the Jews must be stripped of their citizenship and their right to hold public office; all Jews must be deported if the state is unable to feed its non-Jewish population; every Jew who had immigrated to Germany after the start of the Great War must be immediately expelled.

Wolf's performance left me in awe. The dissidents and socialists that remained to the end now raised their voices to embrace a manifesto they tried to shout down hours earlier. Perhaps the ejection of so many from the audience— not to mention their thrashings—accounted for some of this change. Perhaps the realization that the economics of our program mirrored their own socialism satisfied others. In any case, over one hundred new members joined the NSDAP that night. Party membership cards now reached the high nine hundreds.

March 1920

A few weeks after the *Hofbräuhaus* success, German despair turned into a revolution in Berlin.

When word of a putsch in the nation's capital reached Munich, Wolf took me aside. "We're going to Berlin. The *Freikorps* have attempted a coup and installed some unknown civil servant, Wolfgang Kapp, as the new chancellor. Chancellor Ebert has called for a citywide strike. We need to understand what is going on there."

"We have no standing in Berlin. Who will speak with us?"

"My captain authorized me to represent the army on a fact-finding mission. They are flying us there on a military plane. That is all the standing we need."

*

The dominant determinant of Germany's future was its inability to pay the war reparations imposed by the Treaty. *Exorbitant* does not adequately describe them. The burdens piled onto the backs of our people were meant to subjugate Germany for generations. The government met its "responsibilities" the only way it could: it printed more and more money. The resultant inflation drowned us in useless marks and strangled the purchasing power of our people. In 1918, at the end of the war, one American dollar bought 7.9 marks, not quite half its value when the war began in 1914. As we traveled to Berlin in March 1920, the dollar bought twelve times that amount: ninety marks. How could anyone predict the need for a wheelbarrow to transport enough money to pay for a loaf of bread? Still, in 1920, when Wolf and I went to Berlin, the dire situation erupted into a revolt.

*

By the time Wolf and I landed, Berliners were not only weary of revolution, but did not support this "Kapp Putsch." Even while Chancellor Ebert fled the city for safety, the city's population heeded his call for a general strike. All utilities were shut down and public transportation halted. Ebert then hired the same *Freikorps* that overthrew him to now overthrow Kapp and his putschists.

We stalked hotels until we found an empty room. As soon as we checked in, Wolf wrangled a meeting with Kapp's press representative at the headquarters of the failing putsch.

"You're too late," the press secretary said before we introduced ourselves. "Wolfgang Kapp fled the city late last night."

"Your group doesn't control the government?" Wolf asked.

The press secretary shrugged. "We did until Kapp tried to make appointments to key posts. Everyone who said they were with us turned us down. We didn't have the support we thought we had."

"I was sent by the army to investigate this situation. I need to make a full report to my superiors. They will be upset to hear that Kapp ran from the city. They will want to hear from someone in authority."

We both knew he was lying. His superiors wanted the putsch to fail. We, on the other hand, needed to learn as much as possible . . . but not for any report. Wolf was planning his own putsch and needed to avoid Kapp's mistakes.

The press secretary stroked his chin; then his face lit up. "General Ludendorff is on *Unter de Linden*. At the Hotel Adlon. It's only a couple of blocks away. He advised Kapp. He'll give you the answers you need."

Wolf's eyes ignited: Ludendorff was his hero. By the end of the war, Ludendorff was Chief Quartermaster General and second in command of the German armies after Hindenburg. "You can arrange this?"

"We must go at once. The general will leave the city by early morning or face arrest."

Wolf and the press secretary began to move. I remained put. "There is no time to waste, Friedrich."

"I know how much you admire the general." I said as I hung back. "The hotel is safe. You won't need protection there. There's someone I need to see."

I expected Wolf to balk and insist I accompany him. I was surprised when he agreed. "*Ja.* You owe her a visit."

Wolf knew about Anna. His deference to loyalty surprised me, yet it should not have. I came to learn loyalty was the virtue Adolf Hitler prized most. He demanded total loyalty . . . but he also gave it . . . even to friends who disappointed him.

*

Not knowing how Anna would react, I thought it better not to suddenly appear at the hospital. If her schedule hadn't changed, Anna's shift would end in a couple of hours and I could meet her at her apartment . . . and Marta would have gone to work. I burned time by ambling down familiar streets and passing familiar shops that were void of customers. I found a café and ordered a coffee and pastry. I made a project out of the snack until I could wait no longer. I paid the bill and headed to 23 Hannoversche Strasse.

My resolve weakened as I approached the door. Though it might end badly, I owed an explanation to this woman who had done so much to help me. I grasped the doorknocker.

"You are the *last* person I thought would ever stand at my door." Anna was in her nurse's uniform. Cooking smells filled the air.

"May I come in?"

With one hand on the frame, she readjusted her stance and narrowed the opening. The knuckles on her other hand turned white as she clutched the door. "I was a fool to let you take advantage of me. What was I thinking? I should have known better than to hope for something permanent with you!"

"It wasn't the right time."

Anna tossed her head back. "It could never be the right time with you. You are a lost soul, Friedrich Richard. I don't know if you will ever be capable of having a relationship with anyone. Man or woman."

I didn't know what else to say.

"Why are you still here?" She stepped back to close the door. Still, I didn't move. "If you think your pretty face is going to cause me to melt and cave, you're wrong. You are not getting past this door."

Head down, I turned to leave.

She called out before I took two steps. "Marta's at the club. I'm sure *she'd* like to see you."

I turned to tell Anna that I never made an advance on Marta, but she slammed the door to cut me short. I stared at the door for a couple of seconds, hoping she might relent, but it remained closed.

I had a decision to make: I was out of funds. With our business done in Berlin, I simply could not bear to return to the men's shelter in Munich. Although Emil and Wolf were my friends, I was not willing to rely on them or the party for my future. Not until I made an all-out effort to discover my identity. The answer most likely lay in two places, both in Berlin: the German Army personnel records and Dr. Edmund Forster's office in Charité Hospital.

That made up my mind. I would remain in Berlin. But how would I live?

*

"I expected you back months ago." I found Max Klinghofer in his back room office at the Nightingale Club. "I remember telling you to lay low for two or three weeks. That I would take care of that little scrape you got yourself into. It's been what, half a year? Where the hell did you go! I was forced to replace you."

"Hello to you, too. Before I explain, I need to know if the police are still looking for me."

"Don't you trust me? I told you there was nothing to worry about. They came by once. I fed them a story about two customers in a fight. Money changed hands, and the investigation was over. So many die on the streets these days that one more didn't raise a brow. Now tell me, where were you?"

I could not tell Max I was with Hitler and the Nazi Party. Not with their anti-Semitic rants. "Munich. I met some people there. They've been nice to me."

"Then why did you come back if everything was so good there?"

"There are matters I need to attend to in Berlin." I turned sheepish. "Max, I'll never forget what you did for me. I do need a job, though. Do you have something?"

Max toddled over to his desk and lit a cigar. Plumes of blue-gray smoke spiraled around his balding head.

"We need to be crystal clear with each other. I fixed your problem once. That used up currency with the police." He gave me a crooked smile. "If you know what I mean. If you lose control again, there are no more favors coming to me." While he meant what he said, his tone indicated that when it came to Berlin there was always a way to get out of a jam. "The times are different."

"What are you talking about, Max? The local police are on your payroll. That hasn't changed, has it?"

He turned serious. "Have you been hibernating in Munich? Germany changes one week to the next. And it is never for the better."

"The Kapp Putsch has been defeated. Ebert is back in power. The government is safe. Why do you look for things to worry about?"

"We could debate how any German government ruling Germany is safe. But that's not what I'm talking about. I'm referring to something . . . more delicate."

At that moment, Max's door opened. The floor manager stuck his head in. He was about to say something when Max barked, "Can't you see I'm busy?"

Undeterred, he said, "Baron von Manstein showed up without calling ahead. Someone is sitting at his favorite table."

Max shot me a look, a reflex from when I fixed problems like these. I moved toward the door. "Stay put Friedrich. We can handle it." He turned back to the manager. "Offer whoever is at the Baron's table a bottle of champagne. Don't make it too good. If that doesn't entice him to move, kick him out."

Once the door closed, Max continued. "Ever since the armistice, the German people have been in denial. They deny that they started the war and, worse still, deny that they lost it."

"We were winning, Max. Everyone knows that. The politicians stole victory out from under us. They made peace just as we were about to bring the enemy to their knees."

"You and millions of others can believe that crap. Look at me, Friedrich. You don't know me that long. But for the time that you have, did I ever lie to you? Did I ever say I would do something . . . and not do it?"

"Never."

"Then listen to me now. You are spouting right wing, made-up nonsense used by charlatans to persuade the people to hand power over to them. When they get it, they will throw people like me out of the country. They have already made us scapegoats. Do you believe, in your heart of hearts, that I caused Germany to lose the war?"

Now I understood where Max was headed.

He pointed to a chair as he made his way around the desk to his; smoke trailed him like exhaust fumes. "Do you think for one minute that I feel safe here? Right now things are not too bad. Even so, I have a packed bag under my bed. I can leave in five minutes when things go sour."

"Max, nothing is going to happen to you."

"Listen, son, the last time my people had their own land was twenty-five hundred years ago. Since then, no matter where we lived, it was only a matter of time before we were chased out. And if we weren't chased out, we were enslaved, and if we weren't enslaved, we were massacred. It started with the Egyptians. Then the Assyrians. The Babylonians. The Romans. We thought we were safe in Spain until the wonderful King Ferdinand and his Queen Isabella threw us out in 1492. Portugal followed on their heels. After centuries of persecution, most of us are in Eastern Europe, Russia, and Germany. How long do you think it will be before we've outlived our welcome and are forced to leave these places? If you haven't learned already, history has a way of repeating itself."

"But Jews run the banks. The newspapers. They have their claws in the movie industry here and in America. Jews run business after business. What are you talking about?"

"Claws? What are you trying to say, that we know how to make money? Since when is it a crime to make money? Let me give you a different way to look at this, Friedrich. We don't have our own country. We don't have an army. We're a few million people spread around the globe. In many cases, we have been denied the rights of citizenship. Often, we are not allowed to own land or have the right to vote. Through the ages, the rich and aristocratic limited us to jobs they thought dirty. Believe it or not, they found moneylending repulsive. So, yes, we learned the intricacies of money. We became good at it out of necessity. Some might say cunning. We didn't choose it; it chose us. We did it for survival. What has that gotten us? Condemnation from the Henry Fords of the world, not to mention most German politicians. We are the same people who first brought the idea of one God to the world. We invented the alphabet and with that, gave the world the Ten Commandments. Keep in mind that Jesus was one of us. We want nothing better than to live in peace with our fellow neighbors. What do we get for all of this? Blame that we caused Germany's ills . . . including losing the war!"

Max and I had never had a conversation of substance like this. Hearing him, it occurred to me that he and Wolf both saw the Jews as a "people," a tribe united by blood . . . rather than as co-religionists with a common belief.

"Max, not everyone blames the Jews for losing the war." I knew, of course, that the men I left behind in Munich did. "I have no idea what the future will bring for you, me, or anyone else. What I do know is that the good Jews are not the reason we lost the war." Rather than appease him, he grew more agitated.

"Friedrich, would you listen to yourself? Good Jews! Tell me what a good Jew looks like."

I was about to explain but couldn't. Instead, I said, "I have no idea."

"I can't tell either."

I motioned for him to slow down. "Your face is beet red, Max. We're only talking."

He drew in a deep breath and then exhaled. "You touched a nerve. The truth is that there are good and bad people in this world. It has nothing to do with what they look like or believe in, or what country they were born in." He tapped his heart. "Goodness comes from here. Either you're good or you're not."

Max saw my confusion. "You're young, Friedrich. You have much to learn." He flashed his signature ear-to-ear smile as he pulled open his desk drawer. "Here, take this." He tossed me a stack of money tied with string.

I caught it with one hand. "Max, you've done so much for me already. I can't take this."

"You need help and I can help. It isn't complicated. Just remember me when the world turns to shit."

"That is never going to happen, Max." I thanked him and pushed off the chair.

"You might want to find Marta on the way out. She's downstairs checking on inventory."

My run-in with Anna still stung. I didn't need another rebuff. "Tell her hello for me."

"You said you needed a place to stay; she has her own place now. I'm trying to help." A lascivious smile matched the twinkle in his eye. "I know she had the hots for you before, shall we say, your abrupt exit."

I shook my head. "I'm not prepared to see Marta. Not now. As for needing somewhere to stay, I have a hotel room tonight."

"In that case, let me see what I can do." Max picked up the phone, said a few words with his hand covering the mouthpiece, and when he finished, wrote a name and address on a piece of paper. "Go now. There's a place for you to stay . . . and a job. Don't keep her waiting."

*

Kitty Schmidt was thirty-nine years old and heavily made up. She had a penciled-in birthmark meant to draw one's eye. It worked. Kitty owned Berlin's top brothel at Eleven Giesebrecht Strasse, which she called *Pension Schmidt.* Her business maxim was simple: hire the prettiest girls, charge the most, create fantasy illusions, and fulfill the client's every wish. All knew that Kitty's girls were clean. Drugs were not tolerated, and a physician examined the girls each week. She greeted me at the door.

As we proceeded into her office, I noted the red velvet wall-paper, the gold wall sconces, the crystal chandeliers dripping with sparkling prisms, the plush chairs, and a baby grand piano tucked in a corner . . . all meant to create a warm and comforting ambiance.

"Max told me you were the best bouncer he ever had. Looking at you, I can see why."

"I kept everyone in line at the Nightingale, if that's what you mean."

"Are you willing to do the same for me? We run an honest establishment. Our clients are the crème de la crème of Berlin. Every once in a while, though, someone gets out of hand. It may be too much cocaine or they were drunk before they got here. My girls will not service drunks or addicts but, still, there are, shall we say, situations."

"How is it that I showed up at Max's looking for a job, and you just happen to have an opening?"

She grew flushed, opening an ornate fan to help cool down. "Let's just say that Max is familiar with the workings of *Pension Schmidt*."

"How am I supposed to interpret that?"

"Any way you want." Then Kitty explained. "I didn't mean to be coy. Max and I go way back."

My eye was drawn to a framed photograph on her desk. She followed my gaze and broke into a proud smile.

"That's me and my wonderful daughter." She kissed her fingertips and then touched the picture.

I was fixed on Kitty's chest as it heaved with each breath. "The fellow I have at the door does the best he can," she said, still gazing at her daughter's image. Then she looked at me. "There have been a couple of times things got too far out of hand for him. Max says that won't happen if you're here." Kitty leaned closer, revealing more cleavage. Her French perfume made it hard to breathe.

"Then do I have the job?"

"Honey, you had the job the moment you walked through the door."

*

I took a long route back to our hotel, thinking how best to tell Wolf I was staying in Berlin. Kitty and I agreed on a probationary period that was a matter of form; we both knew she'd be pleased. I was to start the following day. There was an added bonus for both: I could stay in the finished attic loft rent-free, and she had me on the premises more often than not.

I waited for Wolf to return from his meeting with General Ludendorff. I must have dozed off because sunlight pierced through the drawn curtains when I heard Wolf call my name.

"It is time to leave. The plane is ready."

"There is something I need to discuss with you."

Wolf shook his head. "We can talk on the way. There's no time to waste."

I propped myself up on both elbows. "That's just it, Wolf, I'm not going back. I need to stay here." I held my breath waiting for his explosive response. His eyes narrowed. He grabbed the only chair in the room and planted it next to my face. He straddled it, resting his arms on the wooden back.

"Explain."

"It's not that I don't appreciate all that you've done for me, the way you accepted me and kept me by your side." No reaction. "I will come back as soon as I can. For now, I need to investigate my past. You know my problem. I can't go on without knowing who I really am."

His practiced glare made me squirm. Then his face grew lax. "What do you hope to achieve here that you cannot accomplish with me in Munich?"

"There are record offices here I need to check. I can't do that in Munich." I hesitated, not knowing how he would react to what I was about to say next. "Dr. Forster is in Berlin. At Charité Hospital. Maybe there are new treatments. I want to see if he can help me the way he helped you."

Wolf blanched hearing Forster's name. "That man and his techniques are evil. I don't want you to see him."

"But he helped you see again."

"Is that what you think? He jumped to his feet. "Nothing could be further from the truth. Forster tried some hocus-pocus with candles and talking about Jesus and Mohammed."

"But when you returned from your session with him, you were a different person. You saw everything."

Wolf turned his back to face the window. Peering through the window, Wolf waved his hand to banish the subject. "Go to him. See if he's gotten better at unlocking your memory. From my point of view, it's a waste of time." He turned and reached for my arm. "Remember, *Friedrichshen*, you are Friedrich Richard. You have a life with the NSDAP and me. Emil, Hermann, Rudy, and the others are your friends. Important meetings are coming up. Speeches to be made. You should be by my side."

I patted his hand. "You don't need me every moment. You have Röhm and the Brownshirts to protect you. I need to find out for myself if you are right about Dr. Forster. As for the military records, I need to fill this hole inside me of not knowing. Any shred of information will help."

Wolf wagged an index finger. "*Ja Friedrichshen* . . . but do not take too long." As he prepared to leave, Wolf stopped at the door and turned. "I found out why the Kapp Putsch failed."

"Wasn't it that the army didn't support him?"

He shook his head. "That was not the worst part. Remember Kapp's press secretary from yesterday? Somehow we never caught his name, only his position. His name is Trebitsch Lincoln."

"Why would that matter?"

Wolf gave an all-knowing grin. "He's a Jew. Kapp was doomed from the start!"

Chapter 12

Over the next weeks, I came to realize that Kitty Schmidt was an extraordinary businesswoman. So were the girls she employed. She personally trained each of them. If a customer was willing to pay for a service, Kitty and the girls provided it. The girls were beautiful, nurturing, good listeners when listening was called for, and only too willing to please every fantasy. There were those clients that wanted to make love to two women at the same time. On occasion, orgies were ordered.

Who were the customers? Lawyers, judges, doctors, industrialists, and the local police, the latter who were paid to look the other way while sampling.

Working at *Pension Schmidt* gave me time during the day to wander the streets in search of images from my past. I saved my earnings and ate most meals at Kitty's. Unlike the girls at Max's Nightingale that were paid to drink with the patrons, be available for a dance, but kept whatever they made off hours, Kitty's women were pros. *Pension Schmidt* was a brothel, pure and simple. That meant keeping my hands to myself, if I wanted to keep my authority over the house.

I got to see Max on a regular basis . . . not at the Nightingale but at Kitty's. He often visited Kitty in the early morning hours after his clubs closed and her clients left. While Max made no effort to hide his interest in Kitty, he remained secretive about his financial stake in her business.

One morning, when it was still dark, he showed up with a surprise: Marta. One look and we folded into a hug that sent sparks through my body.

"That's enough, you two," Max chuckled. "Have you no decency? Even if it is a brothel?"

We laughed with him, reluctant to pull apart.

"I hope you don't mind me barging in like this." Marta said. "I gave up waiting for you to stop by the Nightingale."

I dug my hands into my pockets and looked at the floor. "I didn't want to do anything to interfere with your relationship with Anna. Besides, I've been busy here." When I raised my head I melted at the way she looked at me.

"You two should be alone," said Kitty. With that, she grabbed Max's hand and led him out of the salon.

"You're such a fool," Marta said. "Didn't you know that I was always interested in you?"

"I had a sense, but you and Anna were friends. I was living with her in your apartment. You know how Anna is . . ."

"Shut up and kiss me. I've waited too long for this." We kissed and clutched, neither wanting to let go.

"What about Anna?"

"What about her! Max told you I have my own apartment, didn't he? You could've stayed with me instead of a brothel."

"It didn't feel right to see you as soon as I returned to Berlin."

She stepped into me. "That's time we could have been together. I left Anna soon after you did. She was convinced we were seeing each other behind her back. It didn't matter what I said. I left to save my sanity."

I kissed her again. "Didn't you say that you wanted to show me your apartment?"

"I thought you'd never ask."

*

One afternoon, before the *Pension* opened, Kitty sent word she wanted to see me in her office. When I knocked she cracked open the door a sliver. "Please wait out there and make certain no one disturbs me. I need absolute privacy." I could hear muffled voices but nothing intelligible. When the door opened, a man of slight build slipped out. His low-slung felt fedora and heavy beard obscured his face. As he passed by me, Kitty called me into her office.

Although before hours, she poured two glasses of cognac. "It kills me to give up ten percent of my money, but I don't see another way. At least the Jews are honest."

Kitty had developed a strategy. While inflation continued to squeeze every German, most believed their wages would rise with the escalating prices and that a rising tide would lift both. But Kitty was saving cash and understood her wealth in Reichsmarks was decreasing. The remedy? Change the marks into stable currencies to insulate from devaluation, and whose value in Germany would increase as the German mark declined. So Kitty changed her marks at black market rates into stable currencies: pounds, francs, and dollars. Every month or two, she haggled with Jewish money merchants to get the best exchange rate. On occasion, like today, she engaged one to transport funds to accounts held abroad.

I began to accompany Kitty when she made the rounds of Jewish moneychangers in Berlin's financial underground. It was my job to protect her and keep her cash safe. While I asked for nothing extra, she always threw money my way.

We were in a dangerous part of town one day, when I asked, "I understand how clever it is to exchange money the way you do, but one thing puzzles me: how can you trust one of them to travel to England or some other country and not take the money for themselves?"

"Friedrich, darling, you're right to ask and you're right about not trusting strangers."

"What do you know about the men you're dealing with? They are never the same person."

"The people I deal with are not strangers in the sense you mean. They're Jews. I trust them more than all others, especially when distant banks are involved."

"How could you, Kitty? There are so many warnings about not trusting them." I blurted before I could stop myself.

She stopped in her tracks. "You, of all people, have no right to say that. Look what Max has done for you."

"Max is not like the others. It's just that . . ."

"Just what? When are you going to realize the world is made up of fools? As big as you are, Friedrich, you act like a newborn sometimes. There are times when you should have more common knowledge than you do and it surprises me when you don't. This is one of those times."

At that moment there was a commotion at the end of the alleyway. I held up my hand. I strained to see if it were two men arguing or a ploy to distract us. I checked behind to make certain we weren't being boxed in. All was good but why take a chance? Without alarming Kitty, I edged her back toward the door we had just left.

"Let me ask you a question," she said, oblivious to the two men. "You were in the army during the war. Correct?" I nodded, still vigilant though the men had stopped arguing and were leaving the alley. "Do you know how many Jews fought for Germany against the enemy?"

"Huh?"

"You were not paying attention." She repeated her question.

Seeing that both ends of the backstreet were clear, I could now focus on what she was saying. "I don't know. A handful, I guess. Fifty? Why do you ask?"

"You are in for a surprise. More than one hundred thousand Jewish soldiers fought for Germany during the war. That's twenty percent of the total number of Jews living here." She repeated it for emphasis. "Twenty percent. Would bad people fight for their country in such high numbers? Most Jews here are Germans first and Jews second."

I spouted what Rosenberg, Frank, Feder, and others would have retorted. "And what did the other eighty percent do? They ran the banks that took our money."

Kitty smacked me in the chest. "Are you as blind as all the others? Most of the Jews who didn't fight were women and children, not to mention a number of men too old or too lame to fight. Granted there must have been some that evaded service, but plenty of Germans did that, too. On the whole, the entire

Jewish population supported the war because they supported Germany. Jews are proud to be Germans."

I could not get past the fact that they thought nothing of charging usurious rates. "Are you saying that you trust Jews with your money because they are patriotic?"

Kitty gave a laugh that started in her belly and rolled up to her shoulders. She needed to catch her breath before she could answer. "When it comes to money, the Jews are as trustworthy as my girls at *Pension Schmidt*. The money changing *yids* and the *shiksa* whores all operate with impeccable integrity . . . because they all want repeat business."

Chapter 13

I found myself drawn to the baby grand in Kitty's salon. When no one was around, I pecked at the keys. To my surprise, I could play songs I did not recall. I was soon playing with both hands. When I discovered I could read sheet music, I bought compilations of well-known composers at a local music store.

"You play surprisingly well," Kitty said one day.

"It relaxes me."

"Why not play in the early evening when guests first arrive?"

The first time I did, the patrons applauded. It soon became a routine. One evening, Kitty placed a large brandy snifter on the piano and tossed in some bills. Patrons took the hint. From then on, money often filled the snifter at night's end.

*

I kept up with Wolf and the party through calls to Emil.

"The man is really clever," Emil said on one call. "No matter how tired Wolf is after speaking, he has me drive him to rallies of other political groups."

"Is he soliciting their members?"

"Nothing like that. Wolf is never satisfied with his performances. He pushes himself to study other speakers."

"How is the party membership?"

"We gain new members whenever Adolf speaks. Money is coming in, too. Even a few rich people donate including a small stable of rich old ladies. Enough about the party, what about Berlin?"

"Day-to-day living is getting tougher. Inflation is out of control, Emil. More and more people are supporting the Communists."

"The Boss—that's what some of us have started calling him—warns about the Bolsheviks in every speech. But the big news is that the Boss tendered his resignation from the army."

"As of when?"

"He'll be a civilian April 1." Emil burst out cackling. "Best part is that he sublet an apartment from some mother/daughter combination. Frau Dachs and her daughter Maria Reichert." Emil let loose a whoop. "My prayers are answered. Finally he has his own apartment and will be out of my hair! How's your job?"

If I told him about *Pension Schmidt* he would never stop making jokes. "There's nothing glamorous about being a bouncer. Things are pretty much quiet every night."

"Is it like the other job you had in Berlin?"

"Same job, different venue. It pays the bills."

"Adolf constantly asks about you, Friedrich. When are you coming back?"

"There are things I still need to do in Berlin."

"He told me you would say that. He wanted me to tell you that while he understands your needs, you are testing his patience."

"Tell the Boss that if there is something imperative that requires me to return, I will be there in a jiffy. Reassure him of my loyalty."

I had never shared my memory loss with Emil and there was no need to mention it this time. But Emil's message introduced a heightened urgency to tackle the search for my identity.

*

I hopped out of bed that next morning, determined to deal with the issue.

"Where are you going?" Marta asked through half-closed eyes. "It's barely light out." She had returned from the club not three hours earlier.

"I made an appointment to see Dr. Forster. He's the doctor who treated me at Pasewalk," I answered, thankful that Anna had remained tightlipped to the end. "I helped him with an experiment when I was there. He asked that I stop by so he could collect more data."

"What kind of experiment?"

"Something about reflexes of patients that had broken bones. He wants to see how these injuries affect patients over time."

She tossed off the covers. "I can certify your reflexes are in good working order. Are you certain you have to leave now?" She reached out with lean arms.

I ran my fingers up and down her bare back. "Nothing would please me more, but I promised the doctor."

I did not like the subterfuge, but I could not let her know I was headed for the Ministry of the *Reichswehr* in an attempt to discover my name, and then to a psychiatrist to discover anything I could about myself.

*

I made my way to the monolithic square building that housed the personal records of the German armed forces. The building complex sat on *Bendlerstrasse* overlooking the Landwehr Canal. Before I entered, I strode across the cobblestones and stood at the edge of the safety barrier where Rosa Luxemburg was shot and her limp body thrown into the canal. I tore myself away from the spot and the memory.

"May I help you?"

After many inquiries I found the right clerk. "I am trying to locate a soldier who was in the bed next to me in the hospital toward the end of the war."

The clerk peered over his wire-rimmed glasses. Temperatures outside were rising. His coat was on a hanger, and his sleeves rolled up.

"Do you have a name?"

"That's what I am trying to find out."

"Didn't he tell you his name?"

I shook my head. "He lost his memory when a shell exploded next to him. He was severely injured. When he recovered, he had no recollection of what happened, including his name."

"Do you have anything else to go on? What was his regiment?"

"I don't know."

"Was he in the trenches? Possibly a tank commander? Perhaps he was in the *Deutsche Luftstreitkräfte?*"

"I am pretty certain he was not a pilot." Then I remembered. "He was in the Second Battle of the Marne."

The clerk removed his glasses and wiped smudges off the lenses with a white handkerchief. "That battle lasted weeks. We started with twenty-three divisions. Hundreds of thousands of men fought in it, not to mention those soldiers in artillery and backup support. You're asking me to find the name of a lone soldier without a shred of useful information. You're wasting my time." He returned to his ledgers.

I pivoted to leave and then swirled back. "One last question. What would have happened if they found a soldier's identification disk in the field after a battle was over, but no body to go with it? At least no body that could be identified. Maybe after a direct mortar hit. How would that have been handled?"

He answered without looking up. "If this is about finding a disk in a battlefield, the soldier would have been presumed dead."

"Would the family have been notified that this soldier had died in battle?"

"Only after suitable inquiries to the man's unit. There would have been no other way to handle it."

That meant my family believed me dead and would not be looking for me. It also meant I had no way to find who they might be. Even recognition through a chance meeting was eliminated. My plastic surgery gave me a different face.

"Last question," I said.

The clerk didn't bother to lift his head. "What now?"

"Another mate of mine went missing. Friedrich Richard."

He stopped writing. "With a name like that I probably could help. Do you know his rank or unit?" The clerk flapped his hand. "I'm sure you don't. No matter."

He rose from his seat, trucked to a wall filled with oversized tomes, hefted one off the shelf, and brought it to his work area.

The clerk removed his glasses and looked up. "He's dead. Friedrich Zalman Richard. Suicide. Pasewalk Hospital. June 24, 1918."

"Zalman? His middle name was Zalman? That's a Jewish name."

"Precisely. Another dead Yid." He closed the book, replaced his glasses. "I suspect that was your last question." This time he pulled down a curtain to close his window.

*

I left distraught. The fact that the army had recorded Friedrich's death meant his family was notified and must have buried him. Even if I ran into a family member of his, it would be taken as a coincidence that we two men had the same name. But that worked as long as I stayed as private as possible. I would never be able to survive an official investigation. So far, my instincts led me on the right course. When I joined the Thule Society and the NSDAP, I avoided signing both applications. I left no record. I knew I would need to be on my guard at all times, and never give anyone a reason to check into the official records of "Friedrich Richard." If they did, they would discover, as I had, that Friedrich Richard was a dead Jew, and that my papers were false.

I left the building burning with fury at that son-of-a-bitch Forster. He lied to me about not reporting Friedrich's suicide. He lied to me that Friedrich Richard had no family. Then there was the matter of concealing from me that the dead man was a Jew.

*

I had a few hours before reporting to Kitty's. I marched to Charité and found the psychiatry department located at Bonhoefferweg 3. There was a small reception desk to the left.

"Do you have an appointment?" asked the secretary, her silver hair pulled tight in a bun.

"No, but Dr. Forster will want to see me."

The secretary pointed to a chair before trying to find him. Too agitated to sit, I planted myself in front of a large window and peered out at the bustling city below, rocking from foot to foot.

"Friedrich!" Dr. Forster appeared less haggard, his face fuller than at Pasewalk. "I expected to see you when you saw Dr. Joseph. Why didn't you make an appointment?"

"We need to talk. But not here."

"I have a cubicle for an office. Of late, I don't see patients. Only research."

"That is all the space we will need."

Dr. Forster's office, if one could call it that, was filled from floor to ceiling with bookshelves that sagged from their load. A small, narrow window let in light. The space was more like a pantry than an office.

Before he had a chance to sit down on the lone chair, I asked through clenched teeth, "Who was Friedrich? You said that the hospital was unable to contact his family after he died."

"That's right."

"How hard did they try?"

He cleared his throat. "I'm not certain."

I grabbed the collar of his white lab coat. Our faces were inches apart. "You lying sonofabitch. You told me his death had not been reported. You told me they were unable to contact any of his family. Now you're not sure. Why is that?"

Forster became flummoxed. He stuttered. "They . . . I gave them orders not to report Friedrich's death. I knew you needed an identity."

"Guess what, Dr. Forster, if you really told them that, they didn't listen. His death was recorded in the army records."

"I swear I told them not to report it."

"Swearing isn't good enough, Dr. Forster. If Friedrich's family finds out about me and starts an investigation, they'll call me an imposter. What's to stop them from informing the police?"

He grabbed my arm to loosen the grip; I let go and stepped back.

"You can't be the only person in Germany with that name." He straightened his lab coat. "Well then, let's hope you don't run into anyone looking for this Friedrich Richard."

"That's you're best answer? Your scheme not only forced me to always keep my head down to avoid any chance of an investigation into my background, but what's worse, you made me a Jew. Why the hell didn't you pick a Catholic? Really, Dr. Forster? Who wants to be a Jew in this country?"

His lips quivered; his voice turned shrill. "You have to believe me, Friedrich. I thought I was helping you."

I wheeled around and left, never wanting to see him again.

Chapter 14

From time-to-time, Marta probed into my past. I always found a way to put her off. She saw the scars on my back and knew there were internal injuries, too. She ascribed my reluctance to speak to the trauma of war. She also knew about the man I killed in front of the Nightingale. So I alluded to prior brushes with the law and then requested that she fence off my earlier life. Thankfully, Anna had never revealed my past to her.

Marta agreed that my past life was off base except for one subject. "Are you married?"

"Not to my knowledge."

"What kind of answer is that? Either you have been or never were. Which is it?"

"Because I never was."

"Then why didn't you say that in the first place?"

"Sorry. It's my sense of humor."

"There are some things you never joke about, Friedrich. Having been married is one of them."

"What about you? Have you ever been married? Anna never mentioned anything about you having been married."

"How could you ask? You know I've never been married."

"How would I know? It never came up."

"What have I ever said that would make you think I have been . . . or want to? For the record, I like the independence my money gives me. Besides, working evenings . . . it was never easy to carry on a relationship with men who had day jobs."

"Then what changed?"

"Max telling me you were back. Anything else you need to know?" Her smile was as alluring as ever. "For you, I'm an open book."

*

After leaving Dr. Forster I headed to Kitty's place to retrieve clothes I had left in my attic dormer. As I mounted the stairs, I heard moans and cries from a "guest" room.

"Give me more, give me more!" the woman cried out. "Don't stop! Don't you dare stop!"

"I'm coming!" bellowed a male.

Bedsprings squealed.

"You greedy sonofabitch. Wait 'til I'm good and ready."

I stood outside the door, enjoying the sound show.

Two whooping screams followed the grunts and yelps. Then it turned still. While the midday entertainment was amusing, this was "after hours" in our establishment. It was my job to know if a girl set up private shop at Kitty's.

I nudged open the door. It was not pretty. Flesh linked to flesh. A pockmarked ass led to Max's face buried in Kitty's subterranean jungle. Her meaty thighs pinned his ears against his head.

I lost any attempt to control myself.

Max surfaced for air when he heard me laughing. We locked eyes. "Shit!" he yelled and scrambled to cover Kitty and himself with a sheet. "Get the fuck out of here, Friedrich."

I winked at Kitty. She flashed a thumbs up. I closed the door, grabbed my clothes, and waited in the salon. Fifteen minutes later, Max appeared. I passed him a stein. "Cheers," he said. We clinked glasses; he took a long draught.

"Sorry, Max. I thought one of the girls opened her own business."

His Cheshire smile reassured me he wasn't angry. "Right place. Right girl. Right price." He finished his beer.

"Now that we're here, I need a favor. It's about Marta. She's been with you since the underground club."

"Customers like her."

"That's my point. The customers like her too much. Waiting on patrons, getting her ass pinched, relying on tips . . . it gets old. Can't you move Marta up to a main hostess position or even as a bookkeeper? She's bright."

"Talk straight. What you're saying is that you want her out of those skimpy clothes."

"That's another way to put it."

"Marta is good at what she does. She gets men to buy more expensive bottles. If I have to, I'll give her a raise."

"That changes nothing."

"That's the idea. Marta's the best I have. If I move her into any other position, I lose money. I don't like losing money."

"There's got to be something else she could do."

"If it were up to me, I'd bring her here to Kitty's. She's got everything it takes." Max saw my face redden and laughed. He had taken his revenge. He held up his palm to stop me. "For some reason beyond my comprehension, she fell for you. That takes tricking off the table. I'm willing to give up those profits because she never started, but not the ones at the club."

"Can't you reconsider?"

Max put his meaty hand on my shoulder. "Not when it comes to Marta. I need her at the Nightingale wearing scanty outfits. From time to time, I'll throw her an extra bonus. Given today's economics, that's the best I can offer. But you need to relax, Friedrich. She only has eyes for you. You should see the way she lights up every time I mention your name."

I refilled our steins. "You win. Have another."

He lifted the mug toward his thick lips, and then tipped it towards me. "By the way, thanks for your generosity. Who do you think supplies Kitty with her booze?"

Spring, 1921

Whenever Emil and I spoke by phone, it was usually toward noon . . . about the time Wolf heaved himself out of bed to start his day in Munich.

"You're missing the action," Emil said on one of our calls.

"I'm not missing any action. Berlin has its fair share."

"I am not talking about the fräuleins, Friedrich. Every time the Boss speaks, new people join the party. We're up to three thousand paid members."

"In less than eighteen months? That's impressive."

"Not only that, the Boss managed to buy the newspaper from the Thule Society, the *Völkischer Beobachter.* One of his old ladies gave him the money. We now have a platform to publicize the party. Hermann Esser and Rosenberg are able to write pieces that contradict the poisonous articles in that *Munich Post.*"

"Letting those two loose will cause fireworks."

"That's why we bought the paper," said Emile. "The Boss is looking to stir the pot, so to speak. Now tell me, when are *you* coming back? We need you here in Munich."

"Soon."

*

It was the last week in June when I received what I thought would be "the call" from Wolf. To my surprise, he did not demand my return to Munich.

"Emil and I will be in Berlin tomorrow morning. Meet us for lunch at the Street Café. It overlooks Potsdamer Platz. Do you know it?" When I told him that dinner would be more practical because of the long train ride, he explained, "We're flying."

The next day I got to the café early and selected a table under a linden tree for shade to wait for my friends.

"Friedrich. We made it." Emil staggered toward me, ashen from his first plane ride. We hugged. Behind him grinned Wolf, wearing a skull-clinging pilot's hat with earflaps that adorned his head, the chinstrap circling his cheeks, and goggles framing his neck. I took his hand.

"You look different, Friedrich," said Wolf. "Softer. Like a man in love." At that, Wolf broke out into a hearty laugh. His magnetic blue eyes twinkled as he peeled off his flying cap.

I poked Emil's arm. "What did you tell Adolf?"

Emil extended his palms upward. "Nothing that wasn't true. That you had a special lady in your life."

I shook my fist at him; he feigned fear.

"I must meet this *fräulein* who captured your heart," Wolf said.

"She's anxious to meet you, too. You didn't have to fly to Berlin to meet her. For that matter, a phone call would have sufficed if you wanted me to return to Munich."

"That is not why we are here." Wolf proceeded to take off his cap, smoothing down his errant forelock. "As for returning to Munich . . . soon, Friedrich, soon. We left Munich for a six-week tour to let those *dummkopfs* run the party which will make them realize I am indispensable. Then they will cede total authority to me. In the meantime, I am here to raise money."

"Why? From whom?" I asked.

"Dues and admission fees at rallies are not enough to fund our next steps. A national party requires large contributions. We need wealthy sponsors. That's why we're here."

"In the past you attacked the wealthy industrialists. After all, we *are* the *Socialist Workers Party*."

"That hasn't changed. Our platform addresses the plight of the workingman and helping the poor. That's the *Socialist Workers* part of the party. But we are *Nationalists* first. Our power cannot come at the expense of the rich, but hand-in-hand with them. We cannot destroy German industry the way the Bolshevik Communists literally took everything from the Russian aristocracy. They have destroyed their society and their standing in the world for years to come. We can't have that in Germany."

Emil broke in. "There are those who want us to keep to the twenty-five points. Your plan will cause irreconcilable chasms in the party."

"I don't see how you can walk the line between keeping the masses happy while catering to the wealthy industrialists," I said. "Each group will hear you pander to the other. Neither will trust you."

"People hear what they want to hear, *Friedrichshen*. The workingman will not perceive that we've altered our principles. The wealthy? In their conceit, they take the words that apply to them and trivialize the rest. And then there are the Jews. That message is the same. Everyone knows they are the common enemy to all."

I was about to repeat what Kitty told me about the Jews' service in the war when Wolf continued. "Frau Helene Bechstein, an ardent supporter of our cause, has arranged a special party in my honor. She wants me to meet her wealthy friends."

"What if we can't convert any of the industrialists to our way of thinking?" I asked.

Wolf grabbed both my hands. "Failure is not an option. We must succeed. The situation is that grave."

A waiter came to take our order.

"We were just leaving," said Wolf. He stood. Emil followed his lead. "Bring your pretty *fräulein*. I must meet her."

Chapter 15

I needed proper clothes for my first high society event. Marta called ahead to Hurwitz & Sohn. Moshe and Nathan Hurwitz—father and son—were the best and fastest tailors in Berlin. Everyone in the Nightingale used them for costumes and their everyday clothing.

Their shop was on *Hausvogteiplatz*, a street populated with talented tailors who, a century ago, began to reproduce Parisian *haute couture*.

"Marta said you needed the latest in Berlin chic," Moshe, the father, said, " . . . by tonight." He whipped off the yellow cloth measuring tape slung around his neck and measured: arms, legs, inseam, neck, and torso. "Oy," he repeated with each new measurement.

"Is there a problem making me a suit?"

He raised his hands. "For us, there are no problems. We pride ourselves in pleasing every customer. What sort of suit did you have in mind?"

I didn't know, nor did I have to. Combining Marta's instructions, Moshe's expertise, and some unknown seamstress toiling somewhere nearby, I owned the latest-styled suit with a perfect fit, in a matter of hours.

*

The taxi chugged past a series of ornate mansions styled after Italian palazzos until we came to *Haus Bechstein*. This two-story villa, with its many turrets pointing skyward, had the feel of a medieval cathedral. The livery turned into one end of a u-shaped driveway. We climbed four weathered marble stairs that lead to arched-shaped doors. A tuxedoed manservant ushered us to a salon filled with walking, talking mannequins from Berlin's grace and wealth.

I spied Wolf wearing a new blue suit with a crisp white shirt and collar, a drab tie, and shiny black patent leather shoes. His uneasiness was palpable. Emil, on the other hand, was in another part of the room with a woman old enough to be his mother.

The women present went from deathly thin to matronly. Most were dressed in ornate silk gowns rimmed with necklaces of blazing jewels. Their fingers were bedecked with diamonds. There was a large fireplace at one end of the room and a concert grand piano with the lid propped open at the other.

Wolf's reputation preceded him. He was surrounded by a cluster of society ladies that made no attempt to hide their fascination with a man connected to violence.

Marta and I ambled toward them. When I caught Wolf's eye, he excused himself and grabbed my arm. "There you are, Friedrich. And with the beautiful Marta." He bowed deeply, cupped her hand, and brought it to his lip in his best Austrian manner. When he straightened, his glowing eyes locked onto hers. "Friedrich told me you were beautiful, but I had no idea you were this wondrous."

"*Danke*, Herr Hitler," she said with a smile meant to conquer. As a Nightingale veteran, Marta took Hitler in stride.

"Fräulein Marta, please call me Wolf." With that, Wolf threaded his arms through Marta's and mine and ushered us to meet our hosts, the Bechsteins.

The Bechsteins were a dozen years older than Wolf. Frau Bechstein could barely stop pawing him. "Isn't he charming," she whispered to Marta.

Wolf bowed. "Frau Bechstein, I am unworthy of your kindness." He brought her hand to his lips and a smile to Frau Bechstein's face.

"Herr Hitler, you must come and meet the others." Before Wolf could answer, Frau Bechstein whisked him away to a knot of men conversing in a far corner.

The dynamic of rich men and women speaking to other rich men and women in hushed tones fascinated me. In the end, I knew people were just people. Take them out of their fancy garb, put them in a sauna, and they looked no different than the rest of us. Yet in this setting, it was their carriage and the way they interacted that made them different.

It soon became clear that Wolf was right to change his approach to access this wealth. Wolf reassured the industrialists they had nothing to fear from us. More to the point, they needed us to fight the Communists who vowed to take everything from them, while we would not.

I was not so sure, however, how this change of attitude would go down with others in our party. Most of the top men called themselves socialists . . . and meant it.

Frau Bechstein was the epitome of the perfect hostess. After introducing Wolf to a knot of men, Frau Bechstein presented me to Hugo and Elsa Bruckmann. Hugo was a wealthy publisher and Elsa had money in her own right. "The Bruckmanns are visiting from Munich. You must introduce them to Herr Hitler. They will be most interested in what he has to say."

As Frau Bechstein glided away, I shepherded the Bruckmanns to Wolf who stood in the center of a group of new admirers.

Frau Bruckmann gushed. "I will forever be in Frau Bechstein's debt for this introduction. Now that we have finally met you, we want to give our support, Herr Hitler. Isn't that right, Hugo?"

Hugo rolled his eyes as if to say, *"Here we go again."*

I searched for Marta who now had her own gaggle of admirers. I studied her from afar. Marta could not have looked more elegant. Her dress hugged in a way that enhanced her athletic form. I was proud of the way men clustered around her. I slipped next to her. "Care to join me where it's less noisy?"

With champagne glasses in hand, we strolled past the large grand piano nestled on three stout, ornate legs. A young girl, perhaps twelve years old, waylaid us.

"My name is Lisolette Bechstein, but most people call me Lotte."

"Are you the daughter?" I asked.

"Is it that obvious?"

"Your name gave it away."

She crossed her arms across her budding chest. "Sometimes I wish it were different so I could be like everyone else."

"If I had your name I would shout it from the rooftops," said Marta.

"Well, Lotte, this is Marta Feidt and I'm Friedrich Richard. We are with Herr Hitler."

Lotte trapped her lower lip under her top teeth . . . forming a question. "Everyone flocks to Herr Hitler. Is he as special as they say?"

"I just met him," said Marta, "but I can already tell he is a most special man."

Lotte clapped her hands in glee. She looked at me with doe eyes. "Can you introduce me?"

"Before I do, I have a question." I stared at the name imprinted across the fallboard above the keys. "Your name is Bechstein and the piano is labeled 'Bechstein.' I am guessing that it is no coincidence."

Lotte's plain-featured face beamed. "My grandfather, Carl, founded the company almost seventy years ago. We're the largest piano manufacturer in Europe." Then her smile faded. "At least we were until the British confiscated our manufacturing plant, our showroom with its inventory, and the concert hall we built in London. The same thing happened in Paris."

"Lotte, your home is beautiful," Marta said.

"I know what you're thinking. How can we afford to still live here?" Her innocence had no filter. "We have lots of money."

"Both pretty and smart," I said. "Is there anything left of your factories?"

"Oh, we still have the one here in Berlin. Papa says we can't afford to lose our trained craftsmen, so we continue to manufacture pianos."

"Who has the money to buy them these days?" asked Marta.

"No one," said Lotte. "We give them away for free so we can keep our workers employed. This ensures that the quality of our pianos continues. Otherwise, Papa says, if our pianos did not maintain their high standards, our name would be tarnished forever."

I ran my hand across the Bechstein logo. "This piano is magnificent."

"Do you play?" asked Lotte

"I dabble." The piano in the salon at *Pension Schmidt* was a poor man's version of this celebrated instrument.

"I would love to hear you dabble . . . except your hands look too large to fit on the keys."

I jiggled my fingers. "Somehow they work."

Marta nudged me. "Do it, Friedrich. I've never heard you play."

"Now? With all these people?"

Wide-eyed, Lotte pushed. "They are so engrossed in their conversations they won't notice."

"It's not that I mind embarrassing myself, Fräulein Lotte, but I don't want to ruin the party."

"Please, Herr Friedrich?" She pointed to the piano bench.

I edged onto the cushioned seat. The bench groaned from my weight. I held my breath, waiting for it to collapse. When it didn't, I pushed down on the right foot pedal, the sustaining pedal, and heard a whoosh. I released it and pressed the middle pedal, the *sostenuto*. The one on the left was known as the soft pedal. I wiggled my fingers, placed them on the keyboard, where they moved across the white ivory with a life of their own. The Bechstein piano had rich and sonorous tones, and the room filled with glorious sounds. Notes soared. I was lost in the beauty of the instrument, in the purity of its sound.

All around guests grew quiet. My heart thumped in my chest, rivulets of sweat poured down my face and in the small of my back . . . and yet I played on. A crowd gathered around the piano. I came to the finale, a crescendo of *prestissimo* octaves that covered almost the entire range of the keyboard. When I struck the last notes, I held them an extra beat. The ordeal was over. I sat exhausted, hunched over, head down. Afraid to look up.

Then the room erupted with cheers. "Bravo! Bravo!"

Marta threw her arms around me and kissed the back of my neck. "You were spectacular. I can't believe you kept this from me!"

"Liszt's Hungarian Rhapsody Number 2," shouted Frau Bechstein. She leaned into Wolf. "Why didn't you tell me your young associate was so talented?"

Wolf, still clapping, answered. "We all have our secrets. This was his . . . until this moment." And then he gave me a look, with raised eyebrows and a quizzical smile, as if to say, "Why the hell did you do that?"

So much for staying out of the limelight.

"That was fabulous, Friedrich. Did you know that Liszt had his very own Bechstein piano? My grandfather made it for him," said Lotte.

"I can't believe I played on this one. Thank you."

Frau Bechstein made her way to my side. "You did not just play on a Bechstein," she said, "you conquered it. You must come back for a recital. I insist."

Edwin Bechstein sidled over to me. "I saw you play in Vienna. It was an all-Schubert program."

"You must be mistaken Herr Bechstein. I've never been to Vienna."

"When it comes to music, I do not make mistakes. Herr Richard, I have heard you play. Perhaps not Vienna . . . but somewhere. You realize this is *Haus Bechstein*. The greatest pianists in the world have played for us. Your phrasing, the way you used the pedals, no, I am certain I have heard you play before." He turned to his wife. "Haven't we, Helene?"

My eyes pleaded with Wolf to rescue me. *Why did I make such a spectacle?*

"Friedrich will soon join me in Munich," said Wolf. "When he does return to Berlin, I am certain he will be pleased to play for you again."

Hearing that, Marta squeezed my hand. When the fuss over my piano playing died down, she blurted, "When the hell were you going to tell me you were leaving Berlin?" Her eyes puddled.

"I just heard about Munich when you did. When I met Wolf and Emil for lunch yesterday, Munich was never mentioned. Not even a hint. He said it to get me out of being obligated to come back soon. Don't make anything of it." I reached to reassure her but she stepped back, dabbing her eyes.

"Are you just saying that to let me down easy?"

I took her by the shoulders. "Marta, I have never cared for anyone as much as I care for you. You must believe me. I had no . . ."

"There you are." We both turned to find Lotte. "There is something I would like to ask you." Lotte's cheeks reddened. "Does he have a special person?"

"Who?"

"Herr Hitler, of course."

"You mean a fräulein? Herr Hitler's romance is with Germany. He has given himself to his country," I answered.

"He is so mesmerizing. So romantic. So mysterious. Mother says I should get to know Herr Hitler better. Can you help me?"

I glanced his way; Wolf was conversing with guests. "At the next opportunity."

Pleased to hear this, Lotte turned away.

Marta waited for Lotte to be out of range. "Just so you know, I do believe that you didn't know about returning to Munich." Then her eyes widened; she kissed me on the cheek.

"What was that for?"

"You were brilliant. Why didn't I know you could play like a virtuoso?"

No matter how close Marta and I became, I would not admit her into the tiny circle of those that knew the truth about me: Wolf, Anna, and a couple of doctors.

"When I was younger, my parents forced me to play the piano while all of my friends played football. They made me practice every day. I hated it. I tried to quit, but they wouldn't let me. My teacher told them I had talent. That was all they had to hear. They forced me to plug on until one day I refused to play anymore. They pleaded for me to reconsider, but I held fast. The truth is I enjoyed playing the piano but not hour after hour. So I stopped. Then the war came . . . that was that."

"There were musicians who entertained the soldiers away from the front."

"I wasn't one of them. I was in the trenches. I wasn't drawn to the piano when I worked at Max's. But something clicked when I went to Kitty's. It called to me. I started to tinker at the keys and when I did, it was like magic. Everything came back. Maybe it's muscle memory. Maybe I liked it because it was my choice and no one else's."

"Whatever the reasons, Friedrich Richard, today you made your parents proud."

I hope so, whoever they are.

Chapter 16

Wolf stayed with the Bechsteins two more weeks, letting Frau Bechstein fawn all over him. She bought him new clothes, introduced him to more well-heeled Berliners, and by the end of the stay, referred to him as *Wolfshen*. Whenever the opportunity arose she sang the praises of her daughter, Lotte, in the hopes that, when the girl became of age, Wolf would become interested in her.

Emil was another matter. Technically, he was Wolf's chauffeur. Of course, he was so much more. But to the Bechsteins he was a servant and therefore not allowed to lodge in the same house with their privileged guest.

"Can I stay with you?" Emil asked when we left the Bechsteins that night.

"There's an alternative you might prefer."

"I get it," he laughed. "You two like to run around naked. I'm okay with that. I promise I won't get in the way. I like to watch."

"That wouldn't bother me," Marta said with a wink, "but Friedrich does have a better idea."

"I have a room at *Pension Schmidt*. I'll move in with Marta. I've made arrangements for you to stay there with the owner, Kitty Schmidt."

"*Pension Schmidt*? Your room? Sounds like an old age home? Is that where you're a bouncer? What do you do? Prevent the old biddies from escaping?"

"Emil, everyone needs protecting. I do admit the clientele there comes in all sizes and ages. There should be one to your liking."

Marta kept up the ruse. "But be careful. The staff is quite demanding,"

"*Mein Gott*! I can't bear to be around old people."

Marta patted his cheek. "No need to frown, Emil. The place offers many attractions. You will be well taken care of . . . and made *very* happy there."

Emil scowled. "I don't see how . . . and it's not funny . . . sending me to an old age home. I'll be miserable."

When we stopped convulsing, I said, "That is the last thing you'll be. The *Pension* is a high-class brothel. Kitty is the madam. I have my own room there. It's yours for as long as you need it."

"You told me that you had a job similar to the last one. You never said anything about a whorehouse."

"The jobs *are* fundamentally the same. Like at the Nightingale, I make certain patrons don't get out of hand. I keep things quiet and in check, and everyone is happy."

Emil's eyes widened. "This is putting the fox in the hen house."

"Exactly," Marta and I said in unison.

*

Ten days later, Wolf received an emergency call. In his absence the Executive Council scheduled a joint meeting at the Hofbräuhaus with a völkisch group from Augsburg, to discuss moving party headquarters to Berlin. This violated two of Hitler's cardinal rules: no merging with other groups and the party must stay in Munich. Wolf's deliberate six-week absence to teach the party a lesson had blown up in his face: the Executive Council intended to do both.

Wolf asked Lotte to deliver a note to her parents that thanked them for their hospitality but pressing matters called him away. I remained in Berlin, knowing that I might be called back to Munich any day.

5 a.m., July 18, 1921

The phone above the desk rang. As I sprang out of bed, Marta reached out. "Friedrich, come back to bed. It can't be important," she mumbled in a sleep-filled voice.

A call at that hour could only mean trouble. It was Emil. "Get back on the first train in the morning. Fly if you have the money."

"Slow down, Emil. Is Wolf injured? What's wrong?"

"Wolf tendered his resignation to the party. He gave them eight days to respond to his demands. If they don't capitulate, his resignation becomes final."

"Emil, there's no way Adolf Hitler would quit the party. He *is* the party."

"Friedrich, the Boss is dead serious. If they don't agree to his demands, he's out!"

"What demands?"

"He wants dictatorial powers. No more voters or voting, only one vote: his."

"Wolf's bluffing," I said.

"The Boss doesn't bluff when it comes to his career and the party. He lives and dies for it. He's the one with the vision. None of the others have it."

"The others know that. How can they let him go?"

"He miscalculated leaving Munich for so long. I told him so at the time, but he wouldn't listen. When we got back he went crazy, smacking the table and chairs with his whip. You should have heard him scream, 'We stay in Munich!' Froth dripped from the corners of his mouth. I have never seen him this way."

"Answer me this: would they even consider giving him total control?"

"He's not giving them a choice. 'Take it or leave it,' he told them. He must be made dictator. You should have been there, Friedrich. It was the Boss's finest moment. For the first time, I saw him as a leader who could accomplish all that he has promised."

"Did they cave?"

"That's the damnedest thing: they didn't. At least not yet. Tomorrow is the eighth day. He needs you here in case there's trouble. More than that, he trusts you. And he misses you, Friedrich. You two have a special bond. He is different with you."

Marta overheard enough from my end of the conversation to know I would be leaving for Munich later that morning, and that nothing she could say would stop me.

"At least come back to bed. We still have these few hours together."

*

I met Emil at party headquarters. We hugged. "How did you get here so fast?"

"I convinced a pilot who works for *Allgemeine Elektrizitats Gesellschaft* to fly me here. Didn't cost anything."

"How did you manage that?"

"I have information that would interest his wife."

"Extortion is a benefit I never considered working in a brothel." He patted me on the back. "Excellent thinking. Come. He's waiting at a café around the corner."

We found Wolf sitting alone, drumming his fingers on the tabletop, in complete equanimity. He nodded and frowned. "The Executive Council just sent a runner."

"And?" we said simultaneously.

At first Wolf said nothing. He hunched his shoulders, raised his brows, and shook his head as if all were lost, only to break out in a broad grin. "They accepted my demands."

"All of them? Including the *Führerprinzip?*" Emil asked.

Wolf nodded. "Some kicked, some shouted, and others cried about making me a dictator. But more were pleased that I would have full control than not. The council voted 'yes.' Now it is up to the membership-at-large to approve. The vote is scheduled for July 29."

"They have to support you, Wolf," I said. "They have no other choice."

"I wish that were true. I've learned that there is always another choice, even if you don't see one." Then he grabbed me with both hands. "*Friedrichen*, stay here in Munich. Knowing you're here gives me strength."

Emil looked as surprised as I felt at Wolf's public demonstration of affection. "This is where I belong, Wolf. With you and the party. I'll stay."

Friday, July 29, 1921

The room was rife with excitement as nearly six hundred party members filed into the hall. Röhm, Hess, Emil, and I stood against the wall.

Wolf stood next to Hermann Esser, who read a to-the-point announcement:

> In recognition of your exceptional knowledge, your unusual sacrifice and honorable accomplishments for the growth of the movement, and your unusual oratorical abilities, we grant you dictatorial powers.

There was a beat of silence, and then the room turned raucous with cheers. Those who did not approve remained stone-faced, knowing they would be outvoted.

Wolf raised both arms for quiet. "I stand before you to prevent this organization from being turned into a tea party. We do not wish to unite with other organizations. On the contrary, like-minded groups must merge into ours so we can maintain absolute leadership." Then he threw down the gauntlet. "Anyone who cannot accept this can leave now."

Emil, Röhm, and I scanned across the faces; no one moved.

Wolf continued. "Our movement came from Munich and will stay in Munich." The crowd cheered. "I make these demands not because I am power-hungry, but because recent events have convinced me that without iron leadership the party will fail. If we cease to be what we are supposed to be—a National Socialist German Workers' Party—we will vote ourselves out of existence!"

The vote was 543 yes to 1 against. Abstentions were not counted.

That day, my friend—whom I called Wolf—was elected *der Führer* of the NSDAP. Years later, I came to understand that by this vote to end democracy in our party, democracy took the first step to its inexorable death in all of Germany.

*

The newly elected Führer gathered his inner circle: Hess, Rosenberg, Frank, Frick, Emil, Röhm, me, plus one or two others. "Now that we have control of the party, steps must be initiated to broaden our base."

"Adolf, may I make some recommendations?" Everyone turned to Rosenberg. Before he could elaborate, Wolf jumped up. He glared at Rosenberg and then cast his penetrating stare at the rest of us.

"I am your Führer," he said in a measured voice. "That is how all of you will address me both here and in public."

Rosenberg bowed his head. "Yes, *mein Führer.*"

Wolf sat down. "Now tell me your idea."

"Publicity—good or bad—is the only path to broad recognition. Our newspaper will cover everything we do, but we need the other papers to cover us as well. We cannot be thin-skinned regarding what they will say about us." Wolf started to comment. "There's more, *mein Führer.* When the Brownshirts disrupt communist meetings, it must be done so that everyone knows we did it. This means we give the press advance notice to assure they will be there."

Wolf agreed. "Whatever you print, include the phrase I will use to start every speech: *Ein Volk, Ein Reich, Ein Führer* . . . One People, One State, One Leader."

Hermann Esser was put in charge of propaganda. We plastered the city. Everywhere people in Munich turned, they encountered signs and articles announcing NSDAP activity.

September 14, 1921

Otto Ballerstedt—who championed the Weimar's socialist programs—infuriated Wolf. He was the only public speaker Wolf feared in a one-to-one contest both for his oratory ability and desire to form a separate Danubian Federation comprised of Austria, Czechoslovakia, and Hungary. This was in stark contrast to Wolf, who dreamed of uniting the old Austrian-Hungary Empire into a unified German nation. When we learned that Ballerstedt was to speak to the Bavarian League at the *Löwenbräukeller*, Wolf vowed to silence him.

Our men mingled among the crowd waiting to hear Ballerstedt in the *Löwenbräukeller*. Some parked themselves on seats near the front.

No sooner had Ballerstedt uttered his greeting, than one of our men hopped onto a chair and shouted, "The misfortunes of Bavaria have been brought about by the Jews. Give Hitler the floor."

Ballerstedt refused to budge from the stage. One of his people turned off the lights in an effort to settle everyone down. I decked him with a right hook and flicked the lights back on. A melee broke out. Hermann Esser and—to our shock—Wolf, jumped onto the stage and pummeled Ballerstedt senseless with folding chairs. Ballerstedt had to be carried out while the hall degenerated into a free-for-all.

After the police restored order, the police chief asked Wolf, "Why did you do it, Herr Hitler? I have no choice but to arrest you."

Hitler stood unperturbed. "We did what we had to do. Ballerstedt won't talk anymore." Then the police booked Wolf and Esser.

*

Soon after the Ballerstedt melee, Wolf introduced me to an army buddy. "This is Herr Max Amann. Max was my sergeant in the List Regiment."

The fact that Wolf didn't flinch when Max wrapped his arm around him indicated their closeness.

"Imagine my surprise when I saw Max walking down the street," Wolf said.

"I was more surprised when I learned you wanted me to join a party you headed."

Wolf smiled. "But you refused!"

Amann turned to me. "You have to understand, Friedrich, I'm a lawyer. My practice is going well. But Adolf would not take no for an answer."

Amann was the first person I met who knew Wolf before Pasewalk. "What stories can you tell me about him back then?"

Amann hesitated. He didn't want to say anything that might offend Wolf.

"It's all right, Max, you can say anything to Friedrich. He will be surprised at how different I was then."

"Different is an understatement. Adolf was boring. He was the quietest soldier in the regiment. He hardly talked. When he did, he spouted obscure historical facts or described the minutest details about famous architectural structures that no one cared about." He tapped Hitler's shoulder. "This is a new Wolf."

Emboldened by Amann's candor, I asked, "Herr Amann. We all know about Wolf's heroism during the war. He received Two Iron Crosses. That he was a corporal makes it all the more unusual. Why was he never promoted beyond corporal?"

Rather than erupt, Wolf smiled and let Max explain.

"Wolf's name came up for a promotion more than once. I put him forward myself. Every time I did, the ranking officer turned him down out of hand. He said, 'Corporal Hitler? Corporal Hitler? The man has no leadership ability. He will never amount to anything.'"

Wolf led the conversation away from any possibility of Pasewalk. "It was Friedrich's doing. He gave me the confidence to achieve my potential. I owe it all to him." He slapped me on the back. Then he added, "Max is the party's new business manager. He will also be in charge of both our party newspaper and our publishing arm: the *Völkischer Beobachter* and *Eher Verlag.*"

Max Amann was a small, rough-hewn, muscular man. But to judge Max Amann on his physical characteristics was misleading. We made profits from the moment Max joined the party. His abilities never ceased to amaze me.

*

The more time I spent with Wolf, the more Wolf's venom towards the Jews troubled me. Why did he make hating them a central theme of our party? More than a few times, I resolved to raise this issue, but backed off each time.

By early November, this inner conflict overwhelmed me. I was unwilling to accept Max Klinghofer, Dr. Joseph, Dr. Kroner at Pasewalk, or any other Jew, as my enemy. I needed to confront Hitler—once and for all—about his fixation on the "Jewish question."

We arranged to meet at Wolf's apartment at 41 Thierschstrasse, which was a stone's throw from party headquarters at the tavern. The building was old; the steps to his room warped. Wolf's lone room on the second floor amounted to a jail cell, less than three meters wide by five meters long. The bed was oversized. Pushed against the wall, the headboard still blocked half of the only window in the room. Two threadbare rugs covered parts of the worn linoleum. On the opposite wall, there was a crude bookshelf filled with books on a variety of subjects. There was a hot plate on the ledge. A small table and single chair filled the rest of the room. The toilet was in the hall.

"How can you live here?" I once asked.

"I don't need more."

"You're the leader of the party."

"It's about appearances, Friedrich. I can't be seen living in luxury. Besides, I still have the other room when needed."

The other room. From the time we opened headquarters in the Sterneckerbräu Tavern, the party paid for a room that Wolf used for his many assignations. Only Emil, Max Amann, Hermann Esser, and I knew about it.

I found the door ajar that day. Wolf waved me in. He sat on the bed, I on the chair.

"Thank you for seeing me, *mein Führer.*"

"You don't have to call me that here, Friedrich. When we're alone, you can still call me Wolf. And use *du*. Röhm, Emil, and you are the only ones who can refer to me that way. In public, of course, we must be formal."

I muttered, "Of course."

"You have the look of a man on a distasteful mission."

I had practiced how best to begin. "I am troubled by one of the points in our party's program."

"If you doubt some part of the platform, ignore it. Restoring the Fatherland to its greatness is all that matters." But he could see that I was not satisfied. "What makes you so uncomfortable?"

"The Jews." No longer blasé, he grew rigid. The blood drained from Wolf's face. He remained silent as I continued. "I hear what you and the others say about the Jews. You know that I don't have a memory. I don't know their history. Why should I hate them?"

Wolf stared at me without responding. I didn't expect him to make this easy, and he didn't.

"I've been told that you had friends, or at least acquaintances, that were Jews. There was the Jew who sold your watercolor postcards in Vienna. And I remember how you admired the doctor who cared for your mother, Dr. Bloch."

Hearing Dr. Bloch's name, Wolf's eyes widened but he remained silent.

"I asked Max Amann about his time with you in the army. He told me you never said anything about Jews during the war. Even at Pasewalk, you never spoke ill of the Jews until you were well into your treatments with Dr. Forster. I was there every day with you. What changed?"

There, I said it. I got out what had been bottled up for so long. I was prepared for the consequences, but not the venom he spewed.

"Friedrich, I don't want to talk about Pasewalk or Forster ever again! The man might as well be dead . . . because that's how insignificant he is to me." The veins in his temple pulsed. He smashed the wall behind the bed with an open hand and then stamped his foot. "I never want to hear his name again. Is that understood?"

"I promise. Never again."

Wolf filled a glass with water from a white-enameled pitcher. I watched during the unnerving seconds that he poured, sipped, and then repeated the process. Finally, he spoke in a calmer voice, "Because it's you, you deserve an answer. I don't care what others think or say. Let me be clear: my beliefs toward the Jews have *nothing* to do with Pasewalk."

"But you changed there."

"What I did there was to find a better way to articulate what I long believed."

"What about Dr. Bloch?"

"There are always exceptions. What you need to understand, Friedrich, is that the Jews consider blood more important than their beliefs. That makes them a race. They are tribal. They identify by blood more than by the countries that house and feed them. Jews are for other Jews, and for no one else."

His calm evaporated. Cords in his neck bulged. His voice ratcheted higher. "These so-called 'nice Jews' you speak of, have caused the destruction of Germany. Because of them, there are thousands of orphans and fatherless families. Millions of workers that cannot find jobs. They idled our factories. Their greed has caused runaway inflation. They do all of this through their control of the banks, the newspapers, and the arts. The Jews are a virus, Friedrich. A disease that needs to be eradicated."

"I hear everything you said, but I have not seen the bad in the Jews . . . not in the ones I know. Is that a problem for you? Do you want me to leave the party?"

He did not reply immediately. "Friedrich," he sighed, "you don't have to agree with everything I say or do. The same is true for me about your opinions. What is important is that we stand on the same side for Germany."

Relief washed over me.

Then he said, "You are the brother I wish I had." Wolf put his hand on my arm. "Stay in the party. Stay with me. You can think whatever you want. I only ask you to keep your own counsel. Do not make trouble. Nothing more."

I walked away from his apartment struck by his genuine hatred for Jews. He could have softened his stance in private but didn't. This enmity toward Jews could only be described as an emotional cancer, in no way a platform to attract votes.

I considered walking away from Wolf and Munich that day. But what were my choices? Find a position somewhere? I had no skill or trade. Return to Berlin to be a bouncer in a whorehouse? I knew Kitty would hire me back, but did I want to return to that? Or, I could remain in the party and work for the betterment of my country, accepting everything in the platform except that about the Jews. Whether out of friendship or a desire to be part of the movement, or simply because it was the easier path, I decided to continue to walk with Wolf. What was critical for me was the belief that I could do so without surrendering my integrity.

*

By the end of 1921 I had been in Munich nearly five months. At the outset, my funds were sufficient to rent an apartment. Once Wolf took command, the party assumed that expense. Overwhelmed by work, time slipped away . . . as did my relationship with Marta.

At first, we spoke twice a week on the telephone. Then once a week. As Wolf increased his speaking schedule—sometimes he would give five speeches in one night—contact with Marta lessened. Finally, she brought matters to a head during one of our infrequent calls.

"When are you coming to see me, Friedrich?"

"You know how busy we are. It's impossible to get away."

"No one is so busy that he can't find a few days. Even the chancellor finds time to holiday."

"Violence follows Wolf wherever he speaks. I need to be here to protect him."

"No one's indispensable, Friedrich. He's got Emil and the others." Her voice cracked. "Why don't you say it? You don't love me anymore."

I could have assuaged her feelings by telling her that it wasn't true, that I did love her and that I would rush to Berlin as soon as the opportunity arose. I could have said those things . . . but I didn't.

"Have you met someone else?" she asked, now sobbing.

"I haven't been with anyone since I left you."

"Then what is it Friedrich? Don't you want to be with me?"

There was much I missed about Marta . . . but not enough to change course. I mumbled that I would call more often, but the calls grew scarcer . . . until there were none.

Chapter 17

January 28, 1922

The Wolf/Esser trial for assaulting Ballerstedt was expected to be brief. The facts were not in dispute. A witness described the attack. I sat in the back of the courtroom to avoid drawing attention. The last thing I wanted was for one of Ballerstedt's followers to point an accusatory finger that would land me in the dock as well . . . with the inevitable police check into my background.

Ballerstedt was the prosecution's last witness. The man made a sympathetic figure. He suffered a severe head wound during the war that cost him an eye. His recent beating left his left arm hanging in a sling; aided by a cane, he shuffled with a pronounced limp. Watching him hobble into the witness box was painful. I cowered in my seat.

After stating his name and training as an electrical engineer, Ballerstedt described founding the Bavarian League.

"And what is the purpose of this party, Herr Ballerstedt?" asked the prosecutor.

"To promote measures that would strengthen our state of Bavaria while supporting the integrity of the Weimar Republic."

"Does your party wish to bring harm to the chancellor and the government in Berlin?"

"Absolutely not. We support the government."

Wolf jumped out of his seat and shouted. "That is a lie! You support an independent Bavaria. You bring dishonor to all Germans."

The judge smacked his gavel. "You are in contempt, Herr Hitler. One more outburst and you will be removed from the court."

The prosecutor continued. "Can you describe what happened on September 14 of last year?"

"The beating was severe. I don't remember much."

"Are the men who beat you in this courtroom?"

"I will never forget them." With a shaky hand, Ballerstedt pointed to Wolf and Esser. "Those are the two."

"Did you say or do anything to incite the defendants to jump up on the stage?"

Ballerstedt struggled to make his crooked frame straighter. "I said nothing. Their attack was premeditated. They knew they were going to assault me before they entered the *Löwenbräukeller.*"

"How can you be certain of this, Herr Ballerstedt?"

"Because their thugs took seats in the front row. They had someone planted in the back to turn the lights off to ensure that mayhem occurred."

Wolf jumped out of his seat again. "That is a lie. Your people turned off the lights thinking it would calm everyone down. It did the opposite."

Again, the judge banged his gavel. "Herr Hitler, I am warning you for the last time. Sit down or you will be sent to a cell."

When the prosecutor finished, Wolf's attorney opted not to question Ballerstedt. There was no advantage to have him repeat incriminating statements or draw additional sympathy from the judge.

The defense was simple. Hermann Esser would not take the stand. Wolf was the celebrity. Everyone wanted to hear him speak. He would use the proceedings as a platform to the public through the press.

Speak he did . . . for two-and-a-half hours. He restated why Germany was in such a deplorable state, why inflation was out of control, why the Versailles Treaty had to be discarded, why Germany was at the mercy of the usurious bankers, that the Jews were behind it all, and concluded with the Communist threat to take over both Berlin and Bavaria. Wolf mesmerized all in the court—including the judge—but not Ballerstedt. All the while Wolf pontificated, Ballerstedt leaned on his cane with a sardonic smile. Every so often, he would nod or chuckle as a man would who appreciated a good performance.

When Wolf ended his soliloquy, Ballerstedt requested the judge's permission to question Wolf. The judge acceded. Ballerstedt was known for his eloquence. I cringed at what might happen next.

Wolf had trouble making eye contact with Ballerstedt.

"Herr Hitler." Ballerstedt pointed his cane at Wolf. "Do you agree that out of the world's nearly two billion people, there are sixty million Germans in this country, not to mention tens of millions of Germans worldwide?"

"There may be," Wolf answered, his voice hoarse from his long speech. "I am not a statistician."

"Do you also agree that it is estimated there are thirteen million Jews on the planet? A bit more than half of one percent?"

"Whatever the number," Wolf motioned to dismiss it, "it is too many."

"Yet you attribute incredible financial and intellectual feats to this mere handful of people." Ballerstedt shook his head in feigned disbelief. "If what you say is true, Herr Hitler, then one Jew is equal to ten Aryans. No, let me correct that: one Jew is equal to one hundred Aryans. Is that the reason you are so afraid of them?"

Wolf was dumbstruck. Speechless. He sat frozen, while Ballerstedt's supporters laughed and jeered. Ballerstedt turned to the spectators and waved his cane, enjoying the moment. Even the judge turned away to conceal a grin, making no effort to bring order to the court. Wolf glared at Ballerstedt. If looks could kill, Ballerstedt was a dead man.

Finally, the judge called the court to order. He found Wolf and Hermann Esser guilty. Each received a three-month jail sentence, with two months off for "presumed" good behavior.

*

Wolf and Esser's appeals were unsuccessful. Five months later, on June 24, 1922, both reported to Stadelheim Prison. As he entered the jail, Wolf said, "Two thousand years ago, the mob of Jerusalem dragged a man to execution in just this way."

This statement should have been laughable. But this was Adolf Hitler, believing that Providence had picked him to save Germany. Others heard that same thing and believed he meant it.

When I heard this, I heard the voice of Dr. Edmund Robert Forster.

1922

While in Stadelheim Prison, Wolf was not idle. He wrote an inventory of speeches to be used in a whirlwind speaking tour upon his release. By mid-October we had thousands of additional members.

In October, the town of Coburg was in the grip of our deadly enemy: the Marxists. The Bolsheviks had the audacity to stage an event called "German Day." We made plans to disrupt their "day." Wolf believed that confronting the Marxists would energize party members.

The party leaders met at headquarters on October 11. Rosenberg waved the morning edition of our newspaper, the *Völkischer Beobachter.*

> On Saturday, October 14, at 8 a.m., a special train for members of the NSDAP will depart from the Munich train station for Coburg. All members of the SA, as well as other male party members, are requested to take part in the trip . . . Quarters in Coburg will be taken care of . . . Local groups are to bring along their flags. The meeting will be an unforgettable memory for every participant.

The core group—Wolf, Emil, Max Amann, Rosenberg, Frick, Frank, Hess, Esser, and me—sat around a large table with two recent recruits: Ernst Hanfstaengl and Hermann Göring.

Hanfstaengl, nicknamed "Putzi," was Wolf's Harvard-schooled Nazi. His mother was American. His maternal grandfather was one of the Union generals who carried Lincoln's coffin. Though schooled in the prestigious Ivy League institution, Putzi was German through-and-through. He ran the family fine arts publishing business in New York during the Great War. After the war, he returned to Munich where he was captivated by Wolf's speeches and contributed much-needed dollars to the cause. This bought him into the party's inner circle.

Hermann Göring was the prize. Descended from a well-to-do family, a decorated pilot, he won every possible war award including Prussia's highest, the coveted *Pour le Mérite*. His twenty-two air victories were far short of the eighty achieved by the legendary Red Baron, Captain Baron Manfred von Richthofen. Yet his prowess qualified him to take over Richthofen's squadron, "The Flying Circus," when the Red Baron was shot down and killed. Göring received national attention when he refused to turn his squadron's aircraft over to the victors after the war ended. Following his example, many of his pilots crashed their aircraft rather than obey the order to surrender.

Within months of joining the party, Wolf put Göring in charge of the *Sturmabteilung*—the *SA*—as *Oberster, SA-Führer*. In short order, Göring had them whipped into an effective fighting force.

"How many fighters have signed up for the train?" Wolf asked.

"Close to seven hundred so far, but there will be more," answered Amann. "We don't have enough money to buy a horse let alone transport a veritable army to Coburg by rail. Thank God our fighters will pay for the trip themselves."

"Don't forget the forty-two-piece band," added Rosenberg.

*

As the train pulled in, Coburg's police captain, flanked by twenty officers, waited for us at the end of the platform. Wolf and I hopped off the train and walked toward the cluster of police, each equipped with a baton and a holstered sidearm.

The captain, hands on his hips, his jaw thrust forward, said, "There will be no parade, Herr Hitler. No band. No flags."

He rocked back on his heels, expecting us to leave with our tails between our legs. I still remember his shocked look, along with that of his men, when I gave the signal for Göring to unload our troops. It took nearly half an hour for the eight hundred *SA* men, sporting striking swastika armbands, to form ranks behind the band. Once assembled, our columns hoisted their banners on high and waited for Wolf's command.

"Captain," I said, "those men say there *will* be a parade, *with* our band and our flags." The police captain was ashen . . . and speechless.

Wolf said softly. "Perhaps you and your men would like to return to other duties, captain?"

Without a word, the captain touched the brim of his hat, ordered his men to about-face. They broke ranks to get as far away as quickly as possible.

We marched in formation toward the town center only to be greeted by Marxists hurling rocks and bottles at us. When they attacked our columns brandishing knives and wielding billy clubs, we broke ranks and went after them. They were overmatched. *SA* troopers captured the streets and drove the Reds from Coburg. By the end of the day we were in control. Wolf was invited to address the town board meeting with the Duke and Duchess of Coburg in attendance. At the end of the speech, they joined the party and became donors.

Years later, the Coburg men received a special badge that read: "Mit Hitler in Coburg."

*

On October 29, 1922, thirteen days after Coburg, Benito Mussolini led twenty-five thousand Black Shirts in a march on Rome. The National Fascist Party of Mussolini had seized Italy.

This event was not lost on us. Indeed we often spoke of Mussolini's Putsch. We were simply waiting for the right moment to launch our own.

Twelve months later, when one dollar bought more than four trillion marks, Wolf judged that the time had come to seize the local government of Bavaria in Munich, and then march onto Berlin and national power, under the dictatorship of Adolf Hitler.

October 1922 – November 1923

During the months that followed Coburg, one new member distinguished himself with great organizational skills: party member Number 14,303—Heinrich Himmler—who was installed to lead the newly formed *Schutzstaffel* (*SS*). This handful of men functioned as a unit within the *SA*, specifically charged with protecting Hitler. Their motto was *Meine Ehre Heißt Treue*—My Honor is Loyalty.

We put great stock in early memberships. A low membership number in the NSDAP carried prestige. Once the *SS* came into existence, Wolf, of course, was Number 1. He offered me Number 2 but I declined. I needed to maintain my low profile. So Emil Maurice was issued *SS* Card Number 2. Himmler became *SS* Number 168 with the minor rank of *SS-Führer* (*SS* leader).

The victorious Allies were most helpful for our party's growth. For example, the Treaty of Versailles required Germany to deliver two hundred thousand telephone poles to France and Belgium each year. When Germany failed to send the poles on time, French and Belgian troops occupied the Ruhr Valley. The Ruhr was the heartbeat of our industries. To counter this seizure our leaders urged the factories to shut down in a show of passive resistance. This caused millions more to go hungry and transformed inflation into hyperinflation. As the economy tumbled, our party rose.

Chapter 18

November 7, 1923

We met in General Ludendorff's house. Seated around the table were Frick, Amann, Himmler, Göring, Röhm, Rosenberg, Hess, Hanfstaengl, and Emil. I sat next to Wolf. While the general lent us his house from time to time, he never sat with us. The night before the Putsch was no exception.

I leaned over to Emil and whispered, "Where's Hermann Esser? He should be here."

Emil rolled his eyes. "He sent word he's sick in bed."

"*Scheisse!* What a shit!"

"Call him a coward. That would be more accurate," said Emil.

Wolf tapped the table to get our attention. "The triumvirate will have no choice but to join us." Wolf referred to Hans Ritter von Seisser, Otto Hermann von Lossow, and Gustav von Kahr. Using the fear of another "Red Threat," Kahr seized control of the government after the *Reichswehr* had snuffed out an earlier Communist rebellion. He enlisted Lossow, who was the local *Reichswehr* commander, and Seisser, who headed the state police, and together, the three ruled Bavaria.

"My informants tell me that Kahr, Lossow, and Seisser plan to march on Berlin to take over the government," Göring said. "It appears that Mussolini impressed them as much as us. There is no time to waste. We must move now!"

We were ready. Since going to Berlin three years earlier to study Kapp's Putsch, we worked and reworked the details to avoid his mistakes. We counted on Frick, who headed the political division of the Munich Police, to neutralize the local *polizisten*. Satisfied that everyone knew their role, Wolf made the announcement, "The hour has come."

November 8, 1923

Three thousand of Munich's elite assembled to hear Generalkommissar Gustav von Kahr speak in the *Bürgerbräukeller*. Perched alongside him on the dais were Lossow and Seisser. Soon after Kahr began, Wolf, Göring, Hess, Amann, Rosenberg, Hanfstaengl, Emil, and I entered the hall. We milled around the rear with steins in our hands. At 8:25 p.m., a messenger informed Wolf that our *SA* men were assembled outside.

Nine minutes later, one hundred elite *SS* troopers stormed through the back doors. As they took positions around the room, Wolf hopped onto a table and fired shots from his Browning revolver into the ceiling. In seconds our machine guns were set up, sweeping left and right, creating an arc of fear.

Men dove to the floor. Some crawled under tables. Earsplitting screams and shouting filled the room.

"Silence!" Wolf thundered.

Forming a phalanx around Wolf, we moved toward the stage where Kahr, Seisser, and Lossow glowered down at us.

Wolf leapt onto the platform. "The National Revolution has begun! This hall is surrounded. No one may leave. The *Reichswehr* and the police have joined the swastika flag! The Bavarian Government is deposed! The Reich government is deposed!"

While Wolf spoke, Hess secured a temporary holding room offstage. Wolf waggled his Browning at Kahr, Seisser, and Lossow. As they marched to this makeshift cell, Wolf turned back to the crowd. "General Ludendorff, our great wartime leader, will arrive any minute to join our putsch. He will take over the *Reichswehr*. Lossow will be the minister of War and Seisser will be the minister of Police. Kahr will retain some sort of power."

Wolf left the stage and burst into the holding room. He jammed documents in front of Kahr, Seisser, and Lossow.

"Sign these."

Had the trio signed, they would have transferred legal command of Bavaria to us. But they stalled. Lossow raised numerous objections. I heard him whisper to Kahr, "Let's play out this comedy." And they did, using every excuse to delay.

As planned, Röhm attended a rally at the *Löewenbräukeller*. When he received word that the putsch was on, he interrupted the speaker to announce the revolution. Cheers erupted. Then Röhm loaded men onto trucks to join us at the *Bürgerbräukeller*. As they headed toward us, Wolf sent orders for Röhm to split into three forces: one would continue to the *Bürgerbräukeller*, another should hurry to the St. Annaplatz monastery to retrieve a cache of arms, and the third group was to seize General Lossow's headquarters in the War Ministry located on *Schoenfeldstrasse*.

Each force succeeded in reaching its destination. While we waited inside, Himmler secured our building with a makeshift barrier topped with barbed wire.

Finally, General Ludendorff arrived sporting a hunting jacket and felt hat. When the former wartime commander entered the room, Seisser and Lossow jumped to attention. The general urged the three men to agree to Wolf's terms. "The step has been taken," Ludendorff said. "We can no longer turn back. Our action is already inscribed on the pages of world history."

Ludendorff's appearance seemed to cap our victory.

Fifty-four minutes after the Putsch began, Kahr, Seisser, and Lossow acceded to our demands. We were exuberant. Munich was ours . . . now on to Berlin!

At 10:30 p.m., two hours after the putsch launched, we received our first bad news: army engineers offered strong resistance to two hundred and fifty storm troopers. Wolf needed to intervene if we were to avoid firing on German soldiers. But to do so, he had to leave the building. Taking most of the troops with us, Wolf asked General Ludendorff to remain in charge of the hall and make certain that the deposed triad—Kahr, Seisser, and Lossow—stayed put.

"Wolf," I said as we headed through the door, "do you think it's wise to leave the general without enough backup troops?" What I wanted to say, but dared not, was, "How can you leave this old man in charge?" I knew through the soles of my shoes that this was a mistake.

Wolf stopped in his tracks. "How can anyone disobey General Ludendorff? But if you're so concerned, I'll leave a few more troopers behind."

That was Wolf's first blunder of the night. As soon as we left, the three begged to return to their respective posts. They entreated Ludendorff to accept their parole, promising to do no harm. The foolish old man accepted and allowed them to leave. That was the beginning of the end of our putsch. Once free, Kahr set out to organize the police to resist us.

Believing the three Bavarian leaders had remained confined at the *Bürgerbräukeller*, Wolf arrived at the confrontation and convinced the army engineers to let our troopers proceed. We then continued our march through the streets of Munich, gathering more and more followers. In those first hours, we met no resistance.

At daybreak, buoyed by our seeming success, Ludendorff joined Wolf at the front of the growing columns of putschists. We headed toward the Ludwig Bridge where a wall of police with drawn guns ordered us to halt.

Wolf called out, "We don't want any martyrs," and continued forward. But the police lines held. They cocked their rifles. We went forward. They dropped to a shooting crouch.

I leaped forward, hands raised. "Don't fire! General Ludendorff is with us."

The police lowered their guns. When they did, Wolf raised his hand to move forward. "The city is ours. Let's finish this march."

Göring, Amann, Ludendorff, Hess, Emil, and I were in the front line with Hitler as we marched toward Odeonsplatz. Behind us were rank and file *SA* troopers, followed by hundreds of Great War veterans sporting medals on their chests. Some held weapons. Behind them was a ragtag group of local supporters and students. By now we numbered two thousand strong.

Someone yelled "Heil Hitler!" Suddenly shots rang out; I crouched to make a smaller target. Who fired first? It was impossible to tell. Though it seemed longer, the battle lasted only minutes. Ludendorff ignored bullets whizzing by and continued to march forward. By some miracle, he passed through the police lines unscathed.

Göring was not so lucky. A deflected bullet bounced off the cobblestone and shrapnel punctured his thigh. He fell to the street. He crawled to safety behind one of the two massive stone lions that guarded the front of the former Kaiser's residence. Two *SA* men then dragged him from there to safety.

Despite being fired upon, Wolf continued to march with men on either side of him, their arms interlocked. Scheubner, the man on Wolf's left, fell gravely shot. As Scheubner crumpled to the ground, his bodyweight yanked Hitler to the cobblestone, wrenching his left shoulder out of its socket.

When Wolf went down, I raced over as bullets strafed the air or kicked up fragments of cobblestone. He cried out in agony as I tugged him to his feet and then pulled him through the streets. Along the way I saw that Ulrich Graff, one of Wolf's bodyguards, lay bleeding. There was no time to stop.

Even though he expected our putsch to succeed, Wolf planned an escape valve. A yellow Fiat was to be waiting at a prescribed spot. As I dragged Wolf there, I prayed the driver had not bolted at the sound of gunfire. But there he was. Wolf writhed in agony as I folded him into the car.

Before they sped off, Wolf said through clenched teeth, "This is the end, Friedrich. I am putting Rosenberg in charge of the party. Max Amann will be his deputy."

"We have to get out of here!" The driver cried, putting the car in gear.

"This is not the end. The party will survive," I said.

"There's time to talk later, Friedrich. Get out of Munich; you're vulnerable here. Run!" I waited until the car turned the corner and then scrambled away before the police caught up with me. I later learned that, besides the wounded, sixteen of our men died, along with three police.

Wolf was driven to Putzi Hanfstaengl's house. There, growing increasingly depressed, wracked with constant pain from his dislocated arm that would not be put back into its socket for days, he threatened suicide. Helene Hanfstaengl, Putzi's wife, talked him out of it.

When the police finally located Hitler, they arrested him on the spot. Röhm, Amann, Hess, and Emil were also apprehended. Göring, though severely wounded, escaped out of the country. Over time, more of the leadership was arrested, including Frick. Others, such as Himmler and me, escaped.

*

My first instinct was to discount Wolf's warning, remain in Munich, and help put the pieces of the party back together. I intended to hide out in the apartment above our headquarters, but when I reached the corner of our street, police were there, demolishing our newspaper, the *Völkischer Beobachter*.

I backtracked and circled around toward Wolf's apartment building on *Thierschstrasse*. Wolf's landladies knew me. I was certain they would let me stay until things quieted down. Rather than go there straightaway, I slid into the fruit store across the street from number 41 to observe the building while taking my time to fill a sack with apples. Just when I thought it would be safe to proceed, cars screeched to a halt and a half-dozen police charged into Wolf's building.

"Is there a back door?" I asked the proprietor.

The shop owner pointed without asking any questions.

"*Danke.*"

I threw him some coins, clutched my sack of apples, and ducked out the back, climbed a fence, and headed for the only place I might find refuge: Berlin.

Chapter 19

November 17, 1923

I found Max at his desk. Blue cigar smoke fogged the room. He glanced up when he heard me knock.

"Well, well. Look what the wind blew in. I was beginning to think I wouldn't see you again."

I leaned against the frame for support. After making my journey from Munich, I was tired, hungry, and in no mood for anything but straight talk. "I had nowhere else to go."

"You look like shit."

"If you went through what I just did, you wouldn't look pretty either."

Max motioned me to sit as he pointed to the latest issue of the Jewish weekly paper, *Jüdisch-liberale Zeitung*. The headlines were stark and searing: Hitler and Ludendorff Putsch Fails. "They likened it to the Kapp fiasco . . . only worse."

I turned wide-eyed at the headlines.

"Were you part of this craziness?" My glazed-over expression was all the answer he needed. "They arrested a bunch of your gang. How did you manage to escape?"

"You name it. Boat. Wagon. Car. Train." I stretched my sore limbs as I recounted my journey. "I stole away soon after everything collapsed. I ran to the station thinking I would hop on any train leaving Munich. By the time I got there, the police blocked every entrance."

More smoke billowed to the ceiling. "That was over a week ago."

A week? It was a lifetime ago. "The moment I saw them I turned around and headed for the Isar. But I could only take the river so far. I made it to Freising thinking I would catch the train from there, but that was guarded, too."

"You probably could have walked past without them suspecting a thing."

"I was afraid to take the chance. My height and all. I managed to get across the Austrian border. From there, I made my way to Prague. That took five days. I considered heading to Warsaw to be safe. But I figured if I could make it to Dresden, I would continue to Berlin."

"Now what? You can't stay here. If you're caught, they'll close me down."

"You just said they probably are not looking for me."

Max poked his chubby finger through a smoke ring. "That's a chance I'm not willing to take."

I stood to leave but fell back into the chair as a pain wrenched through my gut.

Max leaned over the desk. "Were you wounded?"

I shook my head.

"Sick?"

I grabbed my midsection. "Haven't eaten in days. Once I finished a bag of apples, I used what little money I had on transportation or an occasional flophouse. Then my money ran out. I stole a loaf of bread and some fruit. That was a couple of days ago."

Max yanked the cord dangling off the wall behind him and then grabbed a funnel-shaped mouthpiece. He barked an order to someone in the kitchen to bring bread, wurst, and a stein to his office.

"Why are you always so nice to me?"

"I've wondered the same thing myself. Big as you are, I get a sense of vulnerability about you. I don't know where that comes from, but I respond to it. I believe you are a good person."

"Even though you now know I'm connected to Hitler?"

"I'm sorry to hear that. That man is a total fraud. A ridiculous caricature with that toothbrush-looking thing under his nose. And his crazy racial theories!"

"I don't know what to say."

"Say thank you. Now I have to figure out what to do with you. Do you have any relatives you could stay with for a while?"

I wish I knew.

"They're all gone."

Max scratched his head. "Going back to Kitty's is too big a risk. The police stop there all the time to collect. It would only be a matter of time before one of them asks too many questions or catches a glimpse of you. If the police *are* looking for you, there are not many your size." He looked up with a glint in his eye. "There's always Marta's place."

"That door is closed. It has to be somewhere else."

He snapped his fingers. "Marta did tell me that when you went to some event together, she was stunned by how well you played the piano. Kitty also said you were pretty good."

"What about it?"

"I have a cousin who is the financial officer of the *SS Ballin*. It's scheduled to cross the Atlantic in a few days. I might be able to get you a job on the ship."

"I know you think I am some big, strong guy, but I am not going into some ship's hold to stoke coal until I drop."

He gave a big belly laugh. "I hope your brain works better after you eat something. Didn't I just ask you about the piano? I'm talking about a job on a fancy ocean liner playing for the rich people in first class. Can you do that?"

*

I hid in an apartment Max maintained for out-of-town performers while Max cajoled his cousin into giving me a job. When he gave me the "all clear" and some funds, I took a first-class train ride to Hamburg thinking it safer than a lower-class ticket.

I met Max's cousin, Manfred Gewürtz, in the headquarters of the Hamburg-American Lines. He looked nothing like his cousin. Thin and balding, with wire-framed glasses, he was a model of his trade: an accountant. He explained that his company had been building ships for more than seventy-five years. They boasted of having three sister ships built just before the

Great War started, each bigger than the *Titanic*: the *Imperator*, the *Vaterland*, and the *Bismarck*.

"We had the largest fleet of commercial ships in the world," Manfred said, and then turned sullen, "before the British and Americans confiscated them for war reparations. That's a part of the price we paid for losing the war that few know about."

I was more interested in studying Manfred's eyes as he copied the pertinent information off my *Ausweis*—my ID card. My heart beat faster as he turned over the fake *reissepass*—passport— Max provided, that now required prints from two fingers.

Manfred handed back the documents. "All seems in order. The office will make you a special identity card so you can leave and return to the ship whenever we stop in port. We'll be leaving from Cuxhaven tomorrow morning."

"I thought all ships left from Hamburg."

"Smaller boats still do. But once we started building ocean liners, we needed a deeper channel. So twenty-five years ago we built a terminal in Cuxhaven plus a private railway to get there from here. Have you been to America before?"

I shook my head. "What's it like?"

He raised his brows. "Like every country, there is good and bad. The Americans are not very sophisticated. They still have growing pains." I didn't understand what he meant, but had no need to question him about it. "The ship leaves tomorrow," Manfred continued. "The next morning it stops at Boulogne-sur-Mer. From there, it goes to Southampton, England. The voyage to New York begins on the third day."

I thanked him for the opportunity and stood to leave.

"There's one more thing," he added. I thought he was going to ask me why I wanted to be on a ship or why I wanted to leave Germany. I began to prepare answers. "I never asked if you could play the piano."

*

The following morning, I boarded the *SS Albert Ballin*, one of four sister ships—the *SS Deutschland*, *SS Hamburg*, and *SS New York*—that plied the waters between Hamburg and New York. The first class accommodations were lavish. Staterooms were wide and well lit. The lounge had a baby grand piano. Hoping for a Bechstein, I settled for a serviceable Steinway, and a small room I didn't have to share.

I spent many months crisscrossing the Atlantic from Cuxhaven to New York and back again, tinkling the black-and-whites for well-heeled Europeans and Americans. As an "eligible" bachelor, I became a focus of attention by single women passengers, and some married as well. I played in the bar lounge each evening, so my days were free. I discovered that the British and Americans on board were only too happy to teach me English.

I particularly enjoyed New York. My days in port were free, as were some of my nights when I didn't have to entertain those who remained behind. When I could, I ventured uptown to 142nd Street and Lenox Avenue to a "whites only" hip spot—some called it a speakeasy—known as the Cotton Club. A gangster named Owney "The Killer" Madden ran it. The club served his Madden's No. 1 beer that he brewed on West 26th Street in defiance of the Prohibition laws.

The Cotton Club created a modern-day plantation environment: white patrons and a colored staff. The music deliberately exuded a jungle-like atmosphere. Dancers and performers were the exception to the "white only" rule. Great musicians appeared that year including Fletcher Henderson, Count Basie, and Ethel Waters. I enjoyed the lavish revues featuring tall, light-skinned women performing in magnificent costumes.

New York was a city of contradictions. Indeed, so was the whole United States. That point was made clear the day I took a ferry to Bedloe's Island. I was resolved to visit the Statue of Liberty, transfixed by its size and grandeur each time we passed it on the way into New York Harbor. I invariably stood by the railing as we approached, mesmerized by its beauty and enhanced size as we drew near, and then with regret as it grew smaller with our departure.

The day I visited, I stood at the base of the statue, cranking my head toward her face and torch. Before I climbed the narrow steps to the top and the spectacular views, I read the poem by Emma Lazarus, welded into a bronze plaque at the base.

THE NEW COLOSSUS

"KEEP, ANCIENT LANDS, YOUR STORIED POMP!" CRIES SHE
WITH SILENT LIPS. "GIVE ME YOUR TIRED, YOUR POOR,
YOUR HUDDLED MASSES YEARNING TO BREATHE FREE,
THE WRETCHED REFUSE OF YOUR TEEMING SHORE.
SEND THESE, THE HOMELESS, TEMPEST-TOST TO ME,
I LIFT MY LAMP BESIDE THE GOLDEN DOOR!"

At first the words thrilled me, but I soon discovered that this Jewish poet's words were of hope—not reality. Everywhere I turned, from the Cotton Club to schools to country clubs, the Negro and even the Jews of New York City and across the country, were already confronted by the NSDAP program proposed for Germany.

In America white people had subtle and not-so-subtle ways of keeping their *Untermenschen*—"impure sub-humans"—in place. Newspapers ran ads for employment under the heading "white." Housing was subtly, and in some places not so subtly, separated into white and black communities. The "nice" communities kept themselves pure by restrictive covenants in deeds that prohibited sales to Negroes and Jews. In practice and often by law, the Negroes, frequently called "niggers" or "coons," and the Jews, often termed "kikes" or "sheenies," lived and worked largely among themselves. While I came to learn that New York City was more lenient about racial purity than most other places in America, certain parts of the city still had lines that Negroes and Jews never crossed. As for some other places in America, racial lines were not drawn with invisible ink . . . they were proclaimed in indelibly written legal laws.

Chapter 20

One particular crossing sticks in my mind. The waters were calm and the sun shining. I usually exercised by walking the deck clockwise for thirty minutes and then reversing the direction for the next half hour. I had to do something about the quantities of excellent—and free—food and drink I consumed. One morning, I neared a gray-haired man at the rail. He bit off the tip off a cigar, spat the end over the railing, and then returned to his deck chair. He held out a newspaper—*The Dearborn Independent*—whose headlines caught my eye.

JEWISH POWER AND AMERICA'S MONEY FAMINE
JEWISH IDEA MOLDED FEDERAL RESERVE PLAN

As I passed, he offered his hand. "I heard you play," he said. "Great stuff." Then he relit his cigar.

"*Danke* . . . thank you."

"W. W. Wilson from Pennington, New Jersey. Got me a Ford dealership there."

"I'm familiar with Henry Ford. But I never heard of that newspaper."

"Second largest circulation in the US behind New York's *Daily News*." He leaned forward, "Tell you a little secret. Ford owns the paper and makes every dealership buy a ton of them to distribute to their customers. Truth is, I'd buy it anyway. He's the only fellow that's got enough gumption to tell what's wrong with our country." He jabbed his finger at the headline. "Them Jews are the reason the world's in such a pickle."

"Some say we have the same problem in Germany."

"Of course you do. They're controlling the banks and gold reserves all over the world." Disdain dripped from his voice.

"Lucky for us we got people in Washington who are clear-headed about this. Finally passed some laws that make sense."

He explained how the America-first supporters believed in a "shut-the-door" policy, and that President Coolidge shared their beliefs. In his first inaugural message, Coolidge said, "America must be kept American." The Johnson-Reed Act passed both houses of Congress. The aim was to effectively limit Jews from immigrating to the United States, and to totally bar immigration from Asia.

"Congressman Albert Johnson says right here in this paper,"—Wilson poked the page and then looked up at me— "he's the one who co-sponsored the bill, and I quote, 'this law is intended to suspend immigration . . . to Jewish people (because they are) filthy, un-American, and often dangerous in their habits.' End quote."

He was only too happy to share his views with me so I asked, "What about the Jews already here?"

"Got their grubby fingers in everything. They run the banks. They created the Federal Reserve to make certain they could control the money supply. But I'm telling you, son, change is in the wind. Not only because of this new immigration law, but the doors are finally being slammed shut so good Americans will never be pushed aside again. Here, look at this." He presented me with one of the back issues he was catching up on. Others lay on the chaise next to him.

The Peril of Baseball—Too Much Jew
The International Jew: The World's Problem
Jewish Jazz—Moron Music—Becomes Our National Music

"I understand what the immigration laws will do to limit who enters your country, but how can you make the sort of changes you're talking about?"

"Let me put it this way, son. I got my degree from the local college down the road from where I grew up. Princeton. You might have heard of it. It is part of what they call the Ivy League. President Wilson was its president before he became governor of New Jersey and then president of the U S of A. He got the race thing right. He knew the coons couldn't hack it. He's the reason we won the war. Now we're teaching you Krauts a lesson so you never step out of line again . . . if you know what I mean."

I couldn't resist the challenge. "We don't see it that way. Had our leaders not forsaken us, the outcome might have been different." Wolf's and Ludendorff's rants about being stabbed-in-the-back were so ubiquitous they were ingrained in me.

"Once America got in it, son, there was no way you were going to win anything. But that was years ago. No hard feelings, right?"

He stuck his hand out, and we shook on our present civility.

W. W. Wilson then picked up the thread of his thinking. "I was talking about the Ivy League to make a point."

"I know about the Ivy League. One of my acquaintances in Germany went to Harvard: Putzi Hanfstaengl. Maybe you know him? His family has a fine arts publishing business in New York."

"I'm not into art. But your friend's school—Harvard—has got it right. Two years ago, under its president, Abbott Lawrence Lowell, it put in Jewish quotas to limit how many of those folks could worm their way in. Other Ivies followed suit. Same with law schools and medical schools. Finally, these schools got enough sense to keep those places for the original Americans."

"What about the Negroes?"

"Take a seat, son," he gestured to the empty deck chair next to his. "By the way, as I said, I like the way you play the piano. Looking forward to tonight. So is the Missus."

I was more interested in hearing about how Americans dealt with the same issues confronting Germans than with him discussing my piano playing. "The Negroes? I heard that they have to sit in the back of the buses in the South. That there are separate bathrooms for whites and Negroes. Why is that?"

"Southerners know a thing or two about how to keep them in their place," answered Mr. Wilson.

As he spoke, I pictured the Negro performers in Max's Nightingale. They were talented, gracious, and reveled in the applause they received for their top-flight performances. The same held true for those I had seen perform in the Cotton Club. And then there was the revival of Eugene O'Neill's play, *Emperor Jones*, that featured Paul Robeson. I had never heard such a majestic voice.

The car dealer continued. "Do you know why there are lynchings in the South, son?" I shook my head. "The South lost the Civil War,"—I had read about that—"so they passed laws that limited everything those folks could do. They aimed to keep the races separate at all costs. Why, if a nigger so much as looked at a white woman cross-eyed in the south, there'd be a good chance he'd be hung."

Like the way our Brownshirts rough up political opponents at their rallies. But not lynching. Germans were too civilized for that sort of extreme measure.

"I didn't see that kind of violence in New York."

"Too many bleeding-heart liberals. Most of them Jews, too. Not that way in the South. No sir. Down there, niggers can't eat in the same restaurants as whites. They can't go to the same movie theaters, play in the same parks, or swim in the same pools. All that is against the law in the South. They keep the schools segregated. The whites have theirs and the coons got theirs. Then there are the blood laws."

"What are these blood laws?"

"If there's one drop of black blood in a white-looking person, that person is considered black as the ace of spades. We call it the One Drop Rule. And don't forget about the Klan."

"I know about clans. They are large families. The Scots are most proud of their clans."

Wilson shook his head. "No, no, no. That's clan with a *c*. I'm talking Klan with a *K*. Three Ks, as a matter of fact. The Ku Klux Klan. KKK for short. They have over four thousand chapters and four million members."

"What do these KKK people do?"

"They enforce the purity and superiority of Anglo-Saxon blood. Their goal is to protect the integrity of anything that threatens our American heritage."

"Are you saying that if they see something they think is wrong, they take the law into their own hands? How do they get away with that?"

"You would be surprised how much support they have across the country."

"Even when they break the law?"

"Laws that don't protect white folks are meant to be broken."

*

I made nearly a dozen trips to the United States in 1924 alone. More over the next few years. I continued to hear how the Jews maintained their stranglehold on world commerce and witnessed how Americans maintained their racial barriers.

My takeaway from this exposure to America and Americans was that there was little difference between what they practiced in the States and what my NSDAP friends preached in Germany. Both believed in racial purity. We called ourselves Aryans. The dominant Americans were referred to as White Anglo-Saxon Protestants. Catholics were more recent immigrants, and were lower on their pecking order, but well above Jews and Negroes. It became apparent that while we had our Brownshirts, they had their white sheets. And, in terms of race and religion, they both stood for the same things.

What did I believe in?

Rather than find answers to my questions, my confusion increased. I regarded Max Klinghofer as I would a beloved uncle, if I could remember one. Far from inferior, I saw Max as a savvy intellectual who was fair and moral, his businesses notwithstanding. Dr. Joseph was sainted in my eyes. I knew in my heart that there must have been many others . . . like the Jewish tailors

I patronized. I struggled to resolve the questions these discordances raised.

As I reflect on those early years, the answers should have been obvious to even someone without a memory: people are just people, whether they have white skin or brown. But at the time, I was surrounded by conflicting images and beliefs from within both countries that only served to confuse me. Not knowing what to do or whom to believe, I chose the easy path: to sail on and see what life unfurled.

Chapter 21

December 1924, Hamburg

After each return trip, the ship was refitted in Cuxhaven. I repeatedly scoured the papers for snippets about party members. I knew that Wolf, Amann, Hess, Emil, and other Nazis had been convicted for their roles in the Putsch. Some were incarcerated in Landsberg Prison. I didn't know much else. I wrote Wolf one letter, but I dared not put a return address. I had no idea if it was received.

In December 1924, Max's cousin had news for me when I entered the office after a return crossing.

"Max called several days ago looking for you," said Manfred.

"Did he say what it was about?"

"Only that you should call him back."

Max picked up on the first ring.

"What's so important?" I asked.

"Hello to you, too. Didn't your mother teach you any manners?"

Maybe she had. "Sorry. How are you, Max?"

"Stop wasting time." I rolled my eyes. Typical Max. "Your friend, Hitler, is being released from Landsberg three days from now. Thought you would like to know." I turned my back and cupped the phone so Manfred could not hear me.

"After nine months? I understand he was given a five-year sentence."

"They say it's for good behavior. It seems fishy to me."

"I'm sure Hitler was a model prisoner . . . he always did respect authority."

"Being good is one thing. Serving only a few months for trying to overthrow the government is ridiculous. No one is *that* good."

"How did you find out?"

"Your friend Emil called Kitty, Kitty called me."

"Thanks for telling me, Max. Before you hang up, I need to ask you something. Promise to tell me the truth."

"Friedrich, that's an insult!"

"Sorry. I should have known better. Has anybody been looking for me? Asking if you knew where I was? I need to know that if I go to Munich I won't be arrested."

"Not a soul. Not once. It's as if you never existed. Besides, if they were looking for you, Emil would have warned me to tell you not to go to Munich."

What was I thinking? Of course Emil would have had my back if I were in danger.

I thanked Max, apologized again for doubting him, and hung up. I wanted to be there when Wolf was released, but we were scheduled to be at sea during *Weihnachten*—the Christmas Eve celebration. I had prepared to play a German favorite, written a century earlier in Austria: *Stille Nacht*.

"Is everything all right?" Manfred asked.

"I need to be in Munich by tomorrow night."

"We sail in five days. Will you be back in time?"

"I can't promise that I will. Can you find a replacement?"

"This is such short notice. Not many pianists are available to drop what they're doing and travel for the next couple of weeks. Especially during the Christmas holidays."

"It could be longer than a couple of weeks, Manfred."

"You're not quitting, are you?"

"I love working on the *SS Ballin*. I promise to have an answer for you in a couple of days. Until I do, can you find a replacement for the next voyage?"

Manfred and the shipping lines had been good to me. I did not want to disappoint them, but I felt I had to be there when my friend was released.

Manfred opened a humidor and stuffed his meerschaum pipe with a sweet-smelling tobacco. He struck a match on the countertop. "Not to worry. There's a way out. The man whom you replaced would give anything to be back on the *Ballin*. He's a fine pianist."

"Replaced? I was so happy you gave me the job that I never asked how you made it available so quickly."

As he puffed, shards of tobacco blazed orange and crackled. "Max called and explained that you had to be on the next ship that sailed. He gave me no choice. I let the other man go and put you on."

"Now I feel terrible. Does the man have a family? Was he able to get by?"

"No family. Getting by? I wish I had his job. It's a dream."

Then it struck me. "Don't tell me. Max got him a job at *Pension Schmidt*."

"How did you know?"

"Lucky guess. Why would your man want to leave there?"

"He complains that it is too confining. He will be happy to fill in for you. Think of it as giving him a vacation."

"What man wants a vacation from a brothel?"

We both laughed. Then he became serious and repeated, "Tell me, Friedrich, will you be back for the next trip?"

"It all depends on what I find in Munich."

*

Three days later, on Saturday morning, I stood in extreme cold outside the back gate of the Landsberg Prison in Munich to wait for Wolf to appear. I stamped my feet and clapped my hands in an effort to stay warm, trying to stave off frostbite.

Time ticked by and nothing happened. I wondered if Emil sent the wrong information or Max heard him wrong. I turned to leave when a big black Daimler-Benz rolled up. Heinrich Hoffman, Wolf's favorite photographer, jumped out, equipment in hand. He was there to memorialize the event.

We greeted each other. I knew Hoffman only slightly. He was loud, gregarious, and inclined to exaggerate, especially when in his cups—which was often.

"I didn't know you had such a big car."

"Where have you been?" he asked. "The *Führer* has been asking for you."

"Traveling back and forth to New York ever since the Putsch. I didn't know if the police were looking for me. If I was ever needed, Emil knew where to find me."

Hoffman nodded at the driver who remained behind the wheel. "As for the car, it belongs to Adolf Müller."

"The same Müller whose company prints the Nazi pamphlets? Do you think he would let me sit in the car with him? I've been out here so long I will be lucky if I don't lose a couple of fingers or toes."

I reached for the handle when the squeal of a gate stopped me. Müller bounced out of the car. Our expectations were dashed when a uniformed gatekeeper strode to us. He ordered Hoffman to dismantle his tripod and stow away the camera.

Hoffman stood his ground and pointed. "You have no jurisdiction outside those walls."

"I may not, but the government in Berlin does. They issued strict orders that no pictures were to be taken when Hitler leaves prison. They don't want propaganda to come from this."

"Berlin holds no sway over me. I'm here to record history in the making."

The guard pointed to the camera. "Either it goes or Hitler stays in jail." Then he gave Hoffman a slight shove. "Of course the *Führer* might be disappointed that he will not be released because of you."

It was not lost on me that he referred to Wolf as the *Führer*.

Hoffman looked from me to Müller. What choice did we have? With reluctance, we retreated into the car and waited.

Wolf finally strode into view accompanied by two guards. We dashed out to meet him. He looked puffy . . . kilos heavier from sweets and cakes sent by his admirers. As he passed through the gates, Wolf shook each guard's hand before marching to the car, trailed by a uniformed man carrying a package. Wolf saluted

Hoffman and then broke out into an ear-to-ear smile. He pushed my hand away, grabbed me, and kissed me on both cheeks.

"*Friedrichen*, I knew you would find a way to be here."

"*Mein Führer*," said Hoffman, "it is essential that I photograph your release, but they will not let me take a picture here."

"Skip the picture, Heinrich."

"*Mein Führer*. This is an historic moment. It must be recorded." Then he snapped his fingers. "I have an idea."

When we slipped into the car, Wolf took the thick package from the guard and placed it on the seat between us. I thought he would explain what was in it, but he didn't. Instead he gazed out the window appreciating the sights.

Hoffman directed Müller to drive to the old city gates. The hulking edifice had the look and feel of a prison wall. Hoffman positioned the car and Wolf to convey the illusion that this was the moment of Adolf Hitler's release from Landsberg Prison. Hoffman's understated picture of Hitler's first taste of freedom, in time, became iconic.

Wolf rubbed his hands together as he returned to the car. "I forgot how cold it gets in December."

Hoffman turned to face us. "We have a surprise for you, *mein Führer*. There is a party in your honor. Nothing fancy. Some of your closest friends want to see you."

Wolf grunted. He never liked small gatherings.

As we drove to the party, I asked him about the package. He cradled it to his chest. "Friedrich, I made good use of my time in prison. I read many, many books." Then he plopped the package wrapped in brown paper and tied with string into my hands. It was weighty. "More importantly, I wrote one. It's my story."

I had so many questions; I didn't know where to start. "They gave you time to write?"

"They let me spend the days as I wished. I had as many visitors as I wanted. Frau Bechstein came with Lotte, who is growing up very fast. My sister visited with my nieces. Admirers sent gifts. There were so many flowers that I gave some to the guards."

"Did you write the pages yourself?"

"*Nein*. I dictated and Emil and Hess took turns typing. Can you believe it? They even gave us a typewriter. Look at these."

He handed me two photographs taken by a guard. They made me smile. One was of him and Emil. The other was of the two of them, with Rudy, Hermann Kriebel, and Friedrich Weber. I could see that Wolf had put weight on by the time of the second shot. I laughed seeing Emil with his mandolin. "I see they let Emil have his instrument."

"When can I publish your book?" Müller asked, stealing glances to see the wrapped manuscript.

"I want to edit it some more, and then your publishing company may do what it does best."

"What is the title?" I asked.

"Amann didn't like mine, even though it is perfect."

"Don't keep us in suspense," said Hoffman.

"My title was *Four-and-a-Half Years of Struggle Against Lies, Stupidity, and Cowardice.*"

I had all to do to bite my tongue and not tell him how terrible that was.

"That *is* a bit cumbersome," Müller said. "What did Max suggest calling it?"

"*Mein Kampf.*"

Without meaning to, I mumbled its translation.

"What did you say?" Wolf asked.

"I learned English this past year."

"How does *Mein Kampf* translate into English?"

"My Struggle."

*

Putzi Hanfstaengl's house, located in Herzog Park, overflowed with well-wishers. Wolf embraced his freedom in a most uncharacteristic manner: he entertained the assemblage. He used his amazing voice to describe his experience on the western front. He mimicked all types of guns: English, French, and German. Then he put the partygoers through the Battle of Somme, imitating the various guns used by the Allies and our forces, with the skills and timing of a seasoned entertainer. Everyone was in stitches. This was a side of the man none had seen.

Hans Frank stood on a chair and tapped his wine glass. He waited for the crowd to simmer down. "Tonight we honor a giant. There is no other way to describe him." Frank unfolded a leaf of paper. "Let me read the words our *Führer* proclaimed in the trial. Hear them and remember them.

> The man who is born to be a dictator, wills it. There is nothing immodest in this.

The room erupted in cheers. Frank held his hand up for silence and then repeated the *Führer's* challenge when the trial ended.

> You may judge us guilty, but the Goddess of Eternal Justice will tear to tatters the verdict of this court. For she acquits us!

The room's exuberance was palpable. Filled with pride in my friend, I strode to the piano and played the German national anthem: *Deutschlandlied*. At the first note, all rose to their feet and joined:

> *Deutschland, Deutschland über alles* . . . Germany, Germany above all.

It was a glorious homecoming. As the party carried on, I cornered Hans Frank, who was now studying law. "I read an article in which a reporter said, 'What went on there reminded me of a Munich political carnival.' Hans, this reporter made it sound like the Boss had a field day. Is it true that Wolf said whatever he wanted?"

"That's not far off," answered Frank. "Let me answer you this way. Do you know Franz Gürtner?"

"He's the Bavarian minister of Justice. But he wasn't the judge," I answered.

"That's right. George Neithardt presided. The same judge in Otto Ballerstedt's case."

"Why was Neithardt so lenient?"

"Because of Gürtner. He is the judge's boss. As the saying goes: good lawyers know the law, but great lawyers know the judge."

"And in this case we knew the judge's boss."

He slapped me on the back. "You catch on quick, Friedrich. Gürtner arranged for an early release after he decided the Boss learned his lesson."

Chapter 22

January 1925 – July 1927

After prison, Hitler was calmer. More disciplined. More focused. In addition to dictating a draft of *Mein Kampf*, he also used his time to read polemics that transformed his thinking. He now rejected a putsch as his path to dictatorial power. After much study, Hitler concluded that winning democratic elections was the only path to the ultimate defeat of democracy.

This led to his greatest transformation.

Campaigning and winning elections required money, and the only available source of the magnitude of funds needed were the industrialists and the aristocracy. But the original founders of the NSDAP continued to embrace the party's cornerstone twenty-five-point program that would nationalize the wealth of those same individuals. This brought Hitler into direct philosophical conflict with diehards in the party. Trouble was brewing.

The avid party socialists—mostly in the north—were not idle while Wolf was in prison. As Hitler set out to regain power as party chief, Gregor Strasser, his brother Otto, and their new recruit, Joseph Goebbels—and even close allies like Wilhelm Frick and Ernst Röhm, indeed most everyone in the party—continued to embrace the socialist workers' part of their party's name. Hitler knew he had to change the ideology of the party, to get all of them to support the nationalist part of the National Socialist Workers Democratic Party . . . or he could never take power.

*

Wolf and I met for lunch soon after his release. We took an inside table at the Heck Café, located at the corner of

Ludwigstrasse and *Galeriestrasse*, overlooking the *Hofgarten*. As we relaxed over dessert, a more confident Wolf said, "Prison was a liberating experience, Friedrich. It gave me time to formulate ideas, write my story, and comprehend what the party needs in order to succeed."

I admired his upbeat attitude but he needed to know what had occurred in his absence. "The party is in shambles, Wolf. Isolated branches have sprung up across the country. In some instances, they've shifted loyalty from you to others."

Wolf had a dreamy-eyed look about him. "I did more than write a book in prison."

"Did you hear what I said about the party? It demands your attention."

"I wrote a poem about my mother. You know I write poetry. I'm going to add this to my collection."

This stopped me cold. I did not know what to think. Was Wolf talking about the same poem that Dr. Forster told me was really written by someone else? I didn't know which was worse: the possibility that he was recycling this old poem as his or that he was unable to focus on the party's problems? Before I could navigate him back to our subject, he reached into his pocket and produced a piece of light-brown stationery lined with his scribble. A quick scan told me that it matched Dr. Forster's description.

THINK IT

When your mother has grown older,
When her dear, faithful eyes
no longer see life as they once did,
When her feet, grown tired,
No longer want to carry her as she walks—

Then lend her your arm in support,
Escort her with happy pleasure.
The hour will come when, weeping, you
Must accompany her on her final walk.

And if she asks you something,
Then give her an answer.
And if she asks again, then speak!
And if she asks yet again, respond to her,
Not impatiently, but with gentle calm.

And if she cannot understand you properly
Explain all to her happily.
The hour will come, the bitter hour,
When her mouth asks for nothing more."
Adolf Hitler, 1923

I placed the poem on the table. "Wolf, this is very touching. I appreciate how productive you were while in prison, but you are losing your grip on the party." The greater question for me: was he losing his grip on reality?

In a move that startled me, he grabbed my hand, leaned forward, and stared to the point that I squirmed in my chair. "After all this time, *Friedrichshen*, you still underestimate your friend. Don't you think I know Gregor Strasser is trying to undermine me? I know that he has made Himmler his personal assistant. I know that the new man on the scene—Joseph Goebbels—is brilliant and that I have to watch out for him."

"His oratory reminds me of you."

"That may be so," said Wolf, "but he has picked the wrong man to get behind."

"If you know this subterfuge exists in the party ranks, what do you plan to do about it?" At that moment, he let go of my hand and sat tall, his eyes trailing the young waitress bringing us coffee. I cleared my throat. "Did you hear what I said?"

"I heard every word." His eyes never wavered from her backside.

"Then how will you go about it?"

"About what?" He turned to me only after she ducked into the kitchen.

"Strasser and the rest of them. Since the party has been banned, they formed a new party: The National Socialist Freedom Movement. They won thirty-two seats in the Reichstag last year. Röhm and Ludendorff are with them."

He turned back to me. "The jailers brought me newspapers from here and Berlin. Visitors also kept me informed. None of what you are telling me is new."

"Then you must know that the *SA* has been banned, and that Röhm constructed a veritable army of ex-*Freikorps*. It's called the *Frontbann*. Wolf, he's got thirty thousand men behind him."

"That's not a concern." He tapped his temple. "Why do you think I put Rosenberg in charge of the party when I was arrested? I knew he was incapable of running it. I needed the party to splinter and fall apart. The last thing I wanted was a strong leader to take control. Now that I am out of Landsberg, I will put everything together again."

"Even if you manage to rein in the others, how can you trust them?"

Before answering, he glanced to see if the waitress was about. She wasn't. "Friedrich, in time most sheep stray from the flock. It doesn't mean they must be slaughtered when they return. Sheep are sheep." He leaned back. "I realized many things in Landsberg. Politicians preach socialism and promise to redistribute the country's wealth to the masses. This makes the workers feel happy. It gains their votes. We will also preach this, but not do it. Otherwise, we would be no different than communists."

"Your plan is to gain the trust of both the rich and the poor at the same time?"

"It's the only way. We took those first steps at the Bechstein mansion. Those are the people we must target. Who else is going to fund us?"

"I understand, but what does this have to do with those disloyal men?"

"Their message is wrong. Each of these men—Strasser, Himmler, and Goebbels, especially Goebbels—has a talent we need. Strasser and Himmler are great organizers. Goebbels is not only a brilliant speaker, but he understands how to manipulate events to enhance the party's visibility to the public. Before Landsberg, I would have forced them to get in line . . . or worse. Now I realize that by repurposing their talents, they will better serve the party. Do you know why most revolutions fail?"

"For the same reason Kapp's and ours failed: we thought we had the army and police behind us but didn't."

"Precisely. And I take the blame for leaving a fool general in charge of that trio of incompetents. Don't think I've forgotten that Kahr betrayed us when he convinced Seisser and Lossow to abandon the putsch. Had they gone along with us, the putsch would have succeeded." Wolf shook his fist. "We will see to Kahr one day."

"Everything you're saying makes sense. But how will you get the German people behind you to the point that we can take over the country?"

"The only way possible: win elections!"

Seeing that his fire and focus had returned, I needed to know what role I would play as he moved to regain power in the party. "What would you have me do?"

"Friedrich, it is still best to keep you out of the limelight. Once we take control of the government, you will no longer have to remain as guarded."

"There's still Pasewalk. I'm not sure I could ever be in the limelight."

"No need discussing what we don't control. For now, I want you to be my minister without portfolio. My unseen right hand."

"To what end?"

"Remember how many important people attended the Bechstein party? There are countless others to meet. I don't have time for small gatherings or one-on-one meetings. You do. Once the party is back under my aegis, my job is to increase membership so we're a force to reckon with in the next election. I can only do this at rallies."

"Are you forgetting that you are banned from speaking in public?"

He gave a sly smirk. "The way to get around that is for me to speak at private clubs and organizations that have lots of members. These talks will not be under party auspices, yet their effect will be the same. While I do that, you will be on a mission that only you and I know its true purpose."

He reached into his breast pocket and handed me a letter. "Read it."

My eyes sailed across the words. His name was signed at the bottom. I reread it a second time. The document confirmed my authority. The rest took my breath.

"It surprises you, doesn't it?"

"I can't believe you're willing to commit this on paper."

"It's the only way. The industrialists and the bankers *must* know we will protect them. You must explain that the elements threatening them in the twenty-five-point program are a thing of the past. Make them understand that we are capitalistic, not socialistic. This letter—with my signature—promises that. But show it only when absolutely necessary to establish your bona fides. It must never leave your possession."

"If I am going to do this, I need to notify the Hamburg American Line that I'm quitting. They found a temporary replacement for this last trip I missed but will need to look for someone more permanent."

"No. Make your next sailing. For now, arrange appointments between voyages. There is another advantage if you continue on the ship: cruises will give you fertile opportunities to meet wealthy people. In your case, you will have captive audiences. Engage them. Explain what we will do to ensure their wealth. Win them to our side."

"This plan could take years."

"Saplings don't bear fruit overnight. We'll take the time necessary to build a proper base. Keep your job and see industrialists whenever the boat is in for refitting."

"Am I supposed to ask for money at these visits?"

"Strike when they are excited about our program. Some will write you a check. Others will hand you cash. One of our partners

is Deutschebank. The bank has already made a handsome donation to the party. You will have access to their branches across
the country. Open bank accounts as needed, with me as the co-
signature. If you receive a check, deposit it in our account. If you
receive cash—and I know you will—deposit that in a bank vault
in our name. When your business is finished with one industrialist, move on to another"

"What if they won't see me?"

Wolf shrugged. "Some will; many may not. Those who
receive you are the ones who understand that their economic
lives are at stake. Their houses, their factories, their money in the
bank, everything is at risk if the Reds take over Germany. You'll
see. As we grow stronger and our chance for power increases,
they will line up to give us money."

"Setting up meetings with industrialists and wealthy families
costs money. Money we don't have."

"Frau Buckmann—you remember her from the last party—
has opened an account in the party name in Deutschebank. You
will have access to it as needed."

He ended our talk with a simple directive. "Each time you
return from a trip, if I am not available, check with Emil or
Hess to see if I need you. If I do, you'll ask for another leave
of absence. If I don't, continue on these voyages and solicit our
wealthy countrymen. I cannot emphasize how important your
role is to the future of our party."

Even though I wanted to help Wolf and the party, I was glad
that I could continue working on the ship a while longer. Now I
could accomplish both at the same time.

"Tomorrow we start," Wolf said, rubbing his hands together.

"But you just said I should return to my ship."

"I have already checked. It doesn't leave for three days. That's
plenty of time for us to go to *Haus Bechstein*, where we are promised a welcoming audience. I am expected to give a brief speech.
This will give you a chance to arrange for private sessions in
the future, with as many industrialists as you can. Besides, Frau

Bechstein expects you to give another recital. And then there's Lotte."

"She's a child."

"She's older now."

At best, the girl was only sixteen. "Why put yourself in that situation?"

"It's clear Frau Bechstein is angling for me to marry the girl. She calls me *Wölfchen*. She openly speaks of an engagement to Lotte. I'll humor her for a few days. Make her feel special. It's the least I can do for arranging this reception and giving me that new Mercedes. I make both happy . . . and the party gets more money."

Chapter 23

We arrived at *Haus Bechstein* expecting a grand reception. Helene Bechstein did not disappoint. The salon was packed with celebrities and the social elite. They came to see Wolf, whose status had grown as a result of his domination of the trial after the failed putsch.

This time we were dressed to the nines. Wolf was in formal tails and I was lucky enough to find a silk dinner jacket in my size at a shop that specialized in tall men.

After greeting us, Frau Bechstein pointed to a wrapped package I carried in for him. "What is that, *Wolfchen*?"

"That's a little something for Lotte," he answered, as I handed it to a butler who stowed it away for later.

Frau Bechstein then slipped her arm through Wolf's and gushed with pride as she prattled to every guest about the famous party leader who would restore Germany to its rightful position amongst nations. There were questions about the rigors of jail life. What kind of food did they serve? Did they beat him? More banal questions followed during the course of the evening. Given our mission, Wolf exhibited more patience than I thought him capable. This was another Landsberg dividend.

Lisolette Bechstein cornered me. She had matured into a young woman during these past four years. No one would turn their head when Lotte passed. But if one stopped to chat, they would discover she had a soft, deferential way that made her attractive. "Has he changed?" she asked. "I visited him once in . . . you know . . . and he seemed fine. Is he all right now?" She turned dreamy-eyed. "I need to know *everything* about him."

"He emerged out of Landsberg stronger and better for the experience. He is more determined than ever to succeed."

"But does he have a special woman to take care of him?"

I turned my head to the cluster of older women preening over him. "He has more mothers then he needs. Rest assured Herr Hitler is well taken care of."

Lotte's face reddened. "That's not what I meant."

I knew very well what she meant. I also knew Wolf was prepared to spend more than a few moments with her if it meant more funds from the Bechsteins. It was time to do my job. I stuck out my arm. "Come. He asked me to bring you to him."

I pried Wolf away from the gaggle of women. Wolf's face lit up when he saw how Lotte had ripened into a young woman. "Come, I have something for you," he said.

We found our way to the reception hall where the butler waited with the package. Wolf took it from him and then, with his classic Viennese bow, presented it to Lotte.

"For me?" her mouth formed a surprised "O."

"*Schönes Fräulein*, only for you."

Her hands trembled as she fumbled to open it. I reached to help her. When the last wrapping fell to the marble floor, she gasped, "It is beautiful!"

It was a vivid watercolor of the Laon countryside leading up to the walled city that Wolf painted in 1919. It was signed, "A. Hitler," and in the lower left hand corner, the number "nineteen."

"Friedrich," said Wolf, "Do you have a pen?" I handed him a pencil. "This will have to do."

He inscribed the back, "*Meiner lieben* Löttl"—my dear Lotte—and signed it "*Dein* Wolf"—your Wolf.

With that he took the thunderstruck girl by the arm and ushered her into a corner where they sat on a cramped, silk settee. She glowed as he fussed over her, leaning closer and closer. I could only imagine how he complimented her on her dress, her shoes, and the way she brushed her hair. His technique with women usually yielded results.

*

I surveyed the room and recognized Fritz Thyssen. Thyssen was fifty-one, with a long face and dark, beady eyes. He stood to inherit his father's steel and mining business, which controlled three-quarters of Germany's iron ore. Thyssen had already donated small sums to the party.

"Herr Thyssen, allow me to introduce myself."

"I know who you are. Herr Hitler has already pointed you out as a rising star in the party. More to the point, I was present the night you thrilled us with your wonderful performance of Liszt's *Hungarian Rhapsody*. Are you going to play for us again?"

"If Frau Bechstein asks."

He slapped me on the back as he scanned the room. "This party needs to be livened up a bit." Having no more to say to me, he turned to rejoin friends.

I cleared my throat. "Herr Thyssen. I need a favor of you."

He stiffened, turning slowly back to me. "Herr Hitler has given me a special mission to meet industrialists such as yourself." I pulled out the sheet of paper that established my authority. "We want you to know that we will no longer support the anti-capitalist measures described in the twenty-five-point program. Hitler feels strongly that those who have accumulated substantial assets as a result of either hard work or through their families, should be entitled to keep them."

Thyssen scanned the document and turned from guarded to benevolent. "It was always my hope that Hitler would take this approach. As long as the riffraff in the party incited the masses against us, there could never be more than token support from us. Granted, the NSDAP was better than the Reds, but until now its attractiveness was limited. This change is *most* reassuring. How soon will he formalize this new position?"

Wolf never mentioned a timetable. "I need to show this to more industrialists. When enough are on board, Hitler will formalize this as an official part of the platform. Any help you can give to speed this along will be appreciated."

"Start with that man over there. Alfred Hugenberg."

I turned to see a barrel-chested man nearing sixty. He sported a gray handlebar moustache, round glasses, and a full shock of graying hair combed straight back. Hugenberg ran Krupp A.G. during the war. Krupp was Germany's largest company. It supplied the military with all of its munitions during the conflict. Having left Krupp, Hugenberg now headed the Scherl House, Germany's largest publisher.

"Can you make the introduction for me?"

Thyssen took me by the elbow. "Certainly. After Hugenberg, there are one or two more worth meeting here tonight."

*

Over the next two years I continued playing music on the *SS Ballin*, traveling between Germany and America. I was able to save my salary since the cruise line paid for my room and board. During layovers in Cuxhaven, I sought out potential patrons for the party. Among whom were Alfred Vogler of the coal, iron, and steel plants; Ernest von Borsig, manufacturer of locomotives; and Richard Franck, who owned Heinrich Franck Söhne, the world's largest manufacturer of substitute coffee made from chicory.

To each I emphasized that financial support of the NSDAP would ensure favored status when the party came to power. Even skeptics donated money as insurance against the unknown future. And as I met more and more sympathetic industrialists and wealthy future patrons, Wolf skillfully made the party's tectonic shift away from Socialism.

It was during this time that Ernst Röhm, a rabid revolutionary, resigned from the party. Sensing that this was not his time, he departed for South America with a contract to build up the Bolivian army. Even this helped. Wealthy donors viewed his departure as a constructive step.

*

I saw little of Wolf or the party regulars during the many months I continued to sail. I did attend one meeting: Nazi Party Day on July 4, 1926. This was the first time Wolf used the *Blutfahne* or Blood Flag that, after the party came to power, became its most iconic symbol.

Heinrich Trambauer carried that swastika flag during the 1923 Munich Putsch. As marchers approached the Feldhernhalle and the Munich police opened fire, Trambauer fell wounded. Andreas Bauriedl then snatched the fallen flag and marched until he was shot . . . the bullet passing through the flag into his body. Trambauer lifted his head to see the dying Bauriedl's blood soak through the fabric. Trambauer mustered his last ounce of strength, grabbed the flag, and gave it to Karl Eggers for safekeeping. For three years, the flag was shuttled from house to house to avoid confiscation until it emerged for this Nazi Party Day ceremony. Seizing the moment, Wolf had the flag fitted with a new staff and finial. Below the finial, he ordered a silver sleeve fabricated that bore the names of the sixteen dead comrades of the failed putsch. From that day forward, every *SA* and *SS* unit consecrated their own banner by touching it to this bloodstained flag of '23.

*

I found a moment to be alone with Wolf at the end of the rally. "Where is Göring? I didn't see him today."

"Do you remember when he was shot during the putsch?"

"Shrapnel bounced off the cobblestone into his groin. The last I saw he was being dragged away. I've heard nothing since."

"He escaped to Austria. The wound got infected. His doctor was too generous with morphine. Our dear friend, Göring, has turned into an addict."

"That can be treated."

Wolf nodded. "Only for those willing to be helped. Not our Hermann. He went crazy. Last September, they admitted him to Catherine Hospital in Stockholm. He attacked a nurse for not giving him enough morphine. They declared him insane, put him a straightjacket, and sent him to Långbro Mental Hospital."

"Will he ever come back?"

"Time is the great healer," answered Wolf. "If Göring comes back, we'll make good use of him."

Chapter 24

Whenever the *SS Ballin* was being refitted and time permitted between soliciting funds for the party, I visited Max.

"I've got a job for you," Max said on one visit. We were eating lunch at a café table in the Nightingale. The club's stale indoors was in stark contrast to the crisp Bavarian skies or the salty sea air that I had grown to appreciate.

"What did you have in mind, Max?"

"I assume you are aware of Prohibition."

"That's why our cruises are so successful. American ocean liners can't serve liquor. We can. The Americans are our best customers."

"I don't know what they were thinking when they passed that law." Max shook his head. "All that lost business. What a shame." He blew a smoke ring from his ever-present cigar. "I've stayed out of this too long. It kills me to be missing easy money."

"What can you do from here?"

"I have connections in New Jersey. My cousin, Abner Zwillman, has been bringing booze in armored trucks from Canada. Sometimes he uses speed boats to run cargo in from ships outside the twelve-mile zone."

"What good are your connections in New Jersey? Even if it is your cousin."

"I've got it covered at both ends. Manfred will get my goods on and off the *Ballin*. No one is going to question him about some extra containers in the ship's hold. When the *Ballin* lands in New York, it will be met by a barge."

"What about using speed boats? They're faster."

"These containers are far too heavy for small boats. Manfred has already arranged the offloading. I want you to be on the barge to make certain everything goes smooth."

"Don't you trust your cousin?"

Max ground the stump of his cigar out in the ashtray. "This sort of cousin you don't take for granted."

"Let me get this straight: you expect me to hop off the ship onto a barge and float to some port in New Jersey like it's a day at the beach. Max, the police are looking for this sort of thing. You'll never get away with it. More to the point, I'll be arrested!"

Max moved his pudgy hand as if shoving crumbs off an imaginary table. "It's already taken care of. The harbor cops, the custom's officers, everybody is on the take."

"Where does this barge end up?"

"Not far. It's called Port Newark. Watch what my cousin's guys do. Count everything. Collect my money. Get back to the *Ballin*. How hard can that be?"

Then Max reached into a drawer and drew out a handgun. "Take this with you."

"If it is going to be so easy, why do I need a gun?"

"I like to play it safe."

"Doesn't sound safe to me."

"It never hurts to be prepared."

*

Max's cousin, Abner "Longie" Zwillman met us when we docked at Port Newark. The "Longie" nickname reflected his height. His men broke open the containers taken from the *SS Ballin* and loaded them into armor-clad, Mack Bulldog trucks once used during the war. He warehoused them near Prince Street in Newark's Third Ward from where he distributed the booze to the speakeasies in the surrounding towns. I accompanied the trucks. There were no glitches. Once the cases of booze were stacked in the warehouse and I collected Max's money, my job was done.

Zwillman eyed me up and down. "You sure you don't want to work for me? I could use a guy your size. You're even bigger than me. How tall?"

"Two meters."

"Meters? What's that?"

"About six-foot-six. Maybe six-seven."

"How much weight are you carrying?"

I converted kilos to pounds since he and the metric system were strangers. "About two-fifty." I was closer to two-seventy with all the free food on board, but that was immaterial.

"How about giving it a shake? You'd be a natural for what I need."

Max briefed me that when Zwillman was a kid, he would protect elderly Jews from Irish thugs who assaulted them. Wherever trouble appeared in the neighborhood, a cry went up in Yiddish, "*Ruff der Langer.* Call the tall one." Longie would show up and beat up the intruders.

"What are you called?" Longie asked, as he counted out the cash.

"Friedrich Zalman Richard." I stuck out my hand.

"You're a *landsman*!"

Under the circumstances, I let him think I was a Jew. "I'm a piano player, too."

"And I'm Knute Rockne."

I was supposed to know who Knute Rockne was, but I didn't. It wasn't a German name.

I gripped the sack that held Max's money in one hand and fingered the gun in my pocket with the other. If there was going to be trouble, this was the time. "No one told me how I was supposed to get back to the boat. Will they take me back on the barge?"

"Too slow," said Longie. "My men will take you on a speed boat."

I made it back to the *Ballin* without incident.

*

I went to the Nightingale as soon as I returned to Germany.

"This is for you." Max clipped a chunk of bills from one of the stacks I dropped on his desk.

"Don't give me anything, Max. I owe you for all the times you bailed me out of tough spots."

"Max Klinghofer doesn't work that way. You do something for me; you get yours. Besides, I've got more jobs in the pipeline. I can't ask you to do them for free."

Over the next number of trips, I ensured that Max's containers were delivered and his money collected. Longie and I often got to talking. I learned that when he was fourteen, he dropped out of school after his father died to help support his mother and siblings. Longie was practical. For example, after a brief war with Richie "The Boot" Boiardo who controlled Newark's First Ward, Longie agreed to a meeting refereed by a "neutral" mobster: Salvatore Lucania, whom everyone called Lucky Luciano. Territories were defined. In this way both Newark enterprises, Jewish and Italian, thrived without further bloodshed.

I got to know a number of Longie's "associates." To a one, they took me for a Jew, since Longie insisted on calling me Zalman. I was surprised at the number of Jews in the rackets in New York and New Jersey. I was more amazed at how tough—no, how *ferocious*—they were.

During my many trips across the Atlantic, I met Meyer Lansky and Benjamin Siegel. Everyone called Benjamin "Bugsy," but not to his face. What surprised me was how the Jewish and Italian gangsters were willing to join forces.

During one stopover, Zwillman asked me for a favor.

"Zal, I need you to come to a meeting in New York City with me. It's important that I look strong."

"An army of tough guys surrounds you morning, noon, and night. The last thing I'd want is to walk down a dark alley and come face-to-face with any of your crew. What do you need me for? I told you, Longie, I'm a piano player."

"There won't be any pianos where we're going. And this is no dance recital, either. We're forming an organization. The Big Seven Group. You've got smarts to go along with your brawn, Zal. Besides looking tough, I need a good pair of ears by my side."

*

Longie posted me outside the door of a suite in the Waldorf. He was wrong. There was a piano in the hotel, just not where we were. I stood like a potted plant for two-and-a-half hours with a dozen goons belonging to Lucky Luciano. Also in attendance were Meyer Lansky, Frank Costello, and Johnny Torrio, who's protégée would be Al Capone. There were other major players whose names I did not catch.

While I stood outside the door with the other soldiers, the men inside created "The Commission" that would rule the country's underworld for years to come.

Where did Longie Zwillman fit into this scheme? He, Louis "Lepke" Buchalter, Jacob "Gurrah" Shapiro, Benjamin "Bugsy" Siegel, and others formed Murder Incorporated. These American Jews did not mince words or take guff from anybody for any reason. So when the Mafia families pronounced death sentences on those who crossed them . . . they gave the contracts to the Jews to do the killing.

This caused me great confusion.

How could these Jews be considered anything less than a match for the toughest Brown Shirt or *SS* man? How could they be the same people that Hitler railed against?

Chapter 25

1927

The outward passage from Southampton to New York—on what became my last round trip voyage—was rough. Many guests became seasick. Two of my shows had to be cancelled. I was grateful for calm seas on the return leg.

My programs varied with the passengers. Why shouldn't I play music they preferred? This particular group wanted both the classics and modern tunes. To accommodate, I mixed Chopin, Liszt, and Mozart pieces with songs from Broadway shows and pieces from the uptown clubs that featured Louis Armstrong, King Oliver, Kid Ory, and Duke Ellington. Of late, I added Scott Joplin's compositions to my repertoire.

"Do you know how to play 'I Ain't Gonna Play No Second Fiddle?'" a voice asked from behind me.

My head bobbed in surprise. Only someone up-to-date on the current music scene could know that song; it had only been out a month. I had just seen Bessie Smith sing this Perry Bradford song at the Cotton Club. I loved it so much I bought the sheet music the next day.

I looked to see who was so in the know about the latest music. Instead of the usual matron, a beautiful blond woman, barely into her twenties, gazed down at me. Her lips were dark red with a peaked cupid's bow. Her rich brown eyes twinkled under her plucked brows. They were both sexy and appealing. She held a champagne glass by the stem. Her sequined dress shimmered. "I'll play it if you sing it." I don't know what made me so bold, but I made the challenge.

With a giggle she laid her glass on the closest table. "Let's do it."

This goddess eased next to me. She nudged me to make room at the bench. Her scent engulfed me as I tingled from the warmth of her body next to mine. It was a miracle that I played a note. I eked out the first few bars and her sultry voice wrapped the words around the music in exotic delicacy.

I held the last note as long as possible to extend the magic.

My "regulars," it was right to call them that after days at sea, exploded into a standing ovation. My mystery guest curtseyed. She then made a half-turn and extended her willowy arm to acknowledge me . . . her accompanist. When I rose, she took my hand and we bowed as one.

We played an encore: "Someone to Watch Over Me," by George and Ira Gershwin. By the final chord, I was in love.

"Who are you?" I asked after the last congratulatory guest had left.

She tapped her glass for a refill. The guests at the front table had not finished their Dom that was still wedged into an ice-filled silver bucket. Enough remained for a glass of champagne for each of us.

Her lips parted to take a sip, displaying perfect pearly whites. I led her by the arm. "Let's get some fresh air."

When we emerged onto the nightclub's small balcony, she asked, "The program says you're Friedrich Richard. Is that a stage name?"

How do I answer that one?

"It's my given name. Now your turn. What do they call you?"

"Does it matter, Friedrich? Here we are, a man and a woman standing next to each other on a brilliant summer night. The waves are dancing rhythmically in the moonlight. What could be more romantic? Don't spoil it with trivial details."

She inched closer. Our fingers touched, sending bolts of excitement through me. Her perfume addled me. My upper lip grew moist. "You're playing dirty. I have all I can do to control myself. If I could, I would wrap my arms around you and smother you with kisses. Standing here, you are the most beautiful angel I've ever seen."

She probed my face with eyes and lips that invited. "What's stopping you?"

Our thighs brushed against one another. This was too much even for me. I jerked back and grabbed the railing. "When does a stunning woman approach a piano player, sing like a pro, and then challenge the man with looks that would melt an iceberg? It only happens in the movies."

"Maybe that's what we're in. The camera is off to the side and we have our parts to play. Didn't you hear him? The director yelled, 'Action.'"

I didn't need another invitation. Our lips met and our tongues teased each other. She arched into me. After a minute, I broke away. "Now really, who are you? Are you with someone? Why haven't I seen you before? The trip is almost over. We've missed out on so much time together."

"That can be remedied."

We drew two deck chairs together until they touched. The light of the moon shimmered off the dark, black waters, causing the tiny waves to flicker like a thousand candles.

I could scarcely breathe. The mysterious woman flipped open a gold cigarette case, extracted a cigarette, and tapped it on her wrist before wedging it into a tortoise shell holder. I managed to strike a match and cup my hands around the flame with as much aplomb as I could muster. She leaned forward and smiled as she drew the flame to the cigarette, knowing her every move captivated me. She had a British accent yet spoke flawless German.

"My given name is Helene Lilian Muriel Pape. My mother is English, and my father is German. I was born in London. We were living in Magdenburg when the war broke out. My parents sent me to live with my aunt in Switzerland. I stayed there until the war ended when I joined them in Berlin. After high school, I studied dance and voice at the school of the Berlin Opera."

"That explains your singing and why you have such a presence about you."

"You don't know who I am, do you?"

"Should I? What are you, twenty? Twenty-one?"

"Age is a state of mind. Besides you shouldn't underestimate anyone just because they're young. Look at the way you played the piano. You didn't start yesterday. And you're still young."

"Point taken. From the sounds of it, you've accomplished much. But you still haven't answered me: who are you?"

She pouted. "I told you my name."

I loved how she pursed her lips. "Lots of women have the name Helene. Tell me the rest of your story."

"Why do think there is any more?"

"No one stands up in front of a room full of strangers and is willing to sing unless they have a voice like yours and a story to tell."

She drew on the cigarette. "My professional name is Lilian Harvey."

I shook my head. "Still doesn't ring a bell."

"I'm not liking you anymore. You know how to hurt a girl's feelings."

"I've been at sea a long time. I've missed a lot. Please don't take offense. Think of me as someone providing opportunities."

Her perfect eyebrows arched. "Now who is teasing who? Anyone who knows 'I Ain't Gonna Play No Second Fiddle' does not have their head buried in the sand."

Both beautiful and bright . . . and not afraid to speak her mind.

"You got me. Let's get past this. Tell me what I need to know about you so I can build a proper pedestal."

"Nice comeback. You are officially on your way to redemption. I appeared in my first film three years ago. I was eighteen. I played a young Jewish girl in a movie called *The Curse*. That got me the lead alongside Otto Bebühr in *The Passion*. Then I did *Love and Passion*. Last year, I was cast in a movie based on an operetta composed by Jean Gilbert called *Die Keusche Susanne*. I played opposite Willy Fritsch."

"That's quite a résumé. Sadly, I haven't seen any of them."

She wrinkled her forehead in wonder. "Not even the posters?"

"They don't have posters on ships. I assure you, had I seen any, I would have searched heaven and earth to find you."

She took my hand. "You have now officially redeemed yourself."

I brought her hand to my lips à la Wolf. I had never met a woman like this. While Anna was nurturing to the point of being motherly and Marta had a hard, sexy edge to her, Lilian—I liked the ring of her stage name—was by turns sophisticated, coquettish, alluring, mysterious, intelligent, and downright exciting.

I studied her as she took another drag. Her polished fingernails were the same color as her lips: fire red. The burning embers gave off a pungent aroma. She smoked Nestor Gianaclis. "I see you like Egyptian cigarettes."

"They are still the best. When I was in New York, they had an imitation brand. What a laugh. They tried to make it appear Egyptian by calling it Camel. How ridiculous thinking that if they pictured a camel with a pyramid and a palm tree in the background, it could pass as Egyptian and not the imitation it was."

"Were you in New York long?"

"Long enough."

"For what?"

"Just long enough. They think they are civilized, but they are crude compared to the sophisticates in London, Paris, or Berlin. And you?"

"And me what?"

"Have you traveled?"

"Here and there."

"Seems that we are both talking in riddles. Let's start again." Lilian extended her hand; I took it. "My name is Lilian Harvey. I am an actress between movies, taking a much-needed vacation. I decided to explore New York to see if there are any movie opportunities for me there."

How could a studio turn this beauty down? "Were there?"

She frowned. "Just my luck. I am either too late or too early."

"That makes no sense."

"Too late because every movie studio in Fort Lee, New Jersey was shuttered. They all moved to this place called Hollywood."

There was a burgeoning movie company in Queens. "What about the studio in Astoria?"

"You mean the Kaufman studios? They're in the midst of converting to talkies. I should be good at them because of my singing, but they're not ready for someone like me now. It's all about timing."

"They should've signed you on the spot. You're a natural."

"How can you say that? You don't even know me."

"I know talent when I see it."

"Mister, you know a pretty face, that's all."

"That, too."

We both laughed as we sized each other up.

"Since I was too early for the Kaufmanns and too late for Fort Lee, I'm returning to Germany for my next movie."

"America's loss is my gain."

"Aren't you taking a lot for granted?" She brought her glass to her lips. I barely breathed for fear she would say goodbye.

"Your singing created sparks tonight."

She leaned until our faces were inches apart. "I sensed a lot of sparks tonight, too."

I grew lightheaded; I had never felt like this. We kissed.

"I was never one for public displays, especially since someone might have seen one of my movies." Then Lilian added, "But we're safe here. No one on this ship has recognized me."

"They will one day soon." We held hands and enjoyed the moment. "I have a swell idea. There are three more nights until we reach port. Why not join me and sing for everyone? You saw how much they loved you tonight. Think of it as a way to advertise your next movie."

"What would I sing?"

"I have all the latest sheet music. We can practice during the day. You're a natural. Besides, I have no problem playing second fiddle to one so lovely . . . and talented."

"Flattery, Herr Richard, will get you everywhere."

*

Lilian was a hit. She sang Broadway show tunes, German folk songs, and then we cobbled together some of Al Jolson's biggest hits: "California Here I Come," "April Showers," "Swanee," "Rock-A-By Your Baby with A Dixie Melody," and "I'm Sitting on Top of the World." Furious applause followed each song, but when she dropped to one knee for, "My Mammy," the room went wild.

The applause was loudest at our last show. Lilian and I turned sober watching the guests trudge out of the salon. None lingered knowing they had to prepare to disembark early in the morning.

"This show doesn't have to end," I said when the last guest filtered out. "Let's continue to perform together."

Her flawless lips turned into broken crescents. "As much as I want that, I start shooting a new film in three days. It's called *Vacation from Marriage*. It's about how war changes people."

"It's an important topic to explore."

"I'm glad I am doing it. I don't want to be typecast as a song and dance girl."

"I'm sure you're great in everything you do." I grew melancholy. "Then this is our last night together."

"Is that a question or a statement?"

"Neither. I don't want to see you go."

She took my hand. "If you haven't noticed, I'm still here. Let's make this night memorable and see where it might lead?"

The night was memorable yet taut with anxiety. At least for me.

*

"I need to ask you a question," Lilian said. She wriggled until she could lean against the headboard, making no effort to cover herself.

"Don't make it too hard," I said. "All I can think about is you leaving the ship."

She smacked me on the head. "I'm being serious."

"So am I."

"Okay. This is it. We've been together day and night for almost four days. Almost one hundred hours, but who's counting."

"It was too short."

She arched her brows. "Whether it's been enough time or too much, save that for another discussion. What I realize is that you know so much about me and I know next to nothing about you."

"You know plenty."

She stuck out her index finger. "I know that you like to play the piano and could be a virtuoso. Two." A second finger darted out from her closed fist. "You're German." A third finger sprang out. "Your scars tell me you were in the war. After that, Friedrich, I don't know anything else about you."

"What else would you like to know?"

"For starters, where are you from? Who are your parents? Do you have any siblings? Where did you go to school? I want to get to know you better."

This was the moment I dreaded from the minute I knew she was the only woman I wanted. How could I possibly account for myself? Even my name wasn't my own. What could I say: I don't know anything about myself?

I was terrified the truth would drive her away. It had been nine years since the shell destroyed my memory. What could I say that made sense? Should I be transparent and confide that I knew *nothing* about myself? Could I even say that I was single? Maybe there was a family waiting for me? I was horrified at the prospect that the truth would drive her away. Knowing she would ask, I concocted a believable story.

"I grew up in a little village in Bavaria. I come from a family of farmers. They had their successes. My father was the *buergermeister* as was his father before him."

"Were they Junkers?"

"The farm was large, but nothing that would qualify my family as landed gentry. My mother, on the other hand, came from Munich. Her father was a doctor. She was well educated. She met my father and they fell in love. Against her parents' wishes, she married him and moved to our farm. She brought life to the tiny village."

"Did that include a piano?"

I smiled as if nostalgic for the good old days. "That was part of my mother's dowry. She taught me how to play. I preferred practicing the piano to manual labor."

She tapped my arm. "You can't fool me. Someone your size didn't get your strength from only playing the piano."

"Guilty as charged. I did my share of heavy lifting. Now you have the whole story."

"I think not. You skipped what happened to you in the war. You still haven't told me if you were ever married? If you have children? Brothers? Sisters? Are your parents still alive?"

How much more of this can I make up? Maybe it's time to face the music and tell her the truth. Lilian is in the arts. If anyone could understand, she should. But . . . if I confess the truth now, it would reveal me a liar. I never thought I would find someone so special. I wish I had not started this.

I turned away. My voice a whisper. "I had a younger brother and sister. They died with my parents in the influenza outbreak at the end of the war."

Lilian wrapped her arms around me. "I am so sorry. I had no idea."

"Even these many years later, it is hard to talk about it."

"What happened to the farm?"

"My uncle ran it for a couple of years and then he died. Now my cousins run it, if you can call it that. They sold off most of it to survive. There's almost nothing left of the original farm."

"That must be hard for you."

Not as hard as this!

"When I learned that my family had been wiped out, I vowed never to go back. I've had a good run playing on this ship. Seeing new places. Having new experiences. And now meeting you has been the most special of all." I squeezed her tight.

"This ship isn't that old," said Lilian. "You're leaving out a few years after the war."

"You got me. I was in the *Freikorps* with the troops that toppled the Communist takeovers in Berlin and Munich. Along the way I worked in a cabaret and even in a brothel."

Her eyes widened. "What was that like?"

"I was fortunate to see a lot of great acts at the cabaret."

She smacked my shoulder. "I meant the brothel."

"The usual stuff."

"Come on, Friedrich. Don't spoil it for me. I want to know the kinds of things they do there. Is it just men tired of their wives or is there more to it? Like ménage a trois? Women with women? Men and young boys?"

"All the above and more. My job was to make certain no one got out of hand and that the girls were protected. It was not to know what sort of things went on there."

She hung on my every word. "Did you ever have to step in to save a poor damsel?"

"What do you think?"

"I guess that comes with the job, doesn't it?" She clapped her hands in glee. "Do you ever go back there?"

"I've visited for old time's sake. I have good memories from when I worked there."

She poked me in the ribs. "I bet you do."

I wrapped my arms around her, wishing she did not have to make that movie. "Not what you think. Miss Kitty had a piano in the salon. I played it during slow periods. Mostly during the day. Sometimes, I played for the men waiting for their dates."

"Which cabaret did you work in?"

"The Nightingale. Maybe you've heard of it?"

"I've been there many times. I would've noticed you."

"I left years ago. Went to Munich."

"To work in another brothel?"

"Something that could not be more different. I got caught up in a new political party. The NSDAP."

"Were you involved when they tried to take over the government?"

"I was."

"I remember the party was banned for a while. Is that why you've been on the ship for the last couple of years?"

"You don't stop asking tough questions, do you?"

"Should I?"

I kissed her on the cheek. "No. To answer your last question, my former boss at the Nightingale helped me get this job. Then, about two-and-a-half years ago, our *Führer* was released from prison and the party ban was lifted. When I'm not playing piano on the ship, I make appointments with wealthy donors during my layovers. That about fills in the missing gaps."

"Not quite." By now we were in our robes and seated at the lone table in the room. We could see part of the deck and the sea beyond through a tiny window. "I have a notion what you've done most of your life, but I need to know about the man. About your morality."

"I love children and dogs and abide by the rules."

"Good to know but that's not what I'm talking about. Are you an anti-Semite?"

I made no effort to hide my shock. "Where did that come from?"

"Everyone in your party seems to be one. If that's the case, there is no future for us."

"I don't subscribe to that part of the party platform. In spite of what others may say, Jews have every right to be here and live in peace."

"So you *don't* believe they should be expelled from Germany?" I shook my head. "I work with them, you know. Many, actually most, of my best friends are Jews."

"Not a problem. Are there any more issues or questions I need to answer to win your heart?"

She grabbed my hand. "You've answered them all and passed with flying colors."

I squeezed tighter. "Then when can I see you after the ship docks?"

"As soon as you'd like."

"Where is your next movie being filmed?"

"Do you know the Hotel Adlon in Berlin?" I nodded, having stayed there with Wolf. "They take my messages even when I am not in residence. Call there first. If you can't reach me, leave word at the desk. One way or another, I'll get it."

*

Lilian and I joined the departing passengers who stood at the railing as the *SS Ballin* eased into its berth. Lilian had a car waiting to whisk her away while I would take the rail link to Hamburg-American's main office to collect my pay.

I watched her descend the gangway. Would she look back? Long strides carried her to a waiting car. She still had not turned. I prepared to leave the deck dejected when she stepped on the running board, turned, touched her hand to her heart, then to her lips, and sent me an airborne kiss. That painted my world in vivid colors of happiness.

Two hours later I stood in the shipping office.

"There's a telegram for you," said the paymaster.

I ripped open the letter.

URGENT YOU RETURN TO MUNICH AT ONCE.
STOP.
CRISIS.
STOP
TAKE A PLANE.
STOP.
BURN AFTER READING.
WILHELM FRICK AND RUDOLPH HESS

I stepped outside, lit a match, and watched the edges of the telegram turn into black curlicues. I waited until the last second before dropping it to the floor to ground out the embers. I reentered the building and asked the paymaster if he could send a telegram to Lilian Harvey, in care of the Hotel Adlon in Berlin.

EMERGENCY IN MUNICH.
STOP.
WILL CALL WHEN I CAN.
STOP.
MISS YOU ALREADY.
STOP.

PART III

Chapter 26

1927

The next morning, I secured the last seat on a new, twin-engine Albatross L 73 biplane. Sanctions imposed by the Treaty of Versailles were recently lifted that allowed commercial aviation in Germany to expand. As a result German Air (*Deutsche Luft*) merged with Hansa, named for the medieval trading association: the Hanseatic League. The new airline—*Deutsche Luft Hansa*—boasted a fleet of one hundred and sixty planes that flew to most European cities. Compared to the plane Wolf and I took to Berlin during the Kapp Putsch seven years before, this flight was luxurious. The enclosed cabin accommodated eight travelers in addition to the pilot, co-pilot, and engineer!

As our wheels touched the dirt runway at *Oberwiesenfeld*, Frick and Hess stood like sentries on either side of an Adler Standard 6 sedan. Frick motioned me to sit in the back with him while Rudy drove.

"Friedrich, you have some catching up to do," Frick began, once we were underway. It was true. The four years I rode the boat limited my contact with Wolf and the party leadership. I did know that Hess, released from Landsberg ten days after Wolf, now served as Wolf's secretary. Frick, arrested for his role in the putsch, stood trial with Hitler and received a suspended sentence. He was then reinstated in the Munich police.

"Before I explain why we need you here," Frick began, "Have you ever heard of the USCHLA? It represents the *Untersuchungsund Schlictung—Ausschuss*. We set it up as a court to discipline party members. Walter Buch is the chief judge."

"I remember Walter Buch as stiff and pompous."

"You're right on that score. And time has not softened Buch," Frick said.

Hess leaned across the seat and rifled through a bag. The car swerved. "Rudy, are you trying to kill us? Sit up when you're driving. And for God's sake, face forward."

Hess waved a *Brötchen mit Eiweiß glasiert*. "You know I like egg whites on a glazed roll. I was hungry."

"We're on our way to lunch. Can't you wait?"

"You know my diet is restricted."

"Just the same," Frick said, "concentrate on the road."

Hess tossed the roll down and muttered something under this breath.

Frick shook his head. Over the years, we learned that Rudy Hess defied stereotyping. He brought his own food wherever he went and had odd mannerisms that made him . . . well . . . different.

"Where were we?" Frick asked.

"We were talking about Buch."

Walter Buch retired from the war as a major. He was with us during the Munich Putsch. His anti-Semitism eclipsed even Wolf's. Worse, he was a sour stick of a man, always inveighing against the lack of morality in Munich and the infidelities of various party members. But he was a faithful party member . . . I had to give him that much. After the putsch, while the wounded Göring fled to Austria and Röhm was taken into custody, Walter Buch took temporary command of the *SA*.

"Before you explain the rest, where are we going?"

"We have reservations at Café Victoria in Munich. It's on *Maximilianstrasse*, close to the *Jahreszeiten Hotel*," answered Frick.

"Where I first met both of you."

"There's time for nostalgia later, Friedrich. For now, we have to concentrate on the problem at hand."

"Which is?"

"Chief Judge Buch has received eight anonymous letters claiming Hitler had sex with young girls. Some may have been minors."

"Are they named in the letters?"

"Some are named. If not, their physical descriptions could lead to their identification. If you can believe this, the blackmailer even provided the addresses where these rendezvous occurred."

"Do you know who did this?"

He shook his head. "It could only be someone close enough to the *Führer* to lay out the details well enough for Buch."

"Buch must be wild with rage trying to find the culprit who sent the letters?"

"On the contrary. He is not concerned about the author's identity. He wants to determine the truth of the charges. When it comes to issues of morality, the man is a self-righteous ass. He's not even a lawyer. But because his father was a judge, he judges all who come before him. Even the *Führer*."

"How can anyone judge the *Führer*?"

Frick's usually placid face turned sour as he explained that Buch did have that right. "This court was *our* doing. We set it up so the party could control what its members did before the official authorities got hold of them. In this way we could divert proceedings from government tribunals to ours and its decisions would be recognized as valid. Now it has come back to bite us."

"Why would the municipalities agree to this?"

"Most people around here believe in the *Führer*, so they bend to accommodate him."

"But going after the *Führer*? Wilhelm, you're a lawyer. There must be something we can do?"

"Our hands are tied. Any which way we turn, we open ourselves to criticism. If we try to influence Buch, it could backfire. If we remove him from his position, the backlash against us from the authorities would be worse. Imagine if the Munich police arrested Hitler for having sex with minors?"

"There must be a way out of this," I said. "There always is."

"We think so," Hess said.

"Rudy, please *just* drive." Frick turned back to me. "I haven't gotten to the worst part."

My head was spinning. "What can be worse than blackmailing the party and the *Führer*?"

"The answer to that question is in a name: Maria Reiter. The Boss was seeing her for many months. When the anonymous letters identified her, he sent Emil to tell Maria that she and the Boss were finished."

"Well, then it's over," I said, relieved. "What's the problem?"

"If only it stopped there. What did distraught little Maria do? Tried to kill herself."

Hearing that conjured up the memory of Suzi Liptauer and her failed attempt to commit suicide a few years back. "Did she . . .?"

"Her brother-in-law found her in time. Cut her down. That's the only ray of light."

"If the press gets hold of all this—numerous young girls and a suicide attempt—Hitler is finished," I said.

"And so is the party. We would not survive his disgrace."

"What are our options?"

"We thought about stealing the letters from Judge Buch, but he would know it was us," Hess said.

Frick made a sour face. "Rudy, let me handle this." Like others, Frick tolerated Hess because he had endeared himself to Wolf. None of us could figure out why. Then Frick said, "Our saving grace is that Hans Frank is one of the two others that serve on the court with Buch."

"Couldn't Hans convince Buch to make this go away?"

Frick shook his head. "Buch sticks to the letter of the law. There is no convincing him of anything. Our only leverage is that Hans made a list of the named girls or their descriptions when there were no names. He was able to obtain the dates and places where these assignations took place and managed to copy the results of Buch's inquiries to date. Having these gives us the opportunity to do damage control wherever possible.

"That's a good start," I said. "What's the next step?"

"To sit down with you and Hermann Esser. You two know more about the Boss's personal life than anyone else. You both ran with him. We've always known there were women, but not much else. We'll scour the material together, try to identify the remaining girls, and plot a course of action."

The thought of being in the same room with Esser infuriated me. "Don't bring Esser into this. He's a rat. He ducked out of the putsch. Said he was sick in bed . . . but we all know he ran to Austria. He turns my stomach."

"You're overlooking that he came back and did jail time. More importantly, the *Führer* forgave him."

"I didn't forget anything. We don't need Esser. There are three others who know plenty: Max Amann and Emil Maurice, not to mention Hitler's adjutant, Julius Schaub. Schaub probably knows the most. Not only did he drive the girls, but he handled the money for the flowers, gifts, and rooms when needed."

"Schaub is out of the question. Hitler forbids him from speaking to us. Amann is off limits because, as we will explain, he was involved in the Maria Reiter business. Besides, you know more than he does. That's why we need you," he hesitated, "and Esser."

"There's Emil. What about him?"

Hearing Emil's name, Hess turned back to us. "He's the root of this crisis."

"Rudy," pointed Frick, "the road."

"What about Emil?" I asked.

"We were waiting to tell you. We've established—don't ask how—that the author of the blackmail letters is Ida Arnold. She's a doctor."

"Emil dated her," Rudy called out.

"Why would she threaten Hitler?" I asked.

Frick corrected me. "She's not the threat, Emil is . . . through her."

How could Emil be at the root of this? Then it occurred to me. "The only thing I can figure is that this has something to do with Hitler's niece."

Frick connected the dots. "A couple of years ago, the Boss's half-sister, Angela Raubal, came to live with him as his housekeeper. She brought her seventeen-year-old daughter, Geli, with her."

"I met both when I visited him at Berteschgaden," I recalled. "My first impression was that this could be a recipe for disaster. Geli was his type: voluptuous, pretty, and young. But I never thought he would be interested in his own niece in *that* way."

"As far as I know he hasn't . . . you know . . ."

Frick couldn't bring himself to say that Wolf might have had sex with his niece.

"A year-and-a-half ago," Frick picked up the story, "he was more interested in rebuilding the party. He paid Geli no mind. Then twelve months ago, Hitler pursued Maria Reiter. That started in September of '26."

"What was she, seventeen? Eighteen? That's how he likes them."

"Sixteen."

"That's young even for Hitler," I said.

"It doesn't matter what any of us think. By this past March, after she was seventeen, they were sleeping together. Here's where sticky turns to shit. A couple of months later, the Boss caught Emil Maurice in bed with Geli. He went wild. Almost shot Emil on the spot. Soon after, a letter about Hitler and young girls popped up at the party headquarters. By July, Party Judge Buch had eight letters in hand. Ever self-righteous, Buch viewed the Boss's actions as immoral if true, and started to investigate. The Boss got scared and sent Emil to dump Maria Reiter. A few days later, in late July, Maria tried to hang herself."

"Hitler can't be blamed for that?"

"Had she died, the papers would have crucified him. Fortunately, that didn't happen. Our issue is with Buch, not Maria. He holds Hitler's fate in his hands. He's such a moralist. The fool is capable of kicking him out of the party without any comprehension that the party would be crushed in Hitler's fall. That's why you're here, Friedrich. To help us quiet things down, if possible."

"I'm still not clear about Emil."

"Don't you get it? Hitler ordered Emil not to see Geli. After that, the letters started coming. Emil put Ida Arnold, his ex-girl-friend, up to it. Arnold met Maria on a double date: Maurice with her and Hitler with Maria. Maurice saw that Ida Arnold was indignant that the Boss was sleeping with the young girl. This gave Emil the opportunity to get his way. We believe that when Emil asked Ida Arnold for assistance, she was more than willing to stick it to Hitler. Like Buch, Ida Arnold is a bit of a moralist. That's why we can't go near Emil to put a defense together. Until we know more than we do now, we don't know how best to defend the Boss."

"Defend? Has Buch charged Hitler with anything yet?"

"That's what we must prevent. If Buch accuses Hitler, the NSDAP is as good as finished. And if he doesn't take action, there is nothing to stop the Ida Arnold/Emil Maurice team from sending the same stuff to the authorities. We must deflate this now, before it goes *any* further. Before we do that, we need you and Esser to flush out how much else there is in Wolf's closet. We can't afford any more surprises."

I studied Frick. His wizened face and steel gray eyes were cold, calculating . . . and unreadable. He was one of the first men in the movement. Smart. Perhaps the smartest of the original men. One thing was certain: he could never be taken at face value.

"Wilhelm, you didn't ask me to fly here for that. Esser knows as much as I do about Hitler's personal life. If you wanted to, you could get all the information you needed from Hitler himself. Why me? And why so secret?"

Rudy turned to answer my question.

"Rudy, please." Frick pointed forward; Rudy's head whipped back to the road. Then Frick explained. "The *Führer* will not talk about this with anyone but you."

We made our way to a private room in the rear of the restaurant. Esser rose to greet us.

"It's about time," he said. "I was getting lonely back here." He extended his hand. "Friedrich, old comrade, it's been forever. Must be nearly four years!"

I hesitated. Frick glared at me to be civil. I barely touched Esser's hand.

A waiter appeared. Frick shooed him away. "We will eat later."

Frick began. "First, let me thank Friedrich for getting here on such short notice. We're charged with looking into the corners of the Boss's past. As Buch moves forward in his investigation, we must be prepared. There can be no surprises. We'll start with the named girls in the letters, and then try to figure out who the unnamed ones are."

"You made me aware that Maria Reiter is mentioned," Esser said. "I assume you did the same to Friedrich. Do you want to discuss her first?"

Frick adjusted his spectacles and consulted his notes. "No. Let's start with Lotte Bechstein."

Before I could mention the night Hitler presented Lotte with his watercolor and the time they spent together afterwards, Esser chimed in.

"There's no problem with her," Esser reassured. "She and Wolf played with her mother's consent. The old bitch drooled at the thought of Hitler as a son-in-law, but her plans were dashed when Adolf, Emil Maurice, and I rented rooms in student lodging at the University of Berlin. Lotte found out that we brought girls into our rooms. *Alles Kaput.* That ended the Bechstein son-in-law possibilities."

Frick drew a line through Lotte's name. "Domestic troubles aside, to Frau Bechstein's credit, she remains a major contributor to the party." He shuffled through the notes for the next name.

Esser rapped the table. "Let me make this easy for you, Wilhelm. We can save time if I run down my list. I'm sure it's more complete than yours. Let's get this out of the way so we can eat. My stomach is growling."

Frick laid down his papers, removed his glasses, and motioned for Esser to start.

"The first was Suzi Liptauer. Remember her, Friedrich? Back in '20? She was a beauty. Hitler screwed her in one of the party member's apartments. There was also talk of Hitler meeting those musical twins in Berlin. If he was, he was doing all of them at the same time."

"I do know that while he saw Suzi, Wolf went out with Emmi Marre," I added. "When Suzi found out, she tried to hang herself in a hotel room using the belt of a bathrobe. Fortunately she failed."

"She did it to gain his sympathy." Esser shook his head. "She didn't know that the Boss doesn't fall for that stuff. When he's finished, he's finished. Anyway, she got married and lives in Vienna."

Frick held up his hand. "The suicide business is too similar to the Reiter girl. But that was seven years ago, or thereabouts. I don't think we have to worry about that one."

Esser protested that every one of Hitler's escapades was relevant, but Frick dismissed him. "Who was next?"

"Remember Hitler's first driver?" Esser looked at me.

"Of course. Ernest Haug," I recalled. "His sister was a beauty."

"It was 1922 or 1923. Jenny Haug was eighteen. Hitler was smitten with her," Esser's eyes danced as he pictured Jenny. "She was built like an Amazon, and as tall as Adolf. She carried a gun. Said it was to protect him. They had a 'rendezvous room' above party headquarters on *Corneliusstraße*. Julius Schaub paid the landlord. Schaub's fingerprints are on most every affair the Boss had."

"So I understand," said Frick. "When did Jenny Haug end?"

"Just before the putsch."

"You mean just before your sudden illness?" Civil or not, I could not get past Esser leaving us to fight in the streets during the putsch. I wanted him to attack me. I intended to deck him.

Esser hopped out of his chair. Before he could take the next step, Frick growled, "Hermann, sit down. Stop this nonsense!" Then he turned to me. "Enough, Friedrich. Forget the playground antics. This is serious business." Frick scanned his notes. "I haven't heard anything so far that will present a problem, unless these women are angry or vindictive."

Though he couldn't look at me, Esser reveled being in the limelight. "There was one more in the summer of '25. Adelaide Klein. She was another eighteen year old. Lived with her parents. Beautiful girl. Brunette with violet eyes. Maurice let them use his apartment whenever they wanted. That brings us to Maria Reiter. After her we have . . ."

Frick cut him off. "We know about Maria Reiter, Hermann. So before we excuse you, I need to know this: if these blackmail letters come to light, how would these women react?"

"That's easy. They would all stand by Hitler."

Frick laid down his pen. "What makes you so confident they would?"

"Because every time Adolf stopped seeing one of them, he remained in contact. He remembered their birthdays. He had Schaub send them chocolates. Every once in a while, Emil or Schaub would deliver an envelope with cash. He was good to all of them. I am convinced *none* bear him animus. For example, as you noted Mama Bechstein still supports the party . . . even after Lotte."

Frick closed his notebook. "This is all very good news. There does not appear to be any surprises that might fuel Buch's investigation against the Boss."

Esser raised his hand. "I just remembered. There was one who could be trouble. Her name was Irene. Hitler called her Ina. One time, I came across the two of them in Café Heck. She was blond and beautiful. Definitely his type. When she demanded that Hitler marry her, he dumped her. She threatened to go to the press unless she got money."

"How was it resolved?" asked Frick.

"With a bundle of Reichsmarks from Party Treasurer Schwartz. To my knowledge, she has kept her mouth shut ever since."

"Do you think she still poses a problem?" Frick asked.

"As far as I know, she has never resurfaced. If that means anything, then she won't be a problem."

"You've been a great help, Hermann. Thank you for coming today."

Esser remained planted in his chair. "I'm not finished. There's still one more."

Frick looked to see if I knew whom he meant. I shrugged that I didn't. "We don't have any other names," Frick said.

"Then you have not done your homework," Esser answered in triumph. "His niece, Geli Raubal."

"What about her?" Frick asked.

"She's part of the triangle: Emil, Geli, and the Boss."

"For now, these letters and Maria Reiter are the problem. We don't need to stray from them. We appreciate your time and all that you've done to help, Hermann. That's all for now."

"What about lunch?"

"I'm sure you can find someplace to eat."

Hess and I had all to do to stifle our laughter. After Esser stomped out, I asked, "Why make him leave? He still had useful information."

"I didn't want him to hear anymore. Esser tries to come off as one of us . . . but we all know there is a sleazy side to him. If Hermann Esser thought there is something in it for him, *he* is quite capable of blackmailing the Boss."

"And his own mother, too," I added.

"He was about to make a point about Geli Raubal," Rudy said. "I would have liked to hear what he knows."

Frick would not be distracted. "Maria Reiter is the issue. Let's put this Reiter thing to bed—so to speak—before it blows up in our face. Anything to do with Geli doesn't interest me at the moment. She's his niece, and that's all we need to know."

I slapped the table as I stood.

"Where are you going?" Frick asked.

"Hermann had the right idea. I'm getting hungry, too."

"Don't be absurd, Friedrich."

"Listen, Wilhelm. I told you in the car that you didn't need me. This was a waste of my time. Hermann just gave you all the information you needed. I have an important woman waiting for me in Berlin."

Frick slid his spectacles into a case. "What I didn't tell you in the car, and didn't want Esser to hear, is that Buch contacted Maria Reiter's sister, Anni, for permission to question Maria. Hans tried to stop him, but Buch couldn't be dissuaded."

I slid back onto the chair. "Why bring the sister into this?"

"Because both parents are dead. Maria Reiter is still a minor and Anni is her legal guardian. Buch needs Anni's consent to speak with Maria."

"What did Anni have to say?" I asked.

"She talked plenty. Anni was furious—venomous was more like it—over the way Hitler treated her sister. It was a miracle that Anni's husband found Maria in time and saved her. Anni laid out all she knew or thought she knew to Buch, starting with the first time Hitler saw the girl. The sisters were in the park. Maria was walking her German shepherd at the same time Hitler was there walking his." Frick retrieved his spectacles and flipped through his notes, "Hers was 'Marko' and his, as you know, is 'Prinz.'" He continued reading without affect. "Hitler was smitten the moment he saw the girl. He asked the sister for an introduction and permission to take her out. Anni refused. Told him he was too old."

"What's their age difference?"

"Twenty-one years. Maria was only sixteen."

"That would never stop the Boss," added Hess.

"How did he get around the sister?"

"Hitler sent Max Amann to the shop where both sisters worked—it's owned by their family—with an invitation to hear Hitler speak at the hotel *Deutsches Haus*. When Maria refused to go alone, Max was quick to invite both sisters. They went, of course. From the moment Adolf opened his mouth, the girl was star struck. By the end of the evening, Amann and Emil had separated Mimi or *Mimchen*—that's what Hitler called Maria— from her sister. That gave Adolf the chance to be alone with her. He told her to call him 'Wolf,' and made his first move pressing his knee against hers under the table."

"How does Anni know these details?"

Frick gave a languid smile. "From our point of view she knows nothing because we deny any of it is true. But to answer your question, more than being her older sister, Anni is Maria's confidant. Maria told her everything. She never had a boyfriend before Adolf. Never been kissed. The girl gushed with puppy love."

"Then the Boss went for the kill?"

"In a manner of speaking, yes," said Frick. "The crux is that the night of his speech, the Boss learned that the girl's mother died ten days before she met him. When the Boss learned of her mother's recent death, he asked for the 'privilege' of visiting the grave site with Maria—by then, he was already calling her Mimi—so he could share in her grief."

"Let me guess what happened next," I said. "They stood there, side-by-side, in front of Maria's mother's grave. Hitler spoke about his own mother's death. Then, in a moment of shared grief, he whipped out the poem he wrote about *his* mother, read it to her, and they both wept."

"How did you know?"

I was not about to report that Wolf plagiarized the poem nor ever bring up how his fixation on his mother's death contributed to his hysterical blindness. "Let's just say that I know the different ways the Boss can inveigle his way into a girl's heart. Sharing the poem about his mother dying is 'vintage Wolf.' Is that when they consummated the deal?"

"Not according to Anni," said Frick. "She reported that Adolf and Emil showed up unexpectedly in Munich this past March, when the girl was practicing for an ice skating competition. By the way, she's a top skater. Adolf convinced her to leave practice. Maurice drove them to Adolf's apartment. *That's* when Adolf screwed her. Afterwards the four of them met, went to dinner and then to a show." Frick consulted his notes. "They saw *Zirkusprinzessi* at the *Gaertner Platz*."

"Two things don't make sense. You said Emil took them to Wolf's apartment? Wolf would never bring a girl to that dump."

"The sister had the right address: 41 *Thierschstrasse*."

"You also said the 'four' of them. There was Emil, Maria, and Hitler. Who was the fourth?"

"That is the *coup de grace*. Dr. Ida Arnold."

"The blackmailer?"

"The one and only. Anni reported that it was too late and too far to drive back to Berteschgaden that night, so Maria stayed in Arnold's apartment. That was only after Hitler told her it would be too dangerous if they were discovered in his. When they were alone, Ida asked Maria how old she was."

"And?"

"Maria told the truth: seventeen. According to Anni, this upset the Arnold woman. She asked her to repeat it, that maybe she hadn't heard Maria right."

"How much did the Boss see Maria after that?"

"A lot. He set her up in an apartment in Munich." Frick consulted his notes. "He would see her in the daytime. Not at night."

"Does she—I mean Maria—have any physical evidence to support her story?"

"Hitler sent her many postcards, letters, and small gifts. He gave her a watch. He gave her a signed leather-bound copy of *Mein Kampf* for her seventeenth birthday . . . which happens to be two days before Christmas."

"What did Buch do when all of this came to light?"

"That's just it. Buch doesn't have Hitler's letters to the girl or know about the gifts. He wants to interview the girl. To date, Anni has staunchly denied access to her sister."

"I suspect the party has played a role in that. Am I right?"

Frick hesitated. "I promised Hans Frank that I would not answer that."

I put both hands on the table and looked from one to the other. "Look, Wilhelm, I have a better sense of what's happened, but I still have no idea what you want with me."

"For Christ's sake, Wilhelm," Hess said, "Tell him already."

Frick nodded. "You're right, Rudy. It boils down to this: in spite of Buch's high and mighty morality, Hans Frank believes that he doesn't want to hurt Hitler or kill the party. We need to give Buch an excuse he can live with so he won't clamp down on the Boss."

"After listening to all of this, what could possibly alter his stance?"

Frick raised his index finger. "One thing. Get the girl to sign an oath that there was never a sexual relationship . . . only friendship. Adolf signs a similar statement. Then all that exists are anonymous letters and the sister's hearsay. We give the sworn affidavits to Buch, and none of the other stuff matters. He shuts down the whole business and the Boss is in the clear."

I took a moment to digest that. "You brought me here to coerce a false confession out of a seventeen-year-old? Wilhelm, you are far more important and experienced than I am. Why didn't you do it? Why me?"

Rather than answer my first question, he answered the second. "I would have gone to see her, but the *Führer* insists it has to be you. When you meet her, Friedrich, also see if you can get the letters and postcards Adolf sent her. We don't need them hanging around. They are all signed 'Wolf.'"

Chapter 27

Maria Reiter lived with Anni and her husband, Gottfried Hehl, in a house near their shop in the *Deutsches Haus*. It was a tiny white house with a fenced off patch of green. Flower boxes filled with lilac and pink-colored aster in full bloom hung from each window. I passed through the front gate not knowing if she would speak with me.

I knocked.

Footsteps shuffled behind the door. When it swung open, a young girl with blond hair and sky-blue eyes stood there. Her skin was flawless. Her eyes were the color of a cloudless sky. She was striking.

"May I help you?"

"My name is Friedrich Richard. I am looking for Maria Reiter."

With one hand on the doorknob and the other braced to slam it closed, she narrowed the opening. I stepped back so as not to pose as a threat.

"What do you want?"

"First, I wish to say how sorry I am for what happened to you. I'm glad to see that you are feeling better."

"You're not the first who has knocked on the door and said that. If you're here to write a story for a newspaper, I have nothing to say." She closed the door and turned the lock. Yet I did not hear footsteps walking away. She was still there.

I raised my voice. "I am here about the letters Wolf sent you."

At first, nothing happened. Then the telltale clicks of the door unlocking. She poked her head out. "How do you know about these?"

"A mutual acquaintance told me. I'm interested to know if you still have them."

"What did you say your name was again?"

"Friedrich Richard."

She opened the door more. "Are you the piano player? Wolf told me about you."

"May I come in, then?"

"My sister and brother-in-law are at work. They told me not to let strangers into the house."

"How can I be a stranger if you already know of me? I have been close to Wolf since even before the end of the war."

She wavered, lowered her head, and stepped back.

We sat at the kitchen table. After she poured a glass of water, I said, "Let me get right to the point, Maria. Wolf stopped seeing you because someone sent blackmail letters intent on destroying him and the party."

"Wolf told my brother-in-law there were eight letters and that he could not afford a political scandal. I will never forget the words he told Gottfried. He said, 'I love Mimi with my whole heart. Please tell her this, but I have to remain distant from her for a while.'" She placed her hands over her heart. "I know he still loves me."

"I am certain he does."

"Did he tell you this himself?"

"Not in so many words."

Maria slumped. Her eyes watered. "I was hoping you were sent to tell me that Wolf wanted to meet with me."

"I am sure he does want to meet with you, but not at the moment. I'm here because of the letters and postcards Wolf sent you. Do you still have them?"

She crossed her arms over her chest. "I will cherish them until the day I die."

At least it was established she'd kept Wolf's love notes. "Once we received the blackmail letters, the party had to get involved. We formed a committee to investigate them."

"All I hear about are these eight letters. Are they even real?" Then she asked as only a rejected lover could, "Did he ever love me the way he said?"

"Without a doubt, Maria. Wolf is heartbroken that he can't see you. As for the blackmail letters, they're real. The Party Judge has them."

"What can I do? I don't want to cause any trouble for Wolf."

"The trouble is these letters accuse Wolf of seducing you. Of violating you in a way that might be against the law."

Her limpid eyes turned dreamy. "The only law that Adolf Hitler has broken is Nature's Law: the law of not being here with me."

Esser had it right. Maria would never turn on Wolf.

"Maria, forgive me for being indelicate, but I must ask . . . and Wolf's fate may depend on your answer." She blinked. "Are you saying that you gave yourself willingly to him?"

"Only after he earned my love. I held him off a long time."

"When was the first time?"

"Wolf was passionate. He was gentle and caring. I had never been with anyone in my life until him, yet I knew he was special. He didn't force himself on me. Emil took us for a drive out of town. He left us at the edge of a forest. We walked deep into the woods until we stopped in a clearing. It was the first time I had ever been kissed. I knew he wanted more, but I couldn't. Not then. I was only sixteen."

"Did Wolf force himself on you that first time you were alone in the woods?"

"Of course not! We waited nearly six months. When it happened, it was magical. He told me that we would never be separated and that I would stay with him when he got a bigger apartment. He told me that we would pick everything out together: paintings, the chairs, and the furniture. He said he could picture how the apartment would look, including a plush violet sofa." She stared off. "I wanted to marry him." Then she added, "I still do."

"Did he want to marry you?"

"He said for the sake of the party, he couldn't. It had to appear that he was married to Germany, and Germany alone. Even so, he promised we could live together." She pulled an embroidered handkerchief from her sleeve and dabbed away the tears. "In the end, none of it came true."

"Mimi."

Her face lit up. "That's what Wolf called me."

"He told me it would be okay if I called you that."

"I loved when he used names of endearment."

"Would you let me see one of the letters or postcards he sent you?"

She jumped out the chair and called over her shoulder. "I want to show you how much he loved me."

Seeing her attitude, I felt confident that I would be able to accomplish my task here and get back to Berlin. While Maria shuffled through her papers, my thoughts drifted to Lilian.

Maria returned with a stack of cards and letters. I leafed through them. First, I saw an undated Christmas card, and another postcard signed Wolf.

Happy Christmas celebrations
My dear child!
For your birthday and Christmas celebrations, my warm greetings and blessings.
Take this as a small token of my lasting memory!
In warm admiration,
Wolf
Please give my warm greetings to sister and brother-in-law!

Then I came across another, a postcard written by Hitler from the road.

Miss Mizzi Reiter
Berchtesgaden
My dear child!
Receive from me my warmest greetings with the assurance of my remembering you faithfully.
Your Wolf!

Finally, I read a letter to Maria from December 16, 1926. It was shortly after Wolf left Berchtesgaden and before the Christmas card. It was in Hitler's hand. I recognized his signature at the end. Maria explained that this letter was tucked in one of the volumes of *Mein Kampf* that he gave her for her birthday.

> *December 16, 1926*
> *My dear little Mimi,*
> *You don't know how much you have come to mean to me. I would so love to have your beautiful and sweet face in front of me so I could personally tell you what you mean to me. December 23 is your birthday. Now I beg of you to take my greeting which comes from the depth of my heart.*
>
> *From my present, you should see how pleased I am that my sweet love is writing so often to me. You have no idea how happy a sweet little letter from you will make me. Out of it your lovely voice speaks to me. And then I always taken by a desire for you as if it was the first time. Are you also sometimes thinking of me? Tell me so and write me.*
>
> *You know Mimi, whenever I have trouble or cares, I would so much like to be with you, to be able to look into your eyes in order to forget all of life's cares. Yes, Mozzerl, you recall how much you mean to me and how deeply I love you. But read the books! Then you will be able to understand me.*
>
> *Now again my sincerest best wishes for your birthday and for Christmas with whole heart.*
> *From your own*
> *Wolf*

I was about to go on to another letter when I stopped. Two lines caught my attention.

"And then I always taken by a desire for you *as if it was the first time* . . ."

I looked up to see Maria studying my reaction. One thing was clear: she was lying. I needed to be sure. I reread another passage.

"You recall . . . how deeply I love you."

These passages could describe mere infatuation. On the surface, they appeared benign. But when I reread them, their meaning became clear-cut. And they were written in December . . . three months *before* the so-called first sex the following March. "Mimi, did you tell your sister the truth about when you first had sex with Wolf?"

"How do you know I told my sister anything?" Her trembling lip betrayed her, as she glanced at a photo of herself and Anni on a side table.

"Please. Wolf's career is at stake. You told Anni it was March 1927, didn't you? But March was a continuation of what started much earlier. Wasn't it?"

Maria covered her face in her hands. "Yes," she whispered.

"It was when Emil left you and Wolf alone in the woods last September. Isn't that right? That was the 'first time' he mentioned in the letter?"

By now the girl was shaking. Tears streamed down her cheeks. "It was glorious." Then she buried her head again.

I left my chair and put my arm around her shoulders. 'Why, Mimi? Why did you lie? Why did you say it was six months later?"

"Because I was only sixteen when it happened. I knew those letters sent to the judge were causing trouble. I didn't want to make it worse for Wolf, so I said it happened three months after my seventeenth birthday . . . not three months before."

I knelt down and lifted her chin. "Wolf will be extremely grateful when I tell him."

That got me a smile. Now that I knew the truth, I could ask the most important question. "Mimi, will you sign a paper saying that you and Wolf were friends . . . and only friends? That there was never any sex between the two of you?"

She squeezed my hand; it was all the answer I needed.

*

I left Maria with a lighter step. I'd succeeded in my primary task. Wolf would have her sworn declaration. But I knew not to push for the second assignment—to get the letters back. Had I tried she would be lost to us. A partial victory would be enough to save Wolf and the party from Walter Buch.

I headed for my next assignment: to see Emil Maurice. He and Wolf were staying at the *Deutsches Haus.* I prayed I would see Emil first . . . and alone.

The clerk at the front desk informed me that Herr Wolf was expected to return from a three-day trip within the next hour or two. As for Emil, the clerk pointed to the restaurant off the lobby. "He's having lunch." As I entered the room, smells of fresh-baked breads and pastries assaulted me. I had been so consumed with getting Maria to agree to sign an affidavit that I had not realized how ravenous I was.

Emil's back was to me. I cleared my throat and Emil knew who it was. He sprang to his feet and we rocked in a bear hug.

"When Rudy told me you were on some special mission in town, I hoped to see you. Did you accomplish what you came to do?"

"It depends on the talk you and I are about to have."

Emil was no fool. He knew he was about to get grilled. He pushed his plate of food away. "Not you, too," Emil said in disgust.

"Is there something I should know, Emil?"

"It's just that I thought they sent you to . . . never mind. Why *are* you here, Friedrich? Be straight with me. We go back too far to bullshit."

Just then, a waiter appeared. I ordered lunch and when he was out of range, explained, "Wilhelm Frick sent me to speak with both you and Maria Reiter."

"Did the girl talk? She's turned everyone else away."

"I was lucky. She knew my name from Adolf. She still loves him, you know."

"It pained me to tell her it was over. If I knew she would try to kill herself, I wouldn't have delivered that message. Thank God they found her in time."

Real or feigned, his concern was of no consequence. "Here's the question: do you think she will cause problems down the road?"

Emil snickered at this. "None of his former lovers will ever cause him problems. You should know that. He treated them well then and continues to treat them well now."

"Then why the blackmail letters? You know about them, don't you?

"Everyone does."

"They say you had something to do with them. Did you?"

Emil jackknifed out of his chair. He raised his hand to throw a punch. I didn't flinch. As much as he was a brawler, we both knew I could crush him.

He kept his pugilistic stance but unclenched his fist. "It makes me furious every time I hear that. Why would I compromise the Boss? I love him. He's been like an older brother to me."

"Are you finished acting out? Now sit down so we can discuss this." After he sat down I said, "Loose lips chronicled affairs that only someone in Wolf's inner circle could know. It can't be me. I've been away for long stretches. I was clueless about Maria Reiter until Frick told me about this mess."

"It's not me. I would never do anything to harm the Boss."

I decided not to challenge him about the letters . . . for the moment. Instead, I went to the heart of the problem. "Are you fucking Wolf's niece?"

Emil's cheeks reddened. "She loves me."

"What are you thinking?"

He put his hand on my arm. "Friedrich. She's amazing. She's got this wild streak in her that . . . I have never experienced it before. There's nothing she wouldn't do for fun. I can't get enough of her." Then he added with a twinkle, "And she can't get enough of me."

"Emil, when did you ever have a problem finding a woman? Why couldn't you resist this one?"

"She flirted with me when she first visited her Uncle Alf in Landsberg. That's what she called the Boss then. She was only a kid."

"Emil, open your eyes. Geli is still a kid. What is she, seventeen, eighteen?"

"She was nineteen in June, not that it matters. She is all woman. Look Friedrich, it's not my fault. I wasn't the one who brought her mother here to keep his house in Obersalzberg. How did I know Geli would move in after she graduated from high school?"

"How does Wolf know about you two?"

Emil turned beet red. "He walked in on us doing it. I never saw him so angry. I thought he was going to shoot me on the spot. He forbade me to see her."

"Did you stop?" He didn't have to answer. It was written across his face. "Does Wolf know?"

Emil shrugged. "I don't care."

Throughout these questions about Geli, I searched for twitches or rapid blinking that might betray his story. There were none. "I need to ask about Ida Arnold."

"What about her?"

"What is she to you?"

He continued to keep his head down. "Just an old girlfriend."

"Could she be the one writing the blackmail letters to Wolf?"

He looked up. "What does she have to gain by ratting on him?"

I didn't answer him. Instead I asked about that March day when he drove Wolf and Maria Reiter from the ice-skating rink to Wolf's apartment. Emil confirmed all that Frick had said. "You left them alone in Hitler's flat?"

"That is right."

"And afterwards, you and Ida Arnold joined them for dinner and a show?"

"Yes. So what?"

"Why did the girl wind up staying with Ida?"

"The show was over too late to drive Maria back to Berchtesgaden, so she stayed with Ida. What was wrong with that?"

"In and of itself, nothing. How long did you continue to see Ida?"

"Maybe a month or so after that time in March. I stopped when I started with Geli."

"It's curious that about the time you stopped seeing Ida, the letters began to arrive at party headquarters. I don't believe in coincidences."

"What's that supposed to mean?"

"It means that the person who wrote the letters had been told details about Wolf and his past women."

"What are you trying to say, Friedrich? Coy doesn't become you."

"I'm not saying anything. I am asking you straight away: did you talk to Arnold about Adolf's old girlfriends?"

"Bark up some other tree. I would never tell secrets about the Boss."

"Okay then, who do you think is writing the blackmail letters?"

"Hermann Esser."

That made no sense. "Why him?"

"Why the surprise? Esser has been on the outs ever since the putsch. True . . . the Boss brought him back after he groveled, but he is the same slime he always was. You remember that the girl he got pregnant complained to Hitler. The Boss ordered Esser to marry her. How could Esser not resent the Boss?"

"Just to be clear, are you saying that Hermann wrote those blackmail letters?"

"He's the most logical one."

"I'm not buying it. What about you and Geli?"

"Are you ready for the truth?"

"What the hell do think I'm doing here? Spit it out, Emil. And be quick about it!"

"I want to marry the girl, but good old Uncle Alf is the problem. The man is conflicted. He loves her as an uncle—she's the only relative he gives a damn about—but has the hots for her as a man. He salivates every time he's with her. The fact that I bedded her drove him crazy. Now do you see the dilemma?" Before I could answer, he continued. "There's another thing. You have to see them together. When he's out with her, he doesn't hide her the way he did the other girls. He takes her shopping and waits for hours while she chooses. Then he carries her packages like a dutiful servant. When he takes her out for dinner or they are in the presence of party members, he not only lets her speak, he even lets her monopolize a conversation without interrupting her. It's amazing."

"He never let anyone do that!"

"That's what I am trying to tell you. The Boss wants Geli for himself . . . and that is my dilemma."

"You've given me a lot to think about, Emil. Where is this going to end up?"

"I wish I knew. I want to marry her, but that's not allowed. Hitler wants to fuck her and keep her on his arm whenever he wants. But he won't marry her because he doesn't want to be married to anyone. I'm no soothsayer, but this is not going to end well. I'm glad you're here. You need to do something, Friedrich."

*

I left Emil and phoned Frick from the lobby. "Prepare the paperwork. Maria agreed to sign."

"I knew I was right to call you. You've saved Hitler and the party."

"It fell into place, Wilhelm. Now I'm headed back. There is a special person waiting for me in Berlin."

"You can't go, Friedrich. Not yet."

My impulse was to slam the phone down. I couldn't wait to get back to Lilian. I tried to modulate my voice. "I've done everything you've asked. Buch will get what he needs to put this to sleep. What else is there to do?"

"You can't go until we button this up. Who put this Arnold woman up to it?" Frick insisted.

"We will never know for sure . . ."

"You must have some idea."

"I do."

"*Please*, tell me."

"My best guess is that this is the handiwork of Emil Maurice . . .by way of Ida Arnold. Emil can only have a free hand with Geli if the Boss backs off. That's what the letters were intended to do. Scare Hitler away from the niece. It might have fallen Emil's way without this tumult but for the fact that the Boss caught him in bed with Geli. That's when Hitler lost it."

"Is this theory, or do you have something to substantiate it?"

"Emil confirmed that Hitler threatened to kill him. That was said out of emotion. But when the Boss forbid the two of them from seeing each other anymore, the letters started coming. That's not a coincidence in my book. That's cause and effect."

"What did they hope the letters would accomplish?"

"Why, a warning, of course! The words are crystal clear: if Hitler continues to carry on with young girls—Geli included— his secret life would be revealed for the world to see. That's what Esser was trying to tell us when you cut him off and had him leave."

"You think Emil would stoop that low?"

"There's the rub. Emil didn't have to. Ida Arnold became his unwitting tool. He saw Arnold's outrage at Hitler after learning Maria Reiter's age. All Emil had to do was to whisper a few old secrets in her ear. Ida's own morality about men in power who compromise young women took over."

"Can you prove any of this?"

"It's the only possible explanation.

"What do we do now?"

"I don't know what you're going to do, but I need to get back to someone special in Berlin. In case you're wondering, she's over twenty-one."

"You got us this far. You have to see this to the end, Friedrich. Your woman friend will have to wait for you.'

"I've done everything you've asked."

"There is still the matter of Hitler," said Frick.

"He will not need any convincing to sign a document that will save his ass. You can do it. Or Amann."

"It has to be you, Friedrich. Signing the document is not the problem. Anyone of us could get him to do that. But you are the only one who can convince him to lay off Emil and Geli. That's the last piece of this puzzle."

"I'll do it after I return from Berlin."

"We both know this can't wait. What's one more day? Do it for him and the party, Friedrich."

"You had this all planned from the time you and Hess picked me up at the airport, didn't you?"

"Before that."

"With all your scheming, you overlooked the last piece of the puzzle, Wilhelm." There was dead silence on the phone. "Someone has to deal with Geli."

*

Dread overcame me. I did not want to confront Wolf about Emil. Not after what I heard. Knowing that Wolf was expected within the next hour or so, I gave the clerk enough Reichsmarks to let me wait in Wolf's room. Not long after I settled into a chair a key jiggled the lock. I hopped to my feet.

Wolf took one step and froze.

"So they dragged you into this, Friedrich?" His feigned ignorance didn't fool me. Frick told me that it was Wolf who wanted me to step in. After nearly ten years of experience with the man, I learned that he lived behind a façade of self-created images. This was one of the times I could not afford to let him get away with it.

"I didn't kick or scream, but I didn't volunteer either." I smiled and then added, "But you already know that."

He lifted both hands in surrender. "In that case, what is your advice?"

Though he capitulated, I was on thin ice. "Maria is taken care of. She will sign an affidavit that nothing happened. You will sign a similar document. So that part is over. The ancient stuff is no problem. Old and cold."

He nodded.

So far, so good. "There is one issue left to resolve."

"Oh? You did a magnificent job cleaning this mess up, Friedrich. What could possibly be left?"

"Your niece, Geli. She is the remaining issue."

As fast as a summer squall crashes down from the mountains, his demeanor changed. He turned angry in defense. His face twisted into a scowl and he raised his voice. "She cannot be brought into this. She had *nothing* to do with Maria or any of the girls in the past."

"Let's sit down, Wolf. It will be easier to discuss this."

"Standing is just fine." His hand slid toward his whip that was never far from his side. "What are suggesting, Friedrich?"

I knew his movement was a reflex, but still, I clenched my right fist. "We have to demonstrate to Judge Buch that you have an appropriate relationship with your niece."

Wolf bristled. "And just how do you propose to do that?"

I eased into a chair, my eyes never leaving his. "Geli must become engaged to Emil, Adolf. The sooner the better. You have to ensure this happens."

His hand moved off the whip as his shoulders slumped. "You never call me Adolf."

"I'm serious. Buch needs a way to reject the veracity of those letters. When that happens, he drops his inquiry and this whole mess vanishes."

The blood drained from his face. His voice softer. "But why must they be engaged?"

"Because Geli is mentioned in one of the letters. If she and Emil become engaged with your blessing, it distances you from her *and* undermines the letter writer. Any demonstrable lie in the letters weakens the credibility of the letter writer and the rest of what was sent to Buch."

Wolf shuffled to the window. He pushed the curtain aside and made a show of looking at something. After an intolerable number of seconds, he twisted toward me. "She means too much to me. I can't do that."

I had one last gambit. "Permit the engagement on the condition that there can be no sex. As her uncle, you can stipulate that because of Geli's age, she must wait two years until she is twenty-one. Would that suit you?"

I searched his face for a flicker of acceptance.

Wolf remained stone-faced. Unblinking. He turned away.

I held my breath, knowing he might lash out at any moment.

I clasped my hands as a supplicant praying he would set aside his personal feelings. "Wolf, is it a deal?"

He turned slowly back to me. "*Ja.*"

That one word ended the emergency that could have brought everything down.

Then, smiling for the first time, he said, "I understand that you are anxious to return to Berlin."

I wanted to explain about Lilian, but he stopped me cold.

"Go with my blessing. When you get there, there is something I need you to do."

First Frick and now Hitler. Everyone has tasks for me.

"And that is?"

"You remember that young man—Joseph Goebbels—we talked about a few years ago?"

"I remember. You spoke about sheep leaving the flock; that they didn't have to be slaughtered when they returned."

"Well, he's moved away from Strasser's to our way of thinking. I rewarded him. He is now the Gauleiter of Berlin. Please make time to see him in Berlin. He is a hothead, but a great talent. Keep an eye on him for me."

*

Given the difficult tasks I had been given, I could not have been more pleased at the outcomes. The investigation of Maria Reiter and Wolf would end with signed affidavits from each. Maria would cling to a hope that one day Wolf might make himself available to her again. Emil and Geli would be publicly engaged in a way that Wolf could accept. All of this would end Buch's inquiry into eight letters by an "unknown" author. And there would be no open fight with Emil.

Me? I could not wait to get to Berlin and explore a relationship with Lilian Harvey. Once we reconnected and I had some extra time, I would see this fellow Goebbels.

Chapter 28

1927 – 1928

I phoned Lilian before my plane left, but she was not in her room. I was forced to leave innocuous messages with the front desk at the Adlon Hotel. I tried one last time before boarding. To my surprise, I was put through.

"This must be your lucky day, sailor."

My pulsed raced. "I didn't expect you to be there."

"They couldn't get the right equipment or enough extras to make a war scene look real, so I left early. I'm holding your messages as we speak. When will I have the pleasure of your company?"

"Sooner than later."

I heard the excitement in her voice. "I didn't expect you for a couple of more days. How come the early surprise?"

"I finished what I needed to do. My reward for success is to spend time with you . . . that is if you still want my company."

"How fast can you get here?"

"Is tonight fast enough?"

"It will have to do."

*

I was languishing in a semi-dream-state when the bed creaked. I reveled in Lilian's body as she sashayed toward the WC. The lovemaking was glorious. I feared it might be awkward after a few days apart, but it was electric the moment our skin touched. I scooted back and propped myself against the headboard as she wriggled into her outfit.

"We're shooting today. The schedule will be tight, but you might find it interesting. Come with me. Everybody wants to see how a movie is made. Besides, I told a few people about you. They're curious to see if I was telling the truth."

"Let me consult with my secretary." I pretended to speak on an imaginary phone. "She says she can spare me. This is my lucky day."

"You bet your tight ass it is."

I hopped out of bed and pulled her body against mine. She edged back, held me at arms' length, and glanced down. "That thing growing between us will cause me to be late. I'm in the first scene."

*

Lilian was under contract to UFA—Universum Film-AG— the largest film production company in Europe. Two years earlier, they entered a distribution deal with Paramount and MGM to form ParUfaMet. As it turned out, one of the first industrialists I contacted to support the NSDAP—Alfred Hugenberg—purchased the company.

Their sprawling studio—*Neubabelsberg*—was located in southwest Berlin. I got the shock of my life when we drove up in the studio car sent for Lilian. "That is the biggest building I've ever seen."

"The building is eight thousand square meters. Wait until you see the inside. It goes on forever."

The studios were ingenious. There was a great hall that could be divided into any sized room needed by shifting movable bricked-up walls. In this way, any number of major and minor films could be shot at the same time. There were forty dressing rooms on the east side of the terminal and ten rooms set aside to screen films or fabricate set designs. There was a large hair-dressing salon and six bathrooms. There were offices, telephone booths, and a warren of rooms, each large enough for 160 extras to wait until they were needed. The west side of the terminal contained equipment rooms filled with whatever was needed to construct film sets.

I was stunned. "This is a city within a city."

"We have everything we need to compete with America," Lilian said with an air of pride.

She found a place for me to sit where I would be out of the way. I took it all in like a kid in a toy store, not knowing what to look at first. On the drive over, Lilian gave me the story line of the movie she was shooting, *Vacation from Marriage*. A young couple is trapped in a listless marriage when the Great War breaks out. Both embrace the war—with all its trials and tribulations—as a welcomed interlude from their everyday doldrums. The husband joins the navy and the wife—played by Lilian—serves as a nurse in a military hospital. When the husband is injured and is sent to a faraway hospital, he finds romance with the nurse caring for him. At the same time, the wife explores pent up feelings in the arms of a handsome surgeon. After three years, the couple arrange for their leaves to coincide. Each fears that the encounter will be with a stranger. The wife intends to ask for a divorce. But when they meet, they discover that they are not the people they were when the war started. Each now admires the other's positive attitudes and self-assured behavior.

The scene to be shot that morning called for a wounded patient to be wheeled into the wife's— nurse's— ward. The director, Victor Janson, turned to me and said, "You."

I poked myself in the chest. "Me?"

"My patient is nowhere to be found." He pointed off to the side. "Get to makeup. You'll be on screen no more than twenty seconds."

I struggled to my feet and edged toward the set. "I'm sorry, but this is nothing I want to do." Anonymity was my safety net. I could not let the public see my face in a close up on a movie screen or know my name.

"Bullshit," said Victor Janson, "everyone wants to be in the movies. Here's your chance." He turned to Lilian. "You came with this guy, right? Be your sweet charming self and ask him to help us out. It'll be over before he knows it."

I'll know it and I am not going to expose myself or Wolf to possible scrutiny.

Lilian grabbed my hand and pulled me behind a wall. I put my index finger on her moist lips knowing what she was about to say. "I will do it under one condition: my face has to be totally wrapped in bandages. Only my eyes and nose and mouth can be exposed."

"That's not the way the patient is described in the script."

"That's the only way I'll do it."

Moments later, swathed in white gauze, I heard the muffled voice of the director yell, "Action." The gurney jerked forward. I was rolled onto a set designed to replicate a hospital room. It was cleaner, nicer, and smelled fresher than either Charité or Pasewalk. I could hear an orderly tell Lilian about my injuries, and then felt her light touch as she leaned over and stared into my eyes. She said something about me being all right and that the doctor would be here soon to look at my wounds, but all I could think about was Anna the day I awoke from my coma. I was transported back to those first moments of my memory.

I knew where I was. I knew this was pretend. Nevertheless, and I cannot explain why, my entire body started to shake. The director thought I was playing the part of a severely wounded soldier. Lilian thought so, too. But I wasn't playing. I was scared all over again. Tears swelled in my eyes as the director yelled, "Cut!"

Lilian leaned over and kissed me. "You were terrific."

Victor Janson appeared by my side. "Son, you're a natural. You've got a job if you want one." He turned to Lilian. "Tell him he has to do it." I sat up and Lilian unwound my bandages while the director jabbered on. "Valentino died last year. He had a short run. Five years and look what he accomplished. The world will always remember him. With your looks and ability, you could replace Rudolph. Lilian wouldn't like that, but the box office would. What do you say?" Janson spoke so fast he made my head spin.

No matter how many times I said, "No," Victor Janson took a different line to convince me to say, "Yes." The man was a contagion to be avoided. I stayed as far from him as possible, watching other productions until Lilian finished her day.

*

Lilian let loose once we were back in the hotel. "Why won't you consider Janson's offer? Do you know how many years I trained to become an actress—singing lessons, dancing lessons, acting lessons—and he hands it to you like a free loaf of bread. And what do you do? Turn him down. I don't get it."

I took her hands and guided her to a chair. The setting sun bathed the room in warm golden hues. This light made Lilian look more beautiful than ever . . . coupled with the fire in her eyes and her reddened lips and cheeks.

"I appreciate Janson's offer. I do. But I have no intention of getting a job right away. Even if I did, it could not be a job that tied me down to responsibilities. I need to be able to shift at a moment's notice. Lots of things went on in Munich. The fires I helped put out could erupt, again, at any time. There is no practical way I could commit to acting in a movie knowing that I might leave with the next phone call."

She pulled back. "I thought I was important to you. Now you're telling me you would leave in a flash just to solve some silly problem."

"Adolf Hitler is on the verge of becoming Germany's savior. When he needs me, I have to be at his side."

Lilian scoffed. "Haven't you been reading the news? Germany no longer needs a savior. Germany has been saved. With our new monetary system, the days of hyperinflation are a thing of the past. Factories are at full capacity and workers' wages are rising. People are saving money for the first time in years. How can your *Führer* improve on that? You're backing a horse that will never leave the stable!"

"Someone has been studying their politics."

"Since I met you, I've done a bit of my own research."

She was more adorable than ever. "And what have you learned?"

"I learned that this freakish clown in Berlin, Joseph Goebbels, is connected to your precious *Führer*. He has a big mouth. His followers beat old men who oppose their views. They accost Jews for no reason. Intimidate people walking down the street minding their own business. Do you know he's banned from speaking in Berlin?"

"I know that he's passionate in his beliefs."

"Passion doesn't give him the right to beat up innocents, Friedrich, or say slanderous things about Jews in his stupid newspaper. The truth is, I could care less if you take Victor's offer to act. And I don't care if you don't work for a while, given that you have money saved from your transatlantic crossings. None of that is important to me. What is important is that I like you more than anyone I've ever met, but . . . "

"There is always a 'but.'"

"You're damn straight there's a 'but' when you associate with thugs who beat up Jews and old men."

"Lilian . . ."

"I'm not finished. I work with Jews. Everyone connected with my last film is Jewish. It will be the same with every movie I make. After all, Jews are in the movie business in Germany just like in the United States. Let me be clear about this: I can't be with anyone who hates the people I work with, who are also my good friends. If you hate them, you hate me."

Finished, she crossed her arms.

"Are you through now?"

"It depends on what you say."

"What I have to say is straightforward. I told you on the *Ballin* that I have had only good experiences with Jews."

"You're deluding yourself, Friedrich. You cavort with bigots. You don't even deny it. So what does that make you?"

"I'm sorry you feel the need to lump me in with these so-called bigots. You should know that I am my own man. I take the good and reject the bad. As for condemning these bigots, as you call them, Lilian, know that they believe in Germany. Like you and me, they believe that the treaty wronged us. Give the party time to bring a new form of nationalism to our country. Then you will see that I am right for helping them."

"That will never happen, Friedrich. Your view is too simplistic. You and your cronies live in the past. Like I said before, Berlin is thriving. Germany is on the way to becoming a great industrial power again. No one is hungry anymore. Breadlines and soup kitchens are disappearing. People are happy. It's time for you to move on." She cupped my hands in hers. "If I mean anything to you, forget these people. Come work with me at the studios."

"Sorry, Lilian, the answer is still no. I will never be an actor."

In so saying, Lilian understood that my answer to the rest of her plea was also, "No."

I could not turn my back on what I believed to be true: that the day would come when the German people would need Adolf Hitler, and he would need me.

Chapter 29

"I wondered when I would finally have the pleasure, Herr Richard," Joseph Goebbels greeted me at the restaurant of his choice.

When I returned to Berlin, I saw no reason to rush to see Goebbels. The mention of his name during my spat with Lilian reminded me of my promise to Wolf. "This was the first chance I had to pay my respects."

Joseph Goebbels needed to pick an obscure place to meet when he was without his *SA* guards. Lilian had mentioned the reason: his newspaper *Der Angriff* (The Attack) had launched repeated vicious attacks on the Jewish deputy chief of the Berlin Police, Bernhard Weiss. As a result, Goebbels ran the constant risk of being arrested.

Goebbels was a small, scrawny man. Standing next to me, he was elfin. I followed him to a table. The man had a clubbed right foot, used a special shoe, and walked with a heavy limp.

"Who told you I was back from Munich?" I asked after we were seated.

He bared his crooked teeth. "It's my job to know everything."

As soon as the waitress left with our order, I challenged his virulent attacks on Deputy Chief Bernhard Weiss. "Is it wise to be constantly embroiled with the police?"

"Nothing could be wiser," answered Goebbels. "He is the top Jew in the city. Bring him down, and they all suffer."

"Have you stopped to think about the bad press you're creating against us? It is nothing the *Führer* wants."

"Tell the *Führer* that I know what I am doing. Be sure he knows that I will never stop attacking the Jews."

"The Jews are one thing. Weiss is another matter," I said.

"Did you come to question my tactics or is there something else on the *Führer's* mind?"

"The *Führer* wants to know the temperature of the Reichstag. What are the controversies he should know about?"

"There are none. The government is getting a free pass to do what it wants because the workers are not complaining. Tell the *Führer* that things are too quiet in Germany for us to gain more traction. I will need to invent disturbances, so I have material for the upcoming issues."

"What makes you think the *Führer* will approve of you creating issues just so you can write about them?"

"He gave me a free hand to rough up Jews when we first met. He didn't limit how I would get 'news' for my paper."

I didn't know if I could believe him. My take? He was opinionated, cocksure of himself, and committed to both making life miserable for the Jews while elevating our party's image in the eyes of every German. Bottom line: I did not like him and would tell the *Führer* as much.

*

Before Lilian went on her brief trip to explore possibilities in New York, she completed filming a comedy based on an operetta by Hugo Hirsch. It was out of post-production and the premier of *Fabulous Lola* was Friday night. I arranged for a celebration afterward at the Nightingale; Max and Kitty would join us.

"You look ravishing." Lilian wore a sleek yellow dress that flared to accentuate her slender, dancer's legs. There was a large red flower tucked into the left side of her hair and she held a broad-brimmed hat in her hand. This was the costume she wore for the movie poster.

She eyed me up and down. "You don't look so bad yourself."

Moshe Hurwitz of *Hurwitz & Sohn* had me fitted into a black tuxedo for this event. "If it impresses you, it was worth getting into this starched penguin suit. Where are we going?"

"To the *Kintopp*. Have you ever been there?"

This was one of countless times I wished I had my memory back. "What is it?"

"Alfred Topp built the first cinema in Berlin about twenty years ago on the floor above his tavern. Since then, it has become *de rigueur* to refer to going to the cinema as going to the *Kintopp*."

I asked the doorman to hail a cab.

"That won't be necessary," she said. "Let's take a short walk."

"I thought we had to be there by eight. We'll be late."

"Walking calms my nerves before a premier."

Lilian was in no hurry to be on time. After a few steps I realized she intended to make a grand entrance. When we arrived at the *Kintopp*, Lilian paused in the doorway, made certain most were seated, and with a flourish marched down the center aisle to the row roped off for the picture's cast. She acknowledged the applause with a tip of her hat to the right and to the left. Once we had nestled into our seats, she whispered, "Thanks for making me look good."

"Lilian, you don't need anyone to make you look good."

On the way Lilian explained that the movie was loosely based on the life of Lola Montez, a flamboyant Irish woman who went to Spain to become a dancer. Lola danced her way through the great halls of Europe and became the lover of such notables as Liszt, Chopin, Victor Hugo, and King Ludwig I of Bavaria. In this interpretation, Lilian plays the part of a German woman raised in Madrid—Tilly Schneider—who returns to Germany as the Spanish dancer Lola Cornero.

The lights flickered. As in the silent films of the day, live musicians played music to enhance the viewer's experience. For the premier, a full orchestra had been assembled.

Lilian squeezed my hand as the frames stuttered onto the screen. Lilian (Lola) captivated the audience. Her pleated yellow dress was knee length, twirling about her beautiful legs as she danced. She flicked the skirt of the dress to and fro, and then touched her legs in a sensuous, slow crawl that mimicked a spider creeping ever upward. The faster she flicked at it, the more fever-ish the music played until it climaxed when she stomped on the spider. When she bowed on screen, the audience rose and cheered the celluloid figure.

After the credits rolled, we waded through a sea of congratu-lations and bravos to a waiting car. "I have never seen anything like that dance."

"It had to be as spectacular as possible. After all, Lola Mon-tez's entire career was based on that one dance. It got her quite the list of admirers."

"I'm going to have to fight off hordes of men tonight."

She squeezed my biceps. "My money is on you."

*

God bless Max. Spotlights glared down on a red carpet that stretched from the curb to the front door of the Nightingale. Well-wishers formed on either side as Lilian and I strolled past like royalty. Max reserved the best table in the house for us. We were about to take our seats when Max waddled toward us. Kitty was a step behind.

I introduced Lilian. "This is my good friend, Max Klinghofer."

"You outdid yourself, Max." Lilian pecked him on the cheek.

"I had nothing to do with it," Max explained. "Once I told Kitty that Lilian Harvey was gracing us with her presence, she said I not only needed to behave but insisted I be nice, too." Max turned to Lilian. "Welcome back to the Nightingale, Fräulein Harvey." He took her hand and kissed it.

"You two know each other?" Then I remembered she men-tioned it on the *Ballin*.

Lilian grabbed Max's hand. "Let's just say that Max knows more about me than most." Before I could ask what that meant, Max drew Kitty nearer. "Allow me to introduce Kitty Schmidt."

"I am a great admirer of yours, Fräulein Harvey."

"Please call me Lilian."

"I can't wait to see *Fabulous Lola*," said Kitty.

I embraced Kitty. "So good to see you again."

Kitty took my arm. "If you're back in town for a while, how about playing a little piano at *Pension Schmidt*?"

Lilian's eyes widened. "You're that Miss Kitty of . . . the escort service?"

"Did Friedrich tell you about us?"

"He most certainly did!" Lilian smacked my arm. "But he's not going to be paying visits there any time soon! Nothing personal."

"You have nothing to worry about, Lilian. Friedrich was always the gentleman."

"Even so," said Lilian, "I think I will keep him where I can watch him."

As we took our seats, I raised my hand to get the sommelier's attention. "It's time to toast our guest of honor."

"Put your hand down, Friedrich," Max said. "It's already taken care of." A bottle of 1926 Dom Pérignon Champagne appeared. We toasted Lilian and the night was off to a grand start.

The lights dimmed and the show began. An all-colored revue danced and sang and even got the audience to join in some songs. When they finished Max jumped onto the stage, to the extent that he scaled the steps one by one . . . as if climbing a mountain path. At the top he paused, panting. A light shone on his face; a sheen of perspiration covered his reddened cheeks.

"Attention everyone. Tonight, we are honored to have the celebrated Lilian Harvey in the audience. If we clap hard enough and long enough, perhaps Fräulein Harvey will be kind enough to sing for us."

The spotlight swung over to our table. Lilian smiled, nodded to the clapping patrons, glanced around our table, and then grabbed my hand. "C'mon, let's give them a show."

For the next half hour, we entertained with a medley of show tunes that we played on the *Ballin*, with Lilian finishing with her rendition of *Mammy*. She received a standing ovation. We worked our way back to the table. As I pulled the chair out for

Lilian, Kitty caught my eye and nodded to her right. Marta was headed towards us. It was nearly four years since we last spoke. It didn't occur to me that she might be at Max's. In a flash, my shirt stuck to my skin like a wet rag.

Max, why didn't you warn me!

Marta wore a red camisole top with strings of large beads around her neck. Her head was crowned with a helmet of these same beads that crisscrossed into a diamond-shaped netting that held down her close-cropped hair. She held a fan painted with the image of a peacock in her right hand. She kissed Kitty and Max. Then standing behind Max and opposite me, she asked, "Aren't you going to introduce me?"

I stood. "Lilian, I would like to introduce you to Marta Feidt. Marta, this is Lilian Harvey."

Lilian reached out but Marta ignored her hand. Then through bared teeth she asked, "Why haven't I heard from you?"

My mouth turned desert-dry. "After the putsch I left the country in a hurry. I couldn't risk calling."

"But you managed to find time for Fräulein Harvey. How nice for you."

"I'm sorry Marta, truly I am. Time slipped away. Then too much time passed for me to call you. I thought it best to move on."

I kept my head straight, not daring to steal a glance at Lilian.

"You mean it was best for *you* to move on. You never bothered to call me to find out what *I* wanted."

Nothing I could say could make her stop. I stood there waiting for what she would say next.

"Before I leave, Friedrich, there is one thing you should know. Anna was right about you: you *are* a son of a bitch!" Then she faced Lilian. "If you know what's good for you, you'll find a nice, pretty-boy actor so you don't have to be with the likes of him." Then, with all the flair she could muster, Marta stamped off.

Max and Kitty were agape. Lilian sat thunderstruck.

"Had I known that would happen, I would've kept her away," Max mumbled.

Before I had a chance to explain that I was about to end it with Marta anyway, Lilian overcame her shock. "Is that what happens, Friedrich? You leave women and don't say goodbye? Not even a note? And, by the way, who's Anna?"

Great! I have had a ten-year lifetime—with only three women in it—and it all spills out on a nightclub floor.

"Anna was my nurse. She was there after I came out of my coma."

"And because of that you felt obligated to take up with her? You have to do better than that."

"I was trying to find myself. It was during the *Freikorps* days."

"Who was after her?"

"Only Marta. That ended long ago. For years, I was with no one. Doesn't that count for something?"

"Not if you treated them poorly. Do it once, and you will do it again."

My hands slapped my sides out of frustration, searching to say something to make this go away. The last thing I needed was for Max to explain that Marta and Anna had been roommates.

Kitty intervened. "Lilian, don't blame Friedrich for gravitating to a kind face. It was wartime. He was at death's door. What he did was natural."

"Friedrich could have been with a hundred women and I wouldn't have cared. It's that he left them without a word . . . that's what matters. It's mean. It speaks to a lack of respect."

Kitty took my hand. "Men are nothing more than big children. Most of the time, they don't know what they're doing. You and I, we need to be bigger than that. More understanding." She looked at Max when she said this, who turned sheepishly away. Then Kitty lifted her glass. "I say we forgive and forget."

Lilian took a sip of champagne without a word.

I reached for Lilian's hand. "I'm different now. I've learned."

My words sounded stilted, even to me. Lilian's limp hand offered no comfort. It took the rest of the evening, with lots of champagne and small talk from Max and Kitty, for Lilian to look at me. A squeeze of the hand in the cab ride to the Adlon signaled she was willing to give "us" a chance. By the time we entered our suite, she had thawed a bit more. For the time being, it would have to be enough.

Chapter 30

Lilian did not have to report to the studio the next morning, which gave us time to mend last night's hurts. We tossed a picnic basket prepared by the hotel into the rear of a rented car, drove until we found a grassy meadow, and lunched on a blanket spread under the shade of an ancient beech tree. As expected, talk was tight in the beginning, like scattered leaves that lay close to one another without touching. Then, after the last of the wine was drained and I started to repack the lunch basket, Lilian reached for my hand.

"Don't be afraid that you lost me last night." She pressed harder to reassure. "I can understand that when it is time to move on, there are never right words to say. And I understand how vulnerable you were when you were wounded."

With an overwhelming sense of relief, I wrapped my arms around her and we kissed. With lighter hearts, we loaded the car.

She asked as we rumbled away, "What plans do you have, Friedrich?"

"Do you mean now, tonight, or tomorrow?"

"Those times are taken. I was thinking more of next week. Next month. Next year. Do you have enough money not to work?"

"For now I do, but I know I have to get a job. The days of playing piano on a ship are over."

"So is going back to Kitty's brothel."

"The thought never entered my mind."

"Let's get one thing straight. Small fibs said in jest are no different than big lies. I see how women make eyes at you. And I see how you appreciate a pretty face. It is perfectly okay to dream about working at *Pension Schmidt*. But hear me loud and clear: it will remain a dream. Can you live with that?"

"One hundred percent. Now that we've settled what I can't do, let's talk about what I could do. For starters, I would like a job that's on the same schedule as yours."

"Why not consider Victor Janson's offer to become an actor? You would be a natural."

"What I said before still stands: I do not want to be in front of the camera."

"Okay then. There's behind the camera. But . . . if you're thinking about directing, there is more to it than yelling, 'Action,' 'Cut,' 'Take five,' and 'That's a wrap.'"

I shook my head. "I don't want to be a cameraman either."

"Then what are you thinking? You could write screenplays about your experiences in the war. Those sort of movies will be made forever."

"I was thinking more along the lines of music."

Lilian's lips drooped. "If you play the piano in a *Kintopp*, I'll never see you. I'll be working days and you'll be working nights. That is not being on the same schedule."

"That's not what I meant. I'm thinking about composing musical scores for films. From what I see, it's haphazard at best. The music is uneven from theatre to theatre. No two nights or two places have the same quality of music. I want to write scores that either a soloist or an orchestra can follow. I would standardize what is played."

Music enhanced a moviegoer's experience. At its best it was fluid. But often the music was choppy and out of sync with the scenes. Most films included cue sheets that informed the pianist or orchestra when they should play suspenseful music, romantic music, and so forth. In the end it was left to the musician to pick the music. There were no industry standards. Just hit or miss.

Lilian bubbled with enthusiasm. "*Birth of a Nation* proved that synchronized music enhanced the movie experience. We can work together," she went on. "Have similar schedules. I like the way you think, Friedrich Richard. I'll speak to Victor about this. He will love the idea."

I couldn't help but smile: Marta Feidt had been forgotten.

*

So my journey to find out more about myself yielded another skillset that enabled me to continue to keep a low profile. Lilian and I went to work together each day. She convinced Victor Janson to let me score his next movie: *Girl of Paris*. Lilian was not in it so I could concentrate on the score.

"I could get used to this," Lilian said one early morning after we made love.

"So could I." It had been weeks since I was last in Munich.

Lilian raised herself on one elbow. "Can I take that as a 'yes' that we can play house a while longer? You haven't mentioned the name Wolf or your party in a long time."

"I've had no reason."

"Yet I suspect that you would drop what you're doing the moment he calls. Is that right?"

"Stop, Lilian. He doesn't belong in bed with us. Look around. Wherever we go these days, Germany continues to grow and prosper. As long as that continues, the Nazis will remain in the background. Oh, for sure, they will run their candidates for the Reichstag, maybe win a few seats, make some noise, but in the end, they will be nothing more than a fringe group. If that's how it plays out, I will be by your side as long as you want."

She cupped my face in her hands. "You could be habit forming."

"That's my goal."

Then Lilian turned serious. "If you agree that Germany's future is rosier than ever, why won't you swear off that man?"

"There is such a thing as loyalty. We have been friends since 1918."

"What is there to be loyal to? He's nothing but a local Bavarian politician with extreme ideas that reasonable people don't accept."

I propped myself up on one elbow. "You underestimate Hitler, my love. The man radiates hope. Agreed, on the surface, he's an ordinary man. And Lord knows, I understand his faults more than most. But when he speaks about Germany and his love of the Fatherland, he is larger than life itself."

"I don't know how a girl can compete against that. When he calls, are you going to leave me like you did Marta?"

I pulled Lilian into me. "Nothing would keep me away from you. Not for long. Whatever the reason I might need to go to Munich, know that I will come back to you as fast as possible. I love you, Lilian Harvey. I never said that to Marta or anyone else. You are the first."

*

As the winter months of 1927 slipped into the warming spring of 1928, my career as a film scorer gained momentum. Lilian was equally busy. When both of us had a free night, we made Max happy performing at the Nightingale. Max wanted to pay us, but we refused. I could never charge Max after all he did for me.

"When you two play, you fill the house. Make this a regular engagement," he importuned, tossing a generous contract onto the table.

"It's fun for us, Max," Lilian said, "but we like our day jobs." Then she winked. "And we do like some nights alone."

I could not leave it at that. "Max, if an act doesn't show up one night and you need us, all you have to do is whistle."

"I told Kitty you wouldn't accept, but I had to try. Consider it a standing offer. Change your minds and I will headline you every night."

*

One April evening, Lilian remained late to shoot a scene. She promised to be back at the Adlon in time for us to dine at Berlin's oldest restaurant, *Zur Letzten Instanz*.

I entered the lobby humming a refrain from one of the tunes I had composed for *Homecoming*, when I heard my name called. It was Wilhelm Frick standing next to a potted plant.

"You're the last person I expected to see here." *Or wanted to see.*

Frick appeared gaunt. "We need to talk." I gestured toward the salon off the hotel lobby. Frick shook his head. "Too many ears. Is your room empty?"

"It is for now. How long do we need?"

"An hour."

"Lilian will be home shortly. We have dinner plans. Cut it in half." A minute later, safe behind my door, I asked, "Why all the mystery, Wilhelm? Why not just call?"

"It's not that simple. You're needed back in Munich."

"Don't tell me another girl tried to commit suicide?"

"If that was your attempt at humor, it wasn't funny. This is serious. The Boss fired Emil Maurice back in January. The ungrateful little watchmaker turned around and sued both him and the party for back wages."

I hadn't spoken to Emil in some time. "This makes no sense. Adolf agreed to let Emil and Geli get engaged as long as they waited two years to be married."

"When could anyone trust anything Emil said?"

"Point taken. What did he do this time? How bad was it?"

"Exactly what you would think. Emil opened his pants, Geli welcomed him in, and the boss blew his stack. He fired Emil the moment he found out. Now they are about to fight it out in labor court. It will be an open trial. This has to be squelched like we did the Maria Reiter disaster. Otherwise, the party could go up in flames."

What was Emil trying to prove?

"How much is Emil owed?"

"He's demanding three thousand. He's crazy. He's owed a few hundred at best."

"How far has the case gone?"

"It goes in front of a judge the day after tomorrow. Even the blackmail letters didn't get this far."

"What's the status of the Buch investigation?"

"You always go to the heart of it, don't you? Max Amann got the Reiter girl to sign a document that she and Hitler were only friends . . . that he was like a father to her. Hitler submitted his corroborating statement. Once Judge Buch was informed that Hitler blessed an Emil Maurice-Geli Raubal engagement, the matter of the anonymous letters appeared closed. *Alles in ordnung*—everything was in order for Buch. That was then."

"Where are we now?"

Frick threw his hands up. "About to have all the damn dirty laundry aired again, this time in the labor court."

"What do you want from me?"

"Prevent this court case from destroying the *Führer* and the party."

"I'll try to help, but how can . . ." The door opened, catching me in midsentence.

"Who . . ."

We both jumped to our feet. "Lilian, this is Wilhelm Frick. He's a member of the Reichstag."

"And a fellow Nazi, I presume."

Frick stiffened. "Is that a problem?"

"Should it be? Friedrich is a party member . . . I like him."

"You make it sound like he's different than the rest of us."

"Oh, but he is." Lilian pecked me on the cheek.

Frick clicked his heels and bowed. "Far be it for me to change a pretty fräulein's mind." We shook hands. "I will meet you at the airport for the morning flight." He bowed again to Lilian. "Sorry to have disturbed you. Please accept my apologies."

"No offense taken, Herr Frick. But I do wish you hadn't come here. Friedrich is too busy to break away from his work."

"You entered just when I was about to explain to Herr Frick that I'm in the middle of scoring a movie." I turned to Wilhelm. "I can't leave in the morning. I need to make arrangements to miss a couple of days."

Lilian's lips tightened into ribbons of anger. "Friedrich . . ."

My stone-cold gaze froze Lilian in midsentence. I turned to Frick. "I said I would go, and I will. But I must take the later flight."

"As you wish," he muttered under his breath.

The moment the door clicked shut, hands on hips, Lilian unloaded. "Are you going to jump every time they pull your strings? Why didn't you tell him 'No'?"

"I told you there would be phone calls. I also told you that when I had to go to Munich I would return as soon as possible. This will take two days. Three at the most."

We stood at opposite ends of the couch. I dared not move. Any attempt to embrace would only fan the flames.

"A few days away is not the issue," she said. "My hackles kick up thinking about whom you'll be with during that time."

"The Nazis are not the poison you make them out to be."

"How could you possibly know? You're too close to be objective. You don't see these men for what they are. Take your buddy, Goebbels. His thugs continue to beat innocent Jews in the streets. How can you have anything to do with these people?"

"Lilian, this has nothing to do with the Nazis or party politics. I need to go to Munich to help a friend. Actually, two friends. If Victor Jansen or someone else needed your help, I know you would stop what you were doing and go."

"My friends are not Nazis. I can assure you, none are like Adolf Hitler," she said.

"He's not what you think, Lilian. One day Hitler will speak at a big rally in Berlin. Come with me. See for yourself, how dynamic he is and how important he is for Germany's future. Then make up your mind about him. Will you do that for me?"

She didn't answer. I opened my arms hoping she would move toward me. She remained rigid for a beat, and then edged closer. I took a step, grabbed her hand, and pulled her into me; Lilian rested her head on my chest. Neither of us spoke. When our breathing was in sync, I said, "I love you, Lilian. Nothing will ever get between us."

She looked up. "In one sense I've been unfair. I see how much your Wolf means to you. If it is that important to you, I will hear him speak."

"Just give him a chance."

She took a step back. "But after I hear him, you have to promise to keep an open mind and listen to what I think. No matter what that may be." She held out her hand. "Can you do that?"

I pulled her back into me and kissed her long and hard. "You've got yourself a deal."

Chapter 31

I landed in Munich as the sun set. Frick met me at the airport. I gave him specific instructions of what I wanted him to do after he left me in front of Maurice's building. Before entering, I counted the floors until I located Emil's windows. The lights were out. I took the steps, two at a time, and was huffing by the time I knocked on his apartment door. Nothing stirred. I knocked again. This time I heard scuffling feet.

I moved back certain Emil would crack open the door with a gun in hand. I called out. "It's me, Emil."

"Friedrich?"

"Open the door." The lock snicked and the door edged open enough for me to see a gun and the face of a haggard man with bloodshot eyes.

"Go away. If you're here to talk me into dropping the suit, you're too late. We go before the judge tomorrow and then everyone will know the truth."

He moved to close the door; my foot blocked it. "Emil, let me in. We can't talk standing in the hall."

"Shit we can't! I've got nothing to say to you." But he opened the door anyway. I ignored the gun and stepped inside. I knew every stitch of his three-bedroom apartment from past adventures. We sat at the kitchen table.

"First off, Emil," I pointed to a wooden chest, "put the gun in the cabinet."

"Or what?"

"Or I'm going to shove it up your ass and pull the trigger."

The clicking of a clock grew louder. It was tense until he gave a familiar laugh, stashed the gun, and returned with a bottle. We each gulped down a shot. He refilled our glasses before either of us spoke. "You wasted your time coming here. I'm not going to change my mind."

"You have every right to sue Wolf. In fact, I don't blame you. As a matter of fact, I would've done the same thing."

He tipped his glass. "No one has been on my side since this started."

I shifted. The chair groaned from my weight. "I said I don't blame you. I didn't say it's the right thing to do. As a matter of fact, it is as far from the right thing to do as you can get."

"Wolf didn't give me a choice, Friedrich. He forbade me to see Geli. No one has the right to get in the way of our love."

"The deal was for you to be engaged and get married in two years. After that, you could fuck all you want."

Emil fingered the glass rim, making it squeal. "You don't get it, Friedrich. No one does."

"Then enlighten me. I need to understand why you broke the deal knowing it would hurt him and kill the party."

"A deal to keep us out of bed for two years? That was bullshit. Wolf set me up to fail by making the terms impossible. It was just a matter of time before I caved. When that happened, I was out and he had Geli all for himself."

I emptied my glass. "You tickle me. When did you ever love a woman, Emil? As for getting laid, that was never a problem for you. You were the shill who got girls for all of us."

"You've been gone a long time, Friedrich. I've changed. I love Geli."

"You can't convince me of that, Emil. You wanted Geli because you could . . . and show Wolf up at the same time."

"You don't believe me? Wait here. You need to read the letter Hitler forced Geli to write me, so you can see how ridiculous this is."

Emil bolted out of his chair and went to his bedroom. I could hear him rummage through a drawer. As I waited, I noticed a picture on a side table of Emil and Geli skiing.

He stomped back and shoved a letter written on blue stationery in my hand. "Read this."

I scanned to the bottom; it was from Geli.

24 December 1927
My Dear Emil!
The postman has already brought me three letters from you,
but never have I been so happy as I was over the last. Perhaps
there is a reason for all the suffering we have endured in the
last few days . . . Uncle Adolf is insisting that we should wait
two years. Think of it, Emil, two whole years of only being
able to kiss each other now and then and always having
Uncle Adolf in charge. I can only give you my love and be
unconditionally faithful to you. I love you so infinitely much.
Uncle Adolf insists that I should go on with my studies . . .
Uncle A is now very nice. I would like to give him great
pleasure, but do not know with what . . . But Uncle A says
our love must be kept a complete secret . . . we will see each
other often, and be alone, too. Uncle A has promised me. He
is so sweet . . .

"Emil, how is this unreasonable? It says as plain as day, wait
two years and Geli is yours."

"It was an impossible challenge, and you know it. So I said
the hell with that. She loves me with all of her heart, Friedrich.
Read the rest of her letter."

You must work to make a living for both of us and we can
only see each other in the presence of others, and besides . . . I
will give you my love and be faithful to you unconditionally
. . . I love you so much!
Geli

"You would've done the same thing, so how can you blame
me? A month after this letter, he tossed me out."

"What's so difficult to understand? He's the protective uncle
looking after his niece."

"You're talking to me, Friedrich. Not some goat herder.
There is a reason good old Uncle Alf is called Wolf. We both
know he wants her for himself."

The whiskey was dulling my resolve. I shook my head to clear my thoughts. "What are your plans for tomorrow?"

"What do you mean? I go to court, explain my case to the judge, tell him how I was fired in a fit of jealousy . . . and see how much money I'm awarded. The party owes me three thousand Reichsmarks."

"Do you really want to do this?"

"Wolf is a bully. He needs to know that he can't get away with this. Besides, I need the money."

"And you think that you—Emil Maurice—are the one to teach Adolf Hitler that lesson? More than sully him, you could bring down the whole party. Do you really want that? Destroy our ten years of struggle?"

Emil shrugged.

I took a last stab. "You should know that I'm the one who convinced Wolf to let you and Geli get engaged. Walter Buch had to be stopped from sniffing around Wolf's sex life. Even Hans Frank couldn't sway him. Your engagement was needed to prove that Wolf wasn't doing his niece so Buch would close the case."

"I'm not stupid, Friedrich. I understand the logic behind this. To the outside world, our engagement portrayed Wolf as the kindly, caring uncle. The reality, however, is that it handed Geli to Wolf while it froze me out."

I squared to face him, forcing him to focus. "Listen carefully, Emil. I can't let you go into that courtroom tomorrow and make a mockery of Wolf and the party." When I was certain I had his attention, I asked, "What will it take to get you to back off?"

"We're beyond deal making, Friedrich. This is a matter of principle."

I tapped the table twice with my knuckles. "Principle has a price tag. What's yours?"

He downed his glass and refilled it again. He studied me over the rim as he took another sip. "Are you authorized to negotiate with me?"

"I wouldn't be here otherwise. Twenty thousand Reichsmarks."

"First offers are never the final offer. I expect you can go higher."

"That's the only offer."

"If I don't take it?"

I pointed to the window. "Take a look."

Emil staggered to the window, brushed back the curtain, and leaned against the frame. Below were three cars, each surrounded by five Brownshirts. Frick had carried out my instructions to a T. Emil let the curtain fall. "Why bother offering any money? There are enough men there to convince me to drop the case."

"We both know Wolf takes care of his *Alte Kämpfer*. The three of us go back a long way."

"The Boss will never forgive me for taking up with Geli." Emil was no longer steady. He wobbled to the chair. His voice became a whisper. "What do you want me to do tomorrow?"

I remained standing, peering down at him. "Go to the courthouse. Say as little as possible. I will have Hans Frank take care of everything. Leave after the verdict is rendered, and don't speak to anyone."

He looked up at me. "For twenty thousand Reichsmarks? That will not be a problem. I assume I also get to keep what the court gives?"

Good old Emil.

I knelt down until we were eye-to-eye. "But you can never see Geli again."

"Even if I agreed to that," Emil gave a sly smile, "I can't be faulted if she shows up at my door one night. She does that now, you know."

I seized his arm; he winced in pain. "If that ever happens, your next visitor will be me."

He struggled to free his arm. "Okay. Okay. It won't happen."

I squeezed harder before I released it. "I'm glad you came to your senses. I will be there tomorrow as a reminder."

He tried to stand but fell back into his chair. I helped him up. We embraced. I held him a beat longer, uncertain when—or if—I would see him again after tomorrow.

We broke without another word. I made my way to the elevator, when Emil called out. "Just so you know, everyone thinks he broke off from Maria Reiter because of the blackmail letters. Everyone has overlooked that Wolf was two-timing Maria with his niece."

I stopped short and spun around. "You're telling me that Wolf was fucking Geli at the same time he was doing Reiter?"

"Geli was living with him, wasn't she?"

Emil gave a big grin as he held onto the door for support. Even in his stupor, he planted a seed of doubt to the point that I didn't know what to believe.

"Emil," I said, holding out my hand, "let me have the Geli letter . . . I will make a copy, and you'll get it back after tomorrow."

Back on the street, I ordered the men into the cars. Before we pulled away, I looked up; Emil was at his window. I waved. Emil waved back. Who would have thought—ten years ago— that we three comrades would come to this!

The driver dropped me off in front of *Thierschstrasse* 41. Before tackling the stairs to see Wolf, I considered the building next to his—*Thierschstrasse* 43—where Frick said Wolf rented a more spacious and suitable apartment for Geli.

During the ride, I reflected on what to say and how best to say it. I knocked and was surprised that he opened the door without asking who it was. When he saw it was me, he gave a broad smile and welcomed me inside. We took our usual places: me on his lone chair, he at the edge of his bed. Hitler made it easy by starting with small talk.

"*Friedrichen* . . . how is Berlin these days?"

"I have a job scoring movies and am living with a wonderful woman." Wolf loved movies. It was a surefire way to engage him rather than start with Emil and Geli. Of course, knowing his far reach—and in particular his love of films—I was sure he knew about Lilian and me. His next comment proved me correct.

"Fräulein Harvey is a wonderful actress. Too thin for my taste. I read that soon all pictures in the United States will be talkies. When will our German studios embrace this new technology?" Before I could answer, he continued. "I spoke to Goebbels about making talking movies for us. We will use Fräulein Harvey to explain why the NSDAP is so special." Then he waved a finger. "Be careful of Goebbels. He can't keep his hands off the women who work for him."

I mumbled something about how she would be honored to help . . . knowing it would never happen. Then I asked, "How much longer do you plan to stay in this apartment? Years ago we discussed you moving to a nicer place."

Wolf was enthused. "I have finally acquiesced. Next year I move to a luxury, nine room apartment. Number sixteen *Prinzegentenplatz*." Then he turned serious. "But you're not here to discuss my living conditions."

"I have just come from Emil."

"Frick mentioned something about that." Typical Wolf. Asking questions when he already knew the answers. I was in no mood to make this easy. I said nothing, forcing him to ask. "What was his response?"

"Emil agreed to take money and not make waves in court. He does not want to hurt you or the party."

"He already has. That cannot be undone."

"On the contrary, after tomorrow it will all disappear. When historians write our story, the episode of him suing you will barely rate a footnote."

"Frick, Amann, and Frank have each advised me to avoid bad publicity at any cost. When I told Goebbels what they said, he said . . . "

"I know. Goebbels believes that *all* publicity is good publicity. Wolf, that doesn't apply to you. In this case, Frick, Amann, and Frank are all correct. Bad publicity is bad publicity. Take comfort knowing that Emil will no longer make trouble for you."

"How much did he agree to take to make this go away?"

"Twenty thousand RM plus whatever the judge awards him tomorrow. It will be enough for Emil to open the watch shop he always wanted."

"And Geli?"

"He promised to leave her alone forever."

Wolf was more interested in this last condition of the deal. "Why should I believe him, Friedrich? He promised to refrain from physical contact last time, and broke that within weeks. Maybe even days. What's different this time?"

"Emil has had time to reflect on what he's done to you. He could not be sorrier. What touched him was when I reminded him of the old days, when the three of us spent time together. I am certain he will adhere to all conditions, including never seeing Geli again." My statement about Emil's remorse was bullshit, but it satisfied him.

"If you're satisfied, Friedrich, then I am, too. Party Treasurer Schwarz will deliver the funds to Frick. Wilhelm will pay Emil once he signs the proper papers."

*

The court appearance was *pro forma*. In addition to the twenty thousand RM from the party, the judge awarded Emil five hundred RM. Emil added one condition: he demanded a letter of recommendation from Hitler. He needed this safeguard should he ever seek new employment. Hitler agreed to write one.

This scandal was now behind us . . . or so I thought. And I never expected to see my old comrade again. But, once again, I proved to be a poor soothsayer.

*

It was twilight when I returned to Berlin. Lilian was preparing for the next day's shoot. "I didn't expect you back so soon."

"I told you I would return as soon as possible. Only away one night."

"How did it feel sleeping alone?" she asked.

"I hated every minute away from you."

"Me, too." Lilian grabbed my hand and helped me undress. When we slipped into bed, she asked, "Did you accomplish everything you set out to do? I am not prepared to spare you anytime soon . . . no matter what the issue."

"It was a small matter between party members. They were two children fighting over the same toy. It's settled now."

*

I completed the score for *Homecoming* by early May. As we approached a national election, Goebbels asked if I could get one of the film company's artists to make posters for the party. After being rejected a number of times, I found one artist who would create a series of posters for twenty-five RM. No matter. The elections of 1928 recorded that the NSDAP was trounced, relegated to the fringes of politics where nuisance parties dwell in near-oblivion.

The morning after the election, Lilian and I read the papers over coffee when she said, "I guess this is the end of your little party."

By any measure, this election should have signaled the death knell for any party with such a poor showing. Out of 491 Reichstag seats, the Nazis garnered twelve, a drop from the thirty-two seats we won four years earlier.

We just lost two-thirds of our strength. Feder, Goebbels, Frick, and Gregor Strasser were elected as deputies to the Reichstag. One name I did not expect to see among the winners was Hermann Göring's. Like a phoenix, Göring rose from the ashes of an insane asylum in Sweden to win a seat in the Reichstag. All things considered, Lilian was right: the future of our party was bleak at best.

I lowered my newspaper. "I told you months ago that if Germany continued to prosper, right wing parties would become less relevant."

Her smile turned to a frown. "What concerns me is that no party in the Reichstag has a clear majority. Until one does, even a minor party like the NSDAP could linger on. Still . . ." she could not help but gloat, "your party's prospects do look dismal."

"It does appear that way, doesn't it? But Wolf is no quitter. I know the man. The bigger the challenge, the more resilient he becomes."

Chapter 32

1928 – 1929

I was committed to my musical career. To my surprise, I missed nothing of my past life. The rallies, the speeches, the struggles in the halls and in the streets, all withered into brown-edged memories. I had not heard a peep from Emil and assumed he was content fixing watches and having no trouble making new conquests with his charm, his mandolin playing, and his repertoire of local folk songs. And then, just when I thought he was out of my life, he called. It was early August.

"Do you know what that bastard did?" He shouted into the telephone.

"You're talking riddles, Emil. What's this about?"

"Hitler. Why else would I be calling? Remember the last part of our deal? That he would give me a reference? Well, he just sent it. You can't believe what that son-of-a-bitch wrote. It's dated August 1, 1928." He read it to me.

Herr Emil Maurice was in my employ as a driver between July 1, 1921 and January 1928. Herr Maurice has proved to be an excellent and extremely safe driver and his skills go far beyond those of the average driver.

"What good is a reference like this?"

"I think what he's saying, Emil, is for you to shove it up your ass."

"Message delivered," said Emil. Then he added, "I guess I had that coming. I'll send you a copy for your collection."

*

I had been with Lilian for a year now and decided to do something to commemorate it. I stopped into the Nightingale to harvest Max's advice.

"It's good to see you, Friedrich."

"Life agrees with you, Max. You're fatter than ever."

"Kitty loves the fact that there is more of me to grab. Anyway, that's what she says. Everything all right with Lilian?"

"That is why I'm here." I explained that it had been a year since she and I started dating. Could he recommend a special restaurant for the two of us and then come by with Kitty afterward to join our celebration?

Max's eyes lit up. "I know just the place. Take her to the *Prater Garten*. It's lively with great people-watching. Lilian will love it. They have an orchestra and a dance floor. What do you say?"

"I say we do it."

"Brilliant. We'll meet you for dessert."

It was a sumptuous meal. Lots of champagne. Our forays in public were becoming events as more people recognized Lilian. To my discomfort, people did not hesitate to approach for a handshake or autograph. As was my practice, I shunned photos for the society pages and movie magazines. That particular evening, we were left undisturbed. When Max and Kitty approached, I signaled the waiter to serve a special cake with one candle.

Max made a toast; Kitty threw her arms around Lilian. It was a splendid evening . . . until Joseph Goebbels entered the restaurant wearing a dark navy-blue tailored suit. He had a platinum blond dressed in a tight-fitting dress draped on his arm.

I turned away, hoping he would not see me, but he did. Goebbels limped to our table. With a toothy smile and a deep bow, he introduced his companion.

"Friedrich, so good to see you and your friends. May I present Fräulein Koch."

"I've had the pleasure of seeing Fräulein Koch in a chorus line at the studio," I said.

The young woman almost knocked Goebbels over when she realized she was in Lilian's presence. She reached to take her hand. "Lilian Harvey! I've admired you on the set. I hope we get to work together one day."

Goebbels clicked his heels and bowed. "The *Führer* and I want very much to have you make a film that explains the goals of the NSDAP."

"Will it be a comedy?" asked Lilian, studying her polished nails.

Goebbels snapped upright. "Fräulein, I don't think you understand the privilege we are extending you."

She looked up. "Herr Goebbels. I very much do . . . and I cannot thank you enough for the consideration."

Goebbels hesitated. "I will be in touch when the time is right."

"Nothing would please me more, Herr Goebbels," said Lilian.

When Goebbels saw the anniversary cake, he said, "We've interrupted your celebration." After saying goodbye to me, and bowing to both Lilian and Kitty, he turned to Max and extended his hand.

Max rose slowly. He studied Goebbels's face, making no effort to take his hand. Only when it started to tremble did Max reach out with the broadest smile he could muster. "Hello Herr Goebbels. I am Max Klinghofer . . . the Jew." Goebbels jerked his hand back as if he had touched fire. Without another word, Goebbels grabbed the girl and hobbled away.

Max burst out laughing, as did Kitty. I cast a timorous glance at Lilian, who had her arm around Max, laughing as well.

November 16, 1928

We prepared to leave for Hitler's speech. "Are you ready?" Lilian was about to fulfill her part of our bargain.

"What do you wear to a Nazi rally?" Lilian asked. "The last thing I want is to be a cliché flamboyant actress."

"Wear a tailored suit." In the end, she borrowed a dress from the set of *Princess Olala* that was worn by a young actress named Marlene Dietrich.

We were ushered to a reserved box at Sportpalast. Goebbels worked his publicity magic and filled every seat in the arena. It was not lost on any of us that this was Wolf's audition for the leadership of the disenfranchised right in Germany.

The Sportpalast was the largest indoor arena in Berlin. Designed for multiple uses, it accommodated track meets, ice hockey, boxing matches, and political rallies.

A low murmur filled the room as fifteen thousand waited for the big moment. We sat in the box reserved for Hitler's inner circle. I introduced Lilian to Max Amann, Hans Frank, Hermann Göring, and Heinrich Himmler. Wilhelm Frick needed no introduction. I was gratified Lilian gave him a civil nod in contrast to the scowl when she found him in our suite at the Adlon.

"And this is Rudy Hess." Rudy had a young girl with him . . . not his wife.

Rudy greeted me and bowed to Lilian. Then he said, "Allow me to introduce Herr Hitler's niece. Fräulein Geli Raubal."

Geli was just as I expected: a young girl who had turned twenty in June, with short brown hair, and brown eyes that danced with excitement. She had a full figure. Geli was the antithesis of most of Wolf's women who were often blond, blue-eyed, and athletic. More unusual, Geli was the first woman Wolf spotlighted in public in the ten years I knew him. Indeed, she reigned as queen of the box that evening.

Geli's hand was warm to the touch. Her fingers lingered long enough to make me uncomfortable. I introduced Lilian.

"I saw you in *Fabulous Lola*," Geli said. "An actress's life must be so exciting."

"It's hard work."

"It must be wonderful to see yourself on film." Then added, "I started singing lessons."

"I applaud you for following your dreams." Geli was about to add something when coronets announced the opening of the spectacle. Brownshirts formed two lines on stage through which Goebbels marched to the podium. Behind Goebbels, *SA* men hoisted an array of banners, sacred insignias, and flags, including the Blutfahne—the Blood Flag—stained with the blood from the fallen during the '23 Putsch. The background for these many flags created a brilliant red field that depicted flames rising skyward. It gave the illusion that the stage was on fire.

The cheers deafened. Goebbels mounted a platform to be seen. He raised his small hands for quiet.

"Are the meetings always this loud?" Lilian shouted in my ear.

I pointed to Wolf who was about to set foot on the stage. "This is not loud. Wait."

In moments, pandemonium overtook the crowd as Wolf entered the stage. Hitler basked in the crowd's adulation. The stadium vibrated, sending pulses through our feet. Screams of "*Heil*" and "*Sieg Heil*" filled the air. A sea of arms saluted, fingers stretched, all pointing to their adored *Führer*.

Hitler gave the Nazi salute and fifteen thousand saluted back. Jubilation swept the stadium.

Lilian was no stranger to star power. After all, that was her world. But this was no movie set; it was beyond anything she had ever seen. She gazed over the screaming crowd as her body absorbed its energy. Her head darted this way and that but was always drawn to the man on center stage.

I had seen this before. Cheering, screaming, singing praises went on and on until Wolf timed the perfect moment to step to the microphone, extend his arms, and appeal for quiet. His gestures were artful. Nothing was left to chance.

Every move Hitler exhibited on stage was a preconceived act. When Hitler spoke into the electronic microphone, he did so with the same skills he brought to his gestures. His voice no longer sounded shrill. It was clear. Powerful.

His rhetoric changed, too. Gone were the attacks on Jews, though he did allude to the colored people. Most important, he reconciled the words Nationalism and Socialism to be inclusive of all classes and peoples. "A nationalist stands by his people while a socialist stands up for the rights of his people." In the end, he linked the workers with the wealthy and the unions with the industrialists in one common cause that pitted Germany against the world. It was a deliberate repudiation of factions within the Party and a declaration of common purpose—from every source—to make Germany what she had been. Orchestrated by Goebbels, Wolf avoided alienating anyone that night.

When Hitler finished, unbridled enthusiasm exploded throughout the arena. To my surprise, Lilian jumped up and clapped with everyone else. We joined others in Wolf's circle to offer a champagne toast in a private room behind the stage. Any other time Wolf would have fawned over Lilian. Not that night. He had just given the speech of his life and was drenched in perspiration. With Geli by his side, Wolf made an effort to be chivalrous when I introduced Lilian. He bowed and kissed her hand. In a hoarse voice he said we were lucky to have found each other. Then he begged to be excused.

*

"What did you think?" I asked as we undressed later that evening.

"He's in love with her."

"Who is with whom?"

"Your Wolf with his niece."

"He dotes over her like any uncle would."

"Don't be a fool, Friedrich. A woman knows these things."

"Apart from his niece, how did Wolf impress you?"

"He's amazing. I have never seen blue eyes like his."

"I'm not talking about his eyes or his niece. You have made it abundantly clear that you have been unhappy with me when I go to Munich. You have criticized me for having anything to do with party members. So, now . . . what did you think?"

Lilian was hesitant. "I expected to hate everything about the night. Instead, I loved the drama, the staging. The energy was infectious."

"You can use those words to describe a play. What about Hitler? What about his speech?"

"It was poignant and to the point. He crystallized what many Germans think but are afraid to say. Like every German, I'm angry at the terms of that awful treaty. Hitler made total sense when he said we have to break down the barriers of class distinction so that the workers and wealthy can link arms to fight for what is right for Germany. How can anyone be against that?"

"And the Jews?"

"He was careful. When he spoke about colored people, he meant those words for Jews, too, I think. I can't see how either group has anything to do with solving Germany's problems. I did hear him say that he wanted our country to be filled with Germans of pure blood. I'm not sure what that meant. For now, I want to see the hooliganism promoted by the likes of that twisted dwarf, Goebbels, stopped."

Chapter 33

1929

While Lilian and the rest of the world flourished, the first three quarters of the new year were the winter of my discontent.

Lilian became "Germany's Sweetheart." She turned out a new film almost every other month; all smash hits. She was constantly on the covers of movie magazines. As her fame grew, so did her income. And she loved spending it. Furs. Jewelry. Automobiles. We moved to a multi-bedroom suite in the Adlon. She began to explore the purchase of a house in *Dahlem*, one of the most affluent addresses in Berlin. When she found one, she decided to keep both residences.

The world at large seemed to prosper as well. Employment in Germany was no longer a major concern. The victorious Allies had eased the pressure of their feet on Germany's neck. In July, they agreed to reduce Germany's war debt—eleven years after our surrender—to *only* twelve billion gold marks. This new plan—the Young Plan—modified the Dawes plan. The staggering sums we had to pay would now stretch over the next *fifty-eight years*. This new "leniency" had Germany paying reparations through 1988—seventy years after the Great War had ended!

Disquietude entered my life. The more Lilian succeeded professionally and financially, the more depressed I became. Lilian never mentioned her wealth. She never said "mine." It was always "our house" or "our car." When we went out—as we did to movie openings, plays, and fashionable parties—I was by her side, dressed to the nines. Lilian made sure to introduce me as her beau, else I would be taken as her bodyguard. But my moment was always brief. People were polite. Once they said, "Hello," I was relegated to their indifference. They all wanted to be with Lilian. Be seen with her. She was important and glamorous. Not only did I not know my true identity, I barely existed as Friedrich Richard when I was by her side.

And then there were the men. Young, slim, handsome, aspiring actors buzzed around her seeking to push their careers or simply to bed her. Wealthy aristocrats and industrialists wanted to take a turn with the beautiful "star." In fairness, she never gave any the time of day. Yet it drove me crazy.

These were my insecurities. No matter how I intellectualized that this had nothing to do with Lilian, I remained disappointed in myself. Strangely, my feelings of inadequacy began to turn into resentment of her.

While Lilian worked throughout 1929 shooting movie after movie, I picked up an occasional scoring job. Rather than be with Lilian as a third wheel, more often than not, I journeyed to Munich in the winter to help at party headquarters. In the summer, I visited Wolf at the Alpine house in the *Obersalzberg*, named Haus Wachenfeld, that he rented from Frau Winter, the deceased industrialist's—Otto Winter's—widow.

When the weather cooperated, Wolf loved to picnic in the woods. We stretched out on blankets with various friends, which always included Geli. During the cold months, there were excursions to restaurants, theater, and the opera in Munich. But, no matter the season, there was the omnipresent Geli Raubal. Wolf was a different man with her. She was his sun. He transformed life into a Copernican world that, unlike his past relationships with women, revolved around her.

Everyone speculated over one question: Were they lovers as well?

*

At the outset of September, double-barreled events were planned for the same weekend: a wedding and Wolf moving into his new apartment at 16 *Prinzregentenplatz*. It was September 2 to be exact. Lilian and I were invited to the Munich marriage of Martin Bormann—a minor party official—to Gerda Buch, the daughter of Chief Party Judge Walter Buch. Hitler, as a "favor" to Buch, was to be a witness at the wedding. Ordinarily, a Buch/Bormann wedding would have gone unnoticed by the party elite. With the *Führer* involved, the wedding became an NSDAP event.

My problem? Lilian refused to go. The night before we were to leave for Munich, I made a last attempt to budge her.

"Can't you bend a little for me?" I asked as we prepared for bed.

"I bent when I heard Herr Hitler at the Sportpalast."

"And I remember how energized you became. How he opened your mind to some of the party's programs."

"Everyone can accept the premise that the terms of the Versailles Treaty are meant to cripple us. But your Goebbels sickens me the way he continues to plaster Bernhard Weiss's picture all over the city, calling him a filthy, Jewish pig."

"Are you forgetting that Weiss arrested Goebbels?"

"You should have cheered when that happened. I did. How can you support a man that slanders the most important policeman in Prussia? Weiss could be Jewish, Slavic, colored, or Buddhist, what's important is that he is a loyal German charged with keeping order. To defame Weiss is to disrespect all Germans. Your Nazi friends need to learn that concept."

"I'm not like that."

"If you were, we wouldn't be together. But I can't be two-faced and show up at the wedding or visit Hitler's new apartment knowing how he underwrites Goebbels's actions."

"Just be at my side. I promise you won't have to talk to anyone. I won't even introduce you."

"You've got it all wrong. Having me stand behind you is not protecting me, Friedrich. It's sad that you have not considered the damage this would do to my career."

"What are you talking about? I love you."

"If you loved me, you would understand that I could never attend a Nazi function again, knowing how they treat Jews. Besides me being personally repulsed, what would my fellow actors say when they found out about it? My career would be damaged forever."

"They'll never know."

"You're delusional. When was the Nazi function that did not allow photographs?"

Lilian snapped off the light ending further talk.

*

The wedding was indeed a Nazi event. As the guest of honor, Hitler rode in the open car next to the chauffer, with the bride— in her snow-white wedding dress—and groom in the back seat. Hitler was in full regalia in his Brown Shirt uniform.

The reception was a who's who of Brown- and Black-shirted glitterati. After the ceremony, Wolf sought me out. "Where's the lovely Lilian? I looked forward to seeing her."

"She sends her regrets but could not break away from her filming schedule."

"I almost had the life of an artist," he sighed. "Tell her I understand and send my best wishes." I said I would but had no intention of adding fuel to her fire. I headed for the bar.

Hans Frank, the party lawyer, swayed side to side as I neared the punch bowl. He started to tip over when I caught him. "You know this is payback for dumping the case? Hitler had no choice but to come to this wedding," he said, slurring his words. I knew he was referring to Maria Reiter and the other girls. I had to shut him up.

I squeezed his elbow harder. "You've had one too many, Hans. I'm getting you some coffee."

He tried to shush me. "Friedrich." I turned from his rotten breath. "You want to know what no one else knows?"

"You need coffee, Hans. And someone to take you home."

"Buch." He giggled. "'Scuse me. Chief Judge Buch."

"What about him?"

"Shh. The moralist prick was ready to slam Adolf."

I glanced about. "Lower your voice, Hans. Be careful what you say here."

"We must be quiet," he whispered. He teetered. I caught him as he pulled a folded paper from his breast pocket. "You're the first person to see this."

It was the summation of Buch's findings on the blackmail letters before he received the sworn affidavits.

I have recently acquired an impression about a number of things and feel it is my difficult duty to tell you, Herr Hitler, that you have contempt for humanity that fills me with grave uneasiness . . .

I looked up. "He was going to censor Hitler because of those letters?"

"Worse. He was going to kick him out of the party until you saved the day with that brilliant solution of letting Geli become engaged to Emil."

"That's been settled, Hans. Why show me this now?"

He looked left and then right before answering. "Because Buch is not to be trusted. Keep an eye on him."

At least this explained why Buch glowered at Wolf for most of the wedding.

*

The following morning I met Wolf at his new apartment. As we threaded our way between the painters and craftsmen, he explained the layout of the rooms. "This is the largest and sunniest room in the apartment."

The space was sumptuous. "This room is five times bigger than your old apartment," I said. "You will be so comfortable in it."

"No. No. No. This is not for me. This will be Geli's room."

Had Lilian been here with me, she would have given me an I-told-you-so look. I could not give him a pass. "Which is Geli's mother's room?"

Wolf replied with indifference. "Angela will remain in the Obersalzberg to take care of *Haus Wachenfeld*." The implication was clear.

"You'll need a staff for an apartment this size."

"I am bringing my landlady from *Thierschstrasse,* Frau Dachs and her daughter, as well as Anni and Georg Winter. They will be sufficient to take proper care of this apartment."

Wolf would not let me leave without showing off his study. As we entered, he pointed to a luxurious new desk and chair, which were from Elsa Bruckmann. Then he extracted a gold watch from his pocket with his initials engraved on the outside. He made a show of flipping open the back. "This is from Elsa, too." Inside was inscribed "To Wolf."

Then Wolf said, "I need your help. Hoffman has taken a series of candid shots of me for publicity. I want your opinion as to which to use."

"I've got a plane to catch."

"It won't take long, Friedrich. I trust your judgment. It would mean a lot to me. Besides, it's on the way to the Airdrome."

When we entered Hoffman's shop at *50 Schellingstrasse*—the studio was in the back—it was impossible to miss the girl balanced high on a ladder, stretching for an item on the top shelf of a bookcase. Her legs were, in a word, spectacular—all the more so because her skirt was impossibly short. The view stopped both of us in our tracks.

There was no need to look at Wolf to know what he was thinking. Wolf turned to Hoffman. "A very attractive girl."

"*Ja, mein Führer.*"

"How old?"

"Seventeen."

Hoffman and I both knew what would come next.

"Heinrich," Hitler said in a soft voice, "please present me as Herr Wolf."

"Of course, *mein Führer.*"

Hoffman beckoned the young lady to descend from the ladder. She was young, slim, athletic, and on the blond side with a pleasant face. The attraction was immediate.

"Eva, this is Herr Wolf. Herr Wolf, I would like to present Fräulein Eva Braun."

Upon my return from Munich, my relationship with Lilian was as icy as the day I left. I tried flowers, her favorite candy, even a piece of fine jewelry—but nothing helped. Our relationship would have plummeted further but for calamitous events that overwhelmed the issues between us.

On October 24, 1929, universally known as Black Thursday, the New York stock market suffered huge losses. The markets steadied the next day only to collapse the following Monday and Tuesday. The losses that became known as Black Monday and Black Tuesday cost the New York stock market forty percent of its value. World markets lost more.

The impact on Germany was devastating. Unemployment doubled and then soon tripled to thirty percent of the work force. Twenty million were forced to feed their families from bread-lines. As economic night fell over Germany, the sun rose on the NSDAP. The political and economic seesaw that led people away from us in prosperity tipped the other way, driving the desperate Germans to us.

During the next two months, our party made significant gains in local elections in two states: Lübeck and Thuringia. Goebbels won a seat on the Berlin city council. By the end of 1929 we had 178,000 dues-paying members. No longer a fringe party of unsuccessful putschists, we were now a political force.

*

While the difficulties of the world minimized the differences between us, politics remained a hot potato when we read the morning papers.

"I see that your boys have finally made the grade." Lilian pointed to a headline. "Thuringia, of all places. Of course, it wasn't in a main state like Prussia or Bavaria. Just the same, your friend Wolf must be delighted to have his first Nazi elected to a cabinet position anywhere in Germany."

"It was a dozen years in the making," I answered. "With one foot in the door in Thuringia, we were invited to join the majority."

"What price did your party extract to form that coalition?"

"I see you are no longer the political neophyte. That was a savvy observation."

"And the answer?"

"We head the ministries of the Interior and Education. As a matter of fact, Wilhelm Frick was appointed minister of both. Remember him?"

"He gave me a creepy feeling when I walked in on the two of you here. And I will always blame him for calling you back to Munich for every crisis. Him aside, why would Hitler have one man heading both ministries?"

"Frick is a party man. He is hellbent to cleanse the government of undesirables. This ensures that Nazi policies would be implemented."

Frick wasted no time. He soon instituted prayer in the schools but was thwarted when the court ruled it unconstitutional. Thankfully, Lilian missed reading about that. Then Frick established himself as the chair of Race Questions and Race Science—*Rassenfragen und Rassenkunde*—at the university. Next he promulgated a racist decree: *Wider die Negerkultur für deutsches Volkstum.* This law was meant to protect the German blood and culture from being tainted by Negroes.

When Lilian did read about these efforts, she hit the ceiling. Calling Frick a beast, she threw down the paper, spilling her morning coffee.

"How can you condone anything this hideous? If it spreads from Thuringia to the other states, Germany will be no better than the United States and the way *they* treat coloreds and Jews."

"Please stop. You're reading too much into this. The idea is to separate the races to prevent intermarriage."

"You're deluding yourself, Friedrich. Many of my actor colleagues are prepared to leave Germany for the United States. One of my friends, Peter Lorre, is most serious about it. He is contracted to make a movie with Fritz Lang called *M*. He said if things get worse, he would leave after that movie was wrapped and in the can."

"Peter Lorre is German through and through. Why would he leave?"

"You're proving my point. Prejudice is blind. It's irrational. It has no place in our society or anywhere else."

"What are you talking about?"

"Peter Lorre is a great actor. His given name is László Löwenstein."

"So he's a Jew. You know I don't care, just like Max is my dearest friend."

"Listen to yourself, Friedrich. In your eyes Peter Lorre is another actor and what he is or believes in doesn't matter . . . until you learn he's a Jew. Now you look at him with a different pair of glasses."

"That's not true. Why do you say things like that?"

"Because the minute I told you his real name, you labeled him. You claim to reject the racist part of Nazi doctrine but accept their other positions. I believe you do accept Jews without prejudice. Yet, at the same time, you want me to understand the rationale for Frick's racist laws. You simply can't have it both ways."

I made one last attempt to explain. "Life is not as simple as you're making it out to be, Lilian. It is not always black or white. There is plenty of grey. It's true that our party is far from perfect, but they are our only chance to restore our greatness. Reality says that bad choices need to be tolerated when good choices outweigh them."

Lilian shot daggers at me. "You, Friedrich Richard, are confused as to what good and bad choices are."

*

As a result of the financial crisis, Hitler seized on the worldwide calamity to transform the puny NSDAP into a major political force. Playing on fears of collapse and offering hope of stability to the German people, he preached the need for a strong dictator. He exhorted workers to break the chains that bound them to low wages. At the same time, he courted the industrialists. He risked internal dissent with the Socialists in his party in order to achieve dictatorial power to confront our domestic economic emergency and weakness in the international community. And it worked! Our strength continued to grow. Soon new elections were upon us. We knew that the party would do well—but were anxious to find out how well.

*

It was still dark when I felt the mattress shift. Lilian crawled out of the bed and tossed on her bathrobe. "Where are you going dressed like that?"

The door clicked open and then slammed shut. We had four papers delivered each day: two German papers, the *London Times*, and the *International Herald Tribune*. By the time I tossed on my robe and washed, she had devoured the pages.

I slipped alongside her to read screaming headlines:

NSDAP Wins 107 Seats

Unbelievably, we were now the second largest party in the Reichstag. Thirty-seven different parties ran candidates for Reichstag seats. A remarkable eighty-two percent of the eligible voters cast their ballots. While the ruling Social Democrats received the most votes, their overall numbers dropped.

I expected Lilian to give one of her patented negative remarks regarding the party, but instead she swiped away a tear with the sleeve of her robe.

*

When the new Reichstag assembled a few weeks later, all 107 Nazi deputies marched into the chambers wearing their brown shirts. At roll call, each stood and called out in his loudest voice, "Present, Heil Hitler!" This brought more recriminations from Lilian.

"Your party bullied everyone their first day in the Reichstag. And what do you say? 'I'm not surprised?' Don't you believe in some sort of proper decorum? In tradition? Politicians ought to exhibit a certain grace among themselves. They are an example for young people."

"How I think they should behave is not the issue. A good number of people voted NSDAP party members into office with a mandate to shake things up. These new delegates are doing just that."

"I can't believe you can toss away manners like a crumpled piece of paper."

"Are you really saying that, Lilian? Why not give the new Reichstag members a chance to make changes?"

I knew Lilian wasn't entirely wrong and that the new Nazi deputies would behave differently than traditional politicians. I also knew that our people were tired of representatives who talked politely and got nothing done. If these rough loudmouth men could save the country, I was for them. But rather than continue to battle with Lilian, I buried my head in the paper.

*

Soon after the election, hundreds of *SA* men roamed the streets, shattering windows of small shop owners, cafés, restaurants, and even those of the upscale department stores . . . all owned by Jews.

As the street violence escalated, the studio sent a car each morning to ensure the safety of "Germany's Sweetheart." I rode with Lilian. Most mornings proved uneventful. One wasn't.

We barely settled in for the ride when I spotted three Brown-Shirted hooligans, with swastikas pasted on their sleeves, harassing a black-garbed Orthodox Jew. The man had grey, wavy hair and appeared to be in his seventies. One Brown Shirt held a dagger to the Jew's belly while another knocked off his yarmulke. When the man bent to pick it up, the brute with the knife yanked the frail man up by his beard and pressed the blade against his throat. The other two convulsed in laughter.

I tapped the driver's shoulder. "Stop the car!"

Lilian cried out. "No, Friedrich. There are three of them. Driver, go on!"

Unsure of what to do, the driver slowed down. I couldn't wait for the car to stop. I flung the door open while still moving, landed on my side, rolled, and pushed up to my feet. The Jew was now on the ground. A Brown Shirt pinned each arm down. The third straddled the helpless man, shouting anti-Semitic gibes and brandishing his *SA*-engraved dagger. He was about to slice off the man's beard when I wrenched him by the collar, spun him around with my left hand, and decked him with a right to the jaw. He went sprawling, no longer a threat. The *SA* man holding the victim's left arm popped up with a raised billy club. He misjudged my reach. I grabbed his hand, billy and all, and twisted it behind his back until something popped in his shoulder. He let out an ear-piercing scream. I pushed him aside and he scrambled away.

The third man snatched the fallen dagger and charged as if it were a bayonet. He was clumsy and leaned forward too far. I deflected his arm with my left hand and came deep and hard with a right to his solar plexus. The man doubled over. While he clawed for air, I grabbed his ears and drove my knee into his chin. Chunks of enamel flew out of his mouth as he tumbled to the ground.

Both men lay on the pavement, neither moving. Lilian shouted from behind me, "That's enough, Friedrich!"

She snatched the victim's yarmulke and knelt beside him. The old man covered his head and rocked in place . . . still stunned by the assault.

The two *SA* men might have been in their early twenties. Maybe a little older. I rifled through their pockets for identification. One lifted his head to protest but stopped when I raised my arm. They had party cards, but their names meant nothing to me. Neither was in condition to go anywhere. I reckoned the third man was still running.

I turned to Lilian. "Is he okay?"

"I can't tell. I'll get a doctor."

The man grabbed Lilian's arm. "Please don't do that. I don't want any more trouble. I'm all right." He nodded toward his assailants. "They're the ones that need help."

The shrill of a police siren pierced the air. Lilian could not be found here when the police arrived. I motioned for our driver, who remained close to the car, to lend a hand to Lilian who hooked her arm around the elderly man. I made certain the thugs remained put.

I called out. "Take this man to wherever he wants to go, and then take Fräulein Harvey back to the Adlon."

Lilian shook her head. "I'm late for the studio."

"Depending on what happens, you may need to get me. The studio will understand. Now please go. *You* can't be found here."

The police arrived moments after Lilian and the old man were on their way. I greeted them and handed the dagger to the first officer. "It belongs to him." I pointed to the brute that had tried to cut the old man's beard. "A third one got away."

The policeman sized up the two on the ground. "Who helped you?"

"What do you mean?"

"Those are tough guys. If the one who got away was anything like them, you must have had help."

I shook my head. "I can handle myself."

While I spoke to the policeman, the officer-in-charge approached the assailants; he appeared familiar with them. The longer they conversed, the more the officer-in-charge tossed hard looks my way. Rather than speak with me next, he conferred with a third policeman who had stayed back.

Then the officer-in-charge walked towards me. "Hold out your hands," he ordered, unhooking handcuffs from his belt. "You're under arrest." The other policeman circled behind me.

I balled up my fists. "You have this all wrong. They attacked an old man. I came to his defense."

He drew his pistol. "I won't say it again. Hold out your hands!"

I did not have to turn around to know there was a pistol pointed at my back. Resistance was futile. I held out my hands. With a twist meant to hurt, the officer-in-charge snapped on the handcuffs. One of them dished out sharp jabs in the back with no let up, prodding me toward the van. I had no chance to explain that this was a mistake. At the same time, the officer-in-charge told the *SA* men that they were free to go. Both smirked as they limped away, but not before giving me a Hitler salute.

As I placed my foot on the first step, I was whacked in the back of the head. I tumbled to the floor of the van. The two policemen locked themselves in with me and began kicking and punching before the van even started toward the station. Every bump heightened the beating. I twisted and turned to lessen the impact of their blows . . . without success. By the time the van stopped, they needed to half-carry me into the stationhouse. Blood poured from my face and scalp. My stomach and back and ribs screamed from the beating. When they removed my handcuffs, I had a shred of satisfaction when I vomited on their shoes before they shoved me into the cell.

"Next time you won't be so lucky," said the fat one.

It hurt to breathe. I crawled to the cell bars and then, hand-over-hand, pulled myself to my feet. I squinted through a swollen eye to read their names.

"Weber and Schneider. We'll be seeing each other again." My face was distorted; the words sounded distant.

They broke out into ear-to-ear grins. "Are you going to report us to your Communist comrades?"

"I don't know what those jerks told you, but you couldn't be more wrong. Consider this your lucky day. I am going to let you live to see your grandchildren."

Schneider, who was in charge, tapped Weber on the shoulder. "Klaus, did you know this was our lucky day?"

Weber glanced from Schneider's shoes to his shoes. "We need to teach this Bolshevik a lesson. Give me the key."

Weber slid the key into the keyhole.

Through my pain I stepped back, ready for them. I grinned, my face a bloody mask. "I was kind to those *SA* men. If you are stupid enough to open the door, get ready to piss red."

Weber saw the hate in my eyes; he tapped Schneider's shoulder. "They are only shoes. He's not worth it. Let the chief take care of him." They left without another word.

*

I struggled to find a position where I was not in pain; it was wishful thinking. I did manage to get a few winks in. I awoke sometime later to the clank of metal. Instead of a menacing police officer, a small man dressed in civilian clothes stood by the cell opening. He had a trimmed moustache and sported gold, wire-rimmed glasses that gave him an owlish, professorial look. His voice was low and soft but wrapped with authority. "Please, follow me."

I shuffled down a cell-lined corridor filled with brawlers and drunks, trailing into his private office. The wall to my left was lined with shelves, floor-to-ceiling, filled with legal statutes plus books on law, philosophy, and Judaism. I grabbed the doorjamb to steady myself only to feel a mezuzah. Max had taught me that this was a "mitzvah," a blessing because it fulfilled the Biblical commandment to "write the words of God on the gates and doorposts of your house."

The man pointed to a chair. "Please." It took some seconds to work my way onto the wooden chair. The bespectacled man winced when I yelped. "Can I offer you anything? Tea? Water?"

"I'd prefer scotch . . . but a cup of coffee would do."

His gaze never left my face. After ordering two coffees, he asked, "Do you know who I am?"

I did. He was Bernhard Weiss, the deputy president of the Berlin Police Force. Weiss was the enemy of the Nazi Party. Joseph Goebbels called him the pejorative, "Isidor," a typically Jewish name. Caricatures of him were posted across the city. As deputy president of the Berlin Police, he sued Goebbels dozens of times for defamation . . . and won every case.

"Should I know you?"

He knew I recognized him but let it go. My Ausweis and identity papers were spread out on his desk. He also had my treasured photograph, the one found in my boot those first days at Charité Hospital

Weiss pointed to the documents. "I don't need these to know who *you* are . . . Herr Friedrich Richard." He leaned back and tented his fingers. His calm manner forced me to lean forward. When I did, lancinating pain seared through me. I gasped; he winced again.

"What I want to know is why one of Hitler's closest friends and most powerful advisors would assault three, low-level *SA* men to save a Jew's beard?"

At that moment, a clerk appeared with coffee. I fussed with the sugar and cream, buying time to formulate an answer. All those years I struggled to stay out of the limelight. Now, in an act of kindness to save a Jew, I was about to be exposed.

I blew to cool the coffee, took a sip, and replaced the cup. "You must have me confused with someone else." I pointed to my papers. "As you can see, there is no party card."

He smacked the desk. "Don't take me for a fool, Herr Richard. Your power in the party is not drawn from some manufactured title or rank, but from your personal relationship with the man your people have styled *Der Führer*. Now, Herr Richard, I ask again, why would a man like you beat up three *SA* men who were practicing what your best friend preaches? Even more curious, if you wanted to stop them, why didn't you just identify yourself and order them to leave the old man alone?"

Pain seized my body; I grabbed the arms of the chair.

I beat them up because I hated them. I beat them up because I hated myself for being a part of them. This was my expiation. I did not identify myself to them because I did not want to identify myself with them. Isn't that obvious, Herr Weiss?

After the pain passed, I said, "Well, Herr Weiss . . ."

"So you do know who I am."

"Most Berliners do. As a matter of fact, Dr. Goebbels speaks about you often."

Weiss smoothed his moustache. "I imagine he would." His eyes sparkled. "Knowing that you cavort with such an avowed anti-Semite makes it all the more difficult to understand why you did what you did."

I started to shrug but the pain stopped me in my tracks. I sucked in air. "If you believe that I acted to save an innocent man from an assault, why was I arrested? Still worse, why did your police beat me and toss me in jail for doing a good deed? I sat for hours in my own vomit and piss, with blood dripping down my face. Is that how you treat law-abiding citizens?"

His thin lips creased into an arc. "Ah, yes. All good questions that save you from answering mine. As it turned out, the officer-in-charge recognized that one of the thugs was the son of a policeman. They said you attacked them and their friend without any provocation. They claimed you shouted Communist slogans. The officers thought their story made sense. How else could you have gotten the jump on them unless you started it?"

"All lies. As my car neared, I saw them attack an old Jew."

"So you said at the time. But when my men arrived on the scene there was no Jew or car. Just you and two *SA* men sprawled on the ground. Once my men heard their story, they had no choice but to arrest you until the facts became clear."

"Even if it was an honest mistake, look at me. Is that what your police do? Beat up prisoners for no reason?" He had no response, or at least, didn't offer one. "Perhaps this was payback for the way Goebbels treats you."

This was getting me nowhere. "How did you learn what really happened?"

"Once I knew who you were, I dispatched men to canvas for witnesses. I had to keep you locked up while they made their inquiries. It took time to establish what people saw and cobble the facts together."

"When you knew the truth you could've sent someone to open the cell door, but you didn't. Keeping me longer served no purpose."

"I'm going to let you go as soon as we finish our little chat. Given the facts, I apologize for the way my men treated you. What you did was admirable. Yet I'm not satisfied as to why you did it. But . . ." he shrugged, "it appears that will not be answered today."

"May I go now?"

"For the record, if you wish to make a complaint, we will launch an investigation into my men's conduct."

That was the last thing I needed. I struggled to my feet. "That won't be necessary. I am sure it was an innocent misunderstanding."

"There's a car outside with a rather well-known, beautiful woman waiting for you. She's been making threats for some hours. I promised you would be out after I asked you a few questions."

"I trust you got the answers you needed."

"Not the ones you avoided."

"It's simple, Herr Weiss. I helped an old man. What more is there?"

"So you said." He slid my identification papers to me. He held back the lone photo. "Is this your family?"

My heart stopped. I managed to give him my stock answer. "A dying soldier shoved it in my hand and asked me to find them. I never knew his name. I've carried it with me ever since. Do you recognize them?"

Weiss studied the faces.

I held my breath.

"For a moment, just a moment . . . I thought the father looked familiar." He looked up. "Families with small children all look the same. In any case, take your things and go."

When I reached the door, he said, "Herr Richard. Perhaps one day we will finish our little talk. There are still questions left unanswered."

I started to tell him that there was little chance we would ever meet again, but there was no need. Instead I shuffled out of his office, holding onto the walls as I went. At the time I didn't notice he had slipped a card with his private number into the envelope with my Ausweis, identity papers, and photograph.

*

Lilian turned wide-eyed when she saw me limp to the car. My lips were swollen, my left eye was partially shut, and crusted blood clung to my skin. She pushed open the door and started to say something. I cut her off. I put my finger to my lips and then pointed toward the driver; we rode in silence.

At home, I eased into a chair while Lilian gathered alcohol, cotton, and gauze. She knelt down and began to clean my wounds. The alcohol stung.

"Take off your shirt."

Dried blood trapped the fabric in so many places there was no point in being delicate. I ripped it open; a spray of buttons clattered to the floor. Lilian helped slip off the sleeves with a ginger-like touch. When she saw the welts and bruises and fresh wounds, she cried.

She disinfected the wounds; I jerked from pain.

I made a clumsy effort to kiss her hands. "I'm sorry."

"For what?"

"Putting you through this."

"Me? You're the one suffering. Was it worth it? Why did you do such a crazy thing?"

"I haven't felt like much of a man lately. I thought by stopping those thugs, you would feel better about me."

"You big fool. I love you the way you are."

"But I don't love myself."

"What are you talking about? We have our issues, but we always get past them."

"It's about day-to-day stuff. Your career. It's skyrocketing while mine is going nowhere. I live off of you. Oh, I know . . ." I shook her off when she wanted to say something, ". . . you've been very good about it. Not demanding anything. Not making me feel dependent. But that doesn't make me feel any better. I could come to grips with all this, but your contempt of the party stops me." Her beautiful lips parted but I continued before she could say anything. "Many of your criticisms are right. I know that. But in my heart, I believe that Germany's future lies with the NSDAP."

Lilian shook her head. "You big dummy. The Nazis, the money, none of this is important right now. What I do know . . ." she straddled my lap with great care and cradled my head in her hands with a feather touch, ". . . is that the last thing you need to do is prove your manhood to me. What I do know is that I love you." I tried to say something, but she brushed her lips against mine. "Friedrich. Look at my face. Then, close your eyes and picture me."

I closed my eyes. "Can you picture my face?"

"Of course I can."

"Picture the way I look on screen." I could. "Now imagine me twenty years from now. Then twenty-five. Then thirty. The shape is different. The eyelids droop. The neck sags. I will not be this pretty face in the years to come."

"You'll always be the most beautiful to me."

"You're sweet, but unrealistic. Try harder, Friedrich. Twenty-five years from now I will be in my mid-fifties. Ancient when it comes to actresses. My skin will have blotches. Furrows in my forehead. Wrinkles spreading from my eyes. It's going to happen."

I pictured older actresses I had worked with, and then tried to imagine what they looked like when they were Lilian's age now. I couldn't.

"What I want you to understand, my darling," she continued, "is that no matter how old I will be, I will expect you to love me and need me and want me just as you do now. That's the kind of man I need you to be. That's the kind of man that I know you are."

I blinked until I could focus on the most beautiful woman in the world.

She eased off my legs. "Now take me to bed if you feel up to it. If you're in too much pain, I'll hold you until you fall asleep."

Chapter 35

As 1930 drew to a close, peace descended upon our home life while disparate elements threatened to rip the NSDAP apart. Socialists, like the Strasser brothers and Wilhelm Frick, clung to the original party doctrine against capitalists and industrialists, resisting Hitler's open efforts to court the moneyed classes. At a party conference in Berlin that May, Wolf boldly proclaimed that we wanted people like the Thyssens in our movement. He used a Darwinian analogy: "The capitalists have worked their way to the top . . . which proves they are the higher race." But many of the old guard remained recalcitrant.

"What about the Krupps?" Gregor Strasser demanded that their factories, along with those of the other industrialists, be nationalized once the NSDAP came into power.

"Do you think I should be so mad as to destroy Germany's economy?" Hitler was adamant. "Of course, I will leave them alone."

As the final weeks of 1930 ticked down, funds poured in, and the party membership swelled. Armed with Reichsmarks, we won elections. Six-and-a-half million Germans voted for us! From a seedling party of seven men in a tavern in those first days in 1919, we grew into the second largest party in the Reichstag while winning local elections throughout the country. But as our power and influence increased, so did the rift within the party.

I took to attending Reichstag sessions. On one occasion I sat in the gallery next to Hermann Göring's wife, who glowed with pride. As she nudged me with her elbow, she said, "Look at him. Doesn't Hermann look splendid?"

"Indeed he does, Carin." I wanted to add that the rotund Göring would look better if there was less of him, but I held my peace.

The curiosity that made me a spectator turned into shock as Göring shepherded a bill presented by our party's Socialists—Gregor Strasser and Wilhelm Frick—to cap the interest payments that banks could charge for loans. This bill was meant to cripple the bankers. If that weren't bad enough, our men also offered a law that called for "the entire property of the banks and stock exchange to be expropriated without compensation." The Communist delegates would certainly vote in favor. Perhaps other parties would join them.

I could not credit what was unfolding. The Socialist faction of the NSDAP was on the cusp of achieving their goal to redistribute the country's wealth. I bolted from the gallery, sailing down the steps two-at-a-time, barged into an office, and telephoned Wolf. Lucky for all of us, he answered on the first ring.

"They did what!" He made me repeat what was in progress on the Reichstag floor. "Are they out of their minds? They will ruin everything. Go back. Tell Frick, Göring, and Hess to withdraw the bill *immediately*. There is not a second to waste."

I raced back to the gallery and sent a runner with a note down to Wilhelm Frick on the chamber floor. Frick searched the gallery and when our eyes locked he gave a knowing nod. Thirty minutes later, the Nazi delegates pulled the proposed bill that would have alienated every industrialist Wolf and I had successfully courted.

Pulling the bill created a cascade of events that were as comical as they were prescient. Thinking this was an opportunity to embarrass us, the seventy-seven Communist delegates reintroduced the same bill as their own . . . without altering a single word from the bill we had just rescinded. When *their* bill came to a vote, they laughed as our delegates—*all* of whom previously voted for the bill—unanimously voted against it.

While our party may have been embarrassed, this episode heightened the internal conflicts between the left-leaning socialists of our party—headed by Strasser—versus the rest of us. These differences would recur again and again . . . until there came a final reckoning.

December 5, 1930

"Everyone has been talking about this movie," Lilian said as we dressed for the German premier of *All Quiet on the Western Front*.

"Doesn't it depict German soldiers as cowards who shit in their pants? There is no way I am going to like it."

"That's not the point of the movie," she answered. "It shows how the horrors of war affect young boys. How the insanity of killing other human beings traumatizes them."

"They're killing the enemy."

Lilian stopped applying her makeup and wheeled around from the mirror. "Is that what you believe? That it is fine to kill another human being as long as they are the enemy? None of the soldiers on the ground—you were one of them—made the decision to declare war and fight the French or British. Old farts in smoke-filled rooms, drinking cognac, made that decision for you. They started a war for no reason at all."

I had learned that when Lilian got this way, there was no point in continuing. I looked at my watch. "You don't want to be late, do you?"

"We're not finished talking about the movie. Once you see it, you will change your tune." She applied her trademark red lipstick. "I want to look my best. Besides, these premiers never start on time."

Our car dropped us off at the *Mozartsaal* Cinema just as they were about to close the doors. We were ushered to seats saved for special guests.

The movie opened with a mailman delivering his last letters before reporting for his first day in the army. The scene switched to a teacher exhorting his students to join the army. I marveled at the lighting, the camera angles, and the viewpoint that the American director used to guide the audience through the scenes. Technically, this was one of the best movies I had ever seen.

In short order, it became apparent that joining the army and preparing for war dispelled the recruits—classmates we followed throughout the movie—of any notion that war was grand. We saw how scared they became, their bodies shaking from the terror of it all. We saw the wanton loss of life, soldiers maimed, and watched them cry and shake from fear.

Lilian squeezed my hand. "Is this what you went through?"

How could I answer her? I must have . . . but I didn't remember. Just then, three rows in front of us, Joseph Goebbels jumped up as the lights flashed on. He caught my eye as he ran up the aisle and pointed toward the exit, signaling me to leave. I grabbed Lilian's arm, tugged her out of her seat, and hustled up the aisle. As we neared the door, one hundred and fifty *SA* men poured into the theater wearing gas masks. They exploded stink bombs, set caged white mice free, and threw sneezing powder at the patrons. The sulfurous stench was wretched. By the time we reached the street, we were gagging.

As we held each other coughing, a nearby legion of Brownshirts fell into formation with Goebbels in the lead. They set off to march through the Berlin streets protesting this movie as anti-German. Goebbels shouted, *"Juden Schmutzfilm."* This shocked me. By no stretch of the imagination was *All Quiet on the Western Front* a Jewish smear film.

"Did that just happen?" The last of the marchers passed from view; we were coughing less and less.

I sniffed her dress and then my sleeve. "Without a doubt."

"Nothing about this is funny. Censoring the arts is serious. Sabotaging a premier is so absurd it leaves me speechless. You're one of us now. You should be indignant at what just happened."

"I am also a proud German. That movie may be well-crafted, but it showed us in a bad light."

"Then you didn't understand its meaning. It's not an anti-German film . . . it's an anti-war movie. The message is clear: war is bad for all sides."

Lilian was still angry when we flagged down a cab. The driver crinkled his face and pinched his nose at our smell; it broke the ice. We laughed and apologized to him. I gave him extra money for not throwing us out of his car. The moment we entered the house, Lilian ripped off her dress. "Start the fire. I am burning this."

"Why ruin a perfectly good dress? It can be cleaned."

"I will always associate this dress with what happened today. I will never wear it again. I suggest you do the same to your tuxedo."

I lit the fire. When the flames took hold, I tossed the clothes, one-by-one, onto the burning logs. We watched the smoke curl up the chimney as licks of fire turned the fabrics into twists of black shards.

With bathrobes on, Lilian grabbed my hand and led me to the couch. "Friedrich, time and again, the Nazis prove that they are nothing but hoodlums and thugs. I can't excuse you being part of them any longer. If you care for me, you must quit the party."

I pulled my hand from hers. "You can't be serious."

Her eyes narrowed. "I've never been more serious."

Lilian aside, I had asked myself the same question many times over the years. I always came up with two answers. The first never wavered: my colleagues were the only hope to create a government able to survive in a world intent on devouring us. I was too afraid to admit the second reason to anyone, including myself: I had nothing else to belong to in life. No other friends. No family. No memory. Lilian did not know any of this.

I always knew that I would have to deal with this someday. Now that it was here, my resolve almost deserted me. "Lilian, there's something I have to tell you. You've seen my scars. You know that I was wounded during the war."

She touched my arm. "I've gotten used to them. In a way, I find them sexy."

"I'm thankful for that. But I have other scars that are not obvious. Those scars have never healed."

"I don't understand."

"When the mortar went off that shredded me to pieces, it also caused me to lose my memory. Friedrich is not my real name."

"What are you talking about? If Friedrich is not your name, what is it?"

"I have no idea. I woke up in Charité Hospital in July of 1918 with no memory. I've spent twelve painful years not knowing who I am."

"But . . . but you told me on the boat—when we first met—you told me all about your family."

"I made it up. All of it."

She jumped up, paced a few steps, then asked, "Has anything you told me been the truth?"

"Everything that has happened since then has been the truth. You and I, we're true. I love you."

A torrent of tears streamed down Lilian's face. "Why, Friedrich? Why did you have to lie about your past? It happened during the war. I would've understood."

"All I know is that the moment I met you on the *Ballin*, I fell in love with the most wonderful woman in the world. I was terrified to tell you I didn't know who I was. Think of how it would have sounded. I was afraid you would think me a lunatic. I couldn't risk that, not then."

"How can I ever trust you again?" she said, dabbing her tears.

"I've never lied to you about anything that touched our lives. I only filled in the blanks before we met. I am the same Friedrich—or whatever my name is—that you fell in love with. That you have lived with. Nothing in our lives has changed."

"Omission is a lie. Making up a story about a fake family, is a lie. I've learned that when it comes to men, once a liar, always a liar."

What could I say to make her understand that my love for her was genuine? That I never lied about "us"?

"Lilian. I have no memory of the shell that blew me to pieces. All I know is that I woke up in Charité Hospital. My face was disfigured. I had too many broken bones to count and burns over large areas. I had surgery-after-surgery to put me back together. But nothing they tried brought my memory back. Lilian, can't you understand . . . I didn't know how to tell you all this when we first met? Any choice I made would have been wrong."

"You are right about that. But even if I give you a pass for being a jerk, how do you explain your irrational attachment to the Nazis?"

"I'm coming to that. Dr. Joseph was my surgeon at Charité."

"Everyone knows him. He's world famous."

"It was my good luck to end up in his clinic. He gave me the name Patient X. I even got used to being called that but this troubled him. He said I needed to find my identity, so he sent me to another hospital near the Polish border."

"I still don't see . . ."

"You will in a moment. The fellow in the next bed became my friend: Wolf. For a month, that's the only name I knew him by. Wolf had been blinded in a gas attack. I fed him. Took him to the bathroom. When he walked the floors at night, I walked with him. I was his eyes until he recovered. That is why there's such a special bond between us. On the day we parted, I learned his real name: Adolf Hitler. After I left Berlin, I fell in with him and his fledgling party. They were the only family I had . . . and still have, until I met you."

Lilian collapsed onto the sofa. I sat still as she struggled to process all that I just told her. After a few beats, I took her hand.

"I can't begin to grasp all of this." Her eyes softened and her lips creased upwards. "Now your name sounds awkward. You are a sweet, gentle man, even if you are a big bruiser. It could not have been easy to tell me what happened to you. Thank you for that. It also helps me understand the bond that exists between you and Hitler . . . to the point of being dependent on each other. I haven't been fair judging you without knowing your whole story. But understand this, Friedrich Richard, if things get much worse, there may come a time when you will have to choose between Wolf and the rest of us. Me, included."

1930

The Christmas holidays were upon us. When I opened the door after work, I found Lilian spread out on the sofa. She moaned, "I am tired of all the tumult in the streets. Tired of looking over my shoulder and in every alley. Tomorrow is Saturday. We're going to Solothurn. I haven't been there since I was a little girl. I've made all the arrangements. I won't take no for an answer."

During the war, Lilian lived with an aunt in Solothurn, an idyllic canton near Basil, in northwest Switzerland. The town was pitched on the banks of the Aare River and was minutes from the foot of the Jura Mountains.

"I wish you had discussed this with me before making plans. I'm in the middle of a project that, as is, I don't think I can make the deadline."

Lilian tugged me to the couch. "Deadlines are meant to be broken. You'll love Solothurn. The town square comes straight out of a fairy tale. There are cobblestones and a beautiful tower clock that chimes every hour. Christmas is the best time to be there. That's when dozens of vendors line the square with their stalls. They sell all sorts of wonderful things for the holidays. We can ski. Snowshoe. Take horse-drawn sleigh rides. We both need to get out of here."

As appealing as it sounded, I didn't see how I could spare the time.

"Wait until you see the view from the top of Weissenstein Pass. The Central Plateau stretches out like a magical carpet, punctuated by the peaks from Säntis to Mont Blanc. It's breathtaking."

Her glee convinced me. We hadn't taken a holiday in three years. I took her hand. "Now that I've had a moment to digest the surprise, I'm glad you thought of this. It will give us time to make new memories." Then I looked away.

"What's the matter? Is there a *But*?"

I hated to ruin the moment. "I was going to tell you. I need to make a side trip to Munich."

Her face hardened as she withdrew her hand. "If it has to do with party business, put it out of your mind. This trip is important for us."

"Give me a chance to explain. No one's called or asked that I go there. This is about what's going on in the streets; no one is safe anymore. How many times have you told me that you look every which way even to only walk a block?"

"It will be a wasted effort. The government has failed to stop the violence. What can *you* do about it?"

"I can speak to Wolf. Make him understand that the chaos the *SA* men are causing is harming the party."

"He has the power to stop it. Why hasn't he?"

"He did try. He was preoccupied with building the party base, but did give orders that weren't followed."

"What's different now?"

"We've become a major force in the Reichstag. We have to put an end to people being afraid."

"Will Hitler listen to you?"

"He has no choice."

"And what am I supposed to do while you take your side trip?"

"Munich is not that far out of the way. We can travel there together and then you go on to Switzerland. Or you can go to straight to Solothurn. Either way, it's a half day out of our vacation, and time well spent."

"Only if it works."

"I know it will work." I said it with a great deal more confidence than I felt.

*

We traveled together from Berlin and kissed goodbye at the Munich Central Station. I trotted alongside her window for a number of steps as the train pulled away. I threw a kiss, waved, and then headed for the new party headquarters, aptly named the *Braunes Haus*—The Brown House—in tribute to the, then, one million Brown-Shirted *SA* men. When the party purchased the building, it was known as the Palais Barlow. Wolf's favorite architect, Paul Troost, remodeled it into our new headquarters. Given his penchant for architecture, Wolf "supervised" the renovation with a heavy hand, using funds provided by Fritz Thyssen. It would officially open in two weeks' time, just after the first of the year.

I wove through the streets until I stood in front of *45 Brienner Strasse*. The building's sheer size gave me a pang of pride. From a start in a tavern basement, we had come very far in eleven years. The arc of our journey increased my determination to confront Wolf about containing the riff-raff within our ranks.

An enormous portrait of the *Führer* dominated the spacious receiving room. Under it read: "*Nothing happens in this movement, except what I wish.*" Flanking the staircase was a display of flags that included the famous *Blutfahne*—the blood flag. I passed offices reserved for Hans Frank, Heinrich Himmler, Hess, Göring, and a lavish one for Goebbels.

Wolf greeted me in his spacious office, standing in front of a life-sized portrait of Henry Ford. Seeing it sent me back to the talk I had on the *SS Ballin* with that car salesman who exulted in Ford's anti-Semitism.

Taking his hand, I said, "This *Braunes Haus* is magnificent. It befits our party."

Wolf, ever the frustrated architect, replied with childlike pleasure. "I helped Troost with some of the changes, you know."

"Adolf." I only used his name when there was something serious. "I think we better sit down."

We faced each other in deep armchairs. I had practiced what I was going to say. "Berlin is in chaos. People are afraid. Gangs of *SA* roam the streets." He remained a blank slate. I continued. "Even if the Reds do it and we get blamed. If the party is to succeed, you must stop this anarchy."

I braced myself for the explosion that would surely follow.

"I could not agree more. It has to stop."

"I didn't expect this. I thought you would give me a hard time. Dismiss me out of hand."

"*Friedrichshen*, how could you underestimate me like this? You, above all others, should know better." He leaned forward and lowered his voice. "I have a plan."

"For what?"

"Shhh. Not so loud. There are workmen and cleaning people all around getting the *Braunes Haus* ready for the opening. No one knows what I am about to tell you. Not even Goebbels." I leaned closer. "We thought we learned from Kapp's mistakes, but we made new ones. I've come to realize no party can come to power by violence in the streets. Democracy is Germany's number one enemy . . . but we must end it by democratic means . . . not fighting in the streets."

"Then what are you proposing?"

"Now that we have most industrialists behind us, we can concentrate on winning at the ballot box. To accomplish this, we need to keep the Socialist fringe in our party in line."

"What about Goebbels? No matter what we've asked him to do, he does what he pleases."

"Not anymore. He's come over to our way of thinking."

"There is still the matter of President Hindenburg. Everyone expects him to retire once his term of office ends."

"Don't discount the old field marshal, Friedrich. Hindenburg may only have fourteen months left, but there is a movement afoot to avoid an election by extending his term."

"That will take a constitutional amendment."

"Something our party will never endorse. Without our votes, they lack the two-thirds needed to amend the constitution. This will force the scheduled election. *That's* when I will declare for the presidency."

"I thought your aim was to be Reich chancellor."

"My goal *is* to be chancellor. While I don't expect to win enough votes to unseat Hindenburg, I do expect our party to win enough seats in the Reichstag for a ruling majority. When that happens, I will be chancellor!"

"Hindenburg is no fan of yours. He will never let that happen."

"What he thinks of me will not matter once we have a majority in the Reichstag. Then the law will be on our side and they cannot stop me from becoming chancellor!"

"So your plan is to run for president to become chancellor? Is that it?"

"Exactly."

"Aren't you forgetting a detail?"

He flicked the air. "That's a technicality that will disappear by the elections. By then I will be a German citizen."

"And the *SA* street gangs?"

"I make this promise to you: 1931 will see the end of the *SA* street violence."

"The *SA* men don't listen to anyone." I swallowed before I added, "And what will make them change?"

"For that very reason, I have summoned Ernest Röhm back from Bolivia. While I remain commander-in-chief, he will take command of the *SA* as chief of staff after New Year's Day. Once he brings them to heel, there will be nothing negative to write about us as the elections near."

"Röhm left because we were too conservative for his taste. Are you sure he's the right man for this?"

Wolf grinned. "For years Ernst has been stuck in Bolivia as their military advisor. He will jump for joy to be back with his people."

"The *SA* has run the roost since he left Germany. Röhm will meet resistance."

"For that reason, I have charged Himmler to enlarge the *SS* and establish a Reich security office to not only police the *SA*, but also *all* party members. Himmler has my blessing to use any force necessary to achieve our goals."

Wolf strode to his desk. He rarely said good-bye, so I rose to leave.

"Not so fast, Friedrich. I have something for you." He pressed a card into my hand. "This is an *SS* card. It identifies you as *SS Obergruppenführer* Richard."

"Lieutenant general? Naturally I'm honored . . . but I've been functioning quite well without a formal title. Is this necessary?"

"There will be rapid changes from here on in. It is good to be prepared for any eventuality." Then Wolf arched his brows. "What if, perchance, you should encounter three *SA* men cutting off someone's beard? This card would be of enormous benefit to you then."

My jaw dropped. At that moment I promised myself never to underestimate Adolf Hitler.

He milked the moment. "Don't be surprised, Friedrich. Very little escapes me." Then he added, "Have a photo taken and paste it in the corner. One day you will thank me for giving you this card."

*

I took the train to Solothurn and found Lilian in the hotel lobby, sipping champagne by a roaring fire.

"Was it a success?"

"He could not have been more understanding. By the time we return to Berlin, the street fighting will be under wraps."

"Good for you. You've just reached your quota for political discourse on this vacation. From this moment on, it's only about you and me." She hugged me tight.

*

Our Christmas/New Year's vacation in Switzerland gave us time to smooth over rough spots. Lilian and I grew closer than we had been in months. We laughed and drank and made lots of love. Both the winter weather and the isolation played their parts in helping us achieve serenity. But it was short-lived.

On a snowy day, as we walked into the hotel from a sleigh ride in the countryside, we were greeted by a photographer and reporter from the local paper.

"Fräulein Harvey, may we take a photo of you next to the fire? Our readers love your movies. The headline will read: Local Girl Becomes Famous Star."

Lilian ripped off her mink hat. "If you give me time to fix myself." Minutes later, she grabbed my hand. We moved, arm-in-arm, next to the blazing fire.

The photographer waved me away. "Excuse me, fräulein. We meant only for you to be in the picture."

Lilian started to protest. "It's all right. You are the important one." I stepped to the side. Watching them stage the shoot, I chastised myself for almost breaking my own rule of avoiding being photographed with Lilian, in the same way I tried to stay wide of the camera's lens when near Wolf.

That night we dined at the hotel, the episode with the photographer reduced to an inconsequential event. We were talking about her current project when the lights dimmed. The seconds ticked down to ring in the New Year.

"Make me a promise," said Lilian, as we danced among the other guests, trying to ignore their admiring glances of their local girl-made-good.

"If it is in my power."

"Promise that no matter what your Wolf asks you to do, no matter how troubled the days become, you will always follow your heart."

"Does that mean that your heart will always be available to me if I do?"

"As long as you honor your promise to follow yours."

Three . . . two . . . one.

Horns blared.

The pop of champagne corks ushered in a New Year that would prove to be a turning point for those I cared most about: Lilian Harvey, Wolf, and the Fatherland.

Chapter 36

1931

When the telephone rang on Sunday morning, January 4, I was reading the paper . . . alone. Lilian was at the studio for a weekend shoot.

It was Wolf.

"*Friedrichshen.*" When he called me that, the hairs on the back of my neck tingled; it meant he wanted me to do something unpleasant. "Röhm is back in Berlin. Set up a meeting with him and Goebbels today . . . before Röhm is formally appointed *SA* chief of staff."

"To what end?"

"Röhm knows you represent me. He has his orders to reestablish control of the SA so there won't be any trouble there. But Goebbels! He's obsessed with action and violence. I don't trust him. We cannot have Joseph sabotage Röhm's efforts. Make Goebbels understand that disobeying me will have consequences."

After the attack on *All Quiet*, I detested being in the same room with Goebbels. But I agreed. The saving grace was that Lilian would be at the studio for the entire day which left me free to accomplish Wolf's request.

Minutes later, I called Goebbels. "Do you know where Röhm is?"

"I have a good idea," he answered.

"Then get him. We meet in two hours."

*

The two men waited in a small café. *SA* men were posted near the front door.

I joined them at the back table and said to Röhm, "You look like shit."

"I should after the night I spent. Why am I up so early?" he asked.

"The *Führer* will announce you as the new *SA* chief of staff tomorrow."

"Tell me something I don't know."

"He wants you to outline how you will organize the *SA* and what plans you have to control them."

"Is that necessary, Friedrich? How many years do we know each other? You know what I'm capable of. Tell him not to worry."

Time had not softened Röhm. He was ruthless when I served under him in the *Freikorps* and I had full confidence he would do Wolf's bidding to get the *SA* under control.

I turned to Goebbels. "*Der Führer* needs you to be fully on board and help Ernst accomplish his mission."

"We assault mainly Jews," Goebbels answered. "They should be of no concern to anybody."

"For the time being, they are a concern to Hitler and the party. Consider them Germans."

Goebbels spat on the floor. "Jews are not Germans."

I leaned toward Röhm. "This is the very attitude the *Führer* needs you to control. How will you do it?"

"I think better after I eat," Röhm answered.

"That's not an option. Tell me what you propose."

"My plan is simple," Röhm spoke without lifting his eyes from the menu. "As it is now structured, the Brownshirts are answerable to the Gau leaders in each state. That needs to be changed. I will restructure the *SA* into groups whose leaders are answerable only to me. Then, when I say stop the street violence, it will stop. Simple and direct." He looked from me to Goebbels.

It really didn't matter what Röhm said. Wolf and I knew he would whip the *SA* into a unified force that obeyed orders from the higher-ups. Order would be restored.

"As Ernst gains control of the *SA* men, Joseph, do nothing that might incite the troops. Can I be any clearer?"

"Doesn't the Boss trust me?"

Every fiber in my body longed to answer with the blunt truth. "Let me be clear: The Boss does not want you to give Bernhard Weiss any more reasons to interrupt a speech, close down a rally, arrest you, or have cause to sue for defamation. Any one of those reflects poorly on the party at a time we need to be on our best behavior."

Goebbels used a file to clean under his fingernails. "I only speak the truth about that Isidor."

"The truth has nothing to do with this. Quiet in the streets is paramount if we are to win elections." I sat taller, towering over him, "What do you want me to tell *der Führer*?"

He laid down the file. "That Goebbels is a good soldier."

I'd said what I had come to say. Time would tell soon enough if either man could curtail any public display that would tarnish Hitler or the party. I pushed back from the table leaving Röhm to slobber over the menu and Goebbels to fume as he failed to light his cigarette with a trembling hand. I had all to do to round the corner out of their sight before I gagged from the taste of the bile that filled my throat. Those two epitomized vile.

*

Röhm did implement changes. SA violence did abate—but not to the complete cessation that Hitler demanded. No single button existed that could control a one-million-man mob accustomed to having its way in the streets.

The *SA* leadership balked at the limitations Röhm imposed. Hitler was compelled to issue a simple order: "I understand your distress and rage, but you must not bear arms." For a time, they listened. Then they didn't.

Goebbels, on the other hand, was recalcitrant. He continued to foment trouble through his newspaper.

"You said you were a good soldier, Joseph. You are anything but." I said when I was forced to pay him another visit. "I'm here to tell you that you are on a short leash. Röhm can't do his job if you continue to encourage the *SA* men to street violence. The party message is simple: win elections through legal means, not by breaking heads."

"The Boss needs to understand that change takes time."

"Time is what you don't have, Joseph. *You* change or suffer the consequences."

Goebbels hoisted an imaginary glass in a toast. "In that case, long live legality. Death to violence," he snarled, pretending to take a sip. "Makes me want to vomit!"

"Vomit all you want, as long as you get in line."

*

While Hitler's threat reined in Goebbels, and Röhm did his best to change the course of hundreds of thousands of Brownshirts, street violence continued. Leaders were replaced and, still, order eluded us.

Wolf and I dissected the underlying problem with the *SA*: renegades had infiltrated their ranks and needed to be weeded out. If we failed to do this, then everything we had been working toward was in jeopardy. We met to find a solution.

"The reality of dealing with the *SA* is two-fold," Wolf said. "If we dismiss them out of hand, they will revert into bands of *Freikorps* that will continue to run wild. That accomplishes nothing. The second issue is that we still need the *SA* at large rallies. Our mistake was to take everyone into the *SA* who wanted to join. We must be more selective going forward."

"You're asking the near-impossible. Thousands join the *SA* each month."

"Friedrich, nothing is impossible. It is a matter of will. We need a system that filters out undesirables. I've asked Himmler to create a counter-intelligence service within the *SS*. It will be their job to keep track of the *SA* and any party member who refuses to comply with our rules."

"How can I help?"

"Himmler is set to interview a man Karl von Eberstein recommended to lead this effort. Meet Eberstein and his candidate at the Central Station in Munich. They will drive you to Himmler's farm. I want a full report when you're done."

"Why can't this be done in Berlin?"

"Himmler has the flu and his wife won't let him travel."

Having met Himmler's wife before, there was no need to say more.

"By the way, what's this fellow's name?"

"Reinhard Heydrich."

*

My plane landed and I made my way to the Central Station with time to spare. I found a quiet table and waited. I knew Eberstein. A member of the aristocracy, he joined Himmler's *SS* two years earlier, and held the rank of SS-*Sturmbannführer*—major.

Eberstein was easy to spot; he made a show of rank and wealth by standing ramrod-straight in his uniform next to a new, royal blue Duesenberg J Torpedo convertible. I remained seated, watching, as a tall, blond-haired man with angular features marched up to Eberstein. They greeted each other warmly.

I gave them a few more moments to catch up before I approached. I raised my arm. "Heil Hitler."

"Friedrich! It is good to see you. Allow me to introduce First Lieutenant Reinhard Heydrich."

Taller than most, Heydrich was still a tad shorter and leaner than me.

"Ex-lieutenant," corrected Heydrich. "It is an honor to meet you, Herr Richard."

"*Obergruppenführer*. You'll learn our ranks in short order." I was not there to babysit.

As we sped to Himmler's farm, Heydrich was not bashful boasting that he had been a champion sailor—winner of many regattas—an expert fencer, and an accomplished violinist. While Eberstein gushed over his prodigy's accomplishments, I could find no reason to like the man.

I was more interested in him being an "ex-lieutenant." "Now that you are out of the navy, are you on the reserve rolls?"

Heydrich shifted positions and looked away. "I'd rather not talk about it."

I cared not a whit that this made him uncomfortable. I needed an answer for my report. "That's not an option, ex-Lieutenant Heydrich. I'm here by order of the *Führer*. He needs to know every answer to every question before a decision is made."

His face reddened. "It had to do with a woman. In fact, two."

"It always does," Eberstein said in an attempt to lighten the mood.

"It's not that complicated. I met Lina von Osteen during Christmas holiday last year," Heydrich explained. "We fell in love that first night; I asked her to marry me three days later."

"I know the family," added Eberstein. "They are descended from Danish nobility."

Heydrich picked up the thread. "That didn't insulate them from the stock market crash. They fell on hard times, as did my family."

"I understand love. It's wonderful when it happens," I said. "But that story has nothing to do with the navy releasing you."

"I needed to explain about Lina first. After she accepted my proposal, we sent out engagement announcements. That's when my problems started," explained Heydrich. "You see I had dated a young woman in Berlin and in Kiel before Lina. Because we slept together on a consistent basis, she thought we were engaged. I gave her no reason to think it, but her father, who is a senior officer in the Navy, thought me dishonorable. He convinced my commander, Admiral Raeder, to bring charges of conduct unbecoming an officer against me."

"They should have dismissed the charge out of hand," said Eberstein. "What happened was highly unusual."

I tried to make sense of this. "Why would your personal life impact the sort of officer you were?"

"I can assure you it does not. Whatever the reason, Raeder saw fit to dismiss me. So here I am."

At that point we arrived at the Himmler farm. The day was warm. Even so, Himmler had a blanket wrapped around him. He had a glazed look and watery eyes behind his pince-nez.

After Eberstein introduced Heydrich, Himmler nodded at me. "Good to see you, again, Friedrich. How is Berlin these days?"

"Frenetic."

Not interested or feeling well enough to make small talk, Himmler turned to Heydrich. "What do you know about the SS?"

"I must admit, very little."

"Maybe that's a good thing. Let me start by giving you my vision. SS members are the elite of the party." He nodded toward Eberstein. "Sorry to say this, Karl, I intend to make the SS Germany's new aristocracy."

"I would expect nothing less."

"The SS man will be everything rolled into one: a soldier, an administrator, an academic, and a leader. But together we will be more than that. We will be the twentieth century version of Teutonic Knights."

This was shades of the Thule Society. Himmler could have qualified as a charter member . . . except he came along too late. My mind wandered to when we first created the SS. Wolf held SS card #1. I would have been #2 but turned it down to keep my name off the roster. Emil Maurice took my place. Now, ten years later, Emil was out of the party and this chicken farmer with card #168 was in charge of the SS.

Heydrich had listened patiently. "That is all well and good, Herr Himmler, but what role do you envision for me?"

Himmler held up his hand. "You come highly recommended, so let me explain. At present, the SS is a select corps of men within the larger SA headed by Ernst Röhm. The trouble is that the SA gains more than one hundred thousand new recruits each month, yet little has been done to weed out spies and agent provocateurs. This problem has magnified as the SA has grown into millions of members. I want you to organize an internal intelligence service that will ensure that only the finest young men are admitted into the SA and the SS. Part of your job will include removing any undesirables from our troops. Can you do it?"

Heydrich, who remained standing the entire meeting, clicked his heels. "Without question."

"I need more than your enthusiasm and confidence, I need to know you can do the job before I recommend you to the *Führer*," said Himmler. "I want you to write an organizational plan for an *SS* intelligence agency. Let's see what you come up with in, say, twenty minutes. Will that be a problem, Lieutenant Heydrich?"

"Not at all." Without hesitation Heydrich took pencil and paper and went into another room. He returned twenty minutes later . . . to the second. Heydrich remained at attention as Himmler read Heydrich's plan. When Himmler finished, he took off his rimless glasses, cleaned the lenses with his scarf, and said, "This is quite good."

"Friedrich?" Himmler passed it to me. I read it: it was better than quite good. I passed it back to Himmler without comment.

"Herr Heydrich," Himmler began, "you have impressed me with your clear and organized thinking. Few men could have accomplished this in such a short time."

"Does that mean you will recommend me?"

Himmler glanced at me for a final approval.

Much to Heydrich's consternation, I did not immediately agree. I did not like the man. But I could think of no reason to object. Yet I waited before answering. Himmler's wheezing pierced the air; Heydrich's breathing grew shallow. As the tension grew taut, I finally nodded. With my assent, Himmler turned to Heydrich, "Yes, I will recommend you."

When I said my goodbyes at the airport, they were the first words spoken since we had left Himmler's farm. I headed for the terminal, feeling their eyes on my back every step of the way. Before my plane took off, I found a private office with a phone I could use.

"What is your assessment?" Wolf asked.

"He is strong-willed. Self-assured. Cocky."

"Did Himmler approve of him?"

There was no doubt he and Himmler had already spoken. "Heinrich thought Heydrich would be capable of any task given to him. He is inclined to use him."

"That's what he told me. Then you approve, too?"

"I don't like him, but . . . yes, I approve. In the end, I expect he will prove quite resourceful." And with that, Reinhard Heydrich was put in charge of what would become known as the *Sicherheitsdienst* or *SD* . . . which was destined to become the most dreaded of all the Nazi apparatus.

*

"You have to admire a man like that," Lilian said over our morning coffee.

I was in the middle of picturing a scene that I was scoring with my eyes closed. I hummed the melody louder than I thought.

"What's that?" Lilian asked.

I stopped. "I thought I was being quiet."

"Not quite, my dear. Did you hear what I said?"

"About what?"

"About Bernhard Weiss. He just sued Goebbels again. Here." She handed me the paper that reproduced a picture from Goebbels's rag sheet. It depicted the head of Bernhard Weiss on a donkey with legs splayed on an ice pond. The caption read, "Isidor on thin ice."

Goebbels' vitriolic attacks on the Jews, particularly Bernhard Weiss, were unrelenting. At every opportunity, his newspaper, *Der Angriff,* depicted Weiss as a big-nosed monkey, a slithering snake, or a Caesar using his police to persecute Nazis. Goebbels even put out a booklet with a collection of published cartoons, one of which caught my eye: the head of a donkey turned into a caricature of Weiss, skating on thin ice.

"I despise that twisted dwarf. I can't stand it when he calls him Isidor," Lilian said. "Weiss is suing him for defamation yet again. He seemed so mild when I met him at the police station. It's a wonder that Weiss is still alive."

"Let me tell you about this mild little man. He was a captain in the army in the Great War and won the Iron Cross First Class. He has more guts and gumption than men twice his size."

"You make him sound like a friend."

"A friend? No. But I admire him."

"I don't blame you. His people should be proud of him. And if Goebbels hates him, I'm proud of him, too."

*

Lilian and I plugged away at our crafts. By the summer of '31, unconnected events occurred that would alter my life. The first was a change in Lilian's career.

I was at the piano in my office when Lilian knocked on the doorjamb.

"Have a minute?"

"What sort of question is that? Have a seat. I'm almost done." I continued to diddle notes of a tune that I wanted to use in a new movie.

"I like it. Is that for your current project?"

"I still need to work on the timing so it fits the movie better."

She balanced herself on the edge of the couch and folded her hands in her lap. When she did this, I knew I was in for a serious talk. "Hermann Paley visited me on set today."

"That's great. Who is Herman Paley?"

"He's the talent scout for Fox Films in California," Lilian grew animated. "You can't believe his bio. He's written hundreds of songs and has accompanied Al Jolson and Eddie Cantor."

"You didn't drop in to tell me about the songs he wrote or who he accompanied on the piano. What's he doing here?"

Then she blurted it out. "He offered me a four-movie contract with Fox."

Fox meant America. "Is that something you're interested in?"

"Under normal circumstances, I would have sent him away. We have the best studios in the world, and I love everyone I work with here." She took my hand. "And by and large we've figured out a way to keep politics from getting between us."

I swiveled to face her. "What did you tell Herr Paley?"

"That I had to talk to you."

"We both know you are going to do what is best for your career."

"What's best for my career is anything that makes me happy. You make me happy. Ergo . . ."

"You've never been a liar. Don't start now. We both know that the UFA makes you happy. Your co-actors and directors make you happy. Me? I'm not so sure anymore."

Lilian slid onto the piano bench and held my arm. "Friedrich, in spite of our differences, we've carved out a great life together."

"There is still that wall between us called 'Wolf.' That is never going away."

She pinched her lips together. "That man *does* get in the way."

There was nothing more to add. "So what are you going to do?"

"Herr Paley said it should be a handsome offer. They are sending me the contract."

"It sounds like you've already made up your mind."

"You'll be involved in any decision I make. For now, I'm exploring options."

July 13, 1931

Lilian rushed into my office in a panic. "We're not getting paid. There's been a run on the banks that forced Chancellor Brüning to declare a bank holiday. I don't understand how this could happen."

She dropped onto the couch sobbing.

"Blame France," I said. "President Hoover and the British prime minister both urged the French to grant Germany a one-year moratorium on our payments. The French dragged their heels so long it caused our banks to collapse."

Lilian was too hysterical to hear the whys and wherefores. France's failure to respond was only part of the problem. Time would prove that strict adherence to the gold standard was Germany's ultimate undoing. It was simple: we could not cover our loans. When Chancellor Brüning took a drastic, last measure—taking Germany off the gold standard—he had a choice: spend more money on public projects or tighten the country's collective belt. He chose the latter, pushing Germany deeper into its financial hole.

"What are we going to do?" she asked through tears.

"There's no need to panic. Crises always look worse as they happen. Time has a way of distilling everything into proportion."

"How can you sit there and be so calm?" Her chest heaved as she struggled to gain control. "It's not about my salary. Lord knows I have enough money. But what if money becomes worthless like it once did? I'll be no better than a beggar on the streets."

I wrapped one arm around her and stroked her hair. "I don't know much about banking and currencies. What I do know is that all countries depend on a stable banking system or they couldn't function. There may be some rough days ahead, but tincture of time will heal things."

"What are we supposed to do in the meantime?" There was nothing more I could say that would reassure her. She looked up at me. "Do you think your party can do something to help us out of this trouble?"

"What do you mean?"

"Well," she caught her breath, "The NSDAP is now a force in the Reichstag. Can't they fix this?"

"Aren't you the one who has called them everything from scoundrels to thugs? Now you want their help?"

"If they can give it."

"Am I supposed to understand how your mind works?"

"Can any man understand a woman?" She kissed my cheek.

While I did my best to reassure Lilian that everything would be all right, I knew no miracle could happen soon. The coalition Chancellor Brüning cobbled together to rule Germany was incapable of confronting the hard choices necessary to bring Germany out of this crisis. From our party's viewpoint, the more the shortsighted victors continued to punish Germany for starting the Great War, the sooner Wolf would be called to power.

Chapter 37

Two days after the bank crisis, a perturbed Kitty phoned. "Max is in trouble."

"Is it about money? I've got enough on hand to tide him over until the banks settle down."

"No. Nothing like that. You need to meet us at the Nightingale."

"I can be there in a few minutes."

"Give me two hours. I need to prepare him. Otherwise Max will be furious that I reached out to you. He's too proud to ask you for help."

*

I found the Nightingale empty. I made my way to Max's office and found him slumped in his chair with Kitty holding his hand. Even in the warm, yellow light, Max was pale and had aged since I last saw him.

Kitty whispered that I was there. Max looked up and mumbled, "I need your help."

"I never thought I would hear those words from you. What's wrong?"

Without explaining, he pushed off the desk. "Follow me." He wobbled to the kitchen and pointed. "Look at the mess they made." Pools of melting ice mixed with mounds of dumped food covered the floor. Broken plates and glasses were strewn everywhere. The air was rank.

"Who, Max? Who did this?"

"The police."

"You take care of them. Why would they do this to you?"

Max rubbed his thick thumb over his index and middle fingers. "They tripled their usual take. I balked . . . and then this. I should've paid them. They said next time, they would torch the club."

"This makes no sense. You've been doing business with them for years."

"These were not my usual guys. These guys were tough. Crude. No offense to you, but they were Nazis. I'm sure Goebbels put them up to it."

"Were they wearing armbands?"

"I told you they were cops. On the way out one gave a salute and said, 'Regards from the *Gauleiter*.'"

"Why would Goebbels . . . ?" Then I remembered the night Max made a fool out of Goebbels at our dinner party at the *Prater Garten*.

"Can you speak to Goebbels for me? Get them to leave me alone? Thank God most of this is just mess. Plates and glasses can be replaced. I can buy more food. Lucky for me they left my ovens and stoves alone. I can't have them destroy my place again."

As I scanned the mess, my mind worked fast. Goebbels was vengeful. If I spoke to him about Max, Max's life could be at stake. Goebbels could be that brutal.

"Max, will you be able to take care of tonight's crowd?"

"This won't stop me."

I tiptoed through the congealing guck and spoiling food, thinking so much more damage could have been done. Why wasn't it? What message was being sent?

"You *must* know someone to help," Kitty said. "My salon could be next."

My challenge was to find a way to save Max but not make it worse for him in the process. Then I realized I had the answer in my wallet. "I think I know who can help. Give me a day or two. My bet is that you will never hear from them again."

Kitty hugged Max. "I told you Friedrich could help."

Southwest Berlin

Bernhard Weiss arranged to meet in a secluded part of the forest tucked in the center of the *Düppel* neighborhood. We needed to keep our talk out of earshot not only from his police minions, but also from onlookers finding us a curious pair: Weiss, so short and me, so tall.

"I've been waiting for your call ever since our last meeting."

"You thought me that predictable?"

"Let's say that I hoped you would call. Of course, after the tongue thrashing Fräulein Harvey gave me, I doubted I would ever speak with you again."

"You might be surprised to learn she respects you. If she knew we were meeting, she would have sent her warmest regards and asked me to get your autograph."

"What changed her opinion of me?"

"She admires the way you keep suing Goebbels and winning. My arrest did little to tarnish that. Lilian was also impressed by the way you marched into the Reichstag to arrest one of the Nazi members for assault. The paper reported how the Nazi delegates screamed 'Isidor' and gave the Hitler salute, and yet you went about your business as if they weren't there."

"Reichstag delegates are not above the law. They gave me no choice. But you know these men well, don't you? They're members of your party. Some are even your friends."

"Herr Weiss. Please don't link me to their crazy racial theories or brutality. You know I don't believe in that sort of stuff."

"Then why remain in the party?" He raised his finger as if he had a new idea. "That's right, you're not a party member. Just a good friend of Adolf Hitler."

Sarcasm aside, I countered. "Who else will face down the victors and restore Germany to greatness?"

Weiss walked head down, hands behind his back, strolling as if on a mountain path. "Like you, Herr Richard, I'm a German patriot. But not at the expense of transforming the Fatherland into a dictatorship on the pretext of creating an efficient government."

"Herr Weiss, aren't you being simplistic?"

We stopped. "I assure you, Friedrich . . . may I call you by your first name? I am anything but simplistic."

"The Nazis are not just about efficiency, Bernhard." I followed his cue. "As Germany is now structured, we have more than two dozen parties incapable of agreeing on anything. Their contrary views and refusals to compromise wrap the Reichstag in a layer of paralysis that renders it incapable of governing. When the Roman Republic needed to overcome an emergency, it set aside the Republic and chose a dictator. We need a similar solution to get us out of this mess."

"May I remind you what happened to the Roman Empire?" said Weiss.

"And may I remind you that Woodrow Wilson insisted we depose the Kaiser and create a democracy in order to negotiate peace. What has that gotten us? One inept government after another. Street battles. A generation of malnourished children, and economic wars with the rest of the world. Democracy does not work for Germany."

Weiss sighed. "We can go on like this forever. These problems are bigger than the both of us. Let me change the subject and explain why I sent for you."

I thought I misheard him. "Bernhard, you're mistaken. I called you."

"You may think otherwise after I explain. It was *my* men that made that mess at the Nightingale. The reference to the *Gauleiter* was meant to make Max Klinghoffer believe Goebbels was behind it."

"To what end?"

"I was certain he would ask for your help. It was my way to get your attention."

"Why not just call me?"

"It was safer if you called me about my police. And it served the purpose of a certain test."

"Logic says I would've asked Goebbels to call off his goons."

"That's what I had to find out: would you call Goebbels or me? Of course, you could have done nothing and let your Jewish friend fend for himself."

"Getting my attention at the expense of someone else, especially a fellow Jew, shows a different side of you." Then I realized: why should I be surprised? Longie Zwillman and his cohorts were tough Jews. So was Bernhard Weiss. "Now that I'm here, I presume Max will have no more trouble."

"Tell him I'm sorry. Better yet, tell him nothing other than from now on there will be no more payoffs. No more bribes. He gets to run his business without interference. Let him think you arranged this with your friends in the party. He can never know it was through me."

"Is this protection for now, or can he expect it to last into the future?"

"You have my word it will last as long as I am here."

"That savings will pay for the damage you caused . . . and then some."

"That was my intention."

"Now that Max is taken care of, what do you want from me?"

"An open line of communication."

"For what purpose?"

We were standing next to a wooden bench. Weiss sat at one end and I on the other.

"In a vague way, I've known about you for years. You're a powerful but shadowy figure in your party. I told you as much when we met. Beating up three *SA* men piqued my curiosity. I asked myself, 'Why would a man like you do such a thing? A Nazi saving a Jew?' I asked you, but you wouldn't answer. So I began my own investigation."

My right leg started to bounce. I did not like the direction this was taking. "Given today's uncertainties, there must be more pressing police matters than wasting your time on me, not to mention more interesting members in the party."

"None as intriguing as you, Friedrich Richard."

The way he annunciated my name sent chills down my spine. "I promise I'm not interesting. You probably didn't find much."

Weiss turned both palms up. "That's just it. There is no official record of you anywhere. At least not after 1918. Doesn't that strike you as amazing, especially since this is a country of meticulous record keeping?"

I couldn't believe it. Here I was, challenged by the man who helped create the science of forensic police work, the foremost policeman in Germany. I grew warm. It was time to leave. I jumped up, making every effort to control my voice. "This has been a profitable meeting."

"Not so fast, Herr Richard . . . if that *is* your name. Sit down!"

After I sank back on the bench, he pointed to a small patch of blue. "Just like that bit of sky peeking through the leaves, I know there is more beyond what I can see. And, like everyone else, I like a good mystery." He tapped my arm. "Thank you for presenting me with one."

"I'm glad I provided you with entertainment."

"More than you think. Imagine my surprise when my inquiries turned up empty after 1918."

"As you said, I am shadowy figure."

"Yet we both know that's not the reason. What we do know is that someone carried your name before you, don't we?" There was no need to answer to him. "That person—the real Friedrich Z. Richard—died at Pasewalk Hospital in September of '18."

Sweat drenched my shirt.

Is this how it is going to end after thirteen years of impersonating a dead soldier? On a park bench, arrested by the great Bernhard Weiss?

Weiss continued. "You must know that Friedrich Zalman Richard was a Jew."

"Coincidences do happen."

"Not in my line of work. Let's say for the moment that your explanation is possible. Every resource in Germany is at my disposal. I left no stone unturned. There is no other Friedrich Richard with the middle initial Z. This can only leave me with one conclusion."

"Where are you going with this, Herr Weiss?"

Rather than answer, he recounted his inquiry. "Once I discovered the details about your name, I backtracked from the army records to the last place Friedrich Richard was known to be alive: Pasewalk Hospital . . . where he died. The next step would have been to go to Pasewalk to search the background and understand the miracle of how he was resurrected in you . . ." I blanched. ". . . But that's when I stopped the investigation."

"If you got that far, why stop?"

"I wasn't sure I wanted to know more about who you were until I determined what kind of man you are: a Nazi thug or a man who would attack his own kind to save an old Jew. So I devised a test. I led you to believe it was Goebbels's handiwork at the Nightingale in order to see how you would respond. Had you called Goebbels, you would have been revealed as a Nazi helping an inconvenient friend. Doing so would have placed both you and Max Klinghoffer in great danger with the party. And so, I reasoned your next possible choice was to do nothing."

"And what would that have told you?"

"That you were a Nazi acting—or rather, not acting—to protect himself."

"It never occurred to me to do nothing."

"Doing nothing would have ended my experiment . . . and your anonymity. If you had gone down that path, I would have fed your information to the Nazis. They would have looked into Pasewalk and discovered whatever it is you want to remain hidden there."

"Yet I called you."

"Ah yes, the third option. Because you did, we will continue to communicate."

"What would we have to talk about?"

"1932 is around the corner. If conditions worsen, your party will gain even more influence in the Reichstag. The same holds true for you."

I stopped him there. "If you are suggesting that I become your agent, Herr Weiss, find someone else. I will not spy for you."

"Spying never entered my mind. It's quite the opposite. I will be the one giving information . . . to you."

"Why should I care about what you might have to say? I am well-insulated by the party."

"You may think you are, but that's not always the case. When that happens, I will be there to protect you."

"I've played your game long enough, Herr Weiss. I'm afraid that this has been a waste of time for both of us. I bid you good day."

He grabbed my sleeve. "Friedrich. Hear what I have to say, and then you can leave. In the unhappy event that Hitler comes to power, Germany will need a man like you in a position to contain excesses that are certain to follow."

"I will never betray Hitler."

"That's not what I'm asking. I know people, Friedrich. I also know that if a dark curtain descends on Germany, a man in a position of authority—like you—could poke holes in the walls of tyranny."

Before I tried to parse out what he meant and how it applied to me, Bernhard Weiss spun around and walked away, leaving me cemented to the bench.

Chapter 38

The weather that Saturday morning was expected to be sunny. It did not disappoint. Lilian ordered a picnic basket so we could spend the afternoon in the *Tiergarten*, the inner-city park that Frederick the Great transformed from a primal forest into a pleasure garden for the citizens of Berlin in 1742.

"Are you ready?" I called out, grabbing a Riesling from the wine cabinet.

"I need another moment to fix my face," she answered as the phone jangled. "Let it ring, Friedrich. Whoever it is, can wait until Monday. This is our weekend."

The phone continued to shrill . . . begging to be answered.

I lifted the receiver to hear a familiar voice gush a command. "It's Hess. Get to Munich as fast as you can. The *Führer* needs you. Geli has been shot."

"Is she alive?"

"No!"

"What happened?"

The phone went dead. I was thunderstruck. Wild thoughts entered my mind. Was this an assassination attempt? Did someone try to kill Wolf, miss, and hit Geli? Did Wolf kill Geli in a jealous rage? What about Emil Maurice? Did he have anything to do with it?

Whatever the cause, this news would cause trouble with Lilian. I stepped toward her; she caught my reflection in the makeup mirror.

"What's with the long face? You look green."

"It was Rudy Hess. I have to leave for Munich on the next plane."

The powder cake dropped from her hand and splattered on the floor. She whipped around. "What could be so important?"

"Hitler's niece Geli has been shot."

"Is she dead?"

"Yes."

"Did Hitler shoot her?"

"How could you ask that?"

"Because that's what lovers do in fits of rage."

"That's not what happened."

"Are you certain?"

"As much as I can be from here."

"If she's dead, why do you need to go? It will ruin our weekend. Don't I count?"

"How coldhearted can you be? You know Wolf's my friend. He needs me."

"Friedrich, friend notwithstanding, when it comes to Hitler, there will always be drama. Don't get involved in his mess."

"What are you trying to say, Lilian? That I should abandon my friend because we have a picnic planned?"

She clapped her hands to get my attention. "Think, Friedrich. Think. Even if Hitler didn't shoot her, he's been sleeping with his niece ever since he moved her into his apartment. When the press gets wind of that and connects you to Hitler, it will have repercussions on *my* career. I can't have my name associated with this sordid affair, no matter who shot whom."

Heat radiated from every pore on my face. "Are you telling me that I can't live my life because of the shadow I cast over yours?" Lilian had no answer. "I can't deal with this now. I'll be back as soon as I can. Then we can talk."

"I'm done talking, Friedrich. If you insist on going, then go. But don't expect me to be here when you return."

Lilian turned her back, dabbing away the tears that ruined her partially finished makeup. I considered clutching her shoulders and kissing the top of her head . . . but what was the point?

*

Wolf's apartment on *Prinzregentenplatz* was a beehive of activity. Police, party members, and staff buzzed everywhere. Wolf was nowhere to be seen. I found Hess speaking with a policeman in the hall near the entrance. When he saw me, I gestured: where was Wolf? Hess pointed to his room down the hall. Then I motioned him to follow me into an empty room. I needed to find out what happened.

"Rudy, was it an accident?"

"Deliberate. Geli shot herself using one of the Boss's pistols."

"She was so young. What could have caused her to do such a terrible thing?"

Hess raised his bushy brows. "From what I can gather she found out that the Boss was seeing another woman on the side. Talk to the housekeeper, Frau Winter. She can fill you in."

"Is he alone in his room now?"

Hess nodded. "He won't speak with anyone, that's why I'm glad you are here. The police want to interview him—but we can't get him out of his room. The press is all over this. We need to come up with a story before the politicians make mincemeat of us."

I left Hess and went to Wolf's bedroom. I knocked, but there was no answer. I knocked harder, still no answer. I turned the knob, felt it give, and slipped into the room. The curtains were drawn. I waited a beat for my eyes to adjust to the darkness. Wolf sat in a chair, bent over, his hands cupped on either side of his head. He didn't look up as I eased down next to him. "Wolf, I'm here." I put my arm around him.

He leaned into me. He had never let anyone get this close, not even me at Pasewalk. "Oh Friedrich. She's dead." Tears spilled down his cheeks. "She's dead. What am I going to do?"

"You are going to pull yourself together, get out of this room, and meet the party men here for you. They're in a panic. You need to reassure them that you can function before Geli's suicide is splashed all over tomorrow's papers. When that happens, the Communists will hammer us with it and the Social Democrats will use it against you, too."

He looked up with puddled eyes. "I can't speak to anyone. Not now."

"Adolf," his head jerked up, "you have no choice. The police won't leave until they interview you. Until they are satisfied, nothing can be done."

He grabbed my hand. "Stay with me."

"Do you have to ask?" With that I led him to the detective in charge.

Detective Sauer introduced himself. "I am sorry for your terrible loss, Herr Hitler, but I need to ask you some questions."

"Can this wait, Detective Sauer?" I asked. "You see how distressed Herr Hitler is over the death of his niece."

Wolf straightened his coat and stood taller. "It's all right, Friedrich. We can sit in my room." Wolf led us back to his room. I turned the light on; they sat opposite each other at a small table. I planted myself behind Wolf's chair, my hand on his shoulder.

"Thank you for arranging this, Herr . . . ?"

"Richard."

"Herr Richard," said the detective. "You won't be needed now."

Wolf put his hand up. "He must stay."

Detective Sauer cleared his throat and muttered, "As you wish." He checked his notes. "I will make it as brief as possible, Herr Hitler. The coroner has determined that the time of death occurred during the hour before midnight. Can you tell me where you were at that time last night?"

Wolf stared as if in a catatonic state. He spoke in a monotone —something I never heard him do.

"Heinrich Hoffman and I left after lunch yesterday. We drove to Nuremberg and stayed the night. We headed for a rally in Hamburg in the morning." He restated it. "That was earlier today."

"How did you learn about Fräulein Raubal?"

"Rudolph Hess tried to reach us at the hotel this morning, but we had already left. The hotel sent a car racing after us. When I got the message that he needed to speak to me, we returned to the hotel. He said something about Geli being injured."

"Did he tell you she was dead?"

Wolf shook his head. "He said it was very bad and that we should come as fast as we could." Wolf raised his head for the first time. "I kept urging Hoffman to drive faster. Faster. In fact, we were stopped for speeding. The policeman gave us a summons. Hoffman is here in the apartment. He can show it to you. When we arrived, her body was already gone. Taken away."

Rather than ask another question, Sauer excused himself, went to the door, whispered something to another policeman, and returned moments later, with a gun. He laid it aside without asking any questions about it. At least not right away.

Wolf's eyes beseeched the officer. "Did she suffer?"

"From what we can piece together, your housekeeper, Anni Winter, thought she heard a noise some hours after you and Herr Hoffman left. According to her, she thought Fräulein Raubal had dropped a perfume bottle on the floor. When she didn't call for help to clean it up, Frau Winter dismissed it. Later that evening, she tried to enter the room about nine o'clock but found the door locked from the inside. She assumed that Fräulein Raubal had gone to sleep."

"Geli never goes to sleep that early. Frau Winter should have pounded on the door to wake her. Maybe my Geli would have realized that she was about to make a terrible mistake." For a man whose image was everything, Wolf made no effort to stem the tears streaming down his cheeks.

Grim-faced, the detective continued after glancing at his form of shorthand. "Because of this timeline, the body temperature, and the degree of rigor mortis, the coroner estimated that death occurred sometime before midnight. Assuming the noise Frau Winter heard was the fatal shot, the answer to your questions is that Fräulein Raubal lived two to three hours after she was wounded. I'm sorry."

"Could she have been saved?" Wolf asked.

"Had someone found her right away, it might have been possible. Based on our preliminary investigation, this appears to be a self-induced wound. Fräulein Raubal aimed at her heart. The bullet entered her lung. She appears to have bled to death."

"My Geli hated guns. Even so, I forced her to learn how to use one in case someone got into the apartment to try to kill me. There have already been many threats on my life."

The policeman interrupted Wolf's ramble. "According to Georg Winter, when Fräulein Raubal did not come down for breakfast, he found her door still locked from the inside."

"What about the window?" I asked.

"No one could have been in her room that night and left. Everything, including the window, was locked from the inside." The officer held up the pistol. "Is this your gun?"

Wolf barely glanced at the Walther. "Yes."

"What did you argue about yesterday as you were leaving?"

Wolf tugged his jacket straight. "We did not argue."

"Neighbors claim to have heard you say, 'for the last time, no!' before you and Herr Hoffman drove away. Herr Hoffman has stated that you were silent for the first part of your journey yesterday. That you brooded over what happened during lunch."

"Herr Hoffman is mistaken. Again, I insist: Geli and I did not argue. She wanted to go to Vienna to take one more vocal lesson before her concert. I encouraged her to do so."

"So you contend that you left on good terms?" asked Sauer.

"Geli and I never argued."

That was false. Wolf and Geli had a tumultuous relationship. There were times she wished to go out to a party or to a play, but Wolf would not allow it. Other times he insisted Max Amann escort her. Wolf always claimed he was protecting her virtue, but it seemed more like jealousy to me.

"Detective," I said. "There is no point going further. Herr Hitler and Hoffman were hundreds of kilometers away when Geli locked herself in her room and took her own life . . . either accidentally or on purpose. Herr Hitler is emotionally spent from this ordeal. If you have more questions, could they be posed at another time?"

Sauer closed his notepad. "I have all that I need for now." He stood. "Again, please accept my condolences, Herr Hitler."

Wolf continued to stare at the floor. The moment we were alone, his demeanor changed. "Call Franz Gürtner. He will know what to do." Then he withdrew a small book from his breast pocket, thumbed through the pages, found Gürtner's telephone number, and scribbled it down.

Gürtner, the Bavarian minister of Justice, a Nationalist but not a Nazi, had helped the party after the '23 Putsch with respect to the trial and the light sentences. Wolf's early release from prison and, later, revoking the ban on his speaking, were Gürtner's doing as well.

"Will you be all right?" I asked.

"Go."

The study was empty. I locked the door and called Gürtner's private number. "Herr Minister, my name is Friedrich Richard. I'm here at the *Führer's* apartment and . . ."

"I was notified soon after the police arrived at the scene. Tragic business," said Gürtner.

"Herr Hitler said you would know what to do. He wishes to have his niece sent to her final resting place in Austria without delay."

"I've been in touch with the police. The preliminary finding is that this was a suicide. I will make certain there is no further investigation."

"About the body?"

"Tell Herr Hitler that her dignity will be preserved. There will be no autopsy."

"Thank you, Herr Minister. The family will be most grateful."

When I returned, Wolf grabbed me. "Take me away from here, Friedrich. I cannot stay a minute longer."

My first thought was that Wolf should stay and be available to the press to help curtail damage. But when I looked at him, I saw that he had to leave. Where to go? Then it came to me: the publisher of Wolf's *Mein Kampf.* He had a retreat that was empty this time of year.

I found Hess. "Call Adolf Müller. Tell him I need to bring the Boss to his house in *Tegernsee* right away. Tell Müller that I will be staying as well. Hoffman will most likely join us." Given the money Müller made from *Mein Kampf*, I knew he would make the house available.

While Hess arranged for the fifty-kilometer drive to Müller's house, I searched for the housekeeper, Anni Winter. I found her alone in the kitchen.

"Frau Winter, will you pack a bag for Herr Hitler? We will be staying at Herr Müller's house for a number of days." I had brought clothes with me expecting to stay as long as I was needed.

Winter was a diminutive woman, with dark hair and eagle eyes that missed nothing. She stood motionless.

"It's all my fault, Herr Richard," Anni said.

"What is?"

"Geli."

"How can you think that?"

"I might have done something to stop her."

"What are you talking about?"

"After the *Führer* and Herr Hoffman left on their trip yesterday, I cleared the lunch table. When I finished, I told Geli that I would make up Herr Hitler's room. She offered to help. I thought it would be a good idea that she had something to do after their argument. So we straightened out his room together. But then . . ." Winter started to weep.

"Then what?"

"Geli went through his pockets after hanging up his jacket and found this note."

She fumbled in her apron pocket and brought out a square of blue stationary that had been pieced back together. She held it out to me.

Dear Herr Hitler,
Thank you again for the wonderful invitation to the theater. It was a memorable evening. I am most grateful to you for your kindness. I am counting the hours until I may have the

joy of another meeting.
Yours
Eva

"Where did you find this?"

"Geli left it there on the *Führer's* desk, torn into four pieces. She wanted to be certain the *Führer* would find it and know that she knew about Eva Braun. I put the pieces back together. There was no reason for the police to see this."

She remained steadfast and looked away.

"There's more, isn't there?"

She nodded. "I'm not sure I should mention it."

"Let me decide."

"There was something else on the desk."

"Another note?"

"It was Hansi. Her canary. She loved that little bird. Hansi was cradled on a soft bed of cotton. Dead."

"Do you think she killed the bird knowing she would soon take her own life?"

"What else could it mean?"

Chapter 39

Max Amann and Julius Schaub—Wolf's adjunct—confirmed that while Geli lived with him in 16 *Prinzregentenplatz*, Wolf began to secretly date Eva Braun. Schaub reported that they often drank tea in a dark corner in the Carlton Café. There was nothing to be done except hope the press did not pry deep into his affairs.

Hitler's private life was now under scrutiny. For the next several days, the press published many stories, most of which were inaccurate and vituperative. Against my advice, Wolf insisted on issuing denials and corrections. These statements only caused the papers to dig deeper. They revived old stories from the twenties, when he was called "King of Munich." Names started to reappear, among them Jenny Haug and Emmi Marre. Had Wolf been able to muzzle his mouth, the stories would have petered out because the facts of Geli's suicide were not in question. But he could not control himself and his denials and threats to sue kept the story alive.

*

"*The Führer* still won't eat a thing," Hoffman said. It was our second day at Alfred Müller's house on Tegernsee Lake. "I left him last night pacing back and forth with his hands clasped behind him. This morning he was doing the same thing. How are we going to get him to eat?" asked Hoffman. Then he brightened. "I'm going to call Frau Winter and get her recipe for spaghetti. That's one of his favorites."

But it didn't work. Nothing enticed Wolf to take more than a forkful. He continued to pace day and night . . . until after two days he finally ventured outside. A brisk wind blew off the water. Wolf took a step, and then another. Soon he was taking long hikes around the lake.

When I had a few moments, I tried to reach Lilian without success. No one answered our phone. Messages left at the studio went unanswered.

"I am calling from Fox Studios in Hollywood, California. Please tell Fräulein Harvey that Hermann Paley is on the line."

The phone operators at the UFA studios needed to be multi-lingual. When Lilian came to the phone, she blurted, "Hermann, what a surprise."

"It's not Hermann, it's me."

"You tricked me."

"It was the only way I could get you to the phone," I said.

"What's the verdict?"

"What do you mean? There was no trial."

"Of course there was. You were on trial. You made a promise to follow your heart. It appears that you kept your promise. Hitler won out over me."

"You've got it all wrong. I helped a friend in terrible need. I didn't pick anyone over you."

"I told you not to go. And you . . ."

"Lilian, don't be like that."

". . . went anyway."

"You can't order me to abandon the oldest friend I've ever known, or at least the only one I can remember."

"I don't care what you say. Your friend probably killed that poor girl."

This was never going to get better. "Lilian, I'm sorry for the way things worked out. You deserve better than me."

"You're damn right I do. Marta was right when she warned me about you that night at Max's. I should have listened then."

"If you could, leave my clothes in a trunk in the front hall. I'll find my own place. I won't bother you again."

I didn't know if Lilian heard the last sentences. The line was dead.

*

Two days later, after circling the lake with his face flushed from the fresh air and quick pace, Wolf announced, "Tonight, we drive to Vienna. I want to visit Geli."

Hoffman and I looked at each other in consternation. Back in 1924, after the failed putsch, Wolf renounced his Austrian citizenship to avoid being deported.

"You know," I reminded him, "you're prohibited from going to Austria."

"I know."

"You're risking jail." But I could not move him. He was adamant.

"I've made arrangements to meet with the *Gauleiter* of Vienna. We'll get there early in the morning, switch cars, drive to the cemetery, see her, and then return to Munich so I can resume speaking. No one will know we were there."

*

Eight days after Geli committed suicide, we entered Austria as the sun's first rays pierced the fading darkness. We met the *Gauleiter* outside of Vienna, transferred to his smaller vehicle as planned, and stood in front of Geli's tombstone in the Central Cemetery by ten o'clock that morning. Wolf laid two-dozen roses on her grave. He mumbled a few words and then turned to us. "Now let the struggle begin again."

His concession to the past was to instruct Frau Winter to keep Geli's room exactly as it was on the last day of her life. It was to be locked at all times except when Frau Winter placed a bouquet of roses in a vase on the desktop each day. Soon after, he ordered a bust of Geli's face sculpted in stone and an artist to paint her portrait . . . that he hung in his bedroom.

When it came to Geli, flowers, a painting, and a sculpture were Hitler's only concession to the past. He picked up the pieces of his life and barely skipped a beat. I, on the other hand, had become homeless now that it had ended with Lilian.

The solution? I moved in with Wolf in Munich . . . and saw things I wish I hadn't.

*

"Would you be interested in seeing a movie?" Wolf asked one afternoon, about four weeks after Geli's death.

"What would you like to see?"

He snickered. "I didn't mean with me. I've given the staff off. Perhaps you would like to spend time at the *Braunes Haus.* Take some overnight things. I'm expecting company into the late evening."

Finally I got it. "I'll leave right now."

"That would be a good idea," said Wolf with a twinkle.

I grabbed some clothes and put my toiletries in a Dopp bag. When I reached the hall, the elevator door sprung open and a beautiful woman stepped out.

"Mimi?"

It was Maria Reiter. Five years had changed her. Now, nearly twenty-two, she blossomed from a young girl into a voluptuous young woman. She carried an overnight case in one hand. How was it possible that I was standing outside of Wolf's apartment, talking to the woman who almost ended his career?

"You look surprised to see me."

"I am. Does Wolf expect you?"

"I should hope so. Rudy Hess came to see me a few days ago. I remember his exact words. He said, 'Herr Hitler sent me. He wants to know if you are happy.' You see I am recently separated from my husband. I was feeling lonely and then Hess appeared. Just to know that Wolf still cared lifted my spirits. He gave me Wolf's private number. Do you know what Wolf said when I called?"

"I can only imagine."

"He said, 'I want you this very minute.' Then he told me to go to the apartment of his adjutant, Julius Schaub. Herr Schaub drove me here." Bewilderment was plastered across my face. "You look confused, Herr Richard."

"I . . . I never expected to see you again; now you tell me you're married but estranged from your husband. Forgive me for asking, but how did Wolf know you and your husband were separated?"

"Wolf knows everything about me. When I married, he sent me a beautiful silver goblet as a wedding present, signed 'Wolf.' We've been in contact over the years. He knew I was miserable."

I was dumbfounded. Once Wolf and Maria signed their affidavits, their relationship should have ended with Buch closing the inquiry about the blackmail letters. In a flash, I understood the Hitler merry-go-round of women. Wolf two-timed Maria with Geli, and then two-timed Geli with Eva Braun. Now, four weeks after Geli's suicide, Maria Reiter shows up while Wolf continues to see Eva. It was clear: the man could not be without a female for any extended period.

And I sacrificed my own love for this?

"That explains everything, Maria." I extended my hand. "It was good to see you again. I'd best be on my way."

"You know I am going to marry Wolf one day," she said as we shook.

"That is one wedding I do not want to miss."

*

It was early evening when I entered *Braunes Haus*. Most offices were empty. After passing a warren of rooms, I chanced upon Reinhard Heydrich who was stuffed into a closet converted into an "office" to accommodate the tall ex-navy lieutenant.

I cleared my throat.

"*Obergruppenführer* Richard. It's been a while since Himmler's farm. What are you doing here?" Heydrich remained seated, without standing to salute me or offer his hand.

"The *Führer* asked that I give him a progress report regarding the internal security plan you are developing."

Heydrich pushed back from his desk; his chair smacked into the wall behind him. He stood to his full measure. I still had the advantage.

"I am answerable only to *Reichsführer* Himmler. No one else."

I slipped onto the corner of his desk and deliberately sat on a folder. "You're new to the party, Herr Heydrich. You have much to learn. Regardless of what you think, everyone in the party is answerable to the *Führer*. Even Himmler."

"And I take it you are his guardian angel?"

There was nothing about this man I liked. "Guardian angel doesn't go far enough to describe how close I am to the *Führer*. Our friendship predates the party. Few others can say that." I tapped him on his chest with my index finger. "And don't you forget that."

"You don't know me, Herr Richard. Be aware that I don't intimidate. If you doubt me, ask my mates in the navy." Then he poked his index finger in my chest. "And don't you forget that."

I wanted no more of the *Braunes Haus*. I left and wandered around the city for a bit. I passed a theater playing "No Time for Love." All things considered, the title amused me. But when I discovered this was Lilian's latest release, I kept my money in my pocket and parked myself in an out-of-the-way café. I only returned to the *Braunes Haus* to sleep once I was certain Heydrich had left.

In the morning, I made my way back to the apartment even though I knew Wolf would still be sleeping. I didn't know if Maria would still be there.

I was relieved when Frau Winter answered the door.

"Is it safe?" I asked.

She smiled. "For now."

I rolled my eyes. "Do I have to leave again?"

"Not tonight. But tomorrow."

"Is Maria returning then?"

"This one is Marlene Weinrich," she grimaced. "Do you know her? Her father Karl Weinrich is a party member." Then added, "She's seventeen."

I shook my head at yet another *Wolfette*. "She's new to me."

"She first met Herr Hitler at a performance of *Lohengrin*. Then at the Hoffman's New Year's Eve party last year, Fräulein Weinrich told Herr Hoffmann's daughter, Henny, that she had her sights on Herr Hitler. Now the *Führer* calls her *Lenchen*."

"How do you know this?"

"Henny told me. If you want to learn more, speak with Julius Schaub." She reached for a framed picture perched on a side table. "Here. Herman Esser took this picture of Geli and Marlene together in *Berchtesgaden*."

I studied the photo. Next to it was a candid shot taken in the street of Esser, flanked by Geli and Marlene.

I turned back to Frau Winter. "You're telling me that during a period of, say, three months, Herr Hitler had been with Geli, Marlene Weinrich, and Maria Reiter?"

"And Eva Braun."

I smacked my forehead. "Eva! How could I forget?"

"Yes, Eva. But I don't think he has done any hanky panky with her . . . yet."

Frau Winter served me coffee. I busied myself with the newspaper and books until Wolf surfaced around noon. He got right to business.

"Himmler called. He said that you and his new assistant had some words yesterday."

"Heydrich is arrogant. He thinks he knows everything."

Wolf gave a crooked grin. "He's young and brash. He has a lot to learn, especially how to treat those close to me. But I can already see that he will be an asset to the party."

"If you don't mind, I will reserve judgment until he proves himself."

"Heydrich's feelings don't concern me. Yours do. How are you getting by?"

I knew he could only be alluding to Lilian. "We had our differences from the start. They magnified the more involved I became in the party. It was time for both of us to move on. In her case, she received a lucrative movie contract and is on her way to America."

The whole time I was talking about Lilian and me, Wolf stared with longing eyes at a picture he took of Geli in a bathing suit, patting her dog, with Hitler's dog Mulky in the background.

"Did you hear what I said?" I asked. "She has gone to America to make movies."

Wolf snapped back. "I love movies." Then added, "Maybe she will long for Germany and return one day, to make movies here, again. Don't give up on her."

"I can't imagine that happening."

"Well, that leaves you alone, at least for now, Friedrich. What are you going to do?"

"Regarding what?"

"Your career. Will you return to Berlin?"

I must go back.

"I have a profession now. I have the freedom to work on the projects I like and pass on those I don't. It also allows me to help the party when I'm needed."

"That plan is ideal because you will be needed more and more. Go back to Berlin. Get situated. Next month I want you to join me in Obersalzberg. Julius Schaub, along with his wife, will drive us. Do you know Wilma?"

"Just like Frau Winter, she is an asset to you."

"Hermann Esser will be there, too. You will both stay at the Platterhof Hotel in *Berchtesgaden*." I made a face. "I know how you feel about Esser, but he has his merits."

"I can't see why you took him back after the putsch."

"Everyone has some use, Friedrich. Think of people as a table setting. Some are spoons, some are knives, some . . . forks! Do not throw away the spoon because it can't be a knife. Some can be more than one. Very few of us are an entire table setting. I appointed Hermann first to the Munich City Council where he proved himself. Now he serves in the Reichstag. He will always support the party. That's all I ask of him."

"He's not my cup of tea."

"He doesn't have to be, Friedrich. The two of you will meet with me in the Obersalzberg to plan rallies for the upcoming elections. You can do that for me, can't you?"

I could, and I told him so. "Will anyone else be there besides Hermann and me?"

"Eva Braun."

"Wolf, something is bothering me."

"You should have no concerns."

"But I do. Now that we smoothed over the problems with Buch and buried those blackmail letters, aren't you concerned that you might bring it all back to life by seeing Maria Reiter again? And is seeing all these women simultaneously wise?"

His face darkened. "Friedrich. We've been through much together. But let me be clear about this: what I do is my business. No one else's."

"I am only concerned about your best interests."

"Then respecting my privacy should be your top priority."

Chapter 40

December 19, 1931

Wolf and I attended Joseph Goebbels's marriage to Magda Quandt at the Quandt family–owned estate in Severin, Mecklenburg. It was now hers courtesy of a generous divorce settlement. The weather was cold, with snow blanketing the ground. An honor guard greeted us with arms in salute as we approached the chapel entrance.

After the ceremony, the newlyweds, along with Harold Quandt, Magda's son from her first marriage, garbed in his *Deutsches Jungvolk* uniform, led the procession from the chapel to the reception hall. Adolf Hitler—their best man—was a step behind the bride and groom, sporting a fashionable long coat and a felt fedora.

At the time of the Goebbels's wedding, the Hitler youth program—personified by young Harold—numbered twenty-five thousand.

*

December 1931 appeared to be a month for Nazi weddings. Less notable was Reinhard Heydrich's wedding, which neither Wolf nor I attended. But Himmler did. He was so impressed with the tall, blond, blue-eyed bridal couple that at the end of December he transformed the *SS* from a bastion of unmarried warrior-elite to a family-oriented corps. He issued a "marriage order." All future *SS* men had to be married, and their marriages had to be pre-approved. Couples had to pass a racial purity test: neither groom nor bride could have a drop of Jewish blood.

To this end, Himmler established an *SS* Racial Office to test for racial suitability and fertility. Each person's family was traced for Aryan purity for 130 years, to the year 1800. If found impure, the *SS* man was forced out of the corps.

*

Looking back on this time, one thing is clear: Adolf Hitler changed. It was not that his character or values were altered. Rather, for him, everything intensified. Blacks became blacker and whites whiter. In a sense, he lost a degree of balance.

. . . along with part of his humanity.

During the time since Geli's death, Germany and the party were in the throes of change much the way Hitler was. The more Germany sank into despair, the more the party flourished. As 1931 closed, six million—nearly one-third of the workforce—searched for jobs. Millions more queued on breadlines and depended on soup kitchens for their sustenance.

As for me? It was also a period of change. I had lost the love of my life and felt adrift.

*

I returned to Berlin during the last days of the year. Wolf arranged for Alfred Hugenberg, the head of the studio, to provide me with one of his many apartments, a modest salary, and a small office at UFA studios with the title "consultant."

I planned to spend New Year's Eve alone in my Berlin apartment but grew depressed when I recalled the previous glorious New Year's with Lilian in Switzerland. I hated the thought of welcoming in the New Year alone.

It took several calls, but I reached her. "Kitty, how are you and Max welcoming in the New Year?"

"We're entertaining a small group at the Nightingale." I mumbled something about how that sounded like fun. Kitty understood at once. "Friedrich, I should have thought of it before. You're alone. Come. Join us."

"Well . . . I don't want to intrude."

"Please hush. Friedrich, there is one thing you should know . . ." She paused then said, "These people are Max's friends. They are all Jews."

"For God's sake, Kitty, you know me better than that." I returned the receiver, with my spirits lifted.

*

"Don't you look handsome in your tuxedo?" Kitty kissed me on the mouth, as I entered the club.

I pretended to brush lint off my lapel. "Thank Herr Goebbels. I needed to buy a new one after last year's stink bomb attack at a movie opening."

Max took my hand. "I can't thank you enough for fixing my problem. I don't know how you did it, but instead of paying for police protection, now the club is protected all the time. It doesn't cost me a pfennig. Who did you call?"

I winked. "You know that certain questions should never be answered."

"Was it Goebbels? Because if it was, I might offer the bastard a drink the next time I see him."

I held up my hand. "Save the liquor for paying customers. What's important is that you and the Nightingale are thriving."

Kitty looped her arm through mine. "Enough shop talk. Let me introduce you to our other guests." We left Max to speak with his headwaiter.

We neared their table set for nine; six seats were occupied. I stood behind an empty chair as Kitty made the introductions. All eyes turned to us. "This is our dear friend, Friedrich Richard. Permit me to introduce Herr Hermann Kaufmann and Frau Kaufmann."

I tipped my head in deference. "I don't know if you would remember, Herr Kaufmann, but we once met on the set of *The Congress Dances.*"

"I supplied the costumes. Wonderful movie." Hermann Kaufmann owned *Theaterkunst,* the top décor and costume supplier in the world. Kaufmann gained notoriety when his company provided eight thousand costumes for *Ben Hur.* "Were you in the movie?"

I shook my head. "I score movies."

"We must chat about that later," Kaufmann said.

Kitty nudged me to the right. "Friedrich, may I present Siegfried Franz Oser-Braun and his wife, Johanna."

I bowed. "I've passed your boutique a thousand times when I stayed at the Adlon Hotel."

"You are a hard man to forget," Oser-Braun rose with his hand outstretched. "I remember you accompanying Fräulein Harvey in our shop."

"She appreciated its uniqueness. You have the best goods in Berlin."

We moved to the last two. "And this is Martin Breslauer and his son, Berndt." The lad stood. Berndt had already been bar-mitzvahed. He was tall and lank, displaying the manners of a mature adolescent. When Martin's wife had passed away, he raised Berndt by himself.

Max appeared. "I see that introductions have been made. Why don't we take our seats?"

After a round of drinks, Hermann Kaufmann turned to me. "Would we know any of the films you've scored?"

I ticked off a few movies.

"Friedrich is quite talented," said Max.

I was glad Max did not elaborate that my dinner companions were dining with an *SS* general.

"He also plays the piano," added Kitty.

"See, Berndt. I bet Herr Richard's parents didn't have to force him to practice the piano every day, now did they?" The doting father eyed me for support.

I empathized at the challenges Martin faced raising Berndt alone. "Perhaps you can visit me at the studio one day, Berndt, and I can introduce you to some pieces that might make the piano more interesting."

Before Berndt could answer, Martin turned to the rest of the table. "I don't know how much longer Berndt and I will remain in Berlin. These last months have given me pause. I can sell my books from anywhere." Breslauer had recently discovered the five-thousand-book collection of Napoleon's second wife—Marie Louise—hidden in an Austrian castle and sold it for a handsome profit. Then he added, "If the Nazis take power, there is little chance they will let me stay in business. My books are antithetical to their way of thinking."

"Martin, you're jumping to conclusions. That will never be necessary," said Oser-Braun. "I've already made substantial donations to the Nazis. We finally have someone who will stand up for our sovereign rights."

"How can you give that man money after everything he says about the Jews?" asked Breslauer.

"Hitler will never carry out his claims to rid Germany of its Jews," answered Oser-Braun. "It's empty rhetoric. He is just saying it to get votes. As for your books, I understand he is a voracious reader. It's been reported that he loves history, art, architecture, and more. I tell you, you and your books are safe."

"That man is capable of burning the books he does not read," said Breslauer.

"Nonsense," Oser-Braun scoffed. "What a crazy notion."

While this was not the evening I expected, these unvarnished perspectives of upper strata Jews interested me. I was anxious to hear from Kaufmann and more from Oser-Braun.

Kaufmann cleared his throat. "I gave money to the Nazis, too, but not because I believe they will be good for Germany. Herr Hitler will always protect industrialists and donors like us. It doesn't matter if we are Jews. What's important is that he believes in capitalism, therefore, he believes in us. Look, he started as a socialist before he embraced capitalism against many in his own party. He began as a putschist—now he tells his party to lay down their arms. He has already become quieter about Jews. If he comes to power, I believe he will move even further away from those wild claims to get rid of us."

He turned to me. "You haven't weighed in, Herr Richard. What are your thoughts as to where this country is headed?"

Max coughed into his napkin. This was his way of letting me know that he would come to my rescue if I faltered.

I struggled as to what to say when Oser-Braun said, "No thinking person in Germany can be blind to what is happening around us, Herr Richard. Surely you must have strong beliefs about this."

"All I know is that ever since the kaiser was forced to step down, we've floundered as a nation. We're constantly on the brink of civil war. I am ready to support anyone who will get Germany back on the right track." I glanced at Max for a lifeline.

Max, good soul that he was, came to my rescue. "In spite of all that is happening, our businesses have thrived, haven't they?" He pointed to Kaufmann, Oser-Braun, and Martin Breslauer. "None of you can tell me I'm wrong. I am the first to admit that there are unsavory elements in Berlin we could all live without. But on the whole, things are not that bad for us."

Kaufman agreed. "I couldn't agree more. We are making more movies than ever. Business could not be better in spite of Herr Goebbels's threats to monitor our industry."

"I think you are all missing the point," said Oser-Braun. "This country lacks structure. Even if the victors lifted all of the sanctions against us, we would not know how to steer this country. I, for one, welcome a benevolent dictator. That is why I am supporting Herr Hitler."

Martin Breslauer shifted in his chair. "Now you're getting into the world of Nietzsche. In order to achieve what you are suggesting, the supreme leader has to demand supreme happiness. I don't think happiness is in Herr Hitler's twenty-five-point program."

"All I know is that President Hindenburg is the glue holding this country together. When he goes, all Germans should start to worry," said Kitty.

"Then it's time to worry. The presidential election is this March. I can't imagine the general running again," said Frau Kaufmann. "He's eighty-five."

"I've seen a number of eighty-five-year-olds with plenty of energy still left in them," said Kitty. That brought much needed laughter to the table. Everyone, including the women, knew about *Pension Schmidt*.

Martin Breslauer remained nonplused. "How can we peg the future of our country on the old general? Is there no one else strong enough to fight the extreme right? Even if Hindenburg runs and wins, we're deluding ourselves. He can't live forever. Whether now or in the not-so-distant future, the government will be overrun. Civil war is knocking on our door. When that happens, this will be no place for Jews. As I said before, Berndt and I will leave before that happens . . . and I suggest everyone else at this table consider doing the same."

That sobered everyone. I wanted to put their minds at ease, to tell them that Wolf had no intention of confiscating their properties or seizing their assets. But I couldn't. Even if I unmasked, I couldn't give them ironclad reassurances. I had no confidence that they had nothing to worry about. And yet . . . the fact that they were the very people with the most to lose and were of split opinion, gave me hope that all might end well.

Chapter 41

1932

A week later, an ebullient Wolf arranged to meet me in Berlin. "I have them in my pocket, Friedrich," he said in animated tones when we spoke on the phone the previous night. "They have finally come to their senses to recognize me as a partner in negotiations."

"Who has?"

"Chancellor Brüning. Today he sent a telegram to our paper, the *Völkischer Beobachter*. He requested that I meet with him and Otto Meissner in Berlin."

"If Meissner is to be there, that's serious. He's headed the Office of the Reich President since the republic was formed. The papers refer to him as 'an institution.'"

"That's why it is important for you to be there with me."

"Shouldn't Hess or one of the others be by your side?"

"You are the only one who doesn't tell me what I want to hear. After we're done with Brüning and Meissner, we have matters to discuss. It's about Goebbels."

I curled my lips. "What did the pig-head do now?"

"No matter what I try, I cannot make Goebbels understand that he must stop defaming the Jews. We're knocking at the gates of power. There is no need to incite anyone now."

How would he feel if I told him I ushered in the New Year with Kaufmann, Oser-Braun, Breslauer, and Max?

Wolf snapped me back to attention when he said, "Just the other day, that Jewish policeman shut *Der Angriff* down for a week after Goebbels wrote another article denigrating the Jews."

"Bernhard Weiss?"

"You know him?"

I caught my breath. "Everyone in Berlin knows him. Closing the newspaper for a week is not the worst thing that could happen."

"If only it had stopped there." Wolf shook his head. "That same evening Goebbels gave a speech at the Sportpalast. He smeared the Jews, again. This time Weiss pulled him off the stage and sent the crowd home. Weiss banned Goebbels from public speaking for three weeks."

"Again, that might be a good thing."

Wolf agreed. "At least when I meet with the leaders in Berlin, I won't have to worry about what comes out of Joseph's mouth."

*

"I can envision the day when you will become chancellor," Brüning told Wolf when we met that afternoon. "But now is not your time. We must first make certain Hindenburg remains in office. There must be no contested election."

Besides Brüning, who had a long, narrow face, circular glasses attached to gold rims, and a professional manner, Otto Meissner was present. Meissner was in charge of the Office of the Reich President. He was a bulldog of a man, with a thick, round head, almost no neck . . . and, unlike most others, real ability.

The president's son, Oskar, was also present. Oscar was forty-nine. Tall—my size—with a military bearing to complement his gaunt face, he served as his father's aide-de-camp during the war and was gatekeeper for access to the ailing president. The inside word was that Oskar was an officer of modest abilities, whose career entirely depended on the influence of his devoted father.

Wolf sat in silence after they presented their proposal.

Seeing no reaction from Hitler, Brüning continued, "I am very close to obtaining necessary foreign concessions. In order to do this, Hindenburg *must* continue to be president."

Again they waited for a response, and again Wolf remained still. His silence began to wear on Brüning, who blotted beads of perspiration on his forehead. Afraid that Hitler would get up and leave before he could present his case, Brüning spoke at a faster clip. "The plan is for your party to join our coalition. When you do, we will control two-thirds of the votes. This will allow us to pass an Enabling Act and suspend the constitution. When this happens, we can extend Reich President Hindenburg's term of office without an election. That plan is to reinstate the constitution in two year's time. Then it will be your turn, Herr Hitler. Do I have your support?"

Hitler remained expressionless.

Brüning wiped his nose and brow with his white handkerchief. Again, he asked for Hitler's consent. "Do I have your support?"

"I shall consider it," Hitler said. He then rose and we left, leaving them scratching their heads.

Outside, he turned to me. "Brüning is blind to the fact that his power dangles by a spider's thread. Turmoil rules the streets. The communists are poised to pounce and take over. And what do they ask me to do? Join with them and destroy Germany! Do they think me a fool?"

February 2, 1932

The presidential election was less than six weeks away, but no candidate had come forward to announce a run for the office. A group of us sat around the conference table in the *Braunes Haus* in Munich. Goebbels rapped the table; all turned to him. "This is our time. You must declare for the presidency."

Wolf shook his head. "Now that we have refused to alter the Constitution, Hindenburg must announce his candidacy. He has no choice. Until he does, we do nothing."

"He has all the advantages," said Goebbels. "The sooner you declare, the more time we have to campaign."

"Hindenburg's hesitancy will be our advantage," said Hess.

"I agree with Rudy," I said. Goebbels glared at me. "If we declare first, it strengthens Hindenburg's hand. He will say he has to run to defeat us. But we gain the advantage after the old man declares. Then the *Führer* offers himself as an alternative to a doddering old general who is long past his prime and has no reason to run except to retain power."

All eyes turned to Wolf for the final word. "Friedrich understands. We wait for Hindenburg to declare. Not a minute sooner."

*

On February 15, the eighty-five-year-old president acquiesced to pressure to run for another seven-year term and issued a two-sentence public statement: "The appeal to stand for reelection came to me not from a party but from the broad masses. Therefore, I recognize it is my duty to stand."

Word reached us in the Kaiserhof Hotel in Berlin, where we waited for the announcement.

"Now," Wolf said to Goebbels, "we declare."

The timing was perfect. Weiss's ban on Goebbels's public speaking had expired. A few days later, Goebbels appeared before an overflowing meeting of the party at the Sportpalast to announce that Wolf would run against von Hindenburg and seek the presidency of Germany.

Wolf and I were planted in the lobby of the Kaiserhof Hotel, waiting to hear how Goebbels's announcement was received. Wolf sipped tea; I had a stein. At a table across from us, three women tittered, bemused they were so near the famous Adolf Hitler.

Wolf nodded to them and then turned to me. "It's been a couple of months since you last saw Lilian, Friedrich."

"More like half a year."

"I couldn't be without for that long." Notwithstanding numerous trips across the country, he would steal away to Obersalzberg to spend moments with Eva Braun or Maria Reiter or Marlene Weinrich. "Perhaps one of those women interests you?"

I moved my chair so my back was to them. "When you were with Eva a few weeks back, I met someone special."

"Why didn't you tell me?"

"At the time, it was a brief encounter. I wasn't sure it would turn into anything."

Wolf patted me on the shoulder. "Is it another actress? Have I seen her movies?"

I feigned mock horror. "One actress was enough for me. This is someone you would approve: Trude Mohr. I met her at a youth rally that Baldur von Schirach invited me to attend a few weeks ago."

Schirach married Henny Hoffmann, the daughter of the photographer Heinrich Hoffmann. In short order, he was elevated to head all Hitler Youth programs, including the the recently formed girls' group known as the BDM: *Bund Deutscher Mädel.* Trude founded the Brandenburg district's chapter, which became the second largest in the country.

Wolf knew of Trude and was delighted. "This is a good choice, Friedrich. She will give you perfect Aryan children."

*

Trude, at twenty-nine, was the prototypic German: tall, athletic, blond, and blue-eyed. She had already been a member of the NSDAP for five years when we met, and now made the BDM her singular focus.

There was an immediate attraction. Trude could have posed as the model Aryan woman. She radiated strength and glowed with natural beauty. She needed no makeup. But she did have one imperfection: she was nearsighted. Yet her glasses were part of her allure.

I first encountered Trude when she was giving instructions to a young girl in a play area. Trude towered over her. I waited until she noticed me. When she did, she said, "Hello," displaying a dazzling set of perfect teeth.

The girl scooted away to join her friends.

"You are good with children." I stepped closer. "My name is Friedrich Richard."

"I know." She smiled again. "I've seen you at rallies."

"Why didn't you make yourself known to me?"

"Why would you talk to someone like me? You're dating Lilian Harvey."

"Dated, as in past tense. She didn't approve of my party activities. Besides, she moved to America."

Trude's lips turned upward when she heard that Lilian was out of the picture. We found a nearby bar. I liked that she drank scotch. We answered each other's superficial questions, and I was thankful I did not need to spin a tale of my obliterated past. Finally, I asked, "Why isn't a girl like you married?"

"Most men find me too strong-willed."

"That is a quality to be admired."

"The truth is I have little time for anything but the party. I've dedicated myself to training young girls to embrace their femininity with a healthy mind and body, and not to idolize men . . . when they should feel their equal."

"That would scare most men away."

"I could never be with a man who thinks his every whim needs to be obeyed. I'd rather be with my girls and the party."

"I've never met a woman who thinks like you."

"Until now. And . . ."

"And what?"

"And I notice you're still sitting here."

Over the following weeks, we became close yet remained independent. She had her work. I had mine. We satisfied each other's physical needs, but there was nothing more substantive to the relationship.

*

"Neither of us is ready to have children, Wolf." I could see he was about to remind me how important it was for NSDAP leaders to marry and propagate, when Goebbels, Hess, Frick, and Göring rushed into the Kaiserhof lobby.

"It was glorious!" Göring called out. "They stamped and stomped and roared when Joseph announced that you will oppose Hindenburg."

Wolf looked to Goebbels for affirmation.

"It was a triumph." Ever cocky, Goebbels beamed as if the crowd's adulation had been for him.

When the jubilation subsided, I called attention to the legal obstacle of our candidate. "Wolf, you are still not a German citizen."

Goebbels put his hand on my arm; I tried not to cringe. "Arrangements have been made."

*

Days later, on February 25, Dietrich Klagges, a member of Braunschweig State government and recently elected to the Reichstag, had the honor of swearing Adolf Hitler in as the *Regierungsrat* (a low-rank government official) at the Braunschweig State Culture and Surveying Office. In his new appointment, Hitler would be stationed in the Braunschweig legation in Berlin. In this way, Wolf became a legal German citizen. Klagges would be rewarded when Wolf became chancellor by appointing him *Ministerpräsident* of the Free State of Brunswick (Braunschweig) for the duration of the Third Reich.

Immediately upon taking the oath, Hitler applied for a leave of absence.

"Absolutely, *mein Führer.* Take all the time you need until after the presidential election," said Dietrich Klagges. This ended Hitler's official duties before they began.

When Klagges offered his hand in congratulations, Wolf answered, "You should congratulate Germany, not me."

*

As the March '32 election neared, labor leaders, capitalists, and democratic supporters rallied behind Hindenburg. Wolf courted industrialists in private while posing as the candidate for the masses. "Things have come to such a pass that two workingmen must feed one unemployed," he repeated at every rally.

Election Day results surprised all. While Hindenburg received the most votes, his 49.6 percent fell fractions short of the needed majority. Wolf garnered 30.1 percent. The Communists collected 13.2 percent. The remaining votes were scattered among fringe candidates. This forced an election runoff between Hindenburg and Hitler scheduled for mid-April 1932.

There was little time to rest. I continued to work in our Berlin headquarters while Goebbels arranged for Wolf to speak at as many rallies as possible. We never expected to win the election or even the runoff election, but we did gain ground. This time we received 36.8 percent of the national vote. Of those Germans who voted, 13,400,000 voted for Adolph Hitler for president!

Nearly thirteen-and-a-half years after leaving Dr. Forster's care at Pasewalk Hospital and seven after his discharge from Landsberg prison, Adolf Hitler and the NSDAP were a major political force in Germany.

May 2, 1932

It was late in the evening. Too tired to undress for bed, I was dozing in my chair when the telephone jarred me awake.

"Do you recognize my voice?"

"Yes."

"We need to meet. Tomorrow. At the same park bench."

A time was set.

*

Ready in my black *Obergruppenführer* uniform, I froze in front of a mirror. "This will never do." It would call unwanted attention to a meeting between Berlin's most important police chief and me. I changed into civilian clothes.

I found Weiss waiting on the bench. It was mid-day on a Monday; no one else was around. I sat at the free end. "What is this about?"

"I told you it was more likely that I would be giving you information rather than you to me. You have an enemy."

"Just one?" I laughed, but Weiss did not smile.

"Perhaps you have more, but this one is dangerous."

"Who is it?"

"Reinhard Heydrich."

I shrugged. "I felt disdain for that man the moment I met him. He doesn't bother me."

"You may sing a different tune after you hear what I have to say. Heydrich approached a party member on one of our police teams to install a wiretap on your telephone."

That wiped the smile right off my face. "Why would the party member come to you?"

"He's still a policeman. He needed to requisition the equipment. When I heard about the request, I drilled into it. Your name came up."

"Did they get what they needed?"

"If they had, I would not have used the phone to contact you."

"You didn't identify yourself."

"I did use my voice."

We both fell silent.

"Bernhard . . . may I still call you so?" The small man waved his yes. "I still don't understand why you've taken on the role of guardian angel. You're a Jew helping a Nazi."

"As I told you last time, you are in a position to provide some balance should Hitler succeed in becoming a dictator."

"Balance may not be needed. Hitler has denounced violence. He has ordered the *SA* off the streets and is categorically against taking power by a putsch. He has even moderated his attacks on the Jews."

"And you believe that once he's in power, this benevolence will continue? That he will continue a reasonable stance on the Jews?"

"Look, Bernhard, I was with a group of Jews just a few months ago. They were not all as negative as you are, and for good reason: the leadership of the NSDAP is moving toward the center."

A mixture of doubt, skepticism, and sadness crept into his voice. "Friedrich, Jews are no better at evaluating a present danger or the future course of events than other people. I've talked with many Berlin Jews and, I agree, some *are* hopeful. I've learned one thing studying history: when the climate turns hostile for Jews, it is rarely a passing storm. Hitler is moderating himself now, as he courts power. But if he gets that power, there will be no restraining him. He will impose cold, remorseless logic to stretch the limits of reasonableness and proportionality to the breaking point as he applies his crazy racial theories."

"In the name of Heaven, what the hell are you talking about?"

"In the name of both, I hope we never find out."

*

The news about Heydrich did not alarm me. He knew I could shut him down with one word to Wolf.

As for Weiss and his worries, I was sure that Wolf would moderate his views once he gained power. Why wouldn't he? I pushed Weiss's concerns aside.

Chapter 42

May 7, 1932

In April, Chancellor Brüning banned the *SA* and the *SS* again. Wolf and I were in party headquarters in Berlin, discussing the situation when the phone rang. It was Kurt von Schleicher. When Wolf replaced the receiver, he was jubilant.

"They continue to think up new ways to resuscitate a government on life support. They fail to see that their futile efforts play into our hands."

"What did General von Schleicher want?"

"He wants me to attend a secret meeting this evening. He would not give any details."

"Is it about Chancellor Brüning?"

"It's possible. Schleicher was emphatic that Brüning would not be at the meeting."

"It sounds like Schleicher may be plotting to remove Brüning. If it comes to that, can Schleicher be trusted?"

"Trusted?" Wolf snorted. "He is the last man in Germany to be trusted. He's been at the Old Man's side for the seven years that Hindenburg has been president. Everyone knows that Hindenburg has been at Germany's helm, but few understand that Schleicher is the one who has set the course that's driven us into this bloody mess."

"I thought the 25/48/53 formula was Hindenburg's idea."

This formula—taken directly from the Weimar constitution—created a presidential government that could ignore the popular vote if no party had a majority in the Reichstag.

Under the Constitution, the chancellor was responsible only to the president, not to the elected members of the Reichstag. Article 25 gave the president power to dissolve the Reichstag whenever he chose. Article 48 authorized the president to sign emergency bills without the consent of the Reichstag. Article 53 gave the president the power to appoint the Chancellor. The only counterbalance to presidential power was given to the Reichstag. The Reichstag was able overturn a presidential edict within sixty days of passage by a simple majority. But with no majority party and a refusal to form a coalition because parties refused to compromise, this check was illusory.

"You can say much about the old Field Marshal, but being an innovative bureaucratic manager is not one of his strengths," Wolf explained. "The magic 25/48/53 formula was Schleicher's idea. His and his alone."

"You're telling me that Hindenburg never intended for Germany to be a democracy?"

"That's not quite right," said Wolf. "The Old Man defends the republic because he gave his oath, but he has always been a monarchist at heart. But the more the parties bicker, the more Hindenburg gets frustrated." Wolf threw his hands up. "Who can blame him? We've had eleven chancellors—thirteen, if you count the second stints of Wilhelm Marx and Wilhelm Müller—plus seventeen different cabinets since the war ended. Of course Hindenburg is frustrated."

"It's no wonder we are where we are. We never really had a democracy, did we?"

"Only a bastardized version that was doomed to fail," said Hitler, rubbing his hands. "This discord within the democracy is strangling democracy itself to death."

*

Schleicher's apartment was antique-filled. We sat around an oval mahogany dining room table extended by adding a leaf. Schleicher, the president's secretary Otto Meissner, and the general's son, Oskar, sat across from us.

I studied Schleicher. He was barrel-chested with a short neck. At fifty he was already bald. He had a low brow, hooded eyes, a beak-like nose, and thin lips.

Schleicher's influence on the president was rooted in his relationship with the president's son. Schleicher entered the Prussian army in 1900, where he soon befriended fellow junior officer, Oskar von Hindenburg, when both served in the Third Foot Guards. As the senior Hindenburg's importance grew during the Great War, Schleicher made certain to cultivate the politically green Oskar, who by then served as his father's aide-de-camp. Schleicher moved even closer to Oskar once the old man became president. As senior grew more infirmed and Oskar took control of access to his father, Schleicher became the most powerful man in Germany.

Schleicher took charge of the meeting. "Let me be blunt, Herr Hitler. The president has grown frustrated over Chancellor Brüning's inability to forge a working majority in the Reichstag. Brüning is finished."

"Like those before him, I am well aware of his limitations," Wolf said.

"No one blames you directly, but you have a heavy hand in these matters."

Wolf bowed his head. "If anything, I am a constitutionalist, General Schleicher. I support the wishes of the electorate. They expect us to remain true to our principles, not to compromise them away."

Oskar Hindenburg spoke next. "Brüning hammered the final nail into his political coffin when he proposed to divide up the Junker estates. He plans to hand our lands over to farmer-peasants to serve as a buffer between Germany and Poland. This is foolhardy." He pounded the table with his large fist. "Taking land from the aristocracy is unthinkable. My father will not tolerate this."

"That was the final straw," said Meissner. "It is the field marshal's wish that Brüning must go."

Wolf looked from Meissner to Oskar Hindenburg to Schleicher. "Is this your way of asking me to be chancellor?"

Schleicher answered. "President Hindenburg cannot support you. He is not ready to turn the republic into a dictatorship."

Wolf focused on Oskar. "The moment your father became president, a course was set for dictatorship." Then he turned to Schleicher, ignoring the others. "From the beginning, it was your idea to erode the last vestiges of democracy with your 25/48/53 formula. You knew what you were doing. You never intended Germany to be democratic."

Schleicher bristled. "Herr Hitler. Six million are unemployed. One-third of Germany's working force sits idle, if you include those who have given up searching for a job. How can you run a democracy under those conditions with dozens of parties that cannot agree on anything?"

Wolf conceded nothing. "When Brüning started, half as many were out of work. The economy was in recovery. But when the world markets crashed, you used Article 48 to sign proclamations into law . . ." then he turned to Oskar, ". . . and your father went along."

The silence was deafening. Wolf had struck a chord.

Then he raised both hands to the ceiling, curling his fingers into tight fists in the way he had practiced in those early photo sessions in Hoffman's studio. "Brüning has used the president to rule by fiat for close to two years. What do we have to show for it? Chaos in the streets and the worst unemployment in our history. Our people are hungry not only for food, but for new leadership. Make me chancellor and I promise to change all of this."

While Oskar and Meissner were spellbound, Schleicher remained unfazed. He presented his proposal, ignoring anything Hitler said. "Field Marshal Hindenburg is prepared to give you a number of concessions, Herr Hitler. Specifically, he is willing to lift the ban on the *SS* and the *SA*."

The aura that encircled Wolf began to dissipate. "What else?"

"We know that the NSDAP is on the rise. We also know that your party has garnered close to fifty percent in various Landtag elections. With each election, you grow stronger."

"All the more reason to make me chancellor. I, alone, can form a majority coalition with the Catholic Centre Party."

Meissner offered a compromise. "The Reich president has had enough of chancellors promising to form coalitions only to have them fail. You will be no different. What he is prepared to do is to disband the Reichstag to give you a chance to earn a clear majority. He promises to schedule new elections as soon as Brüning submits his resignation."

"When will these elections be held?" I asked.

"In July," responded Meissner,

Doggedly, Wolf asked a third time, "Who will be the new chancellor in the meantime?"

Oskar delivered a previously scripted answer. "My father is tired. Since no chancellor has a majority, he will form a gentlemen's cabinet made up of aristocrats who are not beholden to any party. Using Article 53, he will appoint Franz von Papen chancellor."

What they proposed was preposterous. It guaranteed failure. My hackles rose. "How is that better than what we have now?" Everyone turned to me, surprised that I spoke. "We need a strong leader with a single purpose. Otherwise, Germany will be relegated to the discarded heap of once great powers."

Oskar directed his answer to Wolf. "We know you intend to transform our country into a dictatorship. Under no circumstances will my father let that happen. He was elected to guide the republic and that is what he *will* do."

I expected Wolf to explode . . . but he didn't.

"What do you require of me?" Wolf asked in a tone belying his anger and disappointment.

"That you give the next chancellor a chance to succeed."

All in the room expected Wolf to say, "No."

His answer shocked us all. "I agree."

I was bursting to ask the obvious, but I had to wait until we left.

Outside, I asked, "Why did you give in to their demands?"

Wolf pinched my cheek. "*Friedrichshen,* a concoction of barons and aristocrats can never make a difference. They're doomed to fail. We have no choice but to go along because Schleicher has the *Reichswehr* behind him. Without the army, we can never succeed. We suffered that painful lesson when our putsch failed. So let them put Papen in. He will have no majority in the Reichstag. In fact, Papen no longer has a party supporting him. The Catholic Centrum threw him out. Rest assured that Papen will only last a few months. The good news is that they handed us a new election and an opportunity to gain a majority in July. With a majority, I *will* be chancellor. In the meantime . . ." his lips curled upward, ". . . the services of the *SA* and the *SS* have just been returned to us in time for the election."

*

Two days later, Schleicher's plan went into motion. Hermann Göring sent a clear message from the chamber floor of the Reichstag. "The people do not exist to be ruined by a government that cannot master a situation. The Brüning cabinet must go so Germany can live!"

Brüning had no alternative: he resigned. Next, Hindenburg appointed Papen as chancellor. Papen, as promised, then lifted the ban on the *SA* and the *SS*. The final step—the call for new elections—would fulfill the last promise to Wolf.

Within three weeks, Minister of Defense Groener resigned. This paved the way for Kurt von Schleicher to assume that post and he wasted no time "advising" Chancellor von Papen who he should appoint to the remaining cabinet positions. Papen accepted *all* of Schleicher's "suggestions."

The year's fourth major election was scheduled for July. We held meeting after meeting to select our best candidates to run against incumbents, with a singular goal: to gain a majority in the Reichstag in order to make Wolf Germany's next chancellor.

Chapter 43

July 18, 1932

Trude had the week off and I took a few days from electioneering to be with her. It was late Monday morning and we were still in bed. "Tell me about the famous Lilian Harvey. Did you sleep with her in this bed?"

"I took this apartment after we split. In fact, you are the only one who has ever stayed here." I swung my legs over the edge, and sat up, hoping to end this line of talk.

Trude grabbed my hand. "Come back. If you don't know by now, let me tell you that I am not the jealous sort. I'm interested in what type of person she was, because she is so famous."

I leaned back. "There were days she was nice and days we battled. She didn't approve of the party or the *Führer's* program for Germany."

"Then she was a fool. We *need* a strong leader like Hitler." But she wouldn't stop there. "She was beautiful and all that, but what about her soul? Was she a good person?"

I did not want to unlock those memories. I hesitated. "Lilian was fair to everyone. She treated minor actors as if they were major stars. She never had to throw a tantrum to get what she wanted. Directors did kowtow to her because most of her movies were successes. In private, she only acted out with me. She couldn't stand the fact that I would cancel our plans and run to Munich whenever the *Führer* needed help."

"Was she a good German?"

We both knew what that meant. "To the extent that she wanted Germany to get out from under the Treaty, she was like everyone else. But supporting the party? No! Not even after she wanted the party to help when her bank account was in danger. Did you know that Goebbels once asked her to make a film for the party?"

"Don't tell me, she refused? Then she's dumber than I thought. It's better that she went to America." Thankfully, that ended all talk about Lilian Harvey.

We dressed, grabbed a cab, and caught a movie at the Kintopp. We emerged into the bright sunlight and set off for an intimate café nearby. Two blocks later, we heard a cacophony of metal clanging and glass breaking.

"What's that?" asked Trude.

Then a scream pierced the air. I stepped into the street and saw a band of wild-eyed, uniformed *SA* tumbling through the streets toward us. I grabbed her elbow and spun her around. "We need to get out of here."

"Why run from them? They're Brownshirts. Tell them who you are. They won't harm us," said Trude.

"You expect a riotous band of men to stop what they're doing because we ask them to check our ID cards? Let's get out of here."

We turned in the opposite direction, rounded the corner prepared to run, when a ragtag group of Reds brandishing truncheons and chains headed our way. Some had pistols in their waistbands. There was no place to hide.

I grabbed her hand. "C'mon." We sprinted back toward the Brownshirts. "I'm *Obergruppenführer* Richard. There are two-dozen Communists coming our way. They are armed and looking for trouble."

He raised his billy club. "And I'm Heinrich Himmler. Where's your party uniform?"

There was no time to waste; I pointed to Trude's collar. "See her swastika? She's one of the *BDM* leaders!"

As he peered for a better look at Trude's pin, he saw the oncoming hooligans rushing towards us. He whipped around, shouting to his comrades. "Here they come! You two get behind us."

The Brownshirts charged. Surprised by their attack, the Reds broke ranks, but were quick to regroup. They surged forward and managed to push the Brownshirts back.

I grabbed Trude. "Let's get out of here," but we didn't have a chance. Three Reds had circled behind us. A fierce blow clobbered me on the back of my neck. I fell to my knees, twisted onto my back, and kicked the Red in the groin. He dropped the pipe as he doubled over. I scrabbled to my feet and came down hard on the back of his neck with the side of my hand. He crumpled to the ground. A kick to the temple made certain he was finished.

Trude was in trouble. She had drawn a party dagger from her purse and struggled against two Reds who had backed her against a wall. One smashed her right forearm as the other twisted her left hand. She screamed in agony. Her knife clattered to the pavement. She lunged to retrieve it and was slammed into a pipe jutting from the wall causing her to collapse in a heap.

I tackled the Red closest to me and drove his head into the pavement. There was the telltale crack of nose cartilage being crushed. I yanked his head up by his hair. Teeth had pierced through his lips. Blood was everywhere. His eyes had rolled back; he was unconscious and no longer a threat.

The last Red tore at Trude's clothes as she lay there. In one move, I lifted him and hurled him through a storefront window. I dropped beside Trude; her right arm was broken and her left shoulder appeared dislocated. I grabbed the assailant's pipe, ripped off part of my shirt, and lashed it to her arm as a splint. I fashioned a sling from the rest of my shirt for her left arm.

She moaned from the pain.

"You're going to be all right. I've got to get you to a hospital."

I helped her to her feet. She took one step and collapsed. I scooped her up in my arms and headed away from the melee. When I found a cab, I ordered the driver to take us to Charité Hospital. "And fast."

Inside the emergency room, I dropped Alfred Hugenberg's name, knowing the head of UFA studios would get Trude immediate attention. It worked. I stayed in the patient waiting area while they whisked Trude to X-ray, set her broken arm, and performed a closed reduction on her dislocated shoulder. While

Trude was treated, another physician examined me to make sure the blow to the back of my head was nothing more than a bruise.

Sometime later, a doctor found me in the waiting area, holding a bag of ice to my bruise.

"How is she?"

"Her arm and shoulder will mend fine. She received quite a blow to her head. The left orbital bone was fractured and there was a contusion that turned the whites of her left eye red. We bandaged it closed."

"Will she be able to see all right?"

"She asked about her glasses."

"In the excitement I forgot to look for them."

"No matter. She may need a new prescription after she heals. We have a great staff, but we can't give patients individual attention all night."

"What can I do to help?"

"It's important to wake her every couple of hours. Make certain she is coherent and can focus. I don't think there is any cerebral bleeding. Neurologically she seemed fine, but we can't be too careful."

Hugenberg's name was magic. Trude was placed in a private room. She fell into a deep sleep. I watched her chest rise and fall, taking slow, rhythmic breaths. There was an IV in her right hand. Her left eye was bandaged shut, the skin around it already deep purple.

I roused her for the first time around midnight. Trude opened her right eye and smiled. "I hope the other guy looks worse than me."

"I guarantee his mother won't recognize him."

"Thanks for saving me."

"We saved each other. Don't talk. The doctor asked me to wake you every couple of hours. Get some rest now."

Even in pain, she managed to pucker her lips and blow a kiss. Within seconds, she closed her eyes and drifted into a deep sleep.

I returned to my chair, comforted by Trude's soft, even breaths. Sitting there, hearing the night sounds of the hospital, the clanging of metal trays, the wheels chirping under rolling carts, and an occasional muffled cough or nighttime cry brought back memories of this hospital all those years back. I pictured the austere room, the ceiling, how I struggled to walk; then I drifted to my days at Pasewalk, and the man in the bed next to me, begging for anyone to help take him to the loo. Now, with elections two weeks away, that man might become the German chancellor.

"Friedrich. Friedrich."

In my dream, someone called my name. I awoke with a start. "What do you want, Trude? I'm here."

A nurse's hand was on my shoulder. I looked up. The face had grown round, the hair streaked with gray. "Anna?" It was nearly thirteen years, but there she was, standing next to me.

"I'm covering for someone tonight. I glanced through the doorway. It's hard to miss you even though you're slumped in a chair in a darkened room. Imagine my surprise to find you here." She motioned to follow her.

Trude continued to breathe in a rhythmic, sleep state. She appeared to be at peace, at least as much as she could be. I thought it safe to leave for a few minutes.

Anna stepped back and surveyed me. "You look well, except for that bruise on your neck." She touched it; her fingers were soothing. "How have you been?"

There was a gold band on her ring finger. "You're married?"

She smiled, the creases deeper than before. "I became a cliché. I married a doctor."

"Is it anyone I might know?"

She shook her head and then nodded toward the room. "Is she your new friend?"

"Trude? Yes, we've been seeing each other for a bit."

"Is it serious?"

"Neither of us is ready to commit. We're both too busy."

Her face tightened. "Friedrich, I know that you're associated with that Jew-hater, Adolf Hitler."

Hearing this from her lips gave me a jolt. "How did you find out?"

"Every once in a while the camera catches you in the background behind Hitler. I am one of the few who understand why you limit your public exposure. But why him? You're better than that."

"Am I?"

"I used to think so. I'd still like to think so."

"Maybe you never really knew me and that was our problem."

She took a tiny step back. "I didn't tap you on the shoulder to stir up old memories. I wanted to say hello to someone who had once been my friend."

My defenses throttled down. Maybe Anna had touched upon something I had been trying to justify in my own mind for some time. "I'm sorry. Challenging me about why I am with Wolf and the others, well, it surprised me. That's all."

"Who's Wolf?"

"Hitler. He called himself that when we first met in Pasewalk. The thing is, Anna, when I left you, I had no place to go. Then I remembered that Wolf was the only other person I knew or could remember. He was in Munich. I found him, joined his entourage, and watched him take a nascent band of men to the brink of taking over Germany."

"And you think this is a good thing?"

I looked her square in the eyes. "With all its warts and obvious problems, I do."

"Cracking people's skulls is more than mere blemishes. But I'm not going to stand here and debate you. Perhaps you see something in your Wolf that I can't understand." She searched down the hall, signaling she had said all she wanted to say. "I need to return to my patients. Before I do, one last question: did your memory ever return?"

"Not a shred."

"Aren't you still curious as to who you really are?"

"I was in those first few years. Now? I'm not sure I want to know anymore. I've lived so long as Friedrich Richard that I can't imagine any other life. I'm not sure I want to discover a bunch of relatives who would expect me to get to know them. I don't need ghosts to appear."

I was rooted to the spot, guilty that I still owed the apology I tried to give her when Wolf and I were in Berlin during the ill-fated Kapp Putsch.

"Anna, about what happened . . ."

She put her finger on my lips. "Don't say anything. It's not necessary. I remember I told you that I should never have gotten involved with you. It was true, but not in the way I made it sound. You were so young, and I was so lonely after my husband died. I knew all the shortcomings and pitfalls starting up with you. But you were there, so handsome and vulnerable. I couldn't admit that we were never meant to succeed." She looked down and twisted her wedding band. "I've been over you for a long time. Life has been good to me. I'm happy now." Then she looked up. "I hope you are, too."

I stepped toward Trude's room, stopped, turned, and kissed Anna on the cheek.

She touched the spot. "What was that for?"

"For being you. Your husband is a lucky man."

July 19, 1932

I woke Trude every two hours as instructed. Each time, she opened her good eye, smiled, spoke a few words of encouragement, and then lapsed back into a deep sleep.

"What kind of soldier are you, sleeping on guard duty?"

The voice was familiar. My lids fluttered open. Morning sunlight filled the room. I rubbed my eyes only to see the pale face of the deputy president of the Berlin Police etched in concern.

"Bernhard. What are you doing here?"

"This may be the last time we can meet," he whispered.

His words didn't register. "How did you find me?"

"We broke up the fight that sent your lady-friend here. When I heard that a big man took out three thugs, well, it sounded like someone I knew. I made some inquiries and learned that you were here with your friend. How is she?"

"Mending. The doctors reassured me her injuries would heal without lasting damage." Now more awake, I sat straighter. His first words hit home. "What do you mean, 'the last time we can meet?'"

Weiss shook his head. "Not here," he checked Trude's sleeping figure. "There is an empty room down the hall."

Moments later we were in the unoccupied room where I was perched on the edge of the bed and Weiss took the only chair.

He spoke first. "Papen was supposed to head a caretaker government until the next elections. But that does not appear to be the case. Did you know that Papen wants to rule Prussia as well?"

"Are you certain?"

"Are you forgetting I have people everywhere? Papen's so-called cabinet has voted in secret to authorize it. President Hindenburg will soon sign the decree that allows the Reich to take over the Prussian government. When he does, this will end the only democratic government left in Germany . . . not to mention its independent police."

This had so many implications. "Who is behind this?"

"Kurt von Schleicher is moving all the pieces."

"I should have known."

"I have to confess I was surprised Hitler gave in to Schleicher when he heard the new cabinet would be headed by an aristocrat."

"What choice did he have? They were not about to make him chancellor."

"At least Franz Gürtner was named minister of justice. That must have made Hitler happy. As I recall, it was Gürtner as the Bavarian minister of justice who made sure your friend could use the putsch trial in '23 as a speaking platform, guided the court to a mild sentence, and then made certain Hitler had an early release."

"Hitler was already a hero to many."

"Was he a hero with his niece?"

"That's old news. Why go there?"

"Oh, I know he didn't pull the trigger, Friedrich, but character *does* matter. Sleeping with his own niece while chasing seventeen-year-old girls matters. It tells us the sort of man he was . . . and still is."

"Where are you going with this, Bernhard? Why did you really come here?"

"Because there is no one else."

"To do what?"

"To make a difference."

"In what way? I hold no position. I have no power. There is nothing I can directly do."

"That may be true for now, but it may not always be so."

"Perhaps if we gain a majority in the Reichstag . . ."

"I can't see that happening," said Bernhard. "There are too many parties for anyone to gain a majority. That includes your Nazis."

"Then what *are* you talking about, Bernhard?"

"The country cannot continue this way. The paralysis, as you call it, caused by this gaggle of parties has to end. The only answer is for a strong man to emerge. My belief is that it will be Hitler."

"That's what we have been angling for. But you of all people . . . why do you say this?"

Rather than answer directly, he mentioned that Hindenburg was tired and had no desire for another term but felt he had no choice. Then he said, "You must be aware that the aristocrats have no intention of keeping Germany as a republic. They all believe—Papen included—that God has ordained them to rule Germany."

"Hitler is no different. He has been clear that once he becomes chancellor, he intends to get rid of democracy. I support him in this."

"You do now, but there will come a time when you won't."

"How can you be so sure?" I asked.

"Because the man who saved the old Jew in the street, who rallied to his friend when he thought Goebbels was persecuting him . . . is not like the others who surround Hitler. Look at the malevolent dwarf Goebbels, the morphine-addled Göring, or the off-balance Hess."

"But . . ."

"Let me finish. None of them can ever be the voice of reason. Not a one will temper anything Hitler wishes to do. And there are worse rising in your ranks."

He could only mean Himmler and Heydrich. I held up my hands to stop wherever this was leading. "You're placing too much on me."

Weiss sighed. "Perhaps I am." Then he stood and looked deep into my eyes. "There is no one else, Friedrich." He held my gaze to emphasize all that this implied, and then handed me a card.

I looked at it. "I already have one of yours."

"Turn it over. I've written my sister's phone and address on the back. While I expect to be removed from office in a day or two, I still have connections. There may come a time when you need my help or simply want to speak with me."

Bernhard thrust out his hand. "Good luck, Friedrich. It is not likely we will meet again. May God give you strength."

After clasping hands, the diminutive deputy president of Berlin's police slipped through the door. I stood holding the door open, and stared at his back until he rounded the corner and the clicking of his heels faded away.

The quiet was momentary. The faint sound of a distant siren pierced the stillness. An announcement was made calling nurses and doctors to the emergency room: scores of wounded were coming in from another street fight. I felt Bernhard Weiss was right in one thing: a strong leader must emerge to save Germany from itself.

Chapter 44

Two days later Trude was released from the hospital. With her left arm in a sling, her right arm in a cast, and her facial wounds healing, she needed time to recuperate. There was no way she could run two-week stints for her girls at summer camp. After an internal debate, I called Wolf, who continued to rent *Haus Wachenfeld* in the Obersalzberg.

"Of course the two of you can stay until she gets stronger," Wolf answered. "How could I not open my house to a hero?"

Trude had gained notoriety getting injured fighting the Reds. Now she viewed our misfortune on the street as a positive. If not for that, she would not be in the Obersalzberg.

"Can you imagine," she said as we mounted the steps, "The *Führer* has invited *me* to stay in *his* home."

Before we entered, I explained, "You need to understand how secretive the Boss is with his private life. He never lets anyone stay here who isn't in his inner circle. You are the first exception."

"Then I'm truly honored."

I sensed she still did not understand the gravity. "This is no trivial matter, Trude. No matter what you see or hear, you must promise not to breathe a word of it to anyone."

Her eyes narrowed. "Why is everything so hush-hush?"

"Hitler wants our countrymen to see him as totally dedicated to the cause. Without any diversions. This includes women. He often says, 'I am married to Germany.'"

"Does he have a woman?"

"At the moment he favors Eva Braun. I expect she will be here."

"At the moment? What is that supposed to mean?"

She could interpret that any way she wanted. I knocked. Before the door opened, Trude reached on her toes and kissed me on the cheek. "Thank you for this special privilege."

"I had nothing to do with it."

"Of course you did, Friedrich."

At that moment, Wilma Schaub, the wife of Hitler's adjutant, opened the door.

"It's good to see you, Wilma," I said.

"*Wilkommen*, Friedrich." I introduced Trude. "The *Führer* is anxious to greet you in the study."

We followed her to the wood-paneled room. Wolf was dressed in a double-breasted gray suit in contrast to his brown uniform that he wore most often in public. Wolf was reading a report at his desk when we entered. He laid down the paper and rose to greet us.

"So this is the brave fräulein who fought the Reds." He touched her hand with the cast and brought it to his lips. "We are forever in your debt." He stared at Trude an extra beat with his magnetic blue eyes. "I have heard much about you from Baldur von Schirach even before you met my *Friedrichshen*. You are doing a magnificent job with our young girls. The party thanks you."

Trude glowed with pride. "The party is my life, *mein Führer*," and made an attempt to curtsy. Wolf caught her before she toppled over; she gasped at his touch and we all laughed.

"Let's have tea," he said, and led us to the living room.

Just as we nestled into our seats, Eva Braun appeared. Wolf rose, took her hand, and guided her to Trude and me. Eva reached out to shake Trude's hand but stopped when she saw the cast. "Does it hurt?"

"Not anymore. My shoulder is worse."

"I dislocated my shoulder during the putsch," said Hitler. "The pain was unbelievable."

"I hope I never experience that again," Trude said.

Eva turned to me. "It's nice to see you again, Friedrich."

I kissed Eva on both cheeks. "How have you been?"

She nodded at Wolf and smiled. "Very well, now that he's here."

Although Trude was Spartan and unconcerned with couture dresses, jewelry, and other fineries, Eva's expensive dress, shoes, and South Sea pearl necklace were not lost on her.

We migrated to the table when Wilma Schaub brought tea and biscuits. It was telling that Wolf poured the tea. Eva was not allowed to play the role of hostess. Meanwhile, Trude turned her head this way and that, taking in the furnishings, the painted plates resting on the wooden moldings that lined the walls, and the many artifacts in the room.

"I understand that you head the Brandenburg chapter of the *BDM*," said Eva. "It must be wonderful to teach our young girls what they need to be good homemakers. Have you seen much of Germany?"

"I've traveled some. Mainly I supervise the girls during their two-week stays at *BDM* camps." She lifted the arm with a cast. "I can't do that very well now, so I've taken a leave."

"Trude is being modest," I said. "She is turning our German girls into fine young women." Then I turned to Hitler. "The elections are around the corner. Where has Goebbels arranged for you to speak next week?"

Eva frowned as Hitler answered. "I have a dozen speeches scheduled. He has me jumping around the country by plane. More of the 'Hitler over Germany' campaign." Then he added, "Friedrich, I need you with me on this last swing."

"Do you have to take him with you?" asked Trude.

"Friedrich would never tell you this, Fräulein, but he is most important to me and the party. He must be with me for this final push for the election." Then he brightened. "Think of lending him to me as your contribution to the success of the party." He waved his hand. "Enough shop talk. I want to find out more about the good work that Fräulein Mohr performs for us."

Trude turned the color of rosé. I touched the small of her back, signalling she should not make more out of this than what it was meant to be: banter over tea and biscuits.

*

On the last weekend before the July 31 Reichstag election, Wolf and I set out to make a final swing across the country. We left Trude and Eva to spend the next few days together.

"I removed my sling this morning," Trude said as I bid farewell.

"That will make it easier to hike up the mountain trails with Eva," I said.

"I'm so glad you brought me here. Obviously meeting the *Führer* has been the highlight of my life."

"What about me?"

"What about you?" She grabbed my hand and kissed it. "No one has ever been as special to me as you are. Being here is a dream. As for Eva, she needs a friend. It's good that the two of us will have time alone."

Wolf and I drove to Munich where he spoke to a midday rally. Next we flew to Berlin where over one hundred thousand gathered to hear him. Over the course of the next few days, Wolf spoke before more than one million people.

Voting took place on Sunday, July 31. We returned to Berlin to await the results. There was no question that we would do well. But well was not good enough. Our goal was to earn a majority—303 of the 605 Reichstag seats—to make Wolf chancellor without either a presidential designation or a patched-together coalition.

When the votes were tabulated, we had a smashing victory . . . but not what we needed to govern on our own. Some fourteen million Germans voted for us, which represented 37.27% of the votes cast. We were now, by far, the largest party in the Reichstag, trailed first by the Social Democrats and then by the Communists. Yet beneath our triumph was the reality that without winning a majority of seats, our only hope was to persuade Hindenburg to appoint Hitler chancellor using Article 53.

In one sense, our election victory left us in worse straits. To induce Hindenburg to order the July 31 elections and Papen to rescind the ban on the *SA*, Hitler had promised to support the Papen chancellorship. Had we won a majority, Papen would have been replaced. But we didn't win. Now Wolf was bound to keep his promise to become Papen's vice-chancellor. In effect, Hitler would be a hostage within a government he did not control.

*

I called Trude from Berlin after receiving the election results.

"When are you returning to *Berchtesgaden*?" she asked, and then added, "Eva and I have been hiking and giggling like school girls. It's been wonderful. Thank you for bringing me here."

"What better place to recuperate?"

"Congratulations on the number of seats you won. All of you must be celebrating."

"We fell short of the majority we needed. We are about to meet to make plans for the next election."

"That's two years away. Why meet now?"

"To see if there is a possibility to move the election date sooner."

"What I do know about politics is that nothing happens overnight. There is time enough for you and the rest to plan your machinations. Me? I only have a few more days until I go back to my *BDM* girls. When can you get here?"

"Is tomorrow soon enough? We're flying down to Munich. The Boss will send a driver for you and Eva to meet us there. We have tickets to see a production of *Tristan und Isolde*. Are you familiar with it?"

"No. But if the *Führer* likes it, I'm sure I will, too."

"How has it been with Eva?"

"There's much to tell you, but not on the phone."

*

Göring, Goebbels, Hess, Frick, and I met in Hitler's office.

"Did you hear the latest?" Goebbels chortled. "Papen arrested Isador July 20, the day he took over the Prussian Government." Goebbels clapped in triumph. "The army commander in Berlin, Rundstedt, clamped that Jew policeman in irons and tossed him in his own jail. How fitting was that?"

While the others rapped the table, I thought back to what Bernhard Weiss said in that hospital room. He knew his days were numbered. "Is he still locked up?"

Goebbels formed a mask of disappointment. "Unfortunately, it was just for one day. I would have given a thousand marks to be there and another thousand to kick the kike's ass into the cell. I would have made sure that he watched as I turned the key and slipped it in my pocket."

To see Goebbels was bad enough, but to hear him speak elicited a visceral response that awakened loathing in my darkest recesses.

"This is our time. We are at our apex." Hitler scrutinized each of our faces. "I will *not* support that fool Papen. I will *not* form a coalition. I will *not* be a deputy chancellor. I represent nearly forty percent of the German people. He represents no one," his face purpled. "No one! Not a single person! No party backs him! Even his own party asked him to leave!"

"What next, *mein Führer*?" Hess asked.

Hitler let out a breath. "The obvious: a meeting with Schleicher. He controls both Papen and Hindenburg."

"To what end?" asked Göring. "They kept their promises. They lifted the ban on the *SA* and we had a smashing success in the elections. Schleicher will demand you become vice chancellor."

Wolf stood. "If Papen were a viable chancellor I could respect, I would keep my promise and be his vice chancellor." Wolf put both hands on the table and leaned toward us. "But he can't cobble together a majority. Chaos will continue in the chambers of the Reichstag and in the streets. I will not join such a mess. I cannot. For the good of Germany, I *must* demand the chancellorship!"

We all rapped the table in accord.

*

Though it was late and I was exhausted, I made my way to Bernhard Weiss's house where. I stood in the shadows for close to an hour. Nothing stirred except a tomcat on the prowl. Convinced that it was safe to approach, I tiptoed to the back door and gave a gentle knock. It was meant to be heard, not alarm.

A light flicked on and I heard the soft tread of a cautious approach. Pistol in hand, Bernhard parted the window curtain, saw me standing there, opened the door, and ushered me in, but not before sticking his head out for nosy neighbors.

"What are you doing here?" he whispered. He lit a candle, and we huddled around the kitchen table.

"I found out about your arrest. I was concerned that you were all right."

He shrugged. "It was meant to give me a taste of my own medicine. They asked a few questions and then told me I was fired along with the heads of all the other police departments in the Prussian state. Then General von Rundstedt put me in a cell."

I blanched.

"It was only for a few hours," Weiss explained.

"Do you need money?"

Bernhard shook his head. "I've enough."

"Did they rough you up?"

"They wouldn't dare."

"What are you going to do now?"

"The only thing I can do: sit tight and wait. If the Social Democrats return to power, perhaps this Nazi phenomenon will fizzle out. Then I can resume my career. Otherwise, I might work for some international organization." Then he changed the subject. "Have you seen what Papen is doing in Berlin?"

"You mean with the night clubs?"

"Yes. His Catholic Centre Party is busy enforcing the sex laws. Prosecuting homosexuals. He's gone too far."

"Max Klinghofer is crying in his soup. He could use your help these days. It has put a huge damper on his business."

"He's not the only one who needs help these days," Bernhard said, laughing at his own predicament.

It was good to see him inject a bit of levity into his precarious situation. We chatted a bit longer. I was reluctant to leave but knew I should. I promised to stay in touch. For the present, I was content that he and his family were not in danger.

It was quite late when I got to bed.

*

The following day, Wolf asked on the way to the airport, "Did you have a late night, Friedrich?"

My heart skipped a beat. Did I miss a sign? Did he have me followed? "I visited an old friend." He didn't ask whom.

He behaved as a co-conspirator. "I had a visit from a new friend."

"Should I ask her name?"

"Not important."

We arrived in Munich and met Eva and Trude for dinner before Wagner's famous opera. After the last curtain call, Wolf explained that he had made arrangements for Trude and me to stay in his apartment on *Prinzregentenplatz*.

"Eva and I will return to *Haus Wachenfeld*. Meet me in Berlin in two days. From there, you and I will travel to Furstenberg where a private meeting with General Schleicher has been scheduled."

Wolf had arranged for our luggage to be driven to his apartment while we were at the opera. Afterwards, as we said our goodbyes, Trude and Eva embraced, whispering and giggling like schoolgirls.

"What was that about?" I asked once we settled into the guest room in his apartment.

"You mean Eva? We bonded when you and the *Führer* canvassed the country. She's a sad, lonely girl. Much the way Isolde could never be with her lover. There was always another condition or event that got in the way."

"Wolf sees Eva as much as he can."

"He treats his dog better than he treats her. If I were Eva, I'd leave him. As much as I admire him as a leader, there's no future being Hitler's lover."

"Try to see it from his point of view. Wolf is a political force on a national scale. Even international. He gives Eva as much time as he can spare. She must understand this."

"A political force notwithstanding," said Trude, "Hitler needs to learn how to treat women better. He doesn't allow her to voice an opinion. He expects her to be there at his beck and call. Do you know what she said? He doesn't consider her his girlfriend. He considers her more of a *liebelei*. That's hurtful."

"She means more to him than a mere flirt," I said. "He cares for Eva."

"Not in the way a man should. When you travel, you call me almost every day. What does Hitler do? He never calls her on the phone. He sends a note once in a while. Even those, she told me, have become less frequent." Trude took my hand and looked me in the eyes. "Eva Braun is one sad girl."

Chapter 45

For two hours, I trailed within earshot of Wolf and General Schleicher as they ambled through a nature park in Furstenberg, about eighty-five kilometers north of Berlin. The dynamic was curious: Hitler talked and Schleicher nodded . . . without agreeing to anything.

Wolf stated the obvious. "We are the largest party in the Reichstag. Momentum is on our side. With Papen as chancellor, we will never have a place at the table of great industrial countries."

Schleicher strolled with his hands clasped behind his back. When Wolf waited for him to say something, all Schleicher did was nod.

Wolf took this as an assent and continued what was tantamount to a monologue. "Papen will fail the same as Brüning. The country needs a strong man with large public support." They faced each other next to a large boulder. "For these reasons, I must be made chancellor now. Do we have a deal?"

Schleicher pumped Wolf's hand twice and scurried away without uttering a word.

The moment we were alone, Wolf turned ebullient. "Friedrich, we must return to Munich at once. When I become chancellor, I will order a plaque installed to commemorate what occurred on this very spot."

I didn't believe anything "historic" just happened, but I held my peace.

*

Two days after I returned to Berlin, Wolf called, raving and ranting. His words were barely intelligible. A shattering noise clanked through the phone; something had been smashed to smithereens.

I shouted into the mouthpiece. "Adolf! Control yourself. I can't understand a word you're saying."

He was carrying on a tirade with himself. Most of it was gibberish. After what I imagined to be more than a couple of broken dishes followed by a tension-releasing whoosh of air, he said in a calmer voice, "Schleicher called. Hindenburg refused to make me chancellor. The old bastard told Schleicher, 'It is my irrevocable will that this Bohemian corporal will never sit in the chancellor's chair of Bismarck!'"

"Wolf, I don't know what to . . ."

He interrupted. "It's not Hindenburg. Schleicher is behind this. He will rue the day he did this to me. Mark my words. His days are numbered."

"Wolf, calm down. We're almost there. No party can govern without you in a coalition. They have to come to you."

A few days later, they did.

August 13, 1932

President Hindenburg called a meeting in his office. Wolf brought Frick and me, along with Ernest Röhm. He hoped that Röhm's military background would put Hindenburg more at ease. Papen was present along with Hindenburg's son, Oskar, and Schleicher, the master schemer. The eighty-five-year-old former field marshal leaned on his cane throughout the meeting, refusing to sit, which forced us all to stand as well.

"I am told, Herr Hitler, that you refuse to join Papen's coalition. We held the elections you wanted. Chancellor Papen lifted the ban on the *SA* and *SS* as agreed upon. Now, you must honor your word."

"Your Excellency, those elections expressed the will of the German people. I would back Papen had he gained the support of any other major party. But not even his old Catholic Centre Party supports him. There is no reason for him to continue as chancellor or for me to join a coalition to try to keep him in office."

Hindenburg glowered at Hitler. "Your broken word aside, I am unwilling to turn total control of the government over to anyone who has no intention of sharing authority with any other party. And . . . there are still questions regarding your party's excesses against people of different political beliefs. Particularly toward the Jews."

The much-decorated veteran of both the Austro-Prussian War of 1866 and the Franco-Prussian War of 1870-71, who, as general field marshal, commanded the German armies at the end of the Great War, was a direct descendant of Martin Luther and now as the Reich president of Germany, remained an imposing figure. Every inch the aristocrat, General Field Marshal Paul Ludwig Hans Anton von Beneckendorff und von Hindenburg lashed out at the former Austrian corporal—and there was nothing Hitler could do but stand there with hands clenched behind his back, and take it.

There was ample reason to chastise Hitler. Just three days earlier, on August 10, five *SA* men stormed into the house of an out-of-work Communist miner—Conrad Pietzruch—who lived in the town of Potempa. Potempa was in Silesia, near the Polish border. For no apparent reason, they tortured and stomped Pietzruch to death in front of his mother, but not before they castrated him. This atrocity was fresh in everyone's mind. I was sickened every time I thought about it.

Hindenburg continued. "It is well known, Herr Hitler, that you cannot control your minions. Your followers ignore our laws day after day. They disregard the rights of our citizens." He banged his cane on the floor. "You must renounce violence and cooperate with other Reich leaders! *I urge you* to take the position of vice chancellor under Papen."

It was plain that the old man, after all the political chess moves, the campaigning, the ups and downs of elections, the failed putsch and more, now offered a path that could lead Hitler to the chancellorship in the future. Anticipation was in the air . . . but Hitler simply stood there saying nothing.

"Herr Hitler," Hindenburg said in a clear voice, "I need an answer. Are you prepared to collaborate with the Papen cabinet?"

Hitler shook his head. "That is out of the question."

"Does that mean you will go into opposition?"

"You give me no alternative."

When we left, Röhm said, "You must be frustrated by their refusal to give you the chancellorship."

"Ernst, in the end, we will prevail. Papen's days are numbered."

"When that happens, what can you do to change Hindenburg's mind?"

"Remain independent and avoid all coalitions. For now, I want you to furlough your troops for two weeks. The streets must be made quiet again."

Just like that, calm was restored to Berlin. But it was short-lived.

August 17, 1932

We returned to Obersalzberg empty-handed, exhausted, and hoping to snatch much-needed rest. Four days after meeting with Hindenburg, I found Wolf in his study. "There are American reporters here to see you."

The day before, Trude, Eva, and I joined Wolf for an afternoon picnic. We laughed, we hiked, we napped, and for a few hours, Wolf and I managed to put aside our disappointments.

The arrival of the Americans thrust us back into the real world.

"You know I don't like reporters. They never get the story right. They make things up."

"These are distinguished reporters, Wolf. There are millions of Germans abroad who support you. They want to read about you in their local papers or hear reports over the radio."

This got his attention. "One of them is on the radio?"

"H. V. Kaltenborn is acknowledged as one of the best radio commentators in America. I used to listen to him when I was in New York."

I ushered the three men into Wolf's study: Kaltenborn, Karl von Wiegand, and Louis Lochner.

After introductions, H. V. Kaltenborn challenged Wolf with the first question. "Herr Hitler, can you explain your views on Jews entering Germany from the East? Do you treat them differently than Jews already from Germany?"

Wolf smiled patronizingly at Kaltenborn. "You Americans exclude any would-be immigrants you do not care to admit. You Americans regulate their numbers. You Americans demand that they come up to certain physical standards; that they have a certain amount of money, and you examine their political beliefs. We demand the same right. We have no concern with Jews of other lands. Our concerns center around anti-German elements in our own country. We demand the right to deal with them as we see fit."

Karl von Wiegand, of the Hearst papers, asked the next question. "If in the end, the electoral path does not lead to the power you seek, would you consider a march on Berlin as Mussolini marched on Rome?"

"You're German, aren't you?" asked Wolf.

"I was born here, if that's what you mean."

"You don't consider yourself German first?"

"I am not the one being interviewed, Herr Hitler. Would you march on Berlin?"

"No! While the parliamentary system has failed, we cannot substitute brute force. A government must have the support of the people. You cannot establish a dictatorship in a vacuum."

"Then you do intend to be a dictator?"

"Yes. A dictatorship is justified if the people declare their confidence in one man and ask him to lead."

August 28, 1932

The summer-long camp experiences for the *BDM* came to an end, which gave Trude and me time together. By the last weekend in August, the cast was off her right hand and her left shoulder had healed.

"Let's do something different," said Trude.

"What do you have in mind?"

"Let's go sailing."

"Do you think you should?"

"I feel strong. Better than ever."

I scuffed the ground like a shy kid.

"What's wrong?"

"I don't know how to sail."

"I'll teach you. Schwielowsee Lake is the most beautiful in all of Germany. It's an hour away. Near Potsdam. Let's spend the night and make a wonderful weekend of it."

We grabbed what we needed, bought train tickets, and settled into our seats, tucking a small travel case on the rack above our heads. Soon we passed lush farmland and rolling hills.

The rhythmic clacking of the wheels was peaceful. My eyes closed. For the first time in as long as I could remember, I thought of nothing . . . until Trude asked, "Is your Wolf satisfied with Eva? He doesn't act like a man in love."

I opened my eyes. "Wolf is so secretive about his personal life. I'm surprised she shared those thoughts with you."

"Eva has no one to talk to. She has kept the relationship away from her parents. When you and Hitler were gone, we were together day and night. We shared secrets and what was in our hearts . . . that's what girls do."

I sat straighter. "Did she put you up to asking me about Wolf?"

"She would be embarrassed if she knew I told you. She's madly in love with him, you know, but he does not return her feelings. He barely gives her the time of day. Even when they're together, he's busy doing work."

"You saw how he doted on her when we went on that picnic."

"One picnic doesn't make a romance, Friedrich. He needs to pay more attention to her. He's breaking her heart."

We found a small hotel near the train station, left our lone bag in the room, and set out to stroll around picturesque Schwielow-see Lake. It was out of a fairy tale, with verdant meadows and stands of trees that came to the water's edge. We found the dock with rental sailboats, but none were available.

"It doesn't matter," I said, "this place is so special. We can still make beautiful memories. There's time enough to sail tomorrow."

"It's supposed to rain all day." At this, Trude let go of my hand and skipped down to the end of the dock. A man in his early fifties was tying a sailboat to a metal cleat. "Excuse me," asked Trude, "are you returning this rental boat?"

He was a small man, with a shock of steel gray hair and a wide salt-and-pepper moustache. The collar of a white shirt peeked out from under a V-neck white sweater. Lightweight, sky-blue summer pants draped over beat-up moccasins. Crinkled lines extended from the corners of his eyes. "I am afraid this is my boat."

Trude's face dropped. She turned back toward me when he called out. "I never need an excuse to take my boat out. If you like, I can give you a ride. Do you know how to sail?"

"I do."

He pointed to me. "Is that your friend?"

"His name is Friedrich. I'm Trude."

"I'm Albert." He patted his boat. "And this is Tümmler."

"That's a strange name for a boat: bottlenose porpoise."

"I really think of it as my 'thick sailing boat.'"

Albert was quite the accomplished sailor. Trude was quick to demonstrate her knowledge of sailing and the two skippered like longtime mates around the lake. As I gained confidence that the boat would not tip over when we heeled, I released my grip on the railing and stretched out. The Tümmler skimmed along. I closed my eyes. I felt the warmth of the sun as the wind ruffled my hair.

When we neared the dock, I jumped off the boat, tying a figure eight around the mooring cleat. We thanked Albert profusely and strolled back to the hotel.

*

I asked the clerk for the room key when Trude called out, "I can't believe it." She waved a magazine in front of me; Albert's name and picture were on the cover. "He's a Jew!"

"Why does that matter? Look how gracious he was to take us for a ride on his boat."

Her face contorted. "You, of all people, should understand."

"I understand kindness and compassion."

"Have you not heard one word our *Führer* has said about *them*? That we must rid our country of their infestation? That we must make our German blood pure again?"

I pointed to the desk. "The clerk doesn't need to hear this."

Trude followed me into a reading alcove, still clutching the magazine. We sat surrounded by shelves filled with books.

"Trude, I've been with Wolf since the beginning. When he announced his twenty-five-point program, I told him I could not accept the part about the Jews. Do you know what he said? As long as I believed in the overall program, I didn't have to believe in every single point."

"He said that?"

"He did, and did you know that every one of the party's inner circle has Jews they favor? It may be a mother-in-law, a former girlfriend, or a favorite professor. Hess. Himmler. They both have theirs. To this day, Wolf talks about Dr. Bloch, the man who treated his mother for cancer, in glowing terms."

"Who is yours?"

"I have a friend in Berlin. He's more like an uncle than a friend. He owns the Nightingale Cabaret. Max Klinghofer. He's been so very kind to me. And I've worked with many Jews in the film industry over the years."

"And you're saying that it is okay for us to like a Jew?" She covered her mouth in disbelief. "I don't know what to say."

"Don't say anything."

She wagged the magazine and pointed to the cover. "I have to admit, he was kindly. But, still," she wrinkled her nose, "he is a Jew."

"Did he say or do anything that would cause you to think he could harm Germany?"

"You could tell he had a gentle soul," she admitted.

"And he is very smart, too."

"How do you know?"

"You see his name?"

"Yes."

"Well, ten years ago, Albert Einstein won the Nobel Prize in physics."

Her only response was to shrug and change the subject.

Chapter 46

Meetings! Meetings! Meetings! Throughout September and October, it seemed as though we met daily. We had formal meetings with Hindenburg and Papen, and formal meetings with Schleicher. We had secret meetings with Papen and with the Reich President Hindenburg's Secretary of State Otto Meissner. Sometimes Hindenburg's son Oskar joined us. At times we met with Oskar alone. There were offers made. Offers rejected. Offers accepted and then reneged. Promises made and promises broken. Each meeting was attended by us in the hope that the Papen-Schleicher axis would come to their senses and relinquish their power to Hitler. For their part, Papen and Schleicher continued to press Hitler and the Nazis to join them in a working coalition. But Hitler would accept nothing less than the chancellorship with dictatorial powers. Only one man had the power to grant this, and that man—Paul von Hindenburg—could not bear the sight of Adolf Hitler.

On September 8, Hess, Goebbels, Röhm, Frick, Gregor Strasser, and Hermann Göring met with Wolf and me in Munich in the *Braunes Haus* to plan for the upcoming November elections. We crammed around an oval mahogany table that was too small for comfort. Röhm squeezed between Frick and Strasser. I could barely keep a straight face as each man squirmed so as not to rub thighs with Ernst.

Hitler began by offering congratulations to Goebbels. "Our good comrade has just had his first child. A daughter."

We all applauded. "What is her name?" Hess asked.

"Helga," said Goebbels. We looked to Hitler and then to Goebbels, expecting the H was to honor Hitler. Rather than insult Wolf and explain that there was a family tradition from his wife's first husband's family that all children's names began with H, Goebbels offered nothing. In the end, Goebbels and Magda would have five more children . . . all first names beginning with H, including Goebbels's stepson Harald.

Röhm brought us back to the role the *SA* would play in the upcoming election, by mentioning the five men who murdered and mutilated Conrad Pietzruch. "Potempa was just the beginning. Did you see the outpouring of support for those men?"

That he lionized their actions was too much for me to tolerate. I burst out, "Those men are beasts!" No one expected the outcry. Even I was shocked that I lost control. All present waited for Hitler's reprimand knowing he publicly supported these convicted *SA* monsters.

Instead, Wolf said, "Our Friedrich is well known for his tender heart." Then he added insult to injury. "Did you know that the Potempa Five have my photograph pasted on their cell wall?"

The thought that these men, who castrated their victim in front of his mother, stared at Wolf's picture day and night sickened me.

Rudy Hess sobered us. "Apathy is setting in across the country. No one wants to go through another election. Look at us! We've lost twenty thousand party members over the last few weeks. By every measure, we're slipping."

"You can't be so negative," Gregor Strasser said. "Just last week the Catholic Centre Party joined us to elect Hermann,"— he referred to Göring—"president of the Reichstag. They are willing to enter a coalition with us." He glanced to see Hitler's reaction before continuing. "Together we can overwhelm the Social Democrats *and* the Communists."

Hitler sprang to his feet. If there were no table between them, he would have grabbed Strasser by the throat. Hitler roared in the man's face. "I have told you, repeatedly, Strasser, no coalition! This perpetuates the dysfunction." He pounded the table. "Fragmentation of the other parties is our power. It demonstrates the failure of democracy. They cannot agree on anything. In the end, this will force them to give me the chancellorship."

Strasser did not flinch. "*Mein Führer.* It makes no sense to avoid coalitions. The moment we become part of the majority, we're thrust to the forefront of power." Strasser stood taller. He smoothed his jacket sleeves. Then with great pomposity said, "Schleicher wants us to join a coalition cabinet . . . with him as chancellor. Why shouldn't we?"

Frick, Hess, Röhm, Goebbels, Göring . . . we all stared at Strasser with incredulity. He was in open revolt. And then it came: not another explosion, but a controlled, lethal condemnation.

"Why do you continue to stab me in the back, Gregor?" Hitler answered his own question. "Perhaps you think you would make a better party leader than me? Are you that much a fool?" He wagged his finger at all of us. "There is only one acceptable path for me and our party: win more seats in November. Then we will own the majority in the Reichstag. I will not be anyone's vice chancellor," he hissed. He stood to his full measure and asked, "Do you have any issue with what I am saying, Gregor?"

Strasser's future in the party—and perhaps even more — hung in the balance of his answer. He raised his hands in mock surrender. "You are the leader, *Mein Führer.*"

It was not lost that he did not explicitly agree with Hitler's strategy.

"The Papen government will fall like a house of cards. We National Socialists will give the Fatherland a display of our strength of will. I head into this struggle with absolute confidence. Let the battle commence! We will emerge victorious!"

"*Mein Führer,*" Goebbels broke the spell, "I wish I could share in your rosy outlook. This will be the fifth major election of the year. The people are tired, the party's coffers are running low."

Hitler slammed the table. "How can you worry about money when power is in our grasp? We *will* find the money. We always do."

That should have ended the discussion . . . but it didn't. Frick spoke for the first time. "Change your message, *mein Führer.* Don't run 'for the sake of Germany.' Instead, run against Papen and the aristocrats. Paint them as reactionaries. Show how you're a man of the people."

"There is a better way, *mein Führer*," I said. "Mount a campaign that paints you the picture of strength. Repeat over and over that you are forty-three and in excellent health. Tell them that impotent and tired men run the government. Hammer home their indifference to the plight of the lower classes. But don't call them that. Call them the middle class or the working class. No one knows what those phrases mean, but no one identifies themselves as 'low class.' And then inveigh against the industrialists who keep the workers and the middle class under their thumbs, and the way they use Papen as their tool of oppression."

"How can I do that after taking their money? I will lose their support."

Encouraged that I had his ear, I answered, "You need not worry. Above all else, industrialists understand business and what it takes to succeed. These men are not stupid. They want you to gain the popular vote. They know that if you win by criticizing them, they win, too. If you lose defending them, they lose. It is what you do *after* the vote that matters to them."

It all hung in the balance. One never knew if a moment like this would produce agreement or an epithet-filled tantrum. When he did speak, it was not in his oratorical voice that could be heard by followers in the last row of the Sportpalast, it was in his every day, softer tone.

He scanned our faces before asking, "Do you all agree with Friedrich?"

"He's right, *mein Führer*." Goebbels grimaced that he had to support me.

The others concurred.

Then Hitler asked, "Are there other ideas on how to achieve the results we need?"

Again I raised my hand. "Bring together an outpouring of youth the likes of which have never been seen. Let's assemble the Hitler Youth boys and the *Bund Deutsche Mädel* girls in a massive rally for Hitler—a show for Germany's future."

"Children cannot vote, Friedrich." Röhm chirped. "As glorious as it might be, it is a waste of our time and resources with the election a few weeks away."

Goebbels sided with me. "*Mein Führer*, it is a brilliant idea. Everyone reacts to children. This will cast the party in a good light and help gain needed votes."

"What about the cost?" Wolf asked.

"As you said before, we will find a way," I answered without any idea how to do it.

There were no further objections.

"Joseph, work out the details with Baldur." Baldur von Schirach headed the Hitler Youth. Then Wolf grinned at me. "I assume your Trude put you up to this. I won't forget her when we come to power." He turned back to Goebbels. "Work fast to make this happen. I will adjust my speaking schedule to be there."

October 1, 1932

"Would you rub my feet?" Trude kicked off her shoes and plopped onto the bed in the Potsdam Hotel. "Thank you for taking me to the New Palace today. The Grotto Hall was spectacular. I loved the painted ceilings." Trude purred. "You're making the pain go away. Your hands are magic."

I looked up. "Do you think we did the right thing pushing for this *Reichsjugendtag*? There is so much at stake."

"Friedrich. Don't stop rubbing when you talk."

My fingers pressed deep into her tissues and elicited a soft moan. "I am here to please. Seriously, what about tomorrow?"

"Tomorrow will give the *Führer* the success he *needs*. From all reports, more than one hundred thousand boys and girls are coming from every corner of Germany and they are paying their own way, to boot!"

*

In a matter of days, the *SA* and *SS* had transformed the heath outside the ancient city into a working, viable, tent city that would accommodate one hundred thousand strong. There was a speaker's platform and even a post office.

For seven-and-a-half hours, the future soldiers—the Hitler Youth boys and the *BDM* girls—marched past the reviewing stand. Each saluted Hitler who returned the salute, rarely lowering his arm.

The gathering lasted two days. It was the sole highlight in what was a dreary, tiring, frustrating attempt to rally Germany not only to vote for the NSDAP, but to vote at all. The voters, sick of a year of constant campaigning, stayed home. Wolf was now speaking to half-empty halls.

*

"You won't believe what happened," Trude said when she settled into my apartment one night. "We left Heidelberg after a great response and were marching down *Breite Strasse* in Manheim when a group of kids—they couldn't be more than ten or eleven years old—threw tomatoes at the girls in the rear of the line. That's never happened before."

"Was anyone hurt?"

She shook her head. "That's not the point. It was the disrespect. We represent the *Führer.*"

"Not everyone supports us, Trude. We get about one-third the vote. That means two-thirds of Germany votes for the other parties."

Trude looked at me in disgust. "Don't you get it? They were Jews. They wore those stupid skullcaps. They called my girls all sorts of terrible names."

"Röhm's men have been breaking their share of store windows belonging to Jews. Those boys might have been retaliating."

"Well," she laughed, "too bad for them. By the time word got to me in the front of the line, the melee was over. My girls chased them down and broke their hooked noses."

Whenever she spoke this way, she no longer appeared attractive. I needed to change the conversation. "We've both been working nonstop on this campaign. I've arranged a treat: we're going to see Claire Waldoff perform at my friend's cabaret tonight."

She pouted. "Do we have to? I liked her records until I heard that she performed at the Sportpalast for the lawyers of the *Rote Hilfe* organization. I am sure they are Communists and Jews."

"Are we going down that path again? Why would it matter? They help all Germans who are wrongly accused. Jews and Gentiles alike."

We had been next to each other on the couch. Trude moved away. "I don't like it that every time talks center on Jews, you take their side."

I threw up my hands. "People are people. They bleed the same as we do."

"How can you say that?"

"How can you not?"

The air remained frosty as we prepared to go out. "Can we at least put this topic aside so we can have a good time tonight?"

She laid down the hand mirror she used to apply makeup. "You're right. There is no reason to let this get between us."

When we entered the Nightingale, Max hurried over, delighted to see me after a long break. I introduced Trude to Max. He clicked his heels and bowed.

"It is an honor to meet you, Fräulein Mohr. Friedrich has told me so much about you."

Trude remained stiff, making no effort to be gracious. Rather than try to lighten the moment as he was wont to do, Max escorted us to a table, bowed again, and moved on to other patrons.

The minute he withdrew, Trude erupted. "Your Max is short, fat, and with cunning eyes. He looks just like a cartoon out of Goebbels paper *Der Angriff* or Streicher's *Der Stürmer*."

This was not good. Her continued bigotry twisted my gut into knots. I had hoped Trude would have grown more tolerant after meeting Einstein. This had to be resolved . . . but not here.

"We agreed to put this aside for tonight. What happened?" I said with all the control I could muster.

"It's not my fault. I feel unclean when those people get near me."

I was about to tell her we were leaving when the lights dimmed and Trude sat down. I remained standing, unsure of what to do next.

She tugged my hand. "The show is about to start."

Max introduced Claire Waldoff. I was so upset that I sat with my arms folded across my chest, not hearing one song. I only knew the show was over when the lights were turned on and the clapping ended.

I stood to leave when Max brought over a bottle of 1920 Clicquot Ponsardin Brut Champagne.

"Not tonight, Max. But thanks, anyway."

"What's the problem, Friedrich? The bottle not good enough?"

Trude could not restrain herself. "I have to ask, Herr Klinghofer, why is it that you allow a woman who performs for the Communists to sing to your patrons?"

"Without qualification, Claire Waldoff deserves to perform at the Nightingale."

Trude would have none of it. "Claire Waldoff is irreverent."

"Is that a bad thing, Fräulein? These are dark times. We need humor to lighten our moods."

"I'm afraid you're misguided, Herr Klinghofer. How you get through your day means nothing to me. What is important is for all of us to be loyal Germans and not support those who associate with Communists. Unless," she glared down at him, "you are a Jew-Communist yourself."

I seized her arm. "Trude! You have no right to talk to Max that way. Apologize this minute!"

Before Trude could utter a word, Max stepped toward her. "Fräulein. The fact that I am Friedrich's friend should tell you exactly who and what I am. It's sad that your intolerance gets in the way of understanding that you and I are both loyal Germans.

It is a shame we cannot be friends. I bid you a good night." With that, Max squared his shoulders and turned away.

Trude turned to me. "How can he think he's a loyal German? He supports a lesbian who performed for the Communists. The thought is preposterous."

"What is preposterous is that we are still here."

"I was hoping you were ready to leave. Back to your apartment?"

"As fast as we can. And do you know what we are going to do there?"

"I certainly do." She grabbed my hand to kiss it. I yanked it back.

"You are going to collect your belongings—the few that you have there—and then make sure you get the hell out of my life!"

Chapter 47

November 1, 1932

The grimmer the predictions of our losses in the upcoming November elections, the harder we labored to overcome them.

On the evening of November 1, five days before the election, Wolf and I were poring over our lists of candidates in our Munich headquarters when the photographer Heinrich Hoffmann called. I answered the phone.

Hoffman bellowed, "Friedrich, it's going to fall down on us. Hard."

"What are you talking about, Heinrich?"

"It's Eva Braun. She shot herself."

I blurted. "What? Like Geli? Is she dead?"

"No."

Hearing this, Wolf jumped to his feet and spun me around. "What's happened?"

He reached for the Bakelite receiver. I turned my back on him and covered the mouthpiece. "Let me hear what Heinrich has to say." To Hoffman, "Tell me what you know."

"The details are sketchy. Thank God she called my brother-in-law before she passed out. He's a physician. He got the emergency team to her parents' house within minutes. She was alone. Eva used her father's gun. She lost blood, but the wound is not serious. She will survive."

"Where is Eva now?"

"I arranged for a private clinic, so the press won't get wind of this. If they connect the Boss to two women who tried to commit suicide thirteen months apart, the papers will eviscerate him. Keep him away until we're sure we have this under wraps."

Hoffmann clicked off.

Wolf grabbed my shirt with both fists and shook me. "Friedrich, tell me what happened. Don't keep anything from me."

"Eva was alone in her parents' house. She tried to kill herself."

"How?"

"With Fritz's gun. They got to her in time. She will be fine."

I wasn't sure that he heard me. Wolf rocked from foot to foot, staring at nothing. He patted his pant leg with a nervous tic, and then pulled a piece of blue stationary from his pocket. It had four-leaf clovers across the top.

He stared at it before explaining. "I received this farewell letter this morning. It made no sense that Eva told me goodbye. Now I understand. Why would she do such a thing?"

"Wolf. We must talk. Sit down."

He stood fast, one hand clutching the chair and the other holding the letter with trembling fingers. He turned toward the door. "There is no time to talk, Friedrich. We must go at once."

"You cannot go. Not now. There is time enough tomorrow morning."

"No one can tell the *Führer* what he can and cannot do. Not even you, Friedrich."

He tried to push past me, but I blocked his path. "Adolf," I raised my voice. "You need to listen to what I have to say. After that, I will respect your decision to go now or, as I suggest, wait until tomorrow morning."

Wolf edged onto the chair. He planted his feet and folded his hands in his lap.

Wolf never forgave himself for not seeing Geli before she passed. "I know how difficult this is for you, but Hoffmann assured me that Eva will survive. This is not about getting there for her last minutes."

"Eva needs me now."

"Of course she does. But at this moment, the party needs you more. The election is in five days. That's why you must remain here tonight. We'll see her in the morning."

"I don't understand. How can seeing my Eva matter to the party?"

"Consider what the doctors and nurses in the clinic will think if Adolf Hitler, the leader of the NSDAP, marches into the hospital minutes after a young clerk from a photography studio tried to kill herself? What possible explanation could there be for this rush to visit a no-name shop girl unless you are involved in a way you shouldn't be? Our enemies will conjure up what happened to Geli. Then no matter what we say, no matter how much we try to explain you being there, the world would know that two women involved with Adolf Hitler tried to kill themselves months apart. That would end your career." I plumbed his face to see if there was a flicker of understanding. "What if a curious reporter got lucky and found out about Maria Reiter? That she tried to hang herself? Think about that."

"That was years ago." Wolf squirmed off his chair and headed for the door. "Friedrich. If I went to the clinic tonight, the press would think that I care about all people, even a young shop girl like Eva. It would be natural for me to be there. That's what politicians do."

He turned to leave.

"Show that you care by seeing her in the morning. That's what politicians do. Lovers show up in the middle of the night. If Eva were in a public hospital, I wouldn't let you go in the morning either. Wolf. Please. You have no choice but to protect your reputation."

He paused at the door. "Friedrich, if everything plays out according to my plan, no one will ever question what I do. Never again."

"That is all the more reason to be prudent now."

Wolf slid back into the room.

"Then you agree not to go there tonight?"

He nodded.

I wrung my hands together. "There's something else. This is not the first time I have seen this stationary. Geli discovered Eva's note to you after she went through your pockets. Anni Winter found it ripped in pieces after Geli killed herself."

The blood drained from Wolf's face. "If that's true, then I killed Geli."

"Geli killed herself," I said. "Now Eva has tried. I suspect for the same reason. She must have found out about the others."

He looked up at me. "What are you talking about?"

"Maria Reiter. Marlene Weinrich. The dancer, Lola Epp. For all I know, you are doing her sister, Inge, too. Maybe there are others I don't know about. Wolf, you have to stop seeing women on the side."

He did not deny any of this. "I have no formal arrangement with Eva."

"According to Trude, Eva believed she was your one and only. So did Geli. If you care about Eva, make it so. Otherwise, there may be a catastrophe."

"I've done nothing wrong."

"That's irrelevant. What matters is that the election is five days from now and you are vulnerable. You need to be careful."

The following morning, I accompanied Wolf to the clinic. With flowers in hand, he tiptoed into Eva's room; I watched from the doorway. She was asleep. Other than a lone bandage on her neck, there were no other visible wounds. A nurse took the flowers and put them in a vase. We left without waking her.

In the hallway, we met Eva's doctor—Dr. Plate—coming to check his patient. Wolf asked about her status.

"Good thing she called for help before passing out. That saved her life." The doctor reassured us that Eva would mend quickly. "She aimed for her heart but missed. The bullet lodged in her neck without damaging a major vessel. I was able to extract it before moving her here."

Wolf took the doctor by the arm. "Did she stage this to gain my attention? Or are you saying this was a real attempt at suicide?"

He met Wolf's piercing gaze with his own. "Herr Hitler, this was real. Make no mistake about it. Eva Braun tried to kill herself."

Outside the clinic, Wolf said, "Friedrich, she did this for the love of me. Now I must look after her."

November 6, 1932

The turnout for Sunday's election was dismal. More than fifty parties offered candidates. When the results were tabulated, we lost two million votes and thirty-four seats in the Reichstag. The Communists gained eleven seats. While we remained the Reichstag's largest party, it was a blow.

Two days after our election, on November 8, 1932, the United States elected Franklin Delano Roosevelt as president. Nine days after that, after repeated failures to entice Adolf Hitler to join his government, Papen resigned the chancellorship.

Even without a controlling majority, Wolf was in line to become chancellor of Germany. Or so we thought. But two weeks later, Hindenburg selected Schleicher to replace Papen.

Wolf and I were having tea in the Kaiserhof Hotel when we heard the news. Hitler was crushed.

But there was another issue that couldn't wait. "We need to talk about Gregor Strasser," I said.

"Is there something I should know?" responded Wolf.

"Schleicher is considering Strasser for vice chancellor. Given that half our deputies support Strasser and would vote for him, and that the Catholic Centre is behind Schleicher, it would end the impasse in the Reichstag. Schleicher would be the first chancellor to have a majority. He would not need a presidential decree to govern. Worst of all, Strasser would replace you as head of the NSDAP."

Wolf slammed the table. "Strasser will never have a chance to get rid of me."

Wolf summoned Strasser to a private meeting. He obviously threatened him behind closed doors, because Strasser immediately resigned as head of the Central Political Commission to leave for an "extended vacation." Hess took his place. Hitler spent the next few days mending fences with the party leaders around the country. But his mood was grim.

Try as we did, we were no closer to our goal. Indeed, it was slipping further away. Shortly before the Christmas holiday, I sat with Hitler in his office in the *Braunes Haus*.

"Friedrich, what if nothing becomes of my dreams? Many industrialists have come to accept us, but not the aristocrats. It appears they never will. As for Schleicher and Strasser . . . God, how I hate them!"

Then his mood turned darker. "The day I am certain that everything is lost, I will face my defeat and end my life with a bullet."

He said the same thing six weeks earlier when we lost delegates in the last election. He didn't mean it then. He did now.

Chapter 48

January 1933

On January 1, Wolf ushered in the New Year by taking Eva to a performance of *Die Meistersinger*. Rudy Hess and his wife joined them; I tagged along. We took strategic seats, so it did not look like Wolf was with Eva. After the show, we drove to the Hanfstaengl's house for a party.

I didn't know which was worse: spending New Year's Eve alone or being alone in a raucous room of revelers. After an obligatory drink, I left to find my own way in Munich. Then it struck me: go back to where it all began.

*

The Hotel *Vier Jahreszeiten*—the Four Seasons—remained unchanged. I ambled into the bar adorned in the same dark wood that I remembered, musing at the fate that took me to the Thule Society meeting thirteen years before. Mirrors still lined the walls above chair rails. I sat in an empty chair and ordered a scotch, oblivious to the buzz around me.

"Care to buy a girl a drink?"

I turned to face a striking woman holding a champagne glass. I held her gaze for a moment before turning back to stare into my drink.

"I am afraid I wouldn't be much company," I said to the glass.

"Let me be the judge of that." She had an accent.

"Maybe another time . . ." I looked up. "What did you say your name was?"

"I didn't. It's Oksana Nikolaevna. And you are?"

"Nobody you need to know."

She slid onto the chair next to mine. "I can see you need to a friend. I will be your friend tonight."

Her auburn hair was wrapped in an elegant knot held in place by a jewel-encrusted pin. She was lean, with a long jawline punctuated by a smile that invited playfulness. She had catlike, hazel eyes. Exotic eyes.

"The last thing I want to start the New Year off with is spending a night with a pro."

She leaned closer. "Is that what you think? You're right. I am a pro: a professional ballerina. I own a studio here in Munich. I intimidate most men and rarely find one interesting enough to talk to for ten minutes. So what do I do? I dress up as if I will be in the company of an elegant man and come to the Vier Jahreszeiten for a drink. If I'm lucky, I will find my ten minutes of conversation. Maybe that is what we are doing now. No matter. Sleeping with me is out of the question."

Oksana made me stop feeling sorry for myself. "Is sleeping with you in the future?"

"That depends how this evening goes."

"How is it going so far?"

"I don't know. You tell me. But first, what is your name?"

"Friedrich Richard."

"Okay, Friedrich Richard, we start again. Would you like to buy a girl a drink?"

I glanced at the one she carried over; it was still full. "The same?"

"What do you think?"

We spent the next couple of hours sharing stories. She was interested in my experiences in New York. I was fascinated by her world of ballet. When she asked what I did, I told her I was a consultant to the UFA Studios.

"May I walk you home?" I asked.

She lived a few blocks from the hotel in an apartment above her studio. We kissed. Her breath was sweet. A soft growl escaped from deep inside her. She pushed back.

"I didn't see that coming," she said.

"What?"

"That I would feel that way with one kiss. I want desperately to invite you upstairs, but I can't. Not after just meeting you."

I melted at her smile. "I can wait."

"Not too long, I hope," said Oksana.

"Then we wish for the same thing."

*

For the next ten days Wolf and I traveled across the country, campaigning for the local Landtag elections. We had a goal: to increase the party's presence in every state. Back in Munich, I had a block of time and found myself standing in front of Oksana's School of Ballet. Inside, I peered through the window of the studio door as she demonstrated the right way to execute a move. Oksana was the epitome of grace and elegance. Once the class ended, and the last student left, I strolled through the door.

"It's been nearly two weeks," she said. "I expected you a week ago."

"Sorry it took so long, but I've been busy."

"Though not making movies," she said matter-of-factly.

"Then you know who I am?"

She nodded. "When I am interested in a man, I do my homework."

"And?"

"I am still interested."

We spoke until the next class filtered into the room. I told her that I would call in a week or two.

"As I said last time, don't wait too long."

*

"Are you Friedrich Richard?" A Berlin police officer stood at the door to my flat.

"Who wants to know?"

"He said you would be cautious." Then he thrust a letter in my land and left.

I locked my door and tore open the envelope. It was from Bernhard Weiss. Seven words:

Your new friend is a Marxist agent.
BW

I burned the note in the kitchen sink. Long ago, I stopped trying to figure out what Bernhard Weiss knew and how far his tentacles reached.

I would not be seeing Oksana again.

Or so I thought.

Chapter 49

In the end, we won. Adolf Hitler did become chancellor. We won because we made it impossible for Hindenburg to continue to deny us power. We won by threatening to expose his beloved son, Oskar. The chain of events began on January 11, 1933 and culminated in Hindenburg's offer of the chancellorship to Wolf on January 30, 1933.

*

In January, a delegation representing the *Reichslandbund*—the Reich Agrarian League—met with President Hindenburg and Chancellor Schleicher. Their claims were straightforward: take steps to protect Germany's big farmers from cheap imports. Moreover, they asked that the government stop the foreclosures of unproductive, bankrupt Junker properties. Hindenburg took these issues to heart; he owned such a bankrupt Junker estate and wanted relief. Chancellor Schleicher, on the other hand, was a military man. He owned no such estate and could not have cared less about their future. He refused to negotiate the matter.

That infuriated the old president.

Two of the four *Reichslandbund* representatives that petitioned Schleicher and Hindenburg were NSDAP members. I sensed an opportunity and reached out to them. While they were circumspect, they mentioned that I should look into the tax rolls of Hindenburg's estate.

It took the better part of two weeks to uncover an inconvenient truth: rather than applying the government funds to shore up failing farmlands, the Junkers lavished the money on gambling, jewelry, prostitutes, and expensive cars. Hindenburg's estate, like others, misused funds. This became known as the *Osthifeskandal*—the Eastern Aid Scandal. I put a plan in motion. The first step was to have NSDAP deputies on the parliamentary budget committee begin to investigate in closed sessions.

Even more to the point, a study of transfer records of the Hindenburg Estate—Neudeck—in East Prussia gave me reason to smile. I now knew that the old general could no longer block Wolf from becoming chancellor.

I approached Wolf in the *Braunes Haus*. "We need to arrange a meeting with Oskar von Hindenburg."

"To what end?" asked Wolf.

"To the desired end. I guarantee that after we meet with him, things will change."

"Not you, too! There is no point to more meetings. The son is a nincompoop. No, Friedrich, I am content to wait until the old man comes to his senses and asks to meet with me." Hitler pivoted to leave.

"Adolf. Stop. Hear me out." After I stated my case, he agreed to arrange the meeting.

*

Two nights later, we met with Oskar in the home of Joachim von Ribbentrop. Ribbentrop, a wealthy businessman, made his house available for clandestine meetings. Hitler, Oskar, and I sat around the dining room table.

Oskar began with an update on the chancellorship. "There is nothing new to report. My father asked Franz von Papen to become chancellor again. Franz turned him down. He believes he would be no more effective now than before."

"Then who is under consideration?" Wolf asked.

"Franz suggested that you be made chancellor on the condition that he become vice chancellor."

I grabbed Wolf's arm. This was the closest he had come to his goal.

"And what did the Reich president say to that?" I was excited; Wolf did not flinch.

"That as long as there was a breath in him, Adolf Hitler would never become chancellor."

Wolf kept his voice on an even keel. "Then who is his choice?"

"There are a number of names under consideration, but as of tonight, no one has been offered the chair. Now, tell me, what is the purpose of this meeting?" asked Oskar.

We'd prearranged that I would lead the discussion. "You are aware of the *Osthifeskandal*—the Eastern Aid Scandal."

Oskar shrugged. "We have been assured that there are not enough votes to bring it out of committee."

"That will change in the next election," I said, "when the NSDAP gains a full majority in the Reichstag. Then the investigation will begin." Wolf remained silent as I continued in a softer voice. "There is also the issue of Neudeck."

"What about my father's estate?"

"Whose estate is it, Oskar? Wealthy landowners bought that property and made a gift of it to your father five years ago, and in return, received preferential treatment for their failing estates."

Oskar raised his voice. "Neudeck had always been in my father's family. My uncle foolishly lost the land. When it became available again, my father's friends arranged to have it returned to our family. There is nothing wrong with that."

"Very touching, Oskar," my smile turned into a scowl, "except for the fact that the land is not your father's. He registered it in *your* name to avoid death duties."

Oskar swallowed. "May I have a glass of water?" There was a crystal pitcher with water on the table. I filled a glass. Water splashed as he tried to sip some.

As we rehearsed, Wolf took over. "None of this needs to be made public. Once I am chancellor, the Neudeck problem and the *Osthifeskandal* will both disappear."

Oskar cleared his throat. "Are you asking me to meet with my father regarding this matter? To look favorably on you becoming chancellor?"

"That is precisely what we are doing," Wolf said.

Wolf stood and extended his hand. "Please tell your father I will moderate my demands. I no longer require exclusive control of the cabinet. I will accept only three cabinet positions: myself as chancellor, Frick as minister of the Interior, and Göring as minister without portfolio. Assure your father that I will accept Papen as vice chancellor." Wolf remained standing, his hand extended. "Do we have an understanding, Oskar?"

Oskar stared at Wolf's outstretched hand, cleared his throat, stood, and clasped Wolf's hand. "We do."

*

On the morning of January 30, counter to every statement he'd previously made, Reich President Hindenburg offered Adolf Hitler the chancellorship. Papen and Meissner assured Hindenburg that this step would actually hasten the end for Hitler, proving him a charlatan incapable of governing. Then Papen, serving as Hitler's vice chancellor, would resume power—leaving Hitler a broken party leader to fade away.

Perhaps it was these assurances that finally moved the old man. Perhaps it was the chat with Oskar. Whatever the reason, the moment to take power had finally arrived.

Chapter 50

Göring, Goebbels, Hess, Röhm, Frick, Wolf, and I waited in the Kaiserhof Hotel for Hindenburg to summon Wolf for the long-awaited anointing.

"We still need a majority in the Reichstag," I reminded Wolf. "Otherwise, you will fail, just like the others who preceded you."

"To that end, Hindenburg must agree to one condition before I accept his offer: he must dismiss the Reichstag and call for new elections. For my part, I will promise that these will be Germany's last elections."

*

Goebbels broke the silence after Wolf left to meet Hindenburg. "Think of it." Goebbels was exultant to the point of being giddy. "We will have the state's resources as our means. The radio and the press will be at our disposal. There will be no lack of money. There is nothing we can't do."

Talk then focused on how the *SA* now numbered in the millions while the *Reichswehr* was still limited to the one hundred thousand permitted by the Versailles Treaty. What was left unsaid was that every one of us knew that Röhm was scheming to take command of the *Reichswehr*. Röhm stood at a window with binoculars, hoping for a glimpse of Wolf, but said nothing regarding talk about his *SA*.

I moved next to him. "Do you see him?"

As Röhm peered through his glasses we were all unaware that Wolf had slid in behind us, unseen, through the rear door. Wolf cleared his throat. The group stopped what we were doing, turned to face him, and held our collective breath.

Wolf wore a mask of calm, revealing nothing. He looked from face to face as tears of joy began to stream down his cheeks. Fourteen years of struggle had come to an end.

*

That evening tens of thousands of uniformed *SA* men marched through the Brandenburg Gate to *Wilhelmstrasse* carrying torches and singing patriotic songs. Their lights formed a river of fire coursing down the arteries of Berlin. They coalesced into a mass of flames that streaked past Adolf Hitler, smiling and waving from an open window in the Chancellery. Berlin had never seen such a spectacle.

A bright spotlight—worthy of a Hollywood star—highlighted Hitler against the dark backdrop of night. When he waved, the assemblage raised their arms in a thunderous salute: "Heil! Sieg Heil!"

From a perch in the nearby Presidential Palace, Paul von Hindenburg leaned on his cane, occasionally tapping in time to the pomp and marching songs that filled the air. Bootjacks crashed to the street in a hypnotic rhythm. Flickering lights illuminated joyous faces as they waved red and black flags.

The outpouring in Berlin was not unique. Torch-lit parades filled the streets of many German cities. The winds of change were everywhere. All sensed it. But few, if any—including me—understood how great those changes would be.

*

There was one who did understand—Erich Ludendorff—our putsch comrade from 1923. One day after Wolf became chancellor, Oskar von Hindenburg sought me out in the Chancellery.

Oskar waved a telegram in my face. "My father wants you to read this so you can understand what you've done."

I unfolded General Ludendorff's telegram addressed to Hindenburg.

Hitler is not who you think. By appointing Hitler Chancellor of the Reich you have handed over our sacred German Fatherland to one of the greatest demagogues of all time. I prophesy to you that this evil man will plunge our Reich into the abyss and will inflict immeasurable woe on our nation. Future generations will curse you in your grave for this action.

PART IV

Chapter 51

February 1933

Hindenburg dissolved the Reichstag and set new elections for March 5. Our goal was to gain more than the mere majority in the Reichstag necessary to end presidential control. We wanted the two-thirds necessary to pass an Enabling Act to alter the Constitution. This would permit a Hitler cabinet to govern without the need to consult the Reichstag.

I waited for Wolf to return from a radio talk in his new office in the Chancellery. When the door opened, his face was taut with tension from speaking into a microphone in an empty room, unable to feed off a cheering audience.

"We are off to a good start," I said. "Congratulations."

He poured himself a glass of water before saying anything. "The old guard thought they would make me a puppet because we have only three in the cabinet. As we speak, Göring is making plans to replace the police presidents across the country. Frick is drafting legislation to remove Jews from civil service and the professions that they dominate: law and medicine. We will soon put an end to Jews taking jobs from German citizens. The new laws will be ready by April.

"Wolf?"

He held up his hand. "Don't start in again about the Jews. That has been our program from the beginning."

"It was never mine."

"We both know that, but the others don't. And they must never know . . . or else I cannot keep you by me."

"Look, Adolf . . ."

"Stop, Friedrich." This time he shouted. "We made an understanding more than ten years ago. You don't have to do anything that you don't want to do . . . as long as you keep your own counsel and don't make trouble. There's no point in discussing this any further."

I then asked about the dinner Hitler had with Minister of Defense General von Blomberg and the heads of the other armed forces. "How did the meeting go last night?"

"I reassured them that the cancerous growth of democracy had to be eradicated, that Germany must be rearmed, and that we will restore the lands taken from our empire."

"What did they say?"

"Say? They stood and cheered! I explained that the army would have no role in domestic issues. Their sole job was to defend the Fatherland from possible aggression."

"Did the role of the *SA* come up?" We knew the *Reichswehr* feared that Röhm would supplant the army.

"I made it clear, in no uncertain terms, that they had nothing to worry about. The *SA* would be kept separate from the army."

I wanted to discuss strategy, but he cut me off.

"Friedrich, I have something only you can do . . . or all of this could be sabotaged."

"You know all you need to do is ask," I said.

"Can't you guess?"

I shook my head.

"Pasewalk."

"Say no more."

I should have thought of it myself. The hospital records. Dr. Forster's treatment notes. We now had the authority to make them vanish.

*

I arrived in Pasewalk as daylight faded and a cold wind whipped through the air. Tired and hungry, I needed to find a hotel room for a hot meal, a soaking bath, and a soft bed. But the information at Pasewalk was a time bomb that needed to be disabled as soon as possible.

Dressed in my black *SS* uniform, I saluted the young, pimply clerk at the hospital. "I am *Obergruppenführer* Richard." I presented my card.

"Are you here to see a patient?"

Antiseptic hospital smells wafted through the halls. I reached into my travel case. "This is an order from Minister of Interior Wilhelm Frick granting me access to the hospital's records."

Frick knew nothing about this . . . and never would. I paid a quiet visit to his office and lifted a piece of his stationery. My *SS* uniform aside, I needed governmental authority for what I was about to do. Of course, an order from Hitler would have been effective, but highly counterproductive.

"Only the hospital administrator has the authority to turn over records, Herr *Obergruppenführer* Richard."

"Do you see who signed that letter . . ." I noted the clerk's nameplate posted on the counter, ". . . Herr Shäfer?"

"I would like to help you, but I can't. Wait here while I call the administrator."

"Make it snappy. I need to get on with my business."

As I stood there, I tried to remember who the hospital administrator was when I was a patient. I couldn't recall if I ever knew.

I twisted toward the clacking of shoes against the hard tiles. A man in his late fifties, thin and balding, approached. He had a trim moustache and round glasses that contributed to his professorial look. "I am Dr. Ferdinand Sauerbruch. May I help you?" He turned quizzical and added, "Do I know you?"

I ignored his question. "I am *Obergruppenführer* Richard. I have orders from the minister of interior."

"Are you sure I don't know you? You look very familiar to me."

"I did not come here for idle chitchat, Doktor Sauerbruch. Now can we get on with the business at hand? The minister is interested in the records of a certain patient."

"May I inquire as to the name and when that patient was here?"

"That's privileged. I need to see the records from 1914 through 1923."

"Records that old are kept in a separate building behind the hospital."

"Lead the way, please."

"There is no heat. You will be cold."

"If your people have been efficient, it should only take minutes to find the chart."

"I am sure you will find all is in order," said Dr. Sauerbruch. "Follow me."

Anxious to be done, I walked so closely behind him that when he snapped his fingers and halted abruptly, my knee hit the back of his leg. He staggered; I caught him. "I'm sorry. I did not expect you to stop."

"I know who you are. Dr. Joseph treated you at Charité Hospital. I was on the surgical team that put you back together." Then he reached for my face and turned my head one way and then the other. "You have healed remarkably well. I see that you remembered your name."

I cursed under my breath. What were the chances that a doctor from Joseph's team would be in Pasewalk? "Yes, I am no longer Patient X."

"That must be reassuring."

I could no longer push this doctor around in my *SS* role, but I needed to get on with it. "I appreciate what you did for me back then, but I am on a time-sensitive mission. The minister expects my report on his desk first thing in the morning."

Dr. Sauerbruch left me to my own devices in the record storage room. A lone ceiling light cast shadows on the stacks of boxes piled from floor to ceiling. The records were posted by year. I found 1918, freed it from the pile, brought it closer to the light, and lifted the cover. The patient files were alphabetical. In no time I found Hitler, Adolf and also Patient X, shoving both files in my case. Replacing the cover, I was about to return the box when it occurred to me to take Friedrich Richard's file as well. Except it wasn't there. I retrieved the boxes from 1917 and 1919 in case it was misfiled. No Friedrich Richard or Richard, Friedrich in either.

Had Dr. Forster made up his name? Fabricated the entire story? That couldn't be. Friedrich Richard was recorded in the minister of Defense's records. I replaced the boxes and searched the room. Then I stumbled across boxes labeled "Deceased." The names were filed by date of death. In no time, I came across Friedrich Richard's file in the box labeled 1918 and added it to the other two in my case.

*

I found a hotel room, luxuriated in a long, hot bath, and then brought Friedrich Richard's file closer to a lamp. Had he lived, he would now be thirty-seven, which I estimated was within a couple years of my own age—give or take. He was much shorter than me. We had the same color eyes: gray. Beyond that, I could find nothing useful. He had been a mechanic before the war, enlisted at the outbreak, and was wounded twice: once in the leg and once in the head. His head trauma led to seizures. Soon after, he became delusional. He was sent to Pasewalk for psychiatric treatment.

One entry caught my eye. The man had a wife, named Ingrid, who was notified of his death.

"That sonofabitch," I said under my breath. Forster had lied to me when he told me that the man had no family, compounding his first lie years before that Friedrich Richard's death was not reported to the Army.

I turned to my file: Patient X. There was no personal or familial history, but reams of entries that chronicled the numerous surgeries at Charité Hospital. The admitting notes for Pasewalk listed my initial diagnosis as "Amnesia."

Dr. Forster's early notes were hostile. Forster questioned whether I was shamming my condition to avoid returning to the trenches. Over time, his entries reflected a shift in tone as Dr. Forster credited my story and began treatment. Closing my eyes

I remembered the books, pictures, and music he used, hoping to trigger a past image.

I tossed my file aside and took Wolf's. It wasn't as thick as mine. I grabbed the back and front covers, turned it over so the pages faced the floor, and jiggled it. Nothing fell out. Should I bring the file to Hitler or destroy it? How could I decide unless I read it first? But what was there to think about? I knew he would want the goddamned thing destroyed. He had no need of this as a memento. On the other hand, the notes of his psychiatrist might help explain the man. It might be useful in dealing with his obsession on the Jewish question.

I switched the file from hand to hand, weighing my options, the file growing ever heavier with indecision. I decided to read it. However, the moment I turned the cover page and saw his name, I slammed it shut. Wolf was my friend. There was only one right thing to do. I found a match on the mantelpiece, bent down, and lit the crumpled newspapers nesting under the dry logs. In seconds, a fire blazed. As the flames leapt higher, I tossed Wolf's file onto the burning wood. I waited until there was no hope of retrieval before adding Friedrich Richard's. Then, with one final look at "Patient X," I tossed him into the now roaring inferno.

I grabbed the bottle of cognac from my opened traveling case, found a glass in the W.C., wiped it clean with my handkerchief, made a generous pour, and downed it in one swallow. I poured another, held it up to the guttering flames, and saluted the charred ashes of three men: one now chancellor of Germany . . . the other two who were—and now are—me.

Chapter 52

The March 5 election was upon us. We worked feverishly to achieve our goal of gaining the two-thirds majority. Hermann Göring summoned two dozen of the wealthiest industrialists to his new home, the official residence of the president of the Reichstag. There, Hitler spoke for ninety minutes, telling them everything they wanted to hear. He reminded them that the Nazi party needed complete control to finally defeat Communism. He praised the importance of private property, promised to protect their businesses, guaranteed that the unions would be kept in their place, and assured them that law and order would be restored to the streets.

After Hitler left, the appeal was made: we asked for three million Reichsmarks. We collected what we really needed: just under 2.1 million Reichsmarks.

*

Göring's role in the party continued to increase as we prepared for the election. Given charge of police operations, his first step was to replace the police heads throughout Germany with party men. He then ordered the police not to interfere with *SA* actions against Bolsheviks. As the campaign gathered velocity, in February, he ordered raids on Communist offices throughout the country. One raid hit the jackpot: the complete list of Communist members in Germany. When I learned this, I went to his office to verify Weiss's information. As expected, Weiss was correct. Oksana's name was on the list.

On February 22, Göring issued a decree that created fifty thousand auxiliary police—*Hilfspolizei*, made up of predominantly *SA* and *SS* men—to "augment" the police in Germany.

Friday night, February 24, two days after Göring's decree went into effect, I was alone in my apartment reading the English newspaper predictions of the imminent demise of the Adolf Hitler's chancellorship when the phone rang. I lifted up the receiver.

"I want to say goodbye."

I recognized the voice. "Where are you going, Bernhard?"

"To my sister's house. It's not safe for me here anymore."

"You're the greatest forensic policeman in all of Europe. They would not dare . . ."

"They've already thrown me out of office, arrested me, and stripped me of my benefits. What makes you think they would stop at that?" hissed Weiss.

"How can I help?"

"I arranged for an apartment in Prague months ago. That's where I sent my family."

"Can't you join them?"

"I can't. Men still loyal to me on the force found out I'm on a list that forbids emigration. I would be stopped at the border. I have to go into hiding until there's an opportunity to escape."

"Be careful, Bernhard."

"*You* be careful, Friedrich."

"Bernhard, if you need help when it's time to leave—call me." It pained me to say goodbye.

"Thank you, my friend."

The line went dead.

*

On the night of February 27, six days before the election, I decided to visit Kitty Schmidt. It had been too long since I had seen her.

"This is a surprise," Kitty said when she saw me at the door. "You know we're closed on Mondays." Then she looked over her shoulder. "Except for one special customer."

"I'm here to say hello, not to be with any of the girls."

"From what I hear, being with one of my girls might just be what you need."

Kitty never did hold back saying what was on her mind. I shrugged. "I wanted to see a friendly face. *Your* friendly face. Is that a crime?"

"It's lonely even when you are surrounded by people, isn't it?" she asked.

"What's that supposed to mean?"

We sat at the bar. She poured two scotches. "I didn't mean to ruffle your feathers. It's just that you're a confidant to the *Führer*. That makes you vulnerable to gossip. You have to be careful where you go and who you're seen with."

"I've learned to manage." I couldn't fathom what was bothering her. "What I want to know is how are *you* doing?"

"Do you mean me and Max, or something else?"

"Talk about Max. You. Anything you want."

"Max and I are good. We care for each other. But now, more than ever, we can't be too public with our relationship." She stopped. "Max . . . he . . . I'm sure you know, Friedrich."

"Know what?"

Kitty turned away before answering and then said, "How much you hurt Max the night you brought that girl—what was her name . . ."

"Trude Mohr."

"That's right. Trude Mohr. How could I forget? Well, Max was very upset at how Trude Mohr treated him and how you stood there and said nothing. Worse yet, you couldn't leave the club fast enough. Was she that good in bed?"

Now I understood why she seemed a bit aloof. "The reason I rushed away was to gather her things and throw her out! I've never seen her since."

Hearing this, Kitty threw her arms around me. "My dear, I'm so glad! Max thinks of you as the son he never had. In his heart he knew you wouldn't let her get away with insulting him like that. Even so, he needs to hear what happened from you."

I hoisted the glass. "To Max. I'm on my way to see him as soon as I finish this drink!"

But I didn't get there. All thoughts of Max and Kitty vanished the moment I took a few steps out the front door of *Pension Schmidt*. In the distance, an orange hue lit up the sky. It was in the vicinity of *Platz der Republik* now renamed *Königsplatz*. I ran toward it. When I got to the edge of the park, I froze: the massive Reichstag was in flames. Smoke filled the skies.

I showed my identity card at a barrier and rushed to where Hitler stood next to Goebbels and Göring. Wolf strode up and down in his raincoat, ranting and shouting, "It's the Communists!" He bellowed their name over and over. He grabbed my arm. "This is the beginning of their revolution."

Papen, who had been dining with Hindenburg, pushed his way through the crowd. When he reached us, Hitler shouted over the din, "This is the work of the Communists. We will crush this deadly pestilence with an iron fist!"

The morning of February 28, 1933

During the course of the night, the Reichstag's glass ceiling shattered and the whoosh of oxygen turned the blaze into an inferno. The fire was out of control. The building was lost. By dawn, the *SS* and the police arrested hundreds of Communists.

In the morning, Hitler convened an emergency cabinet meeting to deal with the Communist "Revolution." In those early hours after the attack on the Reichstag, we all believed that this was the signal for their uprising.

A young Dutchman named Marinus van der Lubbe was caught at the scene setting fires. He immediately confessed not to just setting the fires but also to being a dedicated Communist. Notwithstanding van der Lubbe, it was reasonable to believe—at that early time—that the arson was part of a larger conspiracy rather than an isolated terrorist attack. What was *also* clear is that

Hitler used this fire as the fulcrum to suppress all personal freedom in Germany on the eve of the election.

And he did so quite legally, under Article 48(2) of the Weimar Constitution.

I was present when Frick and our old friend, Franz Gürtner, the minister of Justice, drafted what came to be known as the Reichstag Fire Decree.

> By Authority of Article 48(2) of the German Constitution . . .
> Article I
> Sections 114, 115, 117, 118, 123, 124 and 153 of the Constitution of the German Reich are suspended until further notice. Therefore, restrictions on personal liberty, on the right of free expression of opinion, including freedom of the press, on the right to assembly and the right of association and violations of the privacy of postal, telegraphic, and telephonic communications, warrants for house searches, orders for confiscations, as well as restrictions on property, are also permissible beyond legal limits otherwise proscribed.

Hitler as chancellor, Frick as minister of Interior, and Franz Gürtner as minister of Justice were quick to sign. A messenger was dispatched to obtain the final signature: Hindenburg's. With his signature in place, all civil rights guaranteed by the Constitution in Germany came to an end. It was supposed to be a "temporary" measure.

How did I feel at that moment? With the ashes of our magnificent parliament building still smoldering, I did not believe that one man alone was capable of bringing the building down without help. It also seemed unreasonable to believe he cooked this act up by himself, as he claimed. Logic pointed to a conspiracy. To look at Marinus van der Lubbe was to see a heavy-lidded foreigner, a Communist who spouted the rights of workers, and a man who spoke broken German. It made sense, then, with our government under attack, that it was necessary to suspend civil liberties until order was restored.

*

The day after the fire was hectic. I decided to retire early, but soon after I entered my flat the telephone rang. The voice was unfamiliar.

"Goebbels just ordered the arrest of Bernhard Weiss."

"Who is this?"

"We met for a brief moment when I gave you a message about a certain ballerina."

I hung up without another word and reached for the card Weiss gave me at our last meeting.

Chapter 53

The evening of February 28, 1933

Dressed in my *SS* general's uniform, my hand was about to knock on the door of Weiss's sister's house when a black car raced around the corner on two wheels. It came to a sudden stop. Two *SS* officers jumped out, guns drawn. They loped up the steps by twos, only to find me standing on the top step.

"Halt!" I ordered. "Where are you going?"

When they looked up, they stopped short, clicked their heels, and stood at attention. "Heil, Hitler," they shouted.

I returned the salute. "Answer my question."

"We have orders to search this house, *Herr Obergruppen-führer.*"

"Then I presume you are looking for Bernhard Weiss."

"We just came from his place," stammered the one to my left. "How did you know?"

"You're two steps behind," I said. "I came here after I found his place empty. I wanted the pleasure of arresting that bastard myself. There's a debt he owes for jailing me under false pretenses a couple of years ago. The trouble is he's not here."

"Did you look everywhere inside?" the other asked.

I glared down at him. "Are you insinuating that I do not know what I am doing?"

The two stood flat-footed. Mute.

I demanded their names. "I would like to make certain both of you receive a commendation for discovering that this Jew has a sister here in Berlin."

They saluted without comment, turned, and started down the steps. Then the more assertive one stopped and asked, "Forgive me, *Herr Obergruppenführer*, but do you mind if we take a look anyway? Then we can write a fuller report."

I could have used my rank to order them to leave, but that might have aroused suspicions.

"Certainly. Go inside and check my work. Make certain you include my name in your report, noting that an *Obergruppenführer* did a thorough and complete job searching the house for this Jew. I will wait for your report with great anticipation."

The second man took his comrade's arm. "Horst, what are we doing? Obviously the *Obergruppenführer* has spared us a waste of time."

After their car disappeared, I trotted to both corners to make certain no others lurked about. I returned to Weiss's sister's house and surveyed the street one last time before knocking.

The door opened.

"I am to meet Bernhard Weiss at this address."

March 1, 1933

The passage to the border, the confrontation with the guards, the drive to Prague, and the ensuing discussion with Weiss pressed the time for my return to Berlin before I was missed. The drive from Prague was an endurance race that ended when I collapsed in my bed.

Hours later, refreshed and showered, I dressed in my *SS* uniform . . . ready to report to the Chancellery. As I adjusted my tunic, I studied the reflection that stared back at me. Nothing is pure, I thought. Nothing can be perfect. Facing myself, I made a resolution: as long as Wolf and the party continued to improve the lot of the German people, I would endeavor to help. But—I resolved—if the balance shifted, no promise to Weiss would bind me to stay. Then, as if the person in the mirror was my witness, I raised my right hand and swore to uphold this contract with myself. For that moment, I was at peace.

What the mirror did not reveal was the unreliability of scales to weigh practicality against morality—or the irresistible impulse to use a thumb when taking that balance.

Chapter 54

March 5–23, 1933

"How is the turnout?" I asked the *SS* man posted at the voting station in my neighborhood.

"We've had long lines like this all day."

The party made sure that each person needed to navigate past a phalanx of *SA* men or auxiliary police that thrust party pamphlets at them that urged them to vote for Nazi candidates. In my district, *SS* men, tethered to muzzled German shepherds, were planted to one side of the polling place entrance.

I studied the ballot. The parties were ranked according to their present standings in the Reichstag. The NSDAP candidate was first on the list, the Social Democrat second, the Communist third, and the Zentrum—the Catholic Centre Party led by Monsignor Ludwig Kaas—fourth. In total, dozens of different parties vied for seats in the Reichstag.

The next day, Wolf and I met with Goebbels, Göring, and Himmler at party headquarters to await the election results.

"We will be ready in fifteen days," said Himmler.

Those few words startled me.

"How many can you accommodate?" Hitler asked.

"Forty-eight hundred at full capacity."

"Excuse me, Heinrich, what is this about?" I asked.

"Friedrich," said Wolf, "where do you think we are going to put all the Communists we arrested this past week? Our jails are overflowing."

I hadn't given the matter a thought. "How many are there?"

Himmler shrugged, "By now, several thousand. We don't have a complete list."

"So where is this new jail that will be ready in fifteen days?"

"I found an abandoned munitions factory sixteen kilometers northeast of Munich. It's in the town of Dachau. I modeled it after the concentration camps the British built to contain the Boers in South Africa. Dachau will be used to house political prisoners. As of now, we will limit it to Communists. If I had my way, Ernst Torgler would be the first interred there."

Torgler, the head of the German Communist Party, arrested immediately after the fire, was in a Berlin jail awaiting trial.

Göring shook his head. "He will have to wait. Hindenburg will not move him from Berlin."

Hess shuffled into the room.

"How was the final turnout, Rudy?" Hitler asked.

He forced a smile. "It broke records. Eighty-eight percent of eligible voters cast ballots."

Hitler clapped his hands. "This can only mean that we have gained a majority."

Hess's false exuberance faded. "I am afraid that is not the case, *mein Führer*. We received a little less than 44 percent of the vote. When you add Hugenberg's DNVP party totals to ours, we control just over half the votes in the Reichstag."

The far right *Deutschnationale Volkspartei*—Alfred Hugenberg's party—always supported us. "What is the actual number?" Hitler snapped back.

"We won 288 seats, for a plus of ninety-two. Hugenberg was flat, at fifty-two, so we control 340 seats."

Hitler jumped to his feet. "Then we do have a majority!" he shouted. "We needed 324 out of the 647 seats. We have 340! More than a majority." He slapped the table. "Now we control the Reichstag without presidential decrees!"

The rest of the room remained quiet, knowing we needed 432 seats to pass the Enabling Act. We were ninety-two seats short of the ability to rule without the Reichstag.

Göring spoke gently. "That's not enough to make the changes you want, *mein Führer*."

Hitler ignored Göring. Instead he turned to Goebbels. "There is one change you will approve of, Joseph. On Monday, the 11th, the cabinet will create a new post: minister of Propaganda. You will be its head."

"Brilliant, *mein Führer*," said Hess. "You get another NSDAP in the cabinet and keep your promise of retaining their ministers. The others won't dare challenge you on this."

Hitler extended his hand to Goebbels. "Congratulations, Joseph."

We all murmured congratulations, waiting to see what would happen next.

Hitler turned to the rest of us, more serious than ever. Of course, he heard Göring and recognized our shortfall. "Now to the main question: how can I get my Enabling Act passed?"

There was an obvious solution that no one else saw. The question was: did I want to be the one to light the path to extinguishing democracy in Germany? I grew uneasy at the prospect . . . and yet we simply could not go on as we had. I slapped my knee in frustration.

The others looked at me. "Friedrich, is there something you want to say?" asked Hitler.

I blew out a long breath. "There is a way. Declare all Communist officials traitors. Ban their deputies from the Reichstag. When you remove their deputies from the chambers, you will shrink the votes needed to tally two-thirds. Then the numbers work."

The men rapped the table in support of my idea.

"Not so fast," said Göring. "Do a quick calculation. You're forgetting the Catholic Centre Party. Even if you eliminate the Communists, you need their votes to make a two-thirds majority. They will not support the Enabling Act."

"They will if I offer them what they don't have," Hitler said.

"Boss, for years I have tried to persuade their leader, Monsignor Ludwig Kaas, to see things our way," said Goebbels. "Nothing has worked. Keep in mind that he supported Hindenburg when he ran for president and campaigned hard against us in this election. Hermann is right. We absolutely need the Catholic

Centre Party, but *nothing* will convince them to join our side. I'm afraid Friedrich's plan falls short."

"I beg to differ, Joseph," I said. "One of the advantages that I've had over these years is to sit on the sidelines and observe the players."

"Pray tell. This should be interesting," said Goebbels, leaning back.

I ignored him. "Give Kaas the assurance his party will continue to exist. Promise to protect Catholics throughout Germany. Guarantee that, unlike under Communist rule, the Catholics' religious freedom and civil liberties will continue. They see their schools as the key to their future. Allow their parochial schools to remain open. Promise these things and they will cast their lot with us."

Hitler was born a Catholic, yet the religion held no attraction for him.

"Friedrich is right. It is the way forward." Hitler nodded to Göring. "Set up a meeting. I want the Act passed while images of the Reichstag fire still burn in every citizen's mind."

*

This became Göring's second important task. His first was to find evidence that Marinus van der Lubbe, the Dutch Communist caught at the scene of the fire, was part of a larger Communist conspiracy to destroy the government. The legitimacy of the Reichstag Fire Decree turned on it.

To entice witnesses to come forward, the government offered a reward of twenty thousand Reichsmarks for information leading to the apprehension and conviction of van der Lubbe's confederates. The incentive bore fruit. Johannes Helmer worked as a waiter in the Bayernhof Restaurant. He claimed to have seen Marinus van der Lubbe at the restaurant in the company of three strangers. Four days after the election, on March 9, three men were arrested and charged as co-conspirators: Georgi Dimitrov, Blagoi Popov, and Vassili Taney.

All were Bulgarian refugees; all were professed members of the Communist party.

The next step was to put five men—van der Lubbe, an admitted Dutch Communist; Torgler, the head of the German Communist Party; and the Bulgarian Communists—Dimitrov, Popov and Tanney—on trial before a panel of judges drawn from the Supreme Court of Germany.

We had no concern about the outcome: Franz Gürtner, Papen's minister of Justice—who remained in the cabinet—was an old friend.

March 23, 1933

But first there was the vote on the Enabling Act. The Kroll Opera House served as a temporary Reichstag. On the day of the vote, the Opera House was ringed with Brown-Shirted *SA* men who enforced the ban that prevented the Communist Party deputies from taking their seats. As delegates scampered to their places, *SA* men exhorted them to pass the Enabling Act.

Inside the Opera House, our party deputies were in full regalia. Their votes were assured. As expected, Hugenberg ordered his party's deputies to cast their votes with us. Everything rested on Monsignor Kaas delivering the Zentrum, the Catholic Centre Party's votes.

The morning of the vote, Kaas made an impassioned speech to his party members, urging them to pass the Act. "Fractionation has kept the Reichstag perpetually precarious. On one hand we must preserve our soul. On the other hand, a rejection of the Enabling Act would result in unpleasant consequences for the fraction and our party. What is left is to guard against the worst. Were a two-thirds majority not obtained, the government's plans would be carried through by other means. President Hindenburg has acquiesced to the Enabling Act. We must cast our vote in the affirmative."

Hitler cemented the deal when he rose to speak to the Reichstag. He was conciliatory. "Christianity is the cornerstone of German culture." They needed to hear that the churches would be safe. And Hitler assured they would be. When he sat down, he knew the Enabling Act was as good as passed. Adolf Hitler was only moments away from becoming dictator of Germany.

Yet with all the machinations—banning the Communist deputies, reassuring Kaas and the Catholics that they would not be persecuted, and including the lesser parties who voted for the Enabling Act—the vote was not unanimous. Led by Otto Wels, the same Otto Wels who led the workers strike in Berlin that undermined the Kapp Putsch a dozen years before, and even in the face of certain defeat on the vote at hand, the Social Democrats refused to capitulate.

When Wels rose against the Enabling Act the house grew silent.

"At this historic hour, we German Social Democrats pledge ourselves to the principles of humanity and justice, of freedom and socialism. No Enabling Law can give the power to destroy ideas that are eternal and indestructible. From this new persecution, German Social Democracy can draw new strength." The shouting of the brown-uniformed deputies drowned him out. He waited until their cries stilled.

Then he pointed straight at Hitler. "You can take our lives and our freedom, but you cannot take away our honor."

Everyone in the makeshift Reichstag jeered except the Social Democrats, who gave Wels a standing ovation.

All the while Wels spoke Hitler furiously scribbled notes. After the clapping ceased, Hitler rose and demanded the floor to respond. I groaned. Why did he need to do this? We had the votes necessary to pass the Act. But Hitler was Hitler. He could not contain himself. In his narcissism, he had to respond although the fight was already won.

"You talk about persecution," Hitler thundered from the podium, pointing straight at Wels. "Most of us here were forced into prison for the persecution you practiced." The brown-shirted deputies roared in their collective anger at this. "We were not allowed to speak," he bellowed. Again, the NSDAP deputies cried out in fury. "*I* was not allowed to speak." Hitler pounded the lectern as he said this.

The Social Democrats chided Hitler for his overstatements.

Göring, as president of the Reichstag, admonished them. "Stop talking and listen for once!"

Again and again, Hitler excoriated them. "You are sissies, gentlemen . . . your death knell has sounded . . . I can only say to you: I do not even want you to vote for it! Germany will be liberated, but not by you!"

With a flourish he relinquished the podium and stalked to his seat. The Nazi deputies thundered, "Heil! Heil! Sieg Heil!" When he reached his place, Hitler waved at his deputies; their crescendo of approval grew louder.

I breathed a sigh of relief. Now that his diatribe and histrionics were over, the vote could be taken. Every deputy voted "Aye" except the ninety-three members of Wels's Social Democrats, who all voted "Nay."

With this vote, Adolf Hitler had been democratically voted dictator of Germany, subject only to the authority of Hindenburg. And so, democracy began to die by its own hand that evening—just as Adolf Hitler predicted when he first took the title *der Führer* twelve years before. Then, his title of *Führer* was for our party alone and now . . .

Chapter 55

"You look like shit," I told Max when we sat down for lunch at a nearby café. "Are you well?"

"I didn't get much sleep. My cousin called last night from New York. He told me to listen to a radio broadcast from Madison Square Garden. I was up 'til 4 a.m."

"How is Longie?"

Max shrugged. "You never have to worry about Longie. He's got his fingers in lots of pies. He's living the life."

Living the life was an understatement. I heard that Longie had been dating the famous actress, Jean Harlow. "You started this conversation about not getting enough sleep because of something at Madison Square Garden. Was it a champion boxing match?"

"It's a different kind of fight," answered Max. "It's Jews fighting back."

"Is Max Baer one of the fighters?"

Max huffed in exasperation. "Friedrich, sometimes you can be a knucklehead."

"What did I say? Max Baer is a great Jewish boxer."

"I am talking about the way the Nazis treat Jews. Longie said that more than fifty-five thousand people, mostly Jews, crammed inside and outside Madison Square Garden. Speaker after speaker called for a worldwide boycott against German products. New York's Governor Al Smith spoke. Senator Robert Wagner spoke. Heads of labor unions, and many rabbis, too."

"How can a bunch of speeches there affect what is going on here?"

"First of all, it wasn't just at Madison Square Garden. Longie said they held simultaneous rallies in seventy cities across the

United States. More than a million poured into the streets. They demanded a stop to the anti-Semitic persecution in Germany. But it's not just speeches. Their goal is to boycott German products in order to put pressure here. If that comes to pass, Herr Hitler *will* hear about it."

"Max, I hope they don't do that. It will have serious repercussions here."

"You think Hitler will retaliate against us?"

"Hitler may or may not, but it's Goebbels you need to worry about. He won't let it pass. Goebbels looks for any excuse to stir the pot."

Max puffed on his ever-present cigar. "My old friend, Joseph. How is the weasel?"

"Thrilled to be a minister in the cabinet, if you really want to know." I turned serious. "If your purpose is to let me know that Jews around the world are raising their voices against Hitler and the Nazis, then consider the message delivered."

"Friedrich, these protests are not only about discrimination against Jews. They are about closing down newspapers that have opinions contrary to the government. And that so-called detention camp in Dachau for political dissidents is a violation of human rights. They are even protesting the Reichstag Fire. They believe the Nazis set the fire to get Hindenburg to end civil liberties."

"That shouldn't concern them. No Jews have been sent there because of their faith."

"You don't get it," said Max. "Jews fight for other people's rights, too."

I did not tell Max about the legislation Wilhelm Frick was drafting that would eliminate all Jews from the civil service, as well as the medical and legal professions. There was no sense adding to his worries now. Besides, I hoped to mitigate those laws with a plan of my own.

March 31, 1933

Two days later, not trusting the phones, I rushed to Kitty's place. I found her sitting on the piano bench.

"You picked quite a night to show up without an appointment, Friedrich. Fridays are our busiest night. Every girl is taken."

"This is not a social visit, Kitty. You need to get Max over here, now."

"His place is jammed on the weekends, too. He'll never leave, no matter what I say."

"Make up any excuse you want but get him here fast!"

"Whatever it is, can't it wait?" She ran her hand along the top of the lacquered key cover. "But as long as you're here, why not play a few tunes."

"You don't get it, Kitty. Goebbels has readied a retaliatory one-day boycott of Jewish businesses across Germany. Tomorrow, *SA* and *SS* men will be stationed in front of every Jewish business. They will paint yellow stars on doors and windows and hold signs asking all Germans to avoid patronizing them. I'm afraid Max will do something stupid and get hurt."

Kitty bit her lower lip, bounced off the piano bench, and grabbed the pearl-encrusted phone receiver. She used an empty cigarette holder to dial and asked for Max. "Max, would you be a dear and leave work a little early tonight? I want to share a friend with you."

I could only imagine what Max said.

"No, dear, it is not Angelika. It's a 1928 Chateau Mouton Rothschild. A client brought a bottle and I immediately thought of sharing it with you."

She drummed her finger on the countertop, barely listening to his response.

She shook her head. "It can't wait until tomorrow night. I already opened it so it could breathe. It's got a great bouquet. It won't be the same tomorrow. I need you here as soon as you can free yourself."

She hung up. "He could never turn down a good bottle of wine. He'll be here in a couple of hours."

*

Saturday morning, Goebbels posted Brownshirts in front of Jewish-owned businesses, department stores, and professional offices. They held signs: "Don't Buy from Jews" or "Jews Are Our Misfortune." As Göring instructed, when violence occurred against Jews, the police did not intervene. But to Goebbels' dismay, many Germans ignored the boycott and patronized Jewish shops. The other good news was that Kitty kept Max occupied. Nothing of note happened at his club.

One who did not fare well was Nathan Hurwitz who, along with his father Moshe, ran the tailor shop where I bought suits over the years. Before reaching Kitty, I stopped at their shop. I caught Nathan as he locked the front door. His father had already left for Friday evening services.

"I appreciate the warning, Friedrich, but Goebbels's goons can't scare us. Not for one minute. We have been open every business day for forty-five years. Tomorrow will be no different."

"If something happens, I won't be able to help you, Nathan."

"What can happen? Paint can be removed. Customers can walk around them. We'll be fine." But when Nathan saw the yellow Star of David painted across his door and two *SA* men planted on either side of the entranceway, he was unable to restrain himself. Moshe, Nathan's father, called to tell me what happened.

"I told him to ignore the *SA* men when he got to the shop," said his father, "but he couldn't."

I expected the worst. "What did he do?"

"He tried to chase them away with an umbrella. He was no match for the two of them, with their rubber truncheons."

"How badly was he hurt?"

"I don't know. They took him away and locked him up. Can you make a call?"

I told him I would . . . but I didn't. If I called Goebbels, I was afraid that Nathan would simply disappear.

Nathan would return a few months later, walking with a decided limp. As he was instructed when released, he never spoke a word of what they did to him.

*

Just when I thought that nothing more could happen in the month of March, which already hosted the election; the Enabling Act; the arrest of Bulgarian Communists alleged to be Marinus van der Lubbe's co-conspirators; the arrest of thousands of Communists; the opening of Dachau; the worldwide Jewish boycott of German goods; the Nazi boycott in response; and Frick crafting restrictive laws against the Jews that would soon be enacted, Emil Maurice resurfaced.

I was getting ready for bed when the telephone rang. It was Emil. I had not heard his voice in five years. "Where are you?" I asked.

"Here, in Berlin. Can I come over to see you?"

"Now?"

"Yes."

"Do you know how late it is? How about tomorrow?"

"Please, Friedrich. I need to see you tonight. It's a matter of life and death."

"Always the drama, Emil," I said, half asleep. I gave him the address. Twenty minutes later, Emil was at my door. He looked heavier than before, but retained his swarthy good looks.

The once confident Emil looked terrified and stammered, "I had no place else to turn. They're going to kill me." Then he pushed past me.

"Kill you? You must be imagining things. Sit down. Do you want some water? What is this about?"

He spoke so rapidly I could hardly follow. "Have you heard about this so-called 'felony treachery' charge? They blame me for suing the Boss in labor court. It was not my fault that the party owed me back wages."

"What are you talking about? Who is blaming you?"

"Himmler and Heydrich. They're seeking revenge for something that happened more than five years ago! Can you imagine? I was there at the beginning. I hold card number 2 in the *SS*. I'm an *Alte Kämpfer*. But none of that matters to them. They want me dead. I did nothing wrong, I tell you. Nothing."

Himmler and Heydrich used this vague "felony treachery" term to arrest and detain people based on past conduct against the party. They were free to punish whomever they wanted. Emil made their list.

"The party members were upset that you sued Hitler."

"He wronged me."

"You should have let that go. And what about the mess with the letters to Judge Buch?"

"That was then. None of that matters now, Friedrich. The Boss got what he wanted. He's the chancellor now. Why can't they leave me alone? Do you have anything to drink?"

I pointed to a side table with a bottle of scotch.

He poured generous portions and handed one to me. "Can you stop them?"

"I don't care for either of those two . . . and they know it. However, it would not be a good idea for me to call them on your behalf."

Broken, he downed his drink. After a moment he brightened. "Then get me an audience with the Boss. Once he sees me, he'll order them to leave me alone."

"Do you think that's a good idea, Emil? You embarrassed him carrying on with Geli. You sued him. Do you really want to take a chance to see Wolf now?"

Emil opened both his hands. "What choice do I have? I'm dead if I don't. He's my only hope, Friedrich. He's forgiven others in the past. You remember how he took Esser back. Please. Arrange five minutes with him for me. That's all I need."

Wolf was too busy to see Emil right away, so Emil stayed in my spare bedroom. As long as Emil was with me, Himmler and Heydrich wouldn't touch him. Feeling safer as the days passed, Emil began to relax.

"Remember that brothel I stayed in years ago?" Emil asked a few days later. "Is it still there?"

"*Pension Schmidt*? The girls are more beautiful than ever."

One phone call and Kitty made certain that Emil was treated well.

*

In mid-April Wolf consented to meet with Emil. When Emil returned to my flat, he was the old Emil, full of swagger, and with a cold bottle of champagne.

"I told you Wolf protects those of us from the early days. Actually, he did more than that." Emil shoved a letter in my hand. "Read this."

I unfolded it.

I am agreeable to the appointment of Emil Maurice to the Munich City Council.
Adolf Hitler April 13, 1933

"Welcome back, Emil." We hugged.

"Do you know who used to be on the Munich City Council?" Before I could answer, Emil blurted, "Our old friend, Hermann Esser."

"I still can't forgive that son of a bitch for pretending to be sick when the putsch started."

"Give up on it, Friedrich. The Boss forgave him long ago . . . and now he forgives me."

*

It was clear that Wolf was a very strange duck. One side of him was a pitiless, relentless, ruthless enemy. The other was unending loyalty to old comrades. Anyone with him on or before the '23 Putsch could count on his favor forever. It was the same with old girlfriends. For example, years later, he arranged a promotion in the *SS* for Maria Reiter's second husband. And while he loved children, he had no desire to father any.

But Hitler's hatred and heartlessness toward the Jews was simply unfathomable. He was determined to drive all five hundred thousand out of Germany. Far from a secret, this was his proclaimed agenda from the beginning. And yet, there came a time when I saw him reach out to protect his Jewish family doctor, Eduard Bloch.

Try as I might over the years, I could never piece together the puzzle pieces that explained Hitler's complexities.

Chapter 56

During the days Emil waited for his face-to-face appointment with Hitler, I grappled with the inner voice of Bernhard Weiss, whispering in my ear. *"Do something about the racial laws Frick is drafting to drum Jews out of the civil service."*

When Hitler turned down my appeal to moderate the laws being promulgated against the Jews, I asked to meet with President Hindenburg. That was not to be. The old general wasn't well and did not have the strength to see me. I turned to Oskar.

Shortly after the April 1 boycott of the Jews, I found myself sitting on the veranda of Neudeck, waiting for Oskar von Hindenburg to return from a hunt. It was an early spring day, and the sun felt good on my face. When I saw Oskar galloping in the distance, I walked down the steps to greet him. He dismounted and grabbed two black woodcocks tied to the back of his saddle.

"Had I known you were coming, Friedrich, we could have hunted together. Now that we have access to marshlands teeming with snipe and blackcock, hunting is so much better." He referred to the five thousand acres Hitler granted his family.

A pair of brown pointer dogs trailed him. As he neared the veranda, a servant trotted out from a side door and took the dead birds to prepare for roasting.

Once we got past pleasantries and had drinks in hand, Oskar said, "You didn't travel all this way to pay a social visit."

"I need your help."

"I would say that you got all the help you would ever need from me." He sipped his drink.

"I am glad hunting is better these days. Let me be clearer. In a very few days the interior minister will issue the Law for the Reestablishment of the Professional Civil Service. It will force every Jew to resign from civil service effective immediately. As of now, they haven't been able to decide who is a Jew. They are arguing back and forth. Frick's position is that it should include everyone with even one Jewish grandparent."

"That doesn't surprise me," said Oskar. "That goes hand-in-hand with last week's decree that Jewish doctors in Berlin are banned from performing charity work." Then he added, "From my point of view, these decrees were long overdue."

"And the lawyers? They're issuing a decree that forbids Jews from taking the bar examination."

"Another good rule," said Oskar. He held his glass skyward, rotating the glass so the amber liquid coated the sides. "Nothing like a fine cognac after a successful hunt." Oskar turned back to me. "Get on with it, Friedrich. You came all this way. What do you want?"

"It's about the Jews being kicked out of the civil service, Oskar. I need you to ask your father to make an exemption for those Jews who fought for Germany in the war or are children of Jewish veterans. As a soldier, surely he will understand that our loyalty must extend to them. They cannot lose their jobs just because they are Jewish." By appealing to his military sense of loyalty, I hoped to at least spare some.

Oskar twirled his moustache, milking the moment. "Why are you coming to me with this? Shouldn't you be going to Herr Hitler?"

"I tried, but he is committed. He wants all the Jews to leave the country, sooner rather than later."

"Then these decrees and laws will go a long way to achieving that goal."

I squeezed my palms together thinking how best to move this man. "Oskar, we were both soldiers during the war. You remember how bad it was. The constant shelling, the gas attacks, the rats gnawing at the bloated bodies in the trenches." He flinched at these images. "When it came to fighting for the Fatherland, all soldiers were Germans first. It didn't matter where we came from or what our religions were. Jews shed their blood like everyone else. We can't turn our backs on those veterans or their families. Hitler will listen to whatever your father says."

"While I don't like the Jews any more than the next one, you make a compelling argument. My father has always been loyal to his former soldiers. Even Jews. Let me see what I can do."

"I appreciate that, Oskar. And please have him consider the children of Jews killed in the war. Aren't they entitled to keep their jobs?"

He hoisted his glass. "Enough! Enough! I get your point."

"What about those who lost a son in the war, or those that . . ."

"Friedrich," he growled, "now you're pushing it." Then, in a good-natured gesture, he said, "Might as well include any civil servant who served at home since the war started in August of 1914. What do you think about that?"

"That's the spirit. An excellent addition, Oskar, excellent!" We both laughed.

*

On April 4, President Hindenburg wrote to Hitler: "The removal of officials for the sole reason that they are of Jewish descent is quite intolerable for me, personally . . . I am certain Mr. Chancellor that you share this human feeling and request that you . . . look into the matter yourself and see to it that there is some uniform arrangement for all branches of the public service in Germany."

The old field marshal followed this with a clear direction that left no room for interpretation:

> As far as my feelings are concerned, officials, judges, teachers and lawyers who are war invalids, fought at the front, are sons of war dead or themselves lost sons in the war should remain in their positions unless an individual case gives reason for different treatment. If they were worthy of fighting for Germany, then they must also be considered worthy of continuing to serve the Fatherland.

The letter from Hindenburg caused great consternation in the party. My colleagues were furious. Fortunately, they had no clue of the chain of events. Like it or not, Hitler dared not cross the old man. He promised, in writing, to do as Hindenburg asked. When the new law against Jews went into effect on April 7, it contained all of Hindenburg's limitations.

May–September 1933

It did not take long for word to spread about Dachau. While conditions were severe in those early days, most who behaved—like Nathan Hurwitz—were eventually allowed to return home to family and friends.

In late May, Reinhard Heydrich marched into my Berlin office without an appointment. I looked up from my desk. "To what do I owe this honor?"

His lips were pressed tight. "There is someone in Dachau making a lot of noise about knowing you. I promised to get a message to you."

"So? You're here. What's the message?"

"Her name is Oksana Nikolaevna. At least that's the name she goes by. Do you know her?"

"We met a number of months ago."

"And?"

"And what, Heydrich? You have your information. You must know I only saw her twice. When I saw her name on one of Göring's lists of Communists, I never went near her again."

"You're corroborating what we know."

"Then why are you here?"

"We've been, shall we say, tough on her. Yet she continues to insist she is not a Russian agent. She's stronger than most."

"That doesn't answer my question."

Heydrich stood straighter. "We want you to go to Dachau and persuade this woman to cooperate with us."

"Who are *we*?"

"Himmler, of course." He gave me a crooked smile.

"Tell Heinrich that I'm too busy right now. Perhaps I can find the time in a week or so to help our vaunted *SD* do their job." I returned to my paperwork.

Heydrich did not budge. "That will not do. Himmler expects you there by tomorrow. He does outrank you, you know."

I stood, enjoying the fact that I was one of the few taller and broader than he was. "Himmler may outrank me, but I answer only to one person. Would you care to bring this issue to the *Führer's* attention? You can explain why the report he expects from me will be late because you need me to stop what I'm doing to persuade a woman in Dachau to cooperate . . . because you cannot."

"I see that you have no intention of helping, Friedrich. That will be in my report." He clicked his heels. "When you see your way to cooperate, call my office and they will issue you a pass."

*

A couple of days later, mostly out of curiosity, I picked up a pass from Heydrich's office. A driver brought me to the front building of numerous low-lying brick structures topped with tiled roofs. Guards rimmed the perimeter to ensure that no one escaped.

Dressed in my black uniform, with Heydrich's pass signed by Himmler, I passed through the heavy security without an issue. At my approach to the commandant's office, the *SS* adjutant sprung to his feet. "Heil Hitler!"

"I am here by request of *Standartenführer* Reinhard Heydrich to interview a prisoner."

"One moment, *Herr Obergruppenführer.*"

The adjutant did an about face and knocked on the commandant's door. The commandant emerged.

"Friedrich, how are you? It's been a long time."

I had met this man before but could not place where or when. We shook hands. "You must forgive me, but I . . ."

"How could you remember? It's been a while. Hilmar Wäckerle. It was the putsch of '23. I was on Himmler's team that set up the barbed wire to secure the *Bürgerbräukeller* during the putsch."

"You didn't stay in the party after, did you?"

"No. I went on to become a cattle rancher. But as you can see, I'm back now."

I had no interest in small talk. "How many prisoners do you have?"

"We started with two hundred. All enemies of the state. It fluctuates, but they number in the thousands now. Would you like to see the plans for the camp? We're knocking down all the buildings. There will be rows and rows of wooden barracks. We'll erect a barbed wire fence around the camp. There will be watchtowers with strong searchlights that weave back and forth all night. No one will be able to escape from here."

"Sounds very thorough. I'd love to hear more details, but I have a plane to catch. I'm here to interrogate Oksana Nikolaevna."

"Heydrich told me to expect you."

"Do you have a room where I can interrogate her?"

"This time of day, where they take their meals is empty. You'll be alone."

Minutes later, Oksana was brought to me in chains. I sat on a hard bench on one side of a long wooden table; she sat opposite me. I instructed the SS man who brought her to stand out of earshot.

"That is not permitted," he replied. "I must remain."

"I say what is permitted! You are to move to those benches over there." I pointed to the far corner. "Otherwise I will charge you with disobeying a direct order from a general officer."

He hesitated, weighed the repercussions, clicked his heels, and moved. I focused on Oksana. Her once luxuriant hair was dirty and knotted. Her cheeks were sunken; her porcelain skin had turned sallow.

"You came," she whimpered.

"They tell me that you are a Russian agent."

She stiffened. "Don't you have a kind word seeing me like this? Right to business like the rest of them."

"This is business. Do you deny that you are a Russian agent?"

"I'm a ballet teacher. A former prima ballerina. I am no spy!"

But I knew that was not true. Not because Heydrich or Himmler accused her. I would have discounted them for her sake. No, I knew because Bernhard Weiss had warned me, and I would not discount him.

"Oksana, if that's your real name, it would go easier on you if you told the *SS* what you know. If you do, I'll make certain they treat you better."

"How can I tell them what isn't true? Please, Friedrich," she said, "I will do anything to get out of here." She leaned into me, still coquettish despite Dachau.

I leaned back. "You are where you belong, Oksana . . . and where you'll stay until you cooperate."

She clutched my arm with both hands. I knocked them aside; the chains rattled across the tabletop. "How can you leave me here?" she said, weeping.

"You dare ask how? You used your beauty to attract me. You were willing to compromise me. Had we continued, you would have spied on me to hurt my comrades and my country. No. The only help you will get is what you earn by cooperating with the authorities." I stood and marched away without looking back. As I passed the *SS* man at the end of the room, I barked, "Take her back where she came from."

As the driver put the car in gear to take me away from this awful place, I pulled out the pass. I looked at Himmler's signature and was about to rip it into pieces. Then I thought otherwise. I recalled how the letter Hitler once signed proved useful when I smuggled Bernhard Weiss out of Germany and into Czechoslovakia.

Chapter 57

May – September 1933

The party had control of the government. Now the widespread unemployment had to be solved if we were to win the loyalty of the people. While this was our most important priority, one piece of unfinished business remained: making good on our deal with the Catholic Church. In return for the promised protection of Catholic schools and institutions, the Catholic Centre Party not only delivered its votes to Wolf, but also voted itself out of existence. This solidified one party rule in Germany.

Wolf delegated Vice Chancellor Papen, who had been a leader of Centrum, to negotiate the deal to protect Catholic institutions, schools, and clergy. They met with Monsignor Kaas and Cardinal Secretary of State Eugenio Pacelli.

The Concordat was signed on July 20, 1933. What the public never saw was a secret clause, signed by Papen and Cardinal Pacelli (who would become Pope Pius XII in 1939), that anticipated Germany's violation of anti-military conscription of the Versailles Treaty. The secret clause provided exemptions to churches, priests, and other employees in an ensuing rearmament.

"We campaigned on getting people back to work," Hitler said at a cabinet meeting in May. "Fritz, what programs will make this happen the fastest, so we can keep our promise to the people?"

Now that he was in control, Wolf increased our cabinet positions from three to a majority. Fritz Reinhardt, a party man and expert in taxation, became the new finance minister. "Here's my solution. Create the Law for the Reduction of Unemployment, granting loans to every newlywed contingent upon the woman leaving the workforce. Many will accept. Men will then take their jobs. Simultaneously, let's expand the Volunteer Labor Service to put more unemployed back to work on projects like roads and on farms."

"How much money do you need to implement these programs?"

"One billion Reichsmarks."

Hitler turned to Göring. "See that Fritz gets this money. Implement these proposals as fast as possible."

By the end of the year, we put more than two million men back to work. Construction on the vast Autobahn network increased. Most important, we rearmed, to the tune of thirty-five billion Reichsmarks. By September, the spirit of the country was changed. The people were filled with optimism. Even those who hated us began to admit: Germany was on the march again. And Goebbels made sure that the people were constantly reminded of our accomplishments.

*

September was significant for two reasons. The first was personal. I stopped cold at an article in *Der Angriff.* I read it over three times before believing it true.

I rushed to Wolf, waving the newspaper as I entered his office. "Did you see today's paper?"

He lifted his head from the reports on his desk. "Who did Goebbels roast today?"

"It's Dr. Forster. He was found dead in his bathroom from a gunshot wound. They say it was suicide."

"That's unfortunate," he mumbled, as he buried his head back into his work.

"That's all you can say?"

Wolf barely tilted his head toward me. "I never liked him. He was arrogant. He thought he was better than us."

I kept waving the paper. "This doesn't make sense. The article states this happened the day before his wedding anniversary. A gun was found next to him. It says that his wife claimed he didn't own one."

Wolf shrugged. "There was nothing to stop him from buying one. Men often keep things from their wives."

"Did you know he had just been released after a week of interrogation by the Gestapo? Apparently one of his students reported him for talking against the party."

"That student should be rewarded."

"Forster never seemed the sort to take his own life. He was comfortable in his own skin."

Wolf tossed down his pen and folded his hands. "Does it matter why or how he died? What should matter to both you and me is that he is *dead*."

There was no point in further discussions. Wolf had closed the door.

"Now that you're here, there is something I need you to do," Wolf said.

I snapped out of my reverie. "What?"

"Interrogate Marinus van der Lubbe."

"To what end?"

"He has not named his accomplices," Wolf said.

"He insists that he set the Reichstag Fire alone."

"He is obviously lying. We need the truth before the trial begins."

"You think that I can extract information out of him after everyone else failed?"

"It seems you have a gift to make prisoners see the light."

Why was I not surprised that he knew I had seen Oksana? "What did she tell them?"

"As soon as you left, she had a change of heart. She gave us names we didn't have. She's been useful since. I hope the same will be true after you see van der Lubbe. The trial starts in nine days."

Interrogating van der Lubbe did not concern me. The death of Forster did. It mattered how Forster died. If Forster committed suicide, that would mark the end of the Pasewalk chapter in both our lives. But if he had been *murdered* on orders, someone out there knew something damaging to both Adolf Hitler and to me.

*

The next day, Wednesday, September 13, I went to see van der Lubbe, who had been in jail since his arrest at the scene of the fire in February. A policeman ushered me to an interrogation cell. "No one has been able to get this freak to name his accomplices," he said before unlocking the door. "Good luck to you."

Another guard led van der Lubbe in by the elbow. He shuffled toward me, his hands and feet chained. He bumped into a small table. The guard guided him to a chair. Van der Lubbe felt for the chair with both hands before lowering himself down. He was heavy-lidded, his eyes without expression. He strained to see me. I was surprised by his broad shoulders and thick neck.

He smelled ripe. "Do you know who I am?" I asked.

"Can you come closer, please? I cannot see you that well."

I bent over the table.

"Closer," he said.

I leaned further. We were fifty centimeters apart . . . about the length of my elbow to the tip of my middle finger. "Now can you see me?"

"I see you now." He squinted until his eyes were almost shut. "No. I don't know you. Are you here for my confession like all the others?"

"What's wrong with your eyes?"

"Are you a doctor? I've been asking for one since I've been here."

I needed to gain his trust. "I'm here to determine if you need one. How far can you see?"

"Not more than a meter. Beyond that, everything is a blur. I hurt my left eye when I was twelve. I was playing with my friends and a piece of cement abraded my cornea. Over time, it got worse. One doctor said I have 30 percent vision out of that eye."

"And the right eye?"

"I hurt that in an accident when I was fifteen. I can only see shapes with that eye. This all happened in the Netherlands."

"How did you support yourself?"

"I collected disability insurance for a while, but it was not enough to live on."

"What about your family?"

"My mother died when I was young. I've been roaming about ever since."

"And the rest?"

"My father's dead. I have a half-sister, but I had a fight with her. I've been on my own for a long time."

It was time to get what I came for. "Marinus, why were you at the Reichstag that night?"

"I didn't start out to go there. It only happened because my friend and I were talking about how the workingman always gets shafted at the expense of the politicians and their cronies. Then my friend said, 'If the Reichstag burns down, that will be a signal for the working masses to revolt.'"

"So you *are* a Communist."

"Of course I am . . . but not here. In Holland. I was the local chairman for a while."

"Finish your story about that night."

"I was sneaking around streets, trying to set fire to some buildings. But each time, I failed. It got me frustrated. I started off in a different direction with my head down, going nowhere in particular. Something made me stop. When I looked up, I was next to the Reichstag. I remembered what my friend said. 'Burn it down. Get everyone's attention.' The Nazis call themselves the '*workers*' party. They say they are '*Socialists.*' They lie! They don't believe in better things for the common man and woman. They believe in enriching themselves just like all the others."

"Did you enter the Reichstag?"

"Yes."

"How did you get in?"

"I tried to break a window. I couldn't. You know they are double-paned for protection. But I found a way in through the back."

"Did you have help?"

"No."

I had the answer to my question. But I had to be sure. "How could you do this alone?"

"I didn't need help. At first, it was hard to start the fires. Then I came across old, musty drapes that were easy to light. In one spot, I used my shirt to start the fire."

"But you brought the whole building down. How did you manage that by yourself?"

He hunched his muscular shoulders. "I was as surprised as anyone else. None of the fires caught. Just smoldering. Lots of smoke. I thought I failed—again. But then," he turned animated, "there was an explosion. The rush of air fueled the fires."

His description corroborated the police report that linked the explosion to turning the fire into an oxygen-rich inferno.

"This has been very helpful, Marinus."

"I don't see how it will help my eyes. Will you send in the doctor?"

"I will do my best to bring one to you."

"You're the first kind person I've met here."

There was still an open question. "Marinus, at any time did a Nazi ask you to burn down the Reichstag?"

He scoffed. "I would never talk to a Nazi. They're fascist pigs. They're for the Krupps and Thyssens of the world, not for people like me. The whole purpose of the fire was to signal a workingman's revolution to bring the Nazis down."

"This has been very enlightening, Marinus. One last thing. A waiter claimed that he saw you in a restaurant with three Bulgarians who are accused of being your accomplices."

"I wouldn't know a Bulgarian from a Hungarian or an Estonian. They are all the same to me."

"So they didn't help you?"

"I never met them. How could they help me?"

"And Ernst Torgler?"

"I know he heads the party in Germany, but I never met him." I rose to leave. Marinus grabbed for my hand but missed. "Will the doctor come soon?"

"It's time for me to go, Marinus."

Once I was out the door, I shook my head, knowing he couldn't see me.

*

"Did he confess about his co-conspirators?" Wolf asked the next day.

"He told me the same story he told everyone else: that he burned the Reichstag building alone."

"We all know that is not possible. Fortunately, we have the others in custody. Everything will come out in the trial."

And it did.

Chapter 58

Monday, four days before the proceedings were to start, key members of the Hitler inner circle—Wilhelm Frick, minister of the Interior; Hans Frank, Wolf's personal lawyer; Franz Gürtner, minister of Justice; Herman Göring, Joseph Goebbels, and me—met in the Chancellery to organize the trial.

Once we settled around the conference table, Göring began. "The trial begins Thursday. We all know that there is no evidence against the Bulgarians. Torgler doesn't matter. He's a German Communist, so he will be found guilty."

"The Bulgarians are just as guilty," said Goebbels. "I don't understand why we can't have the trial before the *Sondergericht*—the Special Courts—that we set up in March. Those judges are reliable."

"We can't," said Gürtner, who clung to the fashion of the late 1800s, with his starched wing collars and pince-nez glasses. "The jurisdiction for all treason cases is *exclusive* to the Fourth Criminal Panel of the Supreme Court in Leipzig. This cannot be changed before the trial."

"Herr Minister," Göring broke in, "all that matters is who the judge is, and if that judge is reliable."

"Hermann," Gürtner replied, "you must believe that if we handpick and talk to the judges before the trial, the convictions would be worthless."

"Nonsense," Goebbels scoffed. "I will make sure the propaganda goes our way. As long as public opinion is with us, the public will not care how the judges reach their conclusion—only the conclusion matters."

Gürtner threw up his hands. "The German judiciary has a tradition of independence. It will not—"

"Come now, Franz," Hans Frank—Wolf's lawyer—interrupted. "When you were minister of Justice in Bavaria, you helped us with the judge in the Putsch Trial."

"I sought leniency for Hitler, yes. But I could not get him acquitted," answered Gürtner. "I didn't even try. The same goes for this trial. Nobody can influence our Supreme Court judges."

None of us would admit, even in the privacy of this room, that the party needed a guilty verdict to justify the Reichstag Fire Decree. If the trial demonstrated that there was no imminent Communist threat, our party would be discredited, and Hindenburg could reverse the laws that suspended civil liberties in Germany.

Göring brought his fist down on the table so hard it startled us. He glared at Gürtner. "Don't you understand that Goebbels and I are listed as witnesses?"

"This has been your show all along, Hermann. If you feel your testimony won't hold up, don't take the stand."

"That is not the answer I expected from you, Franz. We need to control the judges."

"Let's all calm down," said Frick. "We know that no matter the verdict, Joseph will make it favor us." Everybody rapped the table in agreement. Frick held out his hands. "As soon as this trial is over, we will create a new court called the Peoples Court—*Volksgerichtshof.* The judges will be vetted ahead of time for their beliefs and moral compasses. This will ensure their reliability." Before anybody could ask, he added, "This already has Hitler's approval."

I sat there in disbelief. Would we really do this? What kind of justice system picked judges in order to reach predetermined judgments?

September 21, 1933

I occupied a reserved seat for the opening of the trial. A feeling of déjà vu came over me when I found myself seated next to Hans Frank. Fourteen years earlier, he was the first man I encountered at the Thule Society. Now we sat in the privileged seats reserved for Germany's leaders.

Frank leaned over and whispered, "It's a good thing we tapped Wilhelm Pieck's phone."

"The head of the KPD?"

"The same. He instructed Ernst Torgler to claim that Göring and Goebbels used van der Lubbe to set the Reichstag on fire."

"That's ridiculous! Van der Lubbe will deny that. He hates us!"

Frank shrugged. "Half the world is convinced we used a mental defective to gain the advantage so we could issue the Fire Decree." Frank pointed at van der Lubbe. "Look at the way his head droops. He has the squint of a dullard."

"That couldn't be further from the truth. That's not why he keeps his head down."

Frank turned wide-eyed. "What do you know that no one else knows?"

"The man is anything but stupid, Hans. Van der Lubbe's problem is that he can't see. It's a long story."

"Whatever his problem, no one doubts that van der Lubbe set the fire. He has confessed to that. For our purposes, he was part of a Communist conspiracy. We can't let it play any other way."

I started to tell him there was no conspiracy, that it was only van der Lubbe, but I was cut short when a hush fell over the court: Dr. William Bünger, the president of the Court, led his colleague judges—five men in red robes—into the room. Would they be unbiased as Franz Gürtner insisted they would? We received a partial answer when they opened the proceedings with the Nazi salute.

The trial lasted two months. It started in Leipzig, moved to Berlin to observe the ruins firsthand where it was held in the only undamaged room left standing in the Reichstag—the Budget Committee Room—and then returned to Leipzig for its conclusion.

October 19, 1933

Max called late Wednesday afternoon. He was in a celebratory mood and wanted company.

"You're lucky you caught me. I've been jumping back and forth to the Fire Trial. I've been buried catching up on work now that it has moved to Berlin. I could use a break. What are we celebrating?"

"Come to the club for dinner. I'm opening my last bottle of Chateau Margaux."

"What year?"

"The greatest: 1900. It's the most amazing wine. With what's going on these days, who knows when I'll get another reason to enjoy it?"

"I'm honored that you want to share it with me. But aren't you being too much the pessimist?"

"When is it ever the right time to open a great bottle of wine?"

"Still, it's the middle of the week. What can be so special?"

"Come and find out," he said before hanging up.

*

We sat in a dark corner of the club. It was too early for most, and only a few patrons were scattered about. With a surgeon's care, Max removed the seal and cork from his precious bottle. He studied the cork before taking in a long whiff, appreciating is bouquet, and then passed it to me so I could do the same. He poured the wine, as if it were liquid gold, into a cut crystal decanter. He caught me staring at the ornate vessel.

"It was my mother's. She got it in Weimar thirty years ago. Maybe longer. Theodore Muller crafted it. As beautiful as it is, I assure you the wine is better."

I was about to savor its bouquet when Max made a toast. "To Longie Zwillman."

I whipped my head toward him. "I didn't see that coming, Max. Why are we toasting Longie?"

"Because he made me proud last night. Actually, it was early morning, our time. He, along with a first-rate boxer, Nat Arno, whose real name is Sidney Nathan Abramowitz, started a Jewish defense organization called the Minutemen. The group includes boxers, Jewish mobsters, and local thugs."

"To what end?"

"Are you kidding? There was no way he was going to let Nazi supporters hold a meeting in his town."

"Why are you telling me this?"

"I thought you would be interested because you know Longie. He did my people proud last night."

"The way Bernhard Weiss did when he was in charge of the police?"

Max left that hanging. He had a pretty good idea that I helped Bernhard escape, but never asked me straight out.

"Unlike Weiss, the Minutemen are anything but law abiding. They are more like your Brownshirts. Last night a group called the Friends of the New Germany held a meeting in the *Schwabenhalle*. It's a large German hall in Newark. Longie, Arno, and the rest of them would have none of it. There would be no Nazi meeting in their town. They used stones, rubber-covered pipes, and stink bombs to break it up. Does any of this sound familiar?" He didn't wait for me to answer. "Apparently this has happened in other cities in America. The difference was that last night's rally was the largest the Minutemen broke up. It's good to know that some of us don't just sit around . . . we fight back." Again, he raised his glass. "To Longie."

I tasted the wine to honor Max, not Longie.

Hearing that Longie and his Minutemen were fighting back in the United States came as a shock. But when I thought about it, I wondered why the same thing had not happened here? It came to me that perhaps most German Jews believed they would be immune from Hitler's anti-Semitic rants and promises. Isn't that what Oser-Braun and Kaufmann thought that New Year's Eve? But they were wrong. Hitler immediately passed laws expelling Jews from the civil service. Had they gone into the streets before he came to power, would it have made a difference? Maybe . . . and maybe not. After all, in the early twenties, we all thought Hitler's extreme anti-Semitic comments were more rhetoric than substance. I myself never thought he would carry through with his threats.

Consider what the *New York Times* wrote in its first coverage of Hitler on May 20, 1922:

> He is credited with being actuated by lofty, unselfish patriotism. He probably does not know himself just what he wants to accomplish. The keynote of his propaganda is speaking and writing violent anti-Semitism.
>
> But several reliable, well-informed sources confirmed the idea that Hitler's anti-Semitism was not so genuine or violent as it sounded, and that he was merely using anti-Semitic propaganda as a bait to catch masses of followers and keep them aroused, enthusiastic and in line for the time when his organization is perfected and sufficiently powerful to be employed effectively for political purposes.
>
> A sophisticated politician credited Hitler with peculiar political cleverness for laying emphasis and over-emphasis on anti-Semitism, saying: "You can't expect the masses to understand or appreciate your finer real aims. You must feed the masses with cruder morsels and ideas like anti-Semitism. It would be politically wrong to tell them the truth about where you really are leading them."

Now, of course, it was too late. And then it came to me: I cannot disparage the victims, certainly not me—who was so close to it all and did so little. I raised my glass again, and this time toasted Longie Zwillman and his Minutemen.

*

As I sat through sessions of the Fire Trial, I became an admirer of the Bulgarian defendant, Georgi Dimitrov. The man had the heart of a lion. Friendless and alone, surrounded by enemies, he attacked the court and its apparatus, with blistering speeches and lethal examinations of witnesses.

Dimitrov rejected his court-appointed lawyer and lobbied to defend himself. When the presiding judge, Bünger, refused to permit it, Dimitrov convinced him to reverse his decision. Bünger, who came to regret that permission, would periodically eject Dimitrov to stop the carnage.

I made certain to be in court November 4 when Dimitrov cross-examined Herman Göring. Göring kept the court waiting an hour. When he finally made his entrance, he was dressed in his formal *SA* uniform. Seeing this, the judges jumped to their feet and gave the Hitler salute.

When Dimitrov rose to cross-examine, he was far from physically imposing. Short and squat, his once black hair was now streaked with silver, but his bushy eyebrows were still jet-black, and his eyes vibrant, alive, and penetrating.

Dimitrov challenged Göring from the outset. "You announced on the night of the fire that van der Lubbe had a German Communist membership card in his pocket. Based on this card, you stated that the fire was the first step in a Communist takeover of the country. As a result of this, the next morning a law suspending civil liberties was enacted. My question for you, Herr Göring, is how did you know van der Lubbe had a Communist membership card in his pocket?"

Göring simpered. "Let me tell you: the police examine all great criminals and inform me of their findings." Göring thought his answer clever, more so as the party members in the audience laughed with him.

Dimitrov laughed, too, and then delivered a crushing blow. "But each of the three arresting officers have testified in this court, under oath, that *no* membership card was found on van der Lubbe. So, please, Herr Göring, tell us where did you get this information about the non-existent party card?"

Göring's face ripened by the second. He jumped to his feet. He stepped away from his seat. Standing, hands on hips, veins bulging in his neck, he shouted, "Your party is a party of crimi-nals which must be destroyed . . . I will not allow you to question me like a judge or to reprimand me! You are a scoundrel who should be hanged!"

Judge Bünger banged on his gavel for order. He did not admonish Göring for threatening Dimitrov; instead he threw Dimitrov out of court for disrespecting the witness. In time, Dimitrov was permitted to rejoin his trial whereupon he contin-ued to attack the proceedings. As the trial progressed, Dimitrov earned the reluctant—and well-deserved—admiration of even Dr. Bünger.

Goebbels was the next witness. Though extra chairs were brought into the court, the overflow was such that spectators were forced to stand in the back.

It was time for the cross-examination. Dimitrov marched in front of Goebbels. "Is the witness aware that the Reichstag Fire was used by the government and the Propaganda Ministry— which you head—as the basis to quash the opposition parties in the election that was less than a week away?"

"We did not need propaganda," answered Goebbels. "The Reichstag Fire was a confirmation of our struggle against the violence of the Communist party."

"But you agree with violence when it is against the left? What about the murders of Rosa Luxemburg and Karl Liebknecht?" Dimitrov asked.

Goebbels's answer was lost in the spectators' protests. But I would not have heard it, in any case. My mind was drawn back to that day in Berlin, fourteen years before. I saw Rosa Luxemburg clubbed to the ground, shot, and then dumped into the canal.

The judge banged his gavel for quiet; I snapped out of my trance.

Dimitrov next asked, "Is it true that the National Socialist Government has granted a pardon to all terrorist acts that carry out the aims of the National Socialist movement?"

Goebbels spread his arms in a gesture of compassion. "We could not leave people in prisons who risked their lives and health to fight the Communist peril."

Goebbels was no ham-fisted Göring. He was clever and made glib answers, but all in the court that day knew the questioner was the only one who spoke for truth.

The trial dragged on for weeks. While journalists around the world described van der Lubbe as slow, retarded, lacking intelligence, and in a perpetual stupor with his head down, I knew different. On December 6, without warning, van der Lubbe sprang to his feet. "I have had enough! This trial has moved back and forth from Leipzig to Berlin, and now back to Leipzig. I burned down the Reichstag. I want my sentence! How long is it going to take to get a verdict?"

The chief prosecutor called out. "It has lasted so long because you will not reveal your accomplices."

Van der Lubbe shouted back at him, "I set the fire. None of these other defendants had anything to do with it!"

*

As the air grew frigid and winter snows arrived, the lengthy trial drew to a close. Dimitrov was irrepressible in his summation. He flagellated the government without mercy. His oration touched on events I personally knew. He accused the Nazis of suppressing the Communist Party on behalf of the industrialists.

"You have the Krupp-Thyssen Circle—the war industry— which has supported the National Socialists for years. Thyssen and Krupp wished to establish a political dictatorship under their own personal direction to depress the living standards of the working class."

Sitting in the gallery, I recalled my efforts to raise funds from these very people. I knew Dimitrov did not have that quite right—it was not our intention to repress the workers' standard of living—we simply were after power. But, all in all, his speech stung.

Dr. Bünger, as president of the Court, read the verdict on the last day of the trial. As expected, Marinus van der Lubbe was found guilty of setting the Reichstag fire and condemned to death by guillotine. It was also no surprise that the court, bowing to pressure, found the Communist Party responsible for the fire, "for the purpose of overthrowing the government . . . and seizing power."

What surprised many, but not me, was that Dimitrov, Popov, Tanev, and Torgler were all acquitted. It was still possible, in those early days of Hitler's chancellorship, for a court to exercise some modicum of independence.

This court drew the line at convicting four innocent men.

*

While the Nazi party should have been delighted with a result that validated the Reichstag Fire Decree, it wasn't. The judges, who, without any evidence in support, went to great lengths to condemn the outlawed Communist Party, were themselves condemned by the party's press for acquitting the four Communists.

True to form, Goebbels put his thumbprint on the Reichstag Fire Trial. The Nazi Party news bureau called it a "Downright Judicial Blunder." The editorial cried out: "We demand reform of our judicial system. To avert another such decision, German justice must be purged of outworn, alien, and liberal conceptions."

Shortly thereafter, the *Volksgerichtshof,* the Peoples Court, was inaugurated for that exact purpose. The Peoples Court was staffed only with judges who could be relied upon to render the "right" verdict. To make this a certainty, all prospective judges were vetted well in advance of their appointment.

Everything considered, I had learned a great deal about courts and the judges who sit on them. This proved useful because soon after the Reichstag Fire verdict, I made my own court appearance.

Chapter 59

February 1934

My phone rang. "Friedrich, I don't know where else to turn," Kitty said in rapid fire. "I submitted an appeal to the Hereditary Health Court. The hearing is scheduled for next week."

"You need to slow down, Kitty. I don't know what you're talking about," I said. "Start over."

Kitty caught her breath. "It's my niece. She just turned eighteen. She slipped on the ice and hit her head so hard it caused her to have a petit mal seizure. There were *SS* in the hospital getting names of those who needed to be sterilized when my niece, Mila, was wheeled into the emergency area. They saw her diagnosis on the chart. Without getting more information, they put her on the list to be sterilized."

Kitty referred to the law that went into effect that past New Year's Day. It was designed to prevent people from passing hereditary diseases on to their children, thereby limiting the births of unproductive persons that drained the country's resources. Persons with congenital mental deficiencies, schizophrenia, manic-depressive conditions, epilepsy, Huntington's Chorea, inherited blindness or deafness, and alcoholics were on the list to be sterilized.

"Is this a genetic condition?" I asked.

"Friedrich, weren't you listening? She fell and hit her head. It will probably never happen again. She is scheduled for a tubal ligation. It must not happen. She wants to get married and have children someday. Please, do what you can to stop it."

"Where is she?"

"I'm not sure. I do know the court date for her appeal is next Monday."

As soon as we hung up, I went straight to see the man who wrote the law, Interior Minister Wilhelm Frick. Frick explained that while a sterilization order could be appealed in court, no appeal had been successful to date.

That Monday, I met Kitty outside of the Hereditary Health Court in my dress uniform. Before we had a chance to greet each other, Kitty grabbed my hand and kissed it. "How can I ever repay you, Friedrich?"

"Let's win the appeal first, and then you can thank me."

The moment we entered the courtroom, I was struck by the number of people appealing sterilization rulings.

"What is going on?" whispered Kitty. "Why are there so many people here?"

I parroted what Frick told me. "The party does not want the country burdened by supporting people that contribute nothing and require care for the rest of their lives. The law will limit offspring that perpetuate these problems."

"Where's the compassion?"

"This is not about compassion, it's about what is good for the country and good for these unfortunate sorts . . . even if they don't know it themselves."

"Listen to yourself. It's one thing to bellyache about the cost of caring for disabled men, women, and children, but it's another matter, altogether, to pass a law that takes away their ability to reproduce."

"Kitty, we're not doing anything different than what they do in the United States," I repeated Frick's lessons. "California, in particular, has been sterilizing people for twenty-five years. Thousands already. Our procedures are based on *their* criteria. To that point, twenty-nine states in the United States perform sterilization. It even made it to their Supreme Court and was found to be legal. But this talk isn't going to get us anywhere. I didn't make the rules. If I am going to help Mila, tell me about her."

"Mila works in the library at the *Friedrich-Wilhelms-Universität*. She lives with my sister. She's never been in trouble and does not have a medical condition such as you have described. It is sheer lunacy to even contemplate sterilizing her."

At that moment, the judge entered the courtroom. Everyone fell silent. Protocols were announced as to how the court would hear the appeals. Kitty and I observed one unfortunate after another parade in front of the judge. Their disabilities ran the gamut: advanced diabetes, schizophrenia, states of insanity, and chronic alcoholism. Some had lawyers; others did not. The presence of legal help did not seem to matter: every appeal was denied.

Then it was Mila's turn. She was led into the courtroom. I studied her. Slim, with lush brown hair and light-colored eyes, she stood shackled before the judge who read the charge against her. He lowered the paper, pushed his reading glasses down to the edge of his nose, and peered down from his bench.

"What do you have to say for yourself, young lady?"

Before Mila answered, I jumped up and strode down the wide aisle to a wooden gate that separated the spectators from the court officials and the assorted men and women fighting for their reproductive rights.

"Your honor," I pushed the gate aside and stepped before the court. "I am here to speak on behalf of Mila Küchler."

The judge was not used to anyone but a lawyer speaking on behalf of a man or a woman in a sterilization appeal. He ran his eyes up and down my black uniform. After I stated my name and rank, the judge said, "This is highly unusual for an *Obergruppenführer* to take an interest in such matters."

"Avoiding a mistake is important to the *Führer*. Each German woman has the obligation to reproduce children for the Reich, especially those that will grow up to be soldiers. Fräulein Küchler does not fit into the *Gesetz zur Verhütung erbkranken Nachwuchses*. This Sterilization Law is to save the country from caring for the chronically ill from debilitating and genetic diseases. A fall on the ice does not place this fräulein in any of the defined categories."

"I must take umbrage with your explanation, *Herr Obergruppenführer*. I have been advised that once a patient has a seizure, they are prone to debilitating repetitions. In some instances, it can worsen to the point they can no longer care for themselves."

Mila stood tall and stared with keen eyes at the judge. Though she worked in the library, she did not appear bookish. She exuded the air of an outdoor person who enjoyed skiing and hiking.

"Judge. This is taking up too much of your valuable time. I take full responsibility that Fräulein Küchler will continue to be productive for the state."

He puffed up in self-importance. "You can't just walk into my court and tell me what to do, *Herr Obergruppenführer*! How do I even know you are who you say you are? A man of your high rank . . . and I have never heard of you?"

"There is no reason for you to know me, but you should trust me." I drew my card from my wallet and wrote on the back of it. "Call this number for the verification you need."

He waved the card. "Whose telephone number is this?"

"Adolf Hitler. It's his direct line. Please call him. I am anxious to hear what he has to say to you."

At the *Führer's* name, the judge dropped the card to his desk. He stared at it, and then considered the long queue waiting for their appeals to be heard. Pursing his lips, he lifted his gavel and hit the wooden block. "Appeal granted."

I bowed to the judge, pleased that my use of outside influence yielded the result I sought in court.

Unshackled, Mila flew into my arms. "*Obergruppenführer* Richard, you saved my life. I would have been ruined."

Outside, Mila said, "I am going to make the most wonderful meal and bring it to your flat tonight."

I looked to Kitty for help, but she stood there amused. I edged back. "There is no need to go through all that trouble, Mila. Rather than cook, let's go to the parade on *Rosenmontag*."

Her smile faded.

Getting older changed the prescription of the lenses through which I saw the world. Having watched Wolf operate over the years, I had no desire to take advantage of a starry-eyed girl—hardly yet a woman—who wanted to show her gratitude. My only satisfaction was that Kitty's grin turned into a nod of approval.

*

That year Rose Monday— *Rosenmontag*—fell in the middle of February. It was the holiday celebrated two days before Ash Wednesday that would kick off the period of Lent. Marching bands played traditional folk tunes. They wore traditional German costumes and were followed by floats that highlighted native folklore. There was singing in the streets, food vendors selling traditional local dishes, and pubs opened in early morning. It was our version of the South American Mardi Gras.

"I don't like seeing them near every street lamp." Mila pointed to SS men planted along the parade route. "Look at that float." Mila pointed to the platform moving toward us that held bearded men sporting black hats and large hooked noses. Most bystanders jeered and laughed. Mila turned away. "That's disgusting."

Mila turned to me. "How can you stand it?"

"You're asking me about how the Jews are treated? I don't like it any more than you do."

"There is no one in the whole country speaking up for them. You're an *Obergruppenführer*. Do something about it."

"I do what I can, Mila. But I can't change the world."

She looked crossly at the SS men near the corner, and then leaned into me. "I fear for the Jews, Friedrich."

"So do I." Most of all, I feared for Max.

I dropped Mila at her apartment.

"Will I see you again?" she asked.

"I had a lovely time, Mila, but you need someone closer to your age."

"Men my age are boring."

"Keep them around until they grow more interesting."

I pecked her on the cheek and left before she could reply.

As I turned the key to my apartment, the phone rang. "I met the one."

It was Emil Maurice. "What are you talking about?"

"Now that I am on the city council, I chair the masquerade ball that concludes *Rosenmontag*. You should have seen me. I was at my best, dressed as a debonair Spaniard. And then I saw her across the room. She was a goddess."

"Who was, Emil? You're talking in riddles."

"Hedwig. She's a medical student. A real enchantress. This is it, Friedrich. I am going to marry her."

I wished him well and hung up, believing this infatuation would last a week, perhaps a month. They rarely lasted longer. As for me, alone in my flat, my nobility crumbled. I thought about calling Kitty for Mila's number. I started to dial but stopped. Instead, I took out a bottle of scotch and, after a time, found comfort in sleep.

*

At the end of March, I was in my office when Emil called to bring me up to date on his affair with Hedwig.

"How long has it been? A month?" I asked.

"Five weeks."

"And she's still talking to you? What's wrong with her?"

"I told you I am going to marry her."

"Am I supposed to congratulate you?"

"Not yet. But when we do get married, I want you to be my best man."

"If I am going to be your best man, I better know your wife-to-be's name. Tell me this beauty's name again?"

"Hedwig Poeltz. We're getting married after she finishes medical school next year."

"Should I mark the date on my calendar?"

"Don't be a wise ass. I know you don't believe I am going to go through with this, but I am. You wait and see. We need to be entered into the *SS* clan book. I'm processing the paperwork with Himmler as we speak."

Chapter 60

Time has a way of distorting what Wolf and the party accomplished. Then, as well as now, it was incorrect to say that we "seized" power. Ours was a quiet revolution. We followed the provisions of the Constitution, stood for election after election, and became the dominant party in a democracy. We made backroom deals as was done in any democracy . . . even while we openly promised to end democratic rule as soon as we came to power. Unlike the American and French Revolutions, we accomplished our revolution in 1933 without firing a shot at the government. Hitler and his dictatorship moved a Germany mired in the muck of an untenable treaty toward a country keen on retaking a position it once held among the great nations of the world.

But our continued success depended on quieting the disenchanted within our own ranks.

The *SA* now numbered nearly four million men . . . but there was no role for them in the new Germany. The *SA*'s original *raison d'etre*—harassing opposing political parties—had been eliminated. Röhm's aspirations to replace the *Reichswehr* with his *SA* and assume Minister of Defense Werner von Blomberg's position more than infuriated the *Reichswehr*. In December 1933, Hitler attempted to placate Röhm by making him a minister without portfolio in the cabinet. This not only failed to satisfy Röhm, it further alarmed the *Reichswehr* leaders.

In February 1934, Hitler continued his efforts to rein in Röhm. He forced Röhm to sign an agreement with Minister of Defense Bromberg that limited the *SA*'s function to that of an internal police force. Their second function was to provide premilitary training for youths—under twenty-one—as they prepared to enlist in the army. We left the meeting thinking the

Röhm/Blomberg dispute had been settled only to learn that Röhm talked behind our backs.

"What that ridiculous corporal says, means nothing to us . . . if we can't get there with him, we'll get there without him."

We expected Hitler to lash out. Instead, he said, "We must let the situation develop." And it did. Weeks later, the "situation" could no longer be ignored.

April 1934

In April 1934, three events changed the direction of German history. The first was Hindenburg's lung cancer; he had only months to live. The second, driven by the first, was that the *Reichswehr* would not countenance Hitler taking Hindenburg's place without first dealing with Röhm's threat to assimilate the army into the *SA*. The third was Vice Chancellor Franz von Papen's overtures to the aristocrats in the army to make him Hindenburg's successor as president. If successful, Papen would have the ultimate authority over Hitler.

In early April, we sought a meeting with Minister of Defense Blomberg. We needed the military's support to secure Adolf Hitler's elevation to dictator of Germany, once Hindenburg was no more. The meeting was held on Blomberg's terms. Hitler, Göring, Goebbels, Hess, and I, along with Blomberg, and leaders of the *Reichswehr*, went on a multi-day maneuver aboard the heavy cruiser *Deutschland*. The *Deutschland* was completed in 1931 and served the *Reichsmarine* as a training vessel. For public consumption, Hitler and his entourage were touring the ship and interviewing the crew. But our true purpose was to come to an agreement with the *Reichswehr* to Hitler's succession. The *Reichswehr* had its own agenda: to eliminate the threat of Röhm and his four million Brownshirts.

"Hindenburg has already expressed he would like the return of some form of monarchy after he dies," Blomberg began once we were out at sea.

"The people will not stand for that," said Hitler.

"Don't be so sure," Blomberg replied. "They want stability. They long for the security the monarchy offered them."

"We both know that the monarchy cared only about perpetuating itself and protecting the Junkers," answered Hitler. "Look around. We've turned a corner. People are working again. I have gone to extremes to protect the industrialists. They couldn't be happier."

"They made money under the kaiser, too."

"General," said Hitler, "the salt air has been invigorating. Talks with the crew have been enlightening. They make Germany proud. We all know why we are here. What will it take to gain the support of the *Reichswehr* for my succession to Hindenburg?"

Rather than answer, Blomberg said, "You realize that if a new Reich president does not want you to remain in office, you are finished."

"Is that what you want? For me to go?"

"I don't want that. Nor does the army. We believe in you. We believe in the Nazi program for conscription, rearmament, and regaining our lost lands. But there are others—Papen, for one, and we suspect Schleicher, too—that have their eyes on the presidency. While both supported you for chancellor, each expected you to fail within weeks. That might have happened, too, if it were not for the Reichstag fire."

"The fire was not planned!" Göring blurted out.

"That doesn't matter now, does it?" said Blomberg. "Everything you have accomplished is in jeopardy if the aristocracy persuades Hindenburg to declare martial law. They will succeed unless . . ."

"Unless what?" Hitler demanded.

"I speak for all the military organizations when I say that we don't want martial law. We want *you* to lead the country. But as you know," he drew it out, "we follow the orders of the president . . . whomever that may be. *He* is our commander in chief."

"Unless what?" Hitler repeated.

"Unless Röhm is removed and you confirm the army as the *sole* military force of Germany. If this is not done before Hindenburg dies, we will support Papen for president. I cannot make it any plainer."

"And if I do these things?"

"We will make certain you gain control of the government upon Hindenburg's death."

I caught the eye of Admiral Erich Raeder, commander of the Navy. We nodded out of respect to each other and for the momentous agreement that had just been reached. I made a mental note to chat with Raeder about the time he dismissed Reinhardt Heydrich from the Navy. One day, it might be useful to know the details.

*

After four days at sea, we docked on April 11.

"Take us to a bar," Hitler ordered the driver waiting for us at the gangplank.

Göring, Goebbels, Hess, and I were surprised. Hitler had stopped drinking years before. He was not morally against imbibing, but he did not like the lack of control that came from drinking alcohol and would not risk damage to his image.

We found a local pub. Hitler, in civilian clothes, pulled his fedora deep down to cover his face, and hiked up the collar of his trench coat. Göring and I, two large men, had little trouble shielding him from front and back view. I asked for a dark, rear corner and handed the barkeep a fistful of money to keep the area private. We all ordered beer; Hitler ordered tea.

After drinks were delivered, I asked, "Did you expect that from Blomberg?"

"Not only did I expect it, I respect the way he isolated us on that big ship. What did he tell us? That Hindenburg will die soon? We all know that. We also know that Papen, who never wanted to be chancellor, is not hiding the fact that he wants to replace Hindenburg. If the *Reichswehr* supports him, Papen will make Schleicher chancellor. Together, they will reinstall those 'Barons' in the cabinet and guide the country back to rule by divine right. We may even see the return of Centrum—the Catholic Party."

Hitler continued. "Papen is the next thing to a religious fanatic. He still carries rosary beads. And Röhm? If only he had waited, I could have done something for him. But no!" Hitler slammed his fist on the table. "He is desperate to get rid of Blomberg and become defense minister. Tomorrow would not be soon enough for him. Why can't Röhm understand that this is impossible? Especially at this critical juncture. What *is* clear is that Röhm has put me in a corner. I can no longer have him around. He has to go."

"How will you go about it?" Göring asked.

"Hindenburg is dying, but he's not dead. He'll hang on long enough for me to formulate a proper plan. In the meantime, Hermann, you need to make preparations to become my right hand."

Hess winced. This was the role he coveted, but his strength lay in Hitler's fondness for him—not in his ability.

"I am already president of the Reichstag and minister of Prussia," Göring stated. "I head the Gestapo. What police I don't run, Himmler does. What else do you expect of me?"

"Make plans to give up control of the police. Give the Gestapo to Himmler."

"What will that accomplish?"

Hitler turned sour-faced. "The mistake you made was incorporating *SA* men into your police departments."

"They function only as auxiliaries," explained Göring.

"No matter, most weren't vetted. Himmler and Heydrich need to do that." Then Hitler's tone softened. "Don't you see, Hermann, we need a strong force loyal only to me—and not Röhm—when we move against him? That means that from now on, the Gestapo will be under Himmler's *SS*!"

*

The following week, Wolf stopped by my office in the Chancellery, which was not much larger than Heydrich's closet in the *Braunes Haus*. "Goebbels has arranged for me to appear at a youth rally to celebrate my birthday this coming Friday. Can you go for me?"

"When we were on the *Deutschland*, I was reminded of how much I missed the sea. I made plans to take a short trip to Usedom, to the town of Swinemünde. The island vacation will do me good."

"Leave Saturday. There is no one else to stand in for me. Everyone has family obligations. I need to be with Eva in Berchtesgaden. She's been despondent of late. I can't have *that* again. You would only be postponing your trip by one day."

I was reluctant to ruin his opportunity to be with Eva, but I was concerned. "Wolf. You know I have to stay in the background."

"I know, I know," he said. "This will be a one-minute thank you in front of some kids. Wear a civilian suit and a hat. I will make certain there are no photographers. Please, do this for me."

April 20, 1934

The rally was held at Lustgarten Park, an island in the center of Berlin that Hitler planned to restore for rallies. Thousands of *Jungvolk* gathered to celebrate Hitler's birthday in a carnival-like atmosphere of bands, food, games of chance, and sporting contests. Both boys and girls performed calisthenics. I was directed to the pavilion where Hitler was expected to make his appearance.

I arrived—on purpose—with five minutes to spare. The youth leader guided me to the largest cake I had ever seen. It was one-meter round, covered in dark chocolate frosting. Around the rim was written: *Unserem Führer Zum Geburtstag*—Happy Birthday to Our Leader. I kept my head down, read the thank you from Hitler post haste, and then stepped aside as the youth leader began slicing into the cake. I said my goodbyes as a dozen smiling faces held out empty plates, anxious for their piece of cake.

I ducked under the flap of the canvas pavilion and found myself face to face with Trude Mohr, with her hands on her hips. "Hello, Friedrich. How have you been?"

"I never considered that you might be here."

"This is a Hitler Youth Program, after all. My *BDM* girls are all around."

"Someone told me that you were about to be married."

"I'm not that lucky. At least not yet. My work keeps me going." She studied me from head to foot. "And you?"

"I've been busy."

"Too busy to have a friend?" She stepped close enough for me to smell her clean soap scent.

I stepped back. "I'm too busy for anyone who doesn't like my friends."

Her face contorted. "Still tolerating those lousy Jews, Friedrich? How is that little fat, greasy friend of yours?" Hate seethed from her pores.

A wave of fury washed over me. I was angry with myself for taking up with her in the first place. I wheeled and left without another word.

*

Trude Mohr left me in a foul mood. Rather than return to my office, I detoured to my apartment to send any lingering trace of Trude and what she represented down the shower drain. I was toweling myself off when there was a knock on the door.

"You're wet," said Emil Maurice.

"What in the world are you doing here in the middle of the day? And for your information, wet is what happens when you take a shower."

He stepped inside. "Anyone with you?" I shook my head. "You've got to help me. I couldn't trust the phones. You know how they listen. It's Himmler, again."

"Emil, I'm not your nursemaid. You've got to fight your own battles."

"But you're my friend."

Without asking, Emil grabbed a bottle of scotch. He held up a glass; I shook him off.

I could not imagine what got him so riled up. "Himmler's not trying to kill you again, is he?"

Emil downed his drink and poured another. "It's worse. So much worse. He's challenging my right to marry Hedwig. He wants to drum me out of the SS. Not only me. Both my brothers, too!"

That got my attention. I broke my own daytime rule and poured myself a drink. "The only way that could happen is if you violated some law or were an alcoholic. Hey, maybe that's it. We drink too much." I raised the glass in a mock toast.

"You know that's not true."

Then it dawned on me. "The only other thing it could be is that you're part Jewish. But that can't be . . ." I didn't finish my sentence when I saw how my words pained him.

Emil sat down. He clutched the bottle. "I never knew." Then he explained. "You know that Himmler requires everyone in the SS to prove they are racially pure. They check lineage back to 1750 now. It turns out that my great-grandfather, Charles Maurice Schwartzenberger, was a Jew. He founded the Thalia Theater ninety years ago in Hamburg. They're still showing plays there."

"That might have been the giveaway. The Jews were in the arts even then."

"Stop making light of this, Friedrich." He refilled his glass.

"Emil. You've been a card-carrying anti-Semite for . . . what is it now . . . the past fifteen years? Now it turns out you are a Jew. You have to admit that is pretty peculiar."

"I'm NOT a Jew. Goddamn you, Friedrich. Stop kidding around!"

"That's not how it works. It's not what you say you are. Him-mler is on solid ground. He's based Aryan purity on America's 'One Drop Rule.' From the sound of it, you've got more than a few drops of Jewish blood in you."

He looked up with pleading eyes. "I don't act like a Jew, do I?"

Emil was too upset to see the irony in the founder of the *SS* being turned out as a Jew. "Talking like this won't get you any-where. What do you want me to do?"

"Isn't it obvious? Speak to the Boss and get Himmler off my back."

"He's rather busy these days, Emil. The *Reichswehr* is put-ting pressure on him to subdue Röhm. I don't know if he would take time for something this trivial."

Emil jumped up at this. "How can you call my future trivial? Marriage aside, how can they kick me out of the *SS*? Besides, I'm not the only one going through this. So is Erhard Milch. He's Göring's minister for Aviation."

"And?"

"And his father, Anton, is Jewish. Göring has already inter-vened on his behalf to get the hounds off him. Hitler has to do the same for me."

May 1934

"I miss the days when Bernhard Weiss ran the police," Max said. I made it a point to visit Max soon after my encounter with Trude. While I had no particular concern, I needed to stay in touch. "I wonder what ever happened to him?"

"From what I've been told, Weiss left Germany." I took a sip of water to avoid telltale eye contact. "Why do you care?"

Max leaned closer and whispered, "Since Weiss left, the police have become avaricious again."

"I'm sorry for that."

Max knew enough not to press the issue. "By the way," he said, "I never thanked you for helping Kitty's niece."

"It would have been a travesty to sterilize Mila."

Max put his fork down. "Most others are not so lucky to have an *Obergruppenführer* for an advocate."

Something was bothering Max or he would not have mentioned my rank. "What are you trying to say, Max?"

"Just this. Why must your crowd keep everyone in a perpetual state of fear?" Though he referred to the general misconduct of the *SA*, he meant how they harassed the Jews.

"We are making every effort to curb those abuses. Until we succeed, it's a tradeoff for the dysfunction we have been forced to live under since the war ended. Look at the bright side: people are working again; factories are up and running; there are no more food shortages. Have you seen the faces of our young people? They're laughing and smiling and feeling good about their lives for the first time in years. Isn't a bit of distress worth the good that we are doing, Max?"

"You won't like my answer, Friedrich."

"Try me."

"Have you ever heard of Heinrich Heine?"

"Are you talking about Röhm's deputy, Edmund Heines?"

"No. Heine without the *s*."

"Is he one of Göring's Gestapo? He doesn't work for Himmler, does he? Goebbels, perhaps?" I prayed he wasn't one of Heydrich's secret agents in the *SD*.

Max shook his head. "He's not a Nazi. He's a Jewish writer. A poet. He wrote a play entitled *Almansor*."

"Oh? What's so special about this play?"

"I couldn't even tell you what the play was about, but there was a line that bears repeating. One I will never forget. It goes something like this: 'That was but a prelude. Where they burn books, they will ultimately burn people as well.'"

"What is that supposed to mean?"

"Whatever you want it to mean. For me, it means that if a society prohibits all forms of dissent, and it only allows one party to exist—then it destroys the very fabric of its own moral-ity. Friedrich, when a society burns books, how can people feel safe? How can they think *they* won't be next?"

"Are you talking metaphorically, Max, or literally?"

"Metaphorically, I pray," he answered. "But they've already taken the step to sterilize those deemed undesirable."

"The Greeks did it. The Americans do it now. That's how great societies cull out the weak."

Max put his hand on mine. "I hope you don't believe what you just said, Friedrich. We're supposed to help the weak. Feed the weak. Nurture the weak. Because out of the weak may come the next Mozart or Einstein. How terrible if they never had a chance to be born."

"Max, you're talking nonsense."

"Am I? I'm talking about an absurd conclusion to a logical thought."

"You're talking in riddles."

"I'm not. If society's goal is to improve the human race, then by logic alone sterilization is a step to its conclusion. Can't you see that this logical thought is totally absurd?"

"Listening to you, I'm beginning to think this Heine is a Communist. Am I right? Did he write this because of the book burning last May?"

"You could say he was there in spirit. Heine wrote his play in 1821."

Chapter 61

May – June 1934

"How is Eva?"

Wolf had returned to Berlin from Berchtesgaden. "She could not have been happier. And what about your trip to Usedom?"

"I never went."

"I gathered as much . . . when you saw your special friend," he said with a twinkle.

Hitler never surprised me anymore, but how could he already know about Trude?

"When did you find out?"

He patted me on the back. "The person in charge of the birthday celebration called to tell me everything went quite well. Then added that you bumped into Trude Mohr. I was hoping you two got back together. Is she the reason you didn't go to Usedom?"

"I didn't go to Usedom because Emil Maurice visited me over the weekend. If you can believe it, he's madly in love with a medical student and wants to marry her. When he sought approval as racially pure, it was discovered that Emil had a distant great-grandparent who was a Jew. Now Heinrich not only turned him down, he is drumming him and both his brothers out of the *SS*."

"It's taken care of. Himmler came to me soon after he discovered this. I would not let Himmler deny the marriage nor have him ask Emil to leave the *SS*. I ordered him to make an exception. You can imagine how much this infuriated Himmler."

"Then you let Emil needlessly stew?"

"I haven't forgotten the lawsuit . . . and other things he did to me."

"What about his brothers? Do they have to leave the *SS*?"

"No. I made all three honorary Aryans. You can give him the news, if you like."

*

At the beginning of June, as the last sands of Hindenburg's life drained out, the old field marshal retreated to his estate at Neudeck. Little time was left for Wolf to implement his agreement with the army to deal with Röhm and, at the same time, contain Papen's ambitions to become the next president.

Men were detached to surveille the comings and goings of Papen's faction: Herbert von Bose, Papen's press chief; Edgar Julius Jung, his political consultant; and his ally, Erich Klausner, at the Ministry of Transportation. Others in his faction were also placed under watch. Simultaneously, Wolf persuaded Röhm to give the entire *SA* a month's leave. Their furloughs were to commence at the end of June.

June 17, 1934

"Friedrich," said Hitler, "I want you to go to the University of Marburg. Papen is giving a speech. I need to know what he says."

"Can't you ask for a copy of the text?"

"What if he says something different?"

*

Every seat in the auditorium was filled. Papen began his speech by declaring his "obligation" to render his opinion of the current government. He took Goebbels to task for false propaganda and suppressing opposition newspapers.

I marveled at the duplicity of this man who, as chancellor, illegally took over the Prussian government, crushed the Social

Democrats, imprisoned Bernhard Weiss, launched prosecutions of homosexuals, and welcomed the Nazi party. Now, campaigning to succeed Hindenburg, he advertised himself as a liberal alternative to Hitler.

The meeting was a success . . . at least for him. With each statement, Papen received a roar of approval. He said, "If democracy is to be saved by the NSDAP, they are a temporary fix pending the emergence of new intelligentsia that is made up of the politically elite." Papen's meaning was clear: he and the aristocracy were prepared to take over the government once Hindenburg passed.

*

"What else did he say?" Wolf asked.

"That he was convinced that Nazi methods would lead to the destruction of Germany."

The more I spoke, the more infuriated Hitler became. When I finished, he jumped up.

"This is the signal I've been waiting for," he shouted. "Papen and his clique are about to move to take power."

For a moment, I second-guessed myself. "Are you certain?"

"After what you told me, I am. Papen thinks he can lull me to sleep. Right after the speech, he had the audacity to send me a telegram that pledged his support. His next move will be to go to the army and to Hindenburg. He will position himself as an alternative to me."

"Given those scenarios, which will he do first?"

"There is no doubt: Hindenburg. Once Papen has Hindenburg's support, the army falls into place." Then Hitler did something rare: he asked for my opinion. "What do you think?"

As I was about to answer, Hitler's adjutant knocked on the door. "Vice Chancellor Papen is here to see you, *mein Führer*."

I moved toward the door. "Should I leave?"

"*Nein*. You were at the meeting. If he sees you, he can't embellish."

Papen stormed into the room. He ignored me. "What is the meaning of banning my speech across the country? I just learned that all radio broadcasts were terminated two minutes after I started."

"Goebbels thought it best that your remarks remained in Marburg."

"I spoke as the president's emissary to the ordinary people, *mein Führer*. You should have heard the roar of approval when I said that you needed to break away from the men corrupting your ideas."

Hitler glanced to see if it were true; I nodded.

Papen continued. "The very notion that Goebbels, a junior cabinet member, banned my talk is an insult not only to me but to Reich President Hindenburg. It also insults the *gewöhnliche Menschen*, as you call your fellow German citizens. I am left with no choice. My resignation as your vice chancellor will be on your desk in the morning." Papen pivoted to leave.

Hitler reached for his arm. "Don't be rash, Franz. Goebbels has blundered. He thought he would lessen tensions across the country by not broadcasting your speech. I agree with you. It was a mistake. Don't resign until you and I journey to Neudeck to see the old man. When we're with him, we won't limit the discussion to just the ban on your speech. We will entertain any topic you wish to bring before him."

"When can we see the Reich president?" Papen asked as fast as he could.

"Slow down. I am not going to go back on my word. I will arrange it as soon as practical."

Assuaged, Papen turned to leave.

"Franz, I have one last question," Hitler said. "Who wrote your most excellent speech?"

"They were my words."

"Oh, I am sure they were. But who wrote the speech?"

"My private secretary, Edgar Jung." With that, the mollified Papen withdrew.

"That was good. You placated him for the moment. Had he resigned, it would have brought everything to a head. But why take him to see Hindenburg?"

Hitler grabbed me by both shoulders. "*Friedrichen*, my dear friend, I have absolutely no intention of taking him to Neudeck. But, as long as he thinks we're going together, he will delay going alone, until it is too late. Regarding his speech, we will do what we can to keep it under wraps."

Two weeks later, it would be too late for Papen . . . and many, many others.

Chapter 62

"We are going to Neudeck." Hitler stood in my office doorway, bedecked in his flying gear.

"Alone?"

"Certainly not with Papen, if that's what you mean. We have an appointment with the old man. General Blomberg will be there, too."

"Is that wise?"

"Wise? It's imperative we meet with Blomberg. Without the army, we're nothing. Regarding Hindenburg, we need to know if Papen's Marburg speech moved him. Papen may already have reached out to Hindenburg in his bid for the presidency."

"Regarding Papen's speech, people are beginning to greet each other with, 'Heil Marburg.'" The blood drained from Hitler's face.

"Is that so? Everyone concerned with that speech, especially Herr Edgar Jung, who wrote it, will soon get their 'Heil Marburg' from me. But, first, on to Neudeck."

We landed and were driven to the Manor house. General von Blomberg met us at the door. Oskar was at his heel.

"The field marshal is very weak," Oskar said in hushed tones. "Go in alone," he told Hitler. Then, in an apology to me, he mouthed that he was sorry.

"Do you also understand what is at stake?" Blomberg asked me while Hitler was with Hindenburg. "If the *SA* is not suppressed, the president will declare martial law and turn control over to the army."

"You made that clear on the *Deutschland*."

"That was ten weeks ago. Nothing has changed since." Blomberg did nothing to hide his irritation. "We thought Hitler would have done what he promised by now. You are forcing us to invite Papen to be president."

I was about to explain the steps that were in motion when Hitler emerged, nodded to Blomberg, and said, "General, you will hear from me shortly."

"Our patience is growing thin, Herr Hitler." That he didn't refer to Wolf as *mein Führer* punctuated his warning.

Hitler put his index finger to his lips. "Soon." He turned to me. "Come, Friedrich, we have much to do."

I was bursting to find out what Hitler and Hindenburg discussed. As per usual, Hitler sat next to the driver in the front seat, forcing me to wait until we were on the plane. The engines whined. Hitler leaned into me. "The die is cast. The old man knows he has little time left. He could not have been clearer. He is ready to declare martial law if I don't move against Röhm."

June 25 – June 30, 1934

Word came from Oskar von Hindenburg—through General von Blomberg—that Franz von Papen would meet Reich President Hindenburg on June 30. This meeting could not take place.

Wolf activated his plan. He ordered Sepp Dietrich, who commanded Hitler's elite bodyguard—the *SS Leibstandarte Adolf Hitler*—to be ready to move against Röhm and his top officers. Simultaneously, the *Reichswehr* was put on notice. Blomberg agreed to have the army on standby in their barracks if Sepp Dietrich's men needed help. Finally, Hitler ordered Röhm and his top leadership to meet with him on Saturday, June 30 at *Bad Wiessee*, a resort in upper Bavaria. It was the first weekend of their "furlough."

While the newspapers and many historians would label our actions during these next high-tension days as the "Röhm Putsch," there was no putsch—at least not by Röhm.

June 28, 1934, Thursday

To give the appearance of normalcy, we honored a long-standing promise to attend Josef Terboven's marriage in Essen. Josef marched with us in Munich in '23. Hess, Goebbels, Hitler, and I attended the wedding breakfast while Göring, Himmler, and Heydrich remained in Berlin organizing the offensive. At a critical moment, Wolf broke away from the celebration and took me aside. "The wheels are in motion. Röhm and some of the top *SA* leadership are already at *Bad Wiessee*."

"When are the rest expected?"

"Most are in transit and will be there soon. The rest are in Berlin. Himmler, Heydrich, and Göring will take care of them. The plan is for Sepp Dietrich and a contingent of *SS* to accompany me to arrest Röhm and neutralize the top *SA* leadership."

"Some will put up resistance. You need me by your side."

"*Nein.* They don't expect anything. They will be overwhelmed. You, on the other hand, must carry out a critical mission if we are to succeed. Much will depend on you."

"You have thought of every contingency. What could be left?"

"Franz von Papen. It is critical to prevent Papen from communicating with his staff. A plane is waiting to fly you to Berlin. Göring and Himmler will expect you early in the morning. Take a squadron of *SS* to surround Papen's house. Cut his phone wires. Place him under house arrest no later than noon. Restrain him if he resists. No one must go in or out once you get there until our mission has been completed."

"Under what pretext can I keep the vice chancellor under house arrest?"

"Tell him . . . tell him that Röhm's Putsch has started in Munich, that his life is in danger, and that I have placed him in protective custody for his own safety. Under no circumstance can he be allowed to reach Hindenburg on the 30th!"

Friday, June 29, 1934, 6 a.m.

I found Göring, Himmler, and Heydrich in a conference room at *SS* headquarters in Berlin. The three were discussing last minute details of the impending action.

Himmler nodded when I entered. "Right on time, Friedrich. I've placed thirty *SS* at your disposal. That should be enough to keep Papen safe."

"Is one good with communications?"

"You mean can one snip the telephone wires? They all can."

I turned to Göring. "Hermann, please send a messenger with updates. I don't want to be left in the dark."

I rode in the lead car followed by a caravan of black vehicles. In a flash, the men surrounded Papen's house and cut the phone lines before I banged on his front door. Papen, dressed in a blue silk robe over his nightclothes, opened the door scratching his disheveled mane of gray hair.

Papen yawned. "Friedrich, why are you here this early? Did something happen to Hitler?"

"It's not safe to talk out here, Franz. Let's step inside." Papen's house was filled with nineteenth-century furnishings and mementos from his long career. We sat on plush club chairs in the salon. "Are your wife and children home?"

"They went to visit friends in Bremen for the weekend. What's wrong with Hitler? Why is it safer inside?"

"I need to stay with you for the next couple of days. Probably through Sunday. Monday at the latest."

"That's preposterous. I have appointments to keep."

"Your safety is more important than any meeting you might have."

"I don't understand," said Papen.

"Hitler got word that Röhm and the *SA* leadership are plotting a putsch."

He jumped up. "If that's so, I must call Hindenburg so he can declare a state of emergency. The *Reichswehr* must be alerted that the *SA* is about to take it over. General Blomberg must take steps."

"That won't be necessary. Hindenburg has been informed and Blomberg has issued orders. By tomorrow, the heads of the *SA* will be arrested. You must remain here until the danger has passed."

"What does Röhm have to do with me? Besides, if he's in *Bad Wiessee*, as you say, and we're in Berlin, then what harm could come to the vice chancellor?"

"There is no telling how his *SA* men will react when Röhm is arrested. Hitler appreciates your value not only to him and the president, but also to the country. We need this extra layer of security to ensure your safety. I'm sure you understand."

"At least let me call my wife and children. Tell them that I'm safe. When they hear what is about to happen tomorrow, they will worry."

"No need. I'll get a message to them."

"I'll do it myself." He walked to the console and lifted the receiver. He clicked the button many times. He shook it. "The line seems to be dead."

I shrugged. "Just a precaution."

Papen's shoulders slumped. He realized our comedy was over. He and I were not going anywhere. Throughout the day, we talked, read, and played chess. Dinner was brought to us. Papen opened a good bottle of wine. We were civilized for the time being.

Saturday, June 30, 1934, Early Morning

Papen came down to the salon dressed in a fine, three-piece gray tweed suit, white shirt, and gray-striped tie.

"Franz, where do you think you're going?"

"I told you I had an appointment today that I must keep."

"I thought I made it clear yesterday: my orders are to keep you here. Please do not make this more difficult than it already is."

Papen headed for the door. When he opened it, five SS men jumped to alert and aimed their rifles his way. Papen froze.

"Can I make it any plainer?" I nodded toward the SS men.

"But Hindenburg is expecting me," his voice pitched higher.

"He is aware that you are unable to attend because of the emergency."

He slapped his thigh and drew himself up straight. "Friedrich, I am the vice chancellor of Germany. I am walking out this door. No one is going to stop me." He pulled the door open.

I yanked him back and slammed it shut. "Franz, if you don't sit down, my orders are to tie you down." Papen twisted away and stomped from room to room, lifting shades or separating curtains. Through each window, he saw clusters of SS men. Defeated, he went to his bedroom to change his clothes without added protest.

When he returned, he found me in his study. "How long are you going to keep me here?"

"Until I hear otherwise."

"How reassuring," he answered.

An hour later, there was a knock on the door.

"Is it for me?" Papen asked.

"No." It was a report from Göring. I opened the envelope.

All hell broke loose Friday night in Munich. Three thousand SA men rioted. Hitler diverted from Bad Wiessee for several hours. The Führer personally arrested SA Obergruppenführer Schneidhuber and Gruppenführer Schmid. Tore badges off their uniforms with own hands. Ordered them shot. Dealing with putschists in Berlin now. Hitler on way to Bad Wiessee to arrest Röhm. Keep you posted.
H.G.

Papen was at my elbow. "What does the message say?"

I shoved it in my pocket. "Last night, some of Röhm's men got out of hand in Munich. They had to be subdued."

"Was that the beginning of Röhm's Putsch?"

I answered with a shrug. The less Papen knew, the better.

"What *is* going to happen today?" Papen asked.

"Something important. That's all I know. Let's take our mind off this. You won the chess game yesterday. I would like a chance to return the favor."

Sunday, July 1, 1934, 1 p.m.

The hours ticked by that morning without word from Göring. Finally, as I was about to order one of the SS to go to headquarters and get me a report, the commander of the men surrounding Papen's house knocked on the door. He gave a heel-clicking salute, "Heil Hitler."

I held out my hand; he remained at attention. "Where is Reich President Göring's report, *Herr Sturmbannführer?*"

"We have been ordered to withdraw, *Herr Obergruppenführer.* The telephone lines have been repaired. Vice Chancellor Papen is free to do as he pleases."

Göring said this would be over by Sunday. He was right. I thanked the commander.

As I walked back into Papen's living room, the shrill ring of the telephone broke the silence. Papen, reading in his study, lunged for the receiver, the leather-bound volume falling from his lap. As he listened, his posture changed from ramrod straight to that of a hunched old man. He shouted, "No!" Then "Oh *mein Gott!*" And finally, "This is not possible!" When he could, he asked a question or two, only to cry out at the answers.

When the call ended, he needed two trembling hands to return the receiver to its cradle. Papen leaned on the table to gather enough strength to hobble back to his seat, plop down, and then clasp his head in his hands.

"Franz, what on earth is it?"

He lifted his tear-stained face. "Your gang has murdered my entire staff. All of my top people!"

"What are you talking about? That can't be."

"What am I talking about?" Papen rose and leaned on his chair for support. "Goddamn you, Friedrich . . . I'm talking about the cold-blooded killing of my staff. My press chief, von Bose. Herbert was shot dead in the Vice-Chancellery; Erich Klausner was shot in his office. And . . ." Papen fell back into his chair sobbing. I stood stone-still until he spoke again. He whispered through rheumy, reddened eyes, "They even killed Edgar Jung. You knew him, Friedrich. Edgar was always by my side. Now I know why Hitler asked me who wrote my Marburg speech."

Papen hobbled to the side table and poured himself a brandy. He finished it and poured another. With glass in hand, he stepped toward me, and gazed off at nothing. "Edgar was found in a ditch in Oranienburg. With a bullet in his head."

Then he stepped into my space and stabbed his index finger into my chest. "Yes, *Herr Obergruppenführer*, you were there when I answered Hitler's question: 'Who wrote your speech?' Now his body lies in a ditch, shot in the head. Tell me, Friedrich, why was he shot? Why were they all shot? What did they have to do with this so-called Röhm Putsch?" With each question he stabbed me harder. "Why didn't you shoot me? It would have been better for me than to hear this."

I stepped back. "I'm sorry, Franz. I didn't know."

He stepped toward the side table. "Liar!" Papen poured another glass of brandy. Drank half, and with a look that tossed daggers, said, "That's not all of them. Do you know who else your gang murdered? Poor Schleicher."

How to process this madness? "Schleicher had nothing to do with Röhm," I mumbled.

"I'm not finished." He gulped the rest of his drink. "Not only did they shoot Schleicher dead in his apartment doorway, but they killed his wife, too. Poor woman. Both murdered." Rivulets of tears streamed down his face as he struggled to stand.

"Who else?" I prayed there were no more.

"Gregor Strasser. Murdered in a basement cell in Gestapo headquarters." Without another word, Papen grabbed the handrail of the staircase and pulled himself to his room, one step at a time.

Schleicher? Strasser? Both were out of politics. Neither had dealings with Röhm. There was only one answer: revenge. More than once, Wolf told me that he wanted both dead.

The phone rang. After four rings, I knew Papen wasn't answering it.

I lifted the receiver.

It was Papen's wife.

"Yes, he is okay. Yes. Yes. I'm sure. I'll have him call you soon."

Sunday, July 1, 1934

It was almost 5 p.m. when I reached Gestapo headquarters. Göring and Himmler were gone, but Heydrich was in his office. I found him behind his desk that sported a framed photo of Heinrich Himmler. He motioned to the lone chair.

"I just left Papen. His people are dead. So are Schleicher and Strasser. What the hell happened?"

Heydrich leaned back. "Papen's lucky. He should have gotten his, but the *Führer* spared him for some reason."

I was numb. I thought about Göring's note. "Why Schneidhüber?"

"He was a traitor," answered Heydrich.

"I don't understand. The Führer stood in a picture with him at the Buch-Bormann wedding."

Heydrich shrugged. "We didn't count on troops rioting in Munich. That had to be quashed before the *Führer* traveled to *Bad Wiessee* to arrest Röhm. That's when we received the call to spring into action here in Berlin. Code name: *Unternehmen Kolibri*. Operation Hummingbird. It went down fast after that."

"Did they have to kill Papen's entire staff?"

"Goebbels ordered it."

"Why Strasser and Schleicher?"

"Isn't it obvious? They both conspired against the *Führer*."

"Did Schleicher's wife deserve to die? How did she wrong the *Führer*?"

Heydrich shook his head. "We didn't mean to kill her. She came to the door with the general. It was a stray bullet."

My stomach convulsed; this was a living nightmare. "This was supposed to be about Röhm. What happened to *him*?"

"The *Führer* took a handful of men and arrested Röhm himself. The rest is history."

"What do you mean by that?"

"The other co-conspirators were rounded up."

None of this made any sense to me. "I don't understand. If Röhm was arrested, what others were rounded up?"

"The top echelons of the SA, of course. Are you that naïve to think the plan was to eliminate one person? Get rid of Röhm and our troubles would go away? That would never have been enough to satisfy the *Reichswehr*."

"You're talking to me like I'm an idiot, *Standartenführer*. I'm hearing all of this for the first time. How would you like me to respond? Maybe you can talk about all these deaths as though they meant nothing to you, but I knew these people."

"Cut the crap, Friedrich. This is about survival. You and I are both survivors. And for the record, I've just been promoted to *Gruppenführer*. I will be your rank soon enough."

This was not the time to deal with his truculence. "You still haven't told me how it ended in *Bad Wiessee*."

"Ask your old friend Emil Maurice. He had quite a heavy hand in all of it."

When I reached for the telephone on his desk, he stopped me. "There's time to call Emil." Heydrich came around his desk. "Come with me. Let's take a ride. You need to see, firsthand, how we dealt with the putsch."

*

We drove to Lichterfelde, a village founded in the Middle Ages, now incorporated into Greater Berlin. Lichterfelde boasted a well-known military academy that the Berlin Police used since the Great War. It now housed Hitler's bodyguard: the *SS Leibstandarte Adolf Hitler*. We rolled up to the four-story red brick building. From the outside, it reminded me of Pasewalk Hospital. The building stood empty. The garrison and its commander were still in Munich.

"Why bring me here?"

"Be patient, Friedrich."

I followed Heydrich through vast halls and out the back into a courtyard. He explained that the arrested *SA* men were detained in the coal cellar until their names were called. They were then brought to the sunlit courtyard where we stood.

Heydrich pointed to a long wall riddled with bullet holes. Shards of brick were strewn about, resting on blackened ground that looked like pools of oil . . . but were globs of congealed blood. I stepped closer. Clumps of flesh were pinned into divots in the brick. Here and there, I saw a part of an arm or a piece of scalp with matted hair stuck to the wall.

Heydrich rocked on his heels, relishing my reaction to the remnants of this butchery.

I began to choke. The taste of bile rose from my gut. Just when I thought I had it controlled, I turned and vomited. I waved away the white handkerchief Heydrich offered, and used my own. My voice was muffled. "How many killed?"

"I need to confirm names, but it tallied one-hundred-and-fifty-three. We were very organized." Heydrich could not have been more matter-of-fact. "Four names were called every fifteen minutes. They were marched out of the coal cellar and lined up by the wall. We ripped open their shirts and drew a circle around their left nipple with a piece of coal."

I struggled to understand what his words meant as I pushed against my knees to stand. "You drew targets?"

"Shooters must have targets," he said. "Eight *SS* aimed their rifles at the traitors; none knew who had live ammunition and who had blanks. Before I ordered them to shoot, I first called out that the *Führer* wills it. 'Heil Hitler!' Fire! I finished each off with a bullet to the head. We used a butcher's wagon to cart the bodies out, then the next four souls would be lined up."

"Did you tell them why they were being executed?"

He laughed. "The odd thing? They believed a Röhm Putsch had succeeded. They thought Hitler had been arrested and that they were all victims of the coup. Many shouted, 'Heil, Hitler,' as we shot them."

"In Munich, who was killed besides Röhm?"

"Buch headed the operation there. As I said earlier, your friend Emil Maurice played a significant part over my and Himmler's objections."

"I want to leave, now."

"You've seen what I wanted to show you."

He dropped me off at my apartment. I ripped my clothes off and took a long, hot shower. With a towel still wrapped around my torso, I grabbed a glass and a bottle of scotch and took a long pull. Then another. I stared at the phone for a time, and then placed a call.

"I didn't think I would find you home, Emil. What the hell happened?"

"It's over, Friedrich. Finished."

"Why didn't I know about the extent of this beforehand?"

"Only the Boss can answer that. But you should have been here, Friedrich. It was amazing. We pulled up to the hotel early Saturday morning. Walter Buch was there."

"It's ironic how you can't get away from him."

"What are you talking about?"

"Remember the letters? Ida Arnold?"

"Ancient history. Anyway, Buch hung back. I was behind the Boss when he knocked on Röhm's door. Röhm was in a deep sleep. He said, 'Heil Hitler,' when he saw the Boss, and something to the effect that he expected the Boss later in the day. Then Hitler stepped into the room by himself and proceeded to curse Röhm about his lewd behavior. He told him he was a disgrace to himself, to the Boss, and to the entire Reich."

"What did Röhm say?"

"He took it. Not a peep. Then someone said that Edmund Heines, Röhm's deputy, was in bed in the next room with some boy-lover. When Hitler heard this, he turned bright red. I thought he would have a stroke then and there."

"Don't tell me they killed Heines, too?"

"How could we let the immoral bastard live? Buch had us haul Heines and his lover outside. As soon as they cleared the doorway, Christian Weber and I killed them. Buch was okay giving the orders but didn't like to dirty his hands."

"Weber is a murderous slob."

"Weber was perfect for what we had to do. After we shot Heines and his lover, we returned to Munich. Hitler. Buch. Weber. Me. Others too. Along the way, we intercepted car after car filled with *SA* headed toward *Bad Wiessee*. Some were Röhm's personal guards. Hitler ordered them to turn around and follow us. We headed a caravan of *SA* that didn't have a clue they were being led to their deaths."

"I've known many of the top *SA* men for years. We were in the *Freikorps* together. We marched shoulder-to-shoulder in the '23 Putsch. You knew them, too."

"Buch told us we couldn't take any chances. We had to kill them all. Orders are orders."

"What happened to Röhm?"

"We took him to Stadelheim Prison."

"That's where Hitler and Esser did thirty days after beating up Otto Ballerstedt," I said.

"I'll come to him in a minute."

I rolled my eyes. *Not Ballerstedt, too!* "I'm not sure I want to hear about him. Go on about Röhm."

"A gun with a single bullet was placed on the table in front of Röhm. The Boss demanded that Röhm do the right thing. He gave Röhm ten minutes to kill himself."

"Was Hitler in the room with Röhm?"

"No. We couldn't take the chance that Röhm would use it on him. Do you know what that arrogant pig said? 'If I am to be killed, let Adolf do it himself.' I tell you, the Boss wept. In his heart, he didn't want to kill Röhm. Röhm was an *Alte Kämpfer*, like both of us. But he had gone too far against the *Reichswehr*. The Boss had no choice. After ten minutes, the order was given. Röhm died in a hail of bullets shot through the door opening."

"Emil, I thought this was about Röhm and the *SA*, but obviously it was more. Strasser and Streicher were killed here in Berlin. Both of Papen's aides and his secretary were killed, too. Who else died in Munich?"

"Gustav von Kahr, for one. Remember how he violated his word and turned on us during the Putsch? Hitler never forgave him for doing that. Kahr's body was found in the marshes outside of Dachau. Hacked to death. A bullet was too good to waste on him."

"Don't tell me you did that?"

"No, but I wished I had."

"This went far beyond the original plan to satisfy Blomberg and the others in the *Reichswehr*. I'm at a loss as to what to call this? A massacre?"

"Call it revenge. Problem solving. Whatever strikes your fancy."

I had no words to describe this bloodbath. I felt trapped in a world I didn't understand. "You mentioned Otto Ballerstedt."

"Ballerstedt paid for how he treated Hitler when he embarrassed him."

"For God's sake, Emil, that was in 1921. The man was a cripple then. He retired years ago. How could he be a threat to anyone now?"

"No matter. Yesterday he got a bullet in the back of the head." Emil continued. "There were others. We cleaned house, Friedrich. Now people know we mean business. Where were you when all this was going on?"

Still processing the news, I couldn't answer.

"Friedrich? Did you hear me?"

"Sorry. I . . . I was locked in Papen's house with him since Friday. Without access to the outside world. I knew none of this until this afternoon."

"I'm glad you kept Papen safe. Heydrich or Himmler might have gotten the idea to do away with him, too."

"Heydrich did get the idea but couldn't act on it because I was guarding him."

"That would have made the old man in Neudeck very unhappy."

As Emil said this, I recalled Martin Breslauer's words that New Year's Eve in Max's club. Breslauer said that in the world of Nietzsche, a benevolent dictator has to demand supreme happiness.

"Emil, today was not a day for happiness."

Chapter 63

While I spoke to Emil, Hitler convened a cabinet meeting to wrap legality around the executions. Reich Justice Minister Gürtner provided an official opinion that was approved by the cabinet.

> The measures taken on June 30, July 1 and 2 to suppress treasonous assaults are legal acts of self-defense by the State.

With these few words, every death was retroactively justified. Hitler, Gürtner, and Minister of the Interior Wilhelm Frick signed this into law.

On July 13, I sat in the gallery in the Kroll Opera House to hear Hitler address the Reichstag. He explained about the summary judgment leveled on the Röhm Putschists:

> If anyone reproaches me and asks why I did not resort to the regular courts of justice, then all I can say is this. In this hour, I was responsible for the fate of the German people, and thereby, I became the supreme judge of the German people. I gave the order to shoot the ringleaders in this treason.

Not yet formally installed as dictator, Hitler needed and sought Hindenburg's blessing for "saving" the German nation from Röhm's Putsch. He reached out to Oskar to arrange a visit with the bed-ridden, ailing field marshal. With Oskar's help, Hitler obtained the old man's blessing.

*

I sought Hitler out after his speech to the Reichstag. He was in his Chancellery office.

He held out his hands as I approached. "*Friedrichshen.*"

"Adolf." This stopped him cold. He pointed to a chair next to his massive desk, but I shook my head.

"I need to stand."

Hitler sat. "I can't say that I'm surprised that you're here."

"How could you do this, Wolf? All those innocent people. The Schleichers. Strasser. Even old Ritter von Kahr, from the '23 Putsch. Why?"

"Just a minute, Friedrich. Except for Kahr, those took place in Berlin. I was in Munich. Himmler and Heinrich went overboard." He made a sweeping arc. "Totally overboard. That Heydrich has no heart. I take that back. He has a heart of iron. I never wanted Röhm killed. You must believe me. Goebbels and the others pounded away at me. They said Ernst had to die or else Blomberg and the *Reichswehr* would never be satisfied. It was to save our future and all that we worked for. I gave the order with tears in my eyes. Can't you understand that, Friedrich?"

We both knew he was lying. Maybe having Röhm executed—who was with us since '19—bothered him, but he cared not a whit about the lives of any of the others.

I threw my hands up. "You kept me out of it on purpose, didn't you? That's why you had me locked up with Papen."

He looked down at papers on his desk. "I could not let anything happen to Papen. We would've lost the old man had we done that."

"It's more than that. You knew I would protest and try to stop some of it."

He kept his head down. "I did not want you to give them a reason to kill you," he said just loud enough for me to hear.

*

Not long after, Kitty called with fear etched in her voice. "Friedrich, have you seen Max? I've tried for days to reach him."

"I've been a bit of a recluse. I haven't seen much of anyone."

"It is not like Max to disappear with no word."

"What about the club?"

"They haven't seen him there either."

I promised Kitty I would make some calls. Still in my robe, I called Max's home number. It rang and rang until I gave up. I slipped into my uniform and decided to go to his place. Max lived not far from the center of town in a charming house built in 1915 next to Schillerpark, in the Mitte-Wedding district. The house had large bay windows that overlooked the park.

I turned the ringer and listened for footsteps. The house was still. I knocked on the door; no one answered. I tried to peer through the large window, but curtains blocked my view. I trotted to the back door, banged on it, and called out Max's name. Nothing.

I returned to the front door prepared to break it down. To my surprise, when I turned the knob, the door swung open. I stepped into the foyer and called out. There were a couple of pieces of mail on the floor. I placed them on the bench of a hall tree with a mirror in its center.

Although the house felt empty, I walked softly through each room on the off-chance Max was sleeping. When I neared the fireplace, I reached for a brass poker and then laughed at myself, drawing my sidearm instead. I scaled the stairs and searched Max's bedroom.

No Max. The wooden floors were stained in the typical oxblood color. His over-sized, four-poster bed with a canopy was unmade. The bathroom had an array of normal male toiletries. Nothing appeared missing. There were no signs of disturbance.

Years back, Max told me about keeping a bag packed under his bed for a fast getaway. I ducked down and peeked under the bed. Empty. Did that mean Max left in a hurry?

When I checked his clothes closet, nothing was out of order. But on the valet was the gold watch hooked to a chain that Max always carried. Then I found his wallet on the floor; his identification cards and money were missing.

The evidence now pointed to Max leaving under duress. I stopped at the hall tree. There was a key ring with a dozen keys on a hook. I fitted them, one-by-one, until one locked the front door. I pocketed the keys and headed for Charité Hospital.

*

"I am *Obergruppenführer* Richard. I am looking for a patient: Max Klinghofer."

The clerk checked the records. "Sorry, there are no admissions by that name."

I asked him to call other hospitals in the city. "This is urgent Reich business. Here are my office and home numbers. Call me day or night if you find Klinghofer."

I went to the next logical place: The Central Police Station. Max was not there, and they had no information about him. I called infirmaries, spas, and even other nightclubs. He was nowhere to be found. I was stymied.

I went to *Pension Schmidt*. "I've looked everywhere. There is no trace of Max."

"So now what? Do we sit around and wait?" Kitty asked.

"I'm not done. I'll keep looking."

I thought about combing the registries of every hotel in town, but why would Max go to a hotel? If he had gone anywhere on his own, he would have locked his door before leaving and taken his wallet, gold watch . . . and keys. That left only one conclusion: someone took him, but who? If it was not the police—and I checked—that left only one prime candidate.

*

I stood before the propaganda minister's secretary. "I wish to see Herr Goebbels."

"I am sorry, *Herr Obergruppenführer*, but he left for the *Bayreuther Festspiele* a couple of days ago. It's always held the third week in July."

The Bayreuth Festival had faithfully reproduced the grand operas of Richard Wagner since the 1870s. The festival continued in our time under the guidance of Winifred Wagner, widow of Wagner's son Siegfried.

I had no choice but to journey there.

I found Goebbels and Hitler sequestered in a conference room.

"I didn't think you were much of an opera lover, Friedrich," Goebbels said. "I thought you preferred that nigger jazz."

"My tastes are eclectic, Joseph."

"Friedrich, do you know our guests?" He introduced me to Theodor Habicht, our NSDAP representative in Austria, and Hermann Reschny, the head of the Austrian *SA*.

"I am sorry to intrude, gentlemen, but I have business with Herr Goebbels. I will wait outside until you are finished."

"Nonsense," said Hitler, "join us. Your insight will be helpful." Then he turned to Habicht and Reschny and picked up the thread of the conversation. "Are you certain the army is behind this?"

His reference soon became clear: they were planning a coup to depose Federal Chancellor Englebert Dollfuss, head of the Austrian government. After more discussion, their meeting ended. Goodbyes were said, leaving me alone with Goebbels.

"Let me help you," Goebbels started before I could say anything.

"How do you know I need help?"

"Oh, but you do, Friedrich. Otherwise, you would not be here."

I folded my hands in my lap. "Go ahead. I'm listening."

"Your old friend came to me a few days ago."

Hearing this gave me a jolt of hope. "What did Max want?" *Maybe it was about the police asking for larger bribes.*

Goebbels licked his lips. "Not your Max. It was Trude Mohr."

"Baldur von Schirach runs the youth programs. If she needed something, she would have gone to him. Why you?"

"Fräulein Mohr had information about a traitor to the Reich."

"She works with young girls. What does she know about traitors?"

"Are you that dumb or that coy, Friedrich? It was Trude who turned in your Max Klinghofer."

"I don't understand."

"When she saw the success of quelling the Röhm Putsch and how certain undesirables were removed from their positions, she brought your Klinghofer to my attention."

"Whatever for? He runs a great business and makes sure that everybody that needs to be, is taken care of."

"Business is one thing. Being a rabid Communist supporter is quite something else," said Goebbels.

"Are you talking about the time he showcased Claire Waldoff? You and I both know she's a well-known artist. She was never a Communist."

"But she performed for them. That makes Klinghofer a Communist sympathizer."

My pulse quickened. My temples pounded. If I was going to help Max, I needed to control my rage. "Where is Max, Joseph? What have you done with him?"

"I never liked your Max. Besides being a Communist-loving Jew, he was disrespectful that time in the nightclub. You were with Lilian Harvey. Do you remember?" Goebbels tapped his temple. "I don't forget things like that, Friedrich. The truth is I never wasted time thinking about your Max until Trude Mohr visited me. After what she told me, I had to do something about him."

"So you grabbed him from his house. Does the Boss know about this?"

"Why would I bother the *Führer* about an insignificant Jew?"

"That's enough, Joseph. Where is Max?"

"He's in Dachau."

*

I should have shot Goebbels on the spot. Instead, I stormed off and drove to Dachau, 227 kilometers away. I arrived there by late evening. Most of the camp was dark; there was a lone light at the office near the entrance.

"I am here to see Max Klinghofer," It was the same clerk when I visited Oksana.

"No one can see inmates without a pass. And not at this time of night."

I shoved the pass Heydrich had given me, signed by Himmler, in his face. "This says I have a right to visit prisoners."

"The hour is late, *Herr Obergruppenführer*."

"Your job is to obey me, not tell time. If I'm here at a late hour, it's because I have a reason. Bring Klinghofer to the dining room. I will speak with him there."

"I'm afraid that's impossible."

"Why?"

"He can't walk."

"What did you do to him?"

"Me," shrugged the clerk, "nothing."

I was led to what served as the infirmary. It was a wooden shack with thin walls. The guard unlocked the door. It was pitch black.

"Is there a light?"

He flicked on a lone light bulb in the center of the room. I counted twenty-four beds, twelve to a row. I stepped deeper into the room. The beds to my left were empty. The beds to my right were empty except for the last one tucked in a corner shrouded in darkness. As I neared, I saw a lump covered with a stained sheet. I imagined it to be blood. I stepped closer. The stench jerked my head back. I went forward with my hand covering my nose.

"Max, is that you?"

Whoever was under the sheet shivered uncontrollably.

"Max, it's me. Friedrich."

A soft whimper arose as I pulled back the sheet. "Max, is that you?" His face was buried toward the wall. I touched his shoulder. "Max, it's me."

This triggered a hacking cough; I pulled away. When it subsided, the limp figure tried to roll over but couldn't. I stepped to the front of the wooden frame, lifted it, and swung it away from the wall. I squeezed in to see his face. The part of the face around the left eye was swollen. The left ear was partially detached from its base. The mouth was twisted. There was a deep gash through the cheek. It might be Max. I wasn't certain.

"Friedrich?" His speech was hard to distinguish . . . his front teeth were missing. His lips were grotesquely swollen.

Tears streamed down my cheeks. "Max, what did they do to you?" I jumped to my feet. "Wait here." I cringed. Max wasn't going anyplace. I found the guard posted outside the door. "Bring the camp doctor to me immediately."

"The doctor comes every Tuesday. He was already here this week."

"Is there a nurse in the camp?"

"*Nein.*"

I found a bowl of water and bandages. I put my arm beneath his shoulders and began to lift him to clean his face.

"Don't . . ."

"I've got to get you to a hospital, Max."

He groaned in agony.

I lowered him gently.

"Hold . . . me."

I got down on both knees and cradled his head to my chest. Max lost consciousness; his breathing grew more labored. While he lay there, I lifted the sheet with my free hand. Both legs were mangled and twisted in different directions. He had soiled himself and was left in his own excrement.

I sobbed. I stroked his hair. "Max. Oh, Max."

After a time, his good eye cracked open. He said something, but I could not make it out. I leaned closer. There was a gurgling sound in his chest. I was no doctor, but I knew enough to know he was drowning in his own blood . . . and there was nothing I could do.

My tears fell onto his cheek. I touched them gently, smearing a glob of blood. "Max, I swear to you, I will kill whoever did this to you."

Blood bubbled onto his lips and down his cheeks.

"Not important . . . better to . . . "

"What's not important, Max? What's better?"

"Help . . ."

"Help who, Max? *Who?*"

I was about to tell him I would do anything he wanted, that I would help the world if it would ease his pain, but I didn't get the chance. At that moment his mouth fell slack, and his head lulled to the side, exposing the white of his right eye.

My Max was dead.

I cradled his head to my bosom, rocking back and forth, crying for the man who gave me unqualified love from the first day we met. I grew angrier by the moment over his cruel, needless death. Finally, I eased his head down on the cot. I leaned over and kissed his matted hair.

"Goodbye, Max."

I pushed against the bed frame to stand; my knees buckled. I caught myself and leaned back against the wall for support. I waited for the lightheaded feeling to pass before I straightened. Erect, I tugged on the flaps of my uniform and stepped around the edge of the cot. When I opened the door, the guard tossed down a cigarette and jumped to attention.

"Heil, Hitler."

"Indeed."

The guard waited for me to speak. It took me a moment. "The inmate died. His body is not to be touched without my permission. I will send for it in the morning."

*

I drove to Munich, found myself at the Four Seasons Hotel, obtained a room, and then made the dreaded call. Kitty shrieked when she heard that Max was dead.

"Did he suffer?" she asked.

"He went fast."

"How did it happen?"

"From all appearances, it was a heart attack."

"Details, Friedrich, details. How did you find him? Where did you find him? Was he alive when you got there?"

Kitty knew about the blind alleys I ran into trying to find Max: hospitals, hotels, spas, other nightclubs, and more. Even jails. There was no holding back. I told her about Goebbels, my trip to Dachau, and finding Max dead.

"Max and I always assumed Goebbels trashed the Nightingale that night. He had it out for Max. But sending him to Dachau? What did Max do to deserve that?"

"Max's biggest problem was being Max . . . and I loved him for it. The way he confronted Goebbels that night at *Prater Garten*. The hiring of Claire Waldoff. He was a thorn in Goebbels's side. But it wasn't Goebbels who called Max a traitor and Communist lover, it was Trude Mohr. She hated him from the moment they met. She turned out to be a raving anti-Semite."

"Dachau is supposed to be for political prisoners," said Kitty.

"It is."

"I've heard stories," Kitty said. "Did they torture him?"

There was no benefit to ruin her memory of Max. "No. They tried to reprogram him. Turn Max into their image of a good German."

"Max would never go for that crap."

"Agreed. Max was too tough for them. He resisted until his heart gave out. Remember you told me his doctor ordered him to lose weight?"

"Max didn't listen to anyone, Friedrich. Not even me. You should know that." Kitty cursed Goebbels and Trude Mohr. "I

cannot tell you how many times I begged him to sell the Nightingale and keep a low profile. I even suggested that he leave Germany. But not Max. The Nightingale was his baby. He would
never abandon either . . . until his luck ran out." She broke down
into sobs.

"There's a small piece of this puzzle that doesn't make sense.
Help me out. Years ago, Max told me that he kept a bag packed
under his bed, for a fast getaway when the shit hit the fan. It
wasn't there when I looked."

She laughed through her tears. "Max told that to everyone.
It was never true. He loved this country. He would never leave it.
Max had the last laugh: there was never any bag."

After a few more reminisces, I asked Kitty if she knew how
to arrange for a Jewish funeral. She said she would take care of
the details, but that it was important to get his body to Berlin
as soon as possible. Max was a congregant at the Neue Syna-
gogue on *Oranienburgerstrasse*. Kitty said she would contact the
rabbi. She was certain he would make all necessary arrangements
that followed Jewish traditions. She mentioned prayers and body
washing.

"What is this body washing?"

"Don't worry, Friedrich. The rabbi will take care of it."

"Can you give me the rabbi's name and telephone number?"

"There's no need, Friedrich. I will take care of everything.
Just bring Max home."

"I want to make a donation in Max's honor. I think that's
how it's done, isn't it?"

At that, she gave me the rabbi's information. When I reached
the rabbi, I could not get all the words out. I broke down. The
rabbi was horrified at the way Max died.

"But who would do such things to a fellow human being?"

"I wish I could tell you. But whatever you do, rabbi, please
do not let anyone at the funeral see Max's condition."

He gave his assurance.

*

I sat next to the hearse driver as we drove straight to the funeral parlor where ancient prayers were said over Max's body as it was ritualistically washed and placed in a simple, pine coffin. This gave me time to return to my apartment and change into a suit. When all was ready, we set off for Weissensee Cemetery—the largest Jewish cemetery in all of Europe—dedicated in 1880 after the other Jewish cemeteries in Berlin had reached full capacity.

It was a graveside ceremony. In addition to Kitty and me, most of the employees of the Nightingale were there. Hebrew prayers were chanted. The rabbi said a few words about Max and what it meant to die—tying them into passages in the Bible—and then we watched in silence, as the casket was lowered into the grave.

The last step was the hardest. Each of us followed the Jewish tradition of hefting a shovel-full of dirt onto the plain casket until it was totally covered. Kitty and I stood there, arm-in-arm, watching the gravediggers fill in the rest until Max was buried deep under a mound of fresh dirt.

"Hello, Friedrich."

The voice was familiar. I turned to see Marta.

"I didn't stop to think that you would be here," I said.

"These days, I run one of Max's other clubs."

Marta was still pretty, even after all these years of late nights in smoke-filled clubs. "How have you been?"

"I manage."

Kitty tugged on my arm. "The car is waiting, Friedrich."

I took her cue, but not before saying, "Marta, I'm sorry we had to meet at such a sad time." She didn't answer.

The car dropped us off at *Pension Schmidt*. Kitty cracked open her most expensive bottle of scotch, poured two glasses, and we toasted Max.

"You know I loved him, Friedrich."

"I know, Kitty. He always talked about how much he loved you, too. You were the one for him."

She downed her drink and poured another. "I would have married him, had he asked."

We clinked glasses. "Why didn't he ask you?"

She shrugged. "Who knows? Maybe because I wasn't Jewish."

"That wouldn't have stopped Max." I took another sip. "You know what I think? He loved you so much that he didn't marry you because he saw the handwriting on the wall."

"It cost him his life."

"It may have spared yours," I said.

At that, we clinked glasses again and downed our drinks. I was numb to the searing liquid.

"You know Max left a will, Friedrich. He gave me a copy for safekeeping. You're in it."

This was a surprise. "He never talked about family. I know he had cousins. I met one in New York and one here."

"But no close relatives. He left me his estate plus the Nightingale and his two other clubs. He left you his house."

"Why would he do that?"

"He couldn't stand that you lived in a small apartment. He always said that if anything ever happened to him, he wanted you to have his house. Maybe it would induce you to marry and settle down."

"Why didn't he give it to you?"

"I have a nice house. I don't need two."

"What about the clubs? Are you going to keep them?"

"Why don't we run them together?"

"They're yours."

"I don't need more money, but I am going to keep them to honor Max's memory."

"He'd like that, Kitty. You've got Marta to help you. She's been with him from the beginning."

"She will be in charge of operations. Sorry I didn't warn you at the cemetery. How did you feel when you saw her?"

"Nothing amorous, if that's what you mean." I refilled our glasses. "I have no spare time for anyone. I'm on a mission now."

"Something to do with the party?"

"Let's just say I've done a lot of thinking since Max passed. A wise man once told me that one day something would cause me to reflect differently on Hitler and the party."

Kitty lifted her glass. "To Max."

"To Max."

We sat for a while, each with our own thoughts. Then Kitty said, "I have known you for many years, my dear. Your words are thinly veiled. Think twice before you do anything rash, Friedrich. I know what you mean when you say you are on a mission: you're talking about vengeance. In fact, you might even be able to kill Hitler."

My mouth dropped. I started to deny her words.

"Don't say anything. Let me finish. If not Hitler, it could be some other in that crowd. But I urge you, don't do anything like that. The Nazis are a many-headed Hydra. If you cut off one, there's another to take its place. They will kill you and we will have . . . nobody."

"Who are the 'we' you speak of?"

She laid her hand on top of mine. "Good Germans who want to do the right thing. For the time being, rethink this. Come into business with me."

When I didn't answer, she stood and embraced me. "Be careful, Friedrich," she whispered. "We need you."

Chapter 64

I was so preoccupied with finding, then burying Max, that I lost track of Hitler's machinations in Austria. Our Austrian Nazi counterparts assassinated their President Dollfuss. They briefly took over the government only to have their rebellion squashed by the Austrian Army with the help of Mussolini, who massed Italian troops on their common border to protect Austrian sovereignty against Germany. Mussolini publicly rebuked Hitler for trying to overtake a country in Italy's backyard. German-Italian relations turned frigid.

None of that mattered to me. What did matter was that we received a report from Neudeck that Reich President Paul von Hindenburg's death was imminent.

Hitler and I got to Neudeck in time. Hindenburg was alive, but barely. I stood behind Hitler as he approached the aged field marshal, stretched out on a metal cot similar to those in army barracks.

Oskar stood near his father's head. "Father, the chancellor is here."

Hindenburg's eyes remained closed, his breathing labored. Oskar repeated that Hitler was there . . . and the dying man grunted that he heard the first time.

Hitler asked if we could leave them alone. Oskar nodded.

We left Hitler and the Reich president to share a last moment together. History will record that the two men spoke but we will never know what was said. Hitler refused to discuss it after he emerged from the room. We left Hindenburg wheezing, struggling for air. We said our goodbyes and returned to Berlin.

Early the next morning, Hitler convened a cabinet meeting. A law was passed that combined the offices of president and chancellor. It would go into effect after Hindenburg's death. Moments after the law was issued, we received word that the old field marshal had died.

As soon as Papen's proxy signature was affixed to the new law—Papen was away at the time—Hitler summoned General von Blomberg and the commanders of the three armed forces to a meeting. Each man took the following oath: "I swear before God to give my unconditional obedience to Adolf Hitler, *Führer* of the Reich and its people, Supreme Commander of the Armed Forces, and I pledge my word as a brave soldier to observe this oath always, even at the risk of my life."

These few words—and what they represented—sealed the fate of Germany. Whereas before, the armed forces swore their allegiance to preserve and protect the country, they now swore only to Adolf Hitler. The German people were told that the Reich presidency was combined into the Chancellorship because—out of respect for Hindenburg—the post of president had been retired. There was simply no one who could ever fill the great man's shoes.

With Hindenburg gone and buried, there was no one to stop Hitler from doing whatever he pleased. Yet it was not enough that the cabinet passed the law making him *Führer und Reichskanzler—Führer* and chancellor—Hitler wanted a vote of acclimation from the German people. A referendum was scheduled for August 19, 1934, on the following:

> The office of the President of the Reich is unified with the office of the Chancellor. Consequently all former powers of the President of the Reich are demised to the Führer and Chancellor of the Reich Adolf Hitler. He himself nominates his substitute.
>
> Do you, German man and German woman, approve of this regulation provided by this Law?

While everyone in NSDAP headquarters mobilized to get as many men and women out to vote for the referendum, I had my own agenda. I returned to Max's house. When I inserted the key into the front door, it was difficult to push it open. A mound of mail was piled high beyond the mail slot. I needed to open and close the door a couple of times, each swing pushing more mail out of the way until I was able to slip inside. I piled it on the hall bench. I would sift through these eventually, but not then. The paperwork transferring title had yet to be started, but there was no reason not to move into the house.

When I returned to my flat to begin the process of moving, I found a package wrapped in brown paper. There was no postmark or return address. I hefted it; it was heavier than I would have expected. I shook it; it jangled.

I ripped the package open. There were two keys attached to a thick metal ring plus a note with a phone number.

> *Call this number at 12:10 p.m. tomorrow from a phone booth in the lobby of the Adlon Hotel. If no one answers after three rings, hang up. Repeat this same procedure each day adding five minutes to the time that you call. Call from a different hotel lobby each time. Continue this pattern until a call is answered.*

The next day I called the number from the Adlon Hotel as instructed. No one answered by the third ring. The same held true when I called from the Kaiserhof the following day. This grew tedious. I didn't like playing games.

On the third day, I traveled to the Savoy Hotel in Charlottenberg. I arrived early, ordered a coffee, and stared at the morning paper, pretending that I cared about what I read. At noon, I closed the paper, found a booth, and asked an operator to make the call at precisely 12:20.

"How are you after losing Max?" It was Bernhard Weiss.

"How could I be?" Then I asked, "How did you know? Don't answer that. I'm glad some of your officers are still loyal."

"Should the need arise, one or two might be in a position to help you."

"Why the keys?"

"As deputy president of the Police, I had access to critical areas of the government. Historical records. Taxes. Ownership of houses and businesses. There are two safety deposit boxes with information inside. Also funds. Those keys open them."

"Where are the boxes?"

"Separate banks. When the time is right, you will be contacted."

"By whom?"

"By a person who will give you a signal."

"What will he say?"

"The *person* will say, 'Have you seen the beard of a Jew before?' Commit it to memory."

"How could I ever forget?"

"A last thing, Friedrich. My family and I are leaving Prague. We are moving to London. The fact Hitler failed in this attempt to overtake the Austrian government only means it is a matter of time before he tries again. Hitler is an Austrian. He will not rest until Austria becomes part of the Reich."

"And then?"

"Then he will try to put the old empire back together. That is what he promised in his campaign pledges. So, it turns out that Prague was not a desirable place for my family to relocate."

"You're that certain he will continue to look eastward?"

"Don't be a fool, Friedrich. He has been promoting his policy of *Lebensraum*—Eastern expansion—from his very first speech. Enough talk. My time is short. My family and I leave tomorrow."

"How will I get in touch with you?"

"I will find you when the time is right. Until then, Friedrich, be on your guard at all times. You are in a position to do more than anyone, but you must never reveal yourself. There is no one to replace you. God be with you, Friedrich."

I stared at the phone after we hung up. I had no way of knowing what I was supposed to do. I believed Bernhard Weiss, that when the time came, I would know. In the wake of Max's death, I came to accept that it *had* fallen on me—a man without a past and not much of a future—to thwart, stifle, or sabotage the Nazi juggernaut that I had helped create.

*

Germany voted on whether to anoint Hitler dictator. Some of the foreign press complained about intimidation in advance of the vote on the referendum. The *New York Times* projected the following:

> CORONATION FÊTE IS SEEN FOR HITLER; VOTE IS EXPECTED TO CONFIRM OVERWHELMINGLY HIS SEIZURE OF PRESIDENT'S POWERS.

> ELECTORS HAVE NO CHOICE CAMPAIGN WILL CONFIRM ISSUE TO THE FUEHRER AS THE SYMBOL OF GERMAN UNITY.

The *Times* was wrong. There was no seizure of power. It would have been better if there had been and the German people given no choice on August 19, 1934. But they did have a choice. They got to vote yes or no: should the offices of chancellor and president be fused to create the sole position of *Führer*?

The results of the plebiscite were overwhelming. Ninety-five percent of the country voted. Ninety percent of the voters—over thirty-eight million Germans—said, "Yes, we want Hitler to be our *Führer*."

I was not one of them. I cast my vote for Max: I voted "No." The vote went against all that I had worked for fifteen years to achieve. But voting for Max was not enough. Now I had to find the path to avenge his death and atone for my sins.

HISTORICAL NOTES

As stated in the Foreword, the vast majority of persons in *Wolf* were real people whose lives, careers, and sentiments are accurately depicted. Only Anna, Marta, Mila, Oksana, and Max, along with Friedrich Richard, are fictional.

We used Friedrich to narrate the sixteen-year account of a time, a people, a movement, and particularly its deranged leader, who was responsible for the most beastly conflagration in the history of the world.

Friedrich, without a memory or prejudices, is a clear window through which we observed people and events. We presented these with as much objective accuracy as our scholarship permitted. The result produced a very different portrayal of Adolf Hitler—who, as the reader now knows, really did use the name "Wolf"—than that presented by well-regarded historians. Sir Ian Kershaw, perhaps the most esteemed of the present historians, offers this evaluation:

> Hitler's *disturbed sexuality*, his *recoiling from physical contact*, his *fear of women*, his *inability to forge genuine friendship* and *emptiness in human relations*, presumably had their roots in childhood experiences of a troubled family life. (Emphasis added)[1]

Not a word of the above is correct—except that Hitler had a troubled childhood.

Adolf Hitler, in fact, forged life-long friendships with numerous people. He was exceedingly loyal to "old fighters"—*Alte Kämpfer*—who were with him prior to the 1923 putsch. Even when they transgressed against him personally, notwithstanding

---

1 Hitler: 1889-1939 Hubris, W.W. Norton, 1998 p. 46.

that Hitler was a lethal killer, he forgave them when others would not have.

As an example, Emil Maurice frequently crossed Hitler. Maurice poached on Geli Raubal. When Hitler fired Maurice, Maurice sued him. And yet . . . Hitler always forgave Maurice. When Himmler and Heydrich threatened to kill Maurice, Hitler not only saved him but found official positions for Maurice. When Maurice applied for permission to marry and it was discovered that his great-grandfather was Jewish, Himmler wanted to drum Maurice and his two brothers out of the SS because of his Jewish "blood." Again, Hitler intervened. Here is the secret memo from Himmler:

The *Reichsführer SS*, München, 31 August 1935 Official Minutes

1. *SS-Standartenführer* Emil Maurice is without doubt, according to his family tree, not of Aryan descent.

2. On the occasion of *SS-Standartenführer* Maurice's marriage when he had to submit the family tree, I reported to the Führer my position to the effect that Maurice must be removed from the ranks of the SS.

3. The *Führer* has decided that in this one and only exceptional case Maurice as well as his brothers could remain in the SS, because Maurice had been his very first companion, and because his brothers and the entire family Maurice had served the Movement with rare bravery and loyalty in the first and most difficult months and years.

4. I decree that Maurice must not be entered in the SS Clan Book, and that none of the descendants of the Maurice family may be admitted into the SS.

5. The Chief of the Race and Settlement Head Office receives a copy of this Minute with the request of most strictly confidential treatment; only the Chief of the Clan Office is to be informed.

6. For myself and for all successors as *Reichsführer SS* I

state that only Adolf Hitler himself had and has the right also for the *SS* to decree an exception with regard to blood. No *Reichsführer SS* has or will have for all future time the right to allow exceptions from the requirements of the *SS* regarding blood.

7. I oblige all my successors to maintain most strictly the position laid down in point 6.

A confession by the authors is appropriate: Himmler's attempt to remove Emil Maurice and his brothers took place in 1935, not in 1934 as depicted in *Wolf.* We changed the timing to bring these events within the time limits of the volume.

Hitler's loyalty exceeded protecting Maurice. Hitler personally paid for Emil's and Hedwig's wedding, which was held in Munich at the *Hotel Vier Jahreszeiten*—the Four Seasons—when work at Hitler's flat made it impractical to have the wedding there. See the illuminating work of Anna Maria Sigmund, *Des Führers bester Freund,* München, 2003.

There were numerous similar relationships between Hitler and others, including friends, colleagues, and staff. These examples, documented in interviews and books written by contemporaries, refute the likewise incorrect assessment by Professor Volker Ullrich in *Hitler Ascent 1889-1939*:

> . . . Apparently, despite all his charm, Hitler was *unable to approach women confidently* in any way that went beyond the mere exchange of pleasantries. His *lack of experience* may have played a role in this, but it may also have been an *inability* or *unwillingness* to *empathise* with the wishes and needs of the women he fancied. Thus Hitler launched sudden advances and then turned his back equally abruptly, if his *clumsy forays* did not meet with approval. *He seemed to have lacked an internal emotional compass.* (Emphasis added)[2]

2 Volker Ullrich, *Hitler Ascent 1889-1939* (Knopf, 2016), 274.

As with the earlier quotation drawn from Sir Ian Kershaw, these statements are *absolutely* incorrect and without the *slightest* basis in fact.

Far from inexperienced, Hitler kept a stable of women. Far from an inability to empathize with women, he both manipulated while simultaneously respecting them. Except for one, his niece Geli Raubal, he kept them secreted and away from the knowledge of the German people. He treated each of them well. When he terminated a relationship, he often kept in touch, giving assistance to a former lover and even to their subsequent husbands. Numerous interviews of those who knew Hitler well, including his housekeeper Anni Winter, Herman Esser, Wilma Schaub, Gretl Braun (Eva's sister), and even Hitler's mistress Maria "Mimi" Reiter, establish this ability to develop and maintain emotional relationships.

By the same token, *Wolf's* portrayal of Hitler as a mental patient in Pasewalk and his treatment by the psychiatrist, Dr. Edmund Foster, is very different from Hitler's own account in *Mein Kampf.* Historians Kershaw and Ullrich accept Hitler's version as factual: that he was blinded by a gas attack.

As presented in *Wolf,* Dr. Kroner was, in fact, an eyewitness to Hitler's admission to Pasewalk. According to Dr. Kroner's statement to the US Government in 1943, upon admission to the hospital in October 1918, Hitler was diagnosed as a "psychopath" whose blindness was an "hysterical symptom" of his mental condition. Dr. Kroner's exact words describing Hitler were: "*A psychopath with hysterical symptoms,*" (emphasis added).

Dr. Kroner reported that Hitler was treated for his condition by the psychiatrist, Professor Edmund Forster. Forster headed the Berlin University Nerve Clinic and was the Consultant Neurologist to the Military Hospital at Pasewalk. By every measure, Dr. Forster was certainly not an ophthalmologist. And yet, not one of the previous historians noted above mention Dr. Kroner by name or detail Hitler's medical treatment in their works.

*

We offer these abbreviated notes to highlight how the storyline in *Wolf* deviates from accepted accounts. For expanded Historical Notes and references, please visit www.NotesOnWolf.com.

Herbert J. Stern and Alan A. Winter

ACKNOWLEDGMENTS

There are many people that must be thanked for their tireless efforts, help, criticisms, and for their willingness to share this journey with us. As our research unfolded, two things became clear: we needed to go to primary sources, and we needed help in translating books and articles in German. Our first acknowledgement goes to the dedicated archivists at the Library of Congress headed by Barbara Bair, to the staff and research librarians at the FDR Library in Hyde Park, NY, to the archivists of the Musmanno Collection at Duquesne University and to the curators of Michael Musmanno's secretary at Ohio State University. Without your help, thoroughness and orderliness and protection of precious documents, we would not have been able to approach *Wolf* the way we did. And thank you to Tamiko Toland, who gave graciously of her time and willingness to search the last remnants of her father's archives for interviews that may have still been in her basement and not with the Toland Collection in the FDR Library.

If patience is a virtue then Mark Gompertz and Caroline Russomanno, our editors at Skyhorse Publishing, are saints. They, along with Tony Lyons, have indulged two compulsive writers that continued to tweak the manuscript even after the "final" version had been submitted. The Skyhorse team has been magnificent. And where would authors be without an agent to help push a project forward; a publicist who shouts to the world that *Wolf* has arrived; and a social media team that created and did things we still don't understand. We are indebted to these wonderful professionals: Susan Schulman of Susan Schulman Literary Agency; Jane Wesman of Jane Wesman Public Relations, Inc.; and Gabriel Blitz Rosen of Townhouse Digital, for their diligence, expertise, and putting up with our many questions, and desire to get this project done and let the world know that *Wolf* exists.

When we came across crucial books by Anna Marie Sigmund, whom we regard as one of the finest historians of the period and who generously gave of her time and expertise, we needed help with her books that had not yet been translated from German into English. Enter Alan Wallis. Alan has been an invaluable resource translating everything we tripped over that needed to be in English. Alan: thank you for dedication to our project that you embraced as your own. Your meticulous translations were crucial for *Wolf.* We asked a lot of you, and you delivered! Special thanks as well to Professor Richard J. Evans whose trilogy on the rise and fall of the Third Reich we regard as the finest history of the period.

No words can acknowledge Denise Penna Shephard's contribution to *Wolf.* Although Denise has full-time responsibilities at a law firm, no matter how late she had to stay or how much time it took away from her family, there was nothing we asked her to do that she did not do. From typing and retyping our many versions of the manuscript, to helping with research and correspondences, and keeping files that a work like this requires . . . she was always there with a smile and the ability to make it happen. Thank you, Denise.

We received critical editorial help from those who toiled over the manuscript, even before we had a publisher or agent. Special thanks to Michael Mandelbaum and Hew Pate (who suggested the title) who were among the first; and to Clyde and Otto Feil whose early editing kept us on course.

And then there were those who read and critiqued along the way: Tom Campion, Ralph Crocker, Daniel D Droog, Pam Drucker, Ezra Fitz, Bill Jaffe, Richard Levao, Brian Machler, Madelene Magazino, Neal Manne, Alan Marcus, Ruth Maron, Mark McGivern, Andres Romero, Daniel Rosen, Thilo Semmelbauer, Samuel Stern, Sarah Stern, Eric Tait, Kathleen Tait, Olga Vezeris, Marc Wein, Derish Wolff. To Dr. Serge Mosovich, thank you for helping us understand Hitler's evil, distorted mind. And to Afrim Berisha and the team at Bistro Seven Three: you've been great, letting us spend hours discussing *Wolf* while serving the finest food in New Jersey. Tom Kjellberg, you were critical in helping us understand copyright law.

Finally, but most importantly, we acknowledge the two people who sacrificed the most to make this work possible: our wives Lori and Marsha. While this book is written in honor of Bernhard Weiss, it is dedicated to both of you.